AFTERWORLDS

ALSO BY SCOTT WESTERFELD

Uglies

Pretties

Specials

Extras

Leviathan

Behemoth

Goliath

The Manual of Aeronautics:
An Illustrated Guide to the Leviathan Series

AFTERWORLDS

SCOTT WESTERFELD

SIMON PULSE   New York   London   Toronto   Sydney   New Delhi

SIMON PULSE

An imprint of Simon & Schuster Children's Publishing Division

1230 Avenue of the Americas, New York, NY 10020

First Simon Pulse hardcover edition September 2014

Text copyright © 2014 by Scott Westerfeld

Jacket photographs copyright © 2014 by Thinkstock

All rights reserved, including the right of reproduction in whole or in part in any form.

SIMON PULSE and colophon are registered trademarks of Simon & Schuster, Inc.

For information about special discounts for bulk purchases, please contact

Simon & Schuster Special Sales at 1-866-506-1949 or business@simonandschuster.com.

The Simon & Schuster Speakers Bureau can bring authors to your live event.

For more information or to book an event contact the Simon & Schuster Speakers Bureau

at 1-866-248-3049 or visit our website at www.simonspeakers.com.

Jacket design and photo-illustration by Regina Flath

Interior design by Mike Rosamilia

The text of this book was set in Minion Pro.

Manufactured in the United States of America

2 4 6 8 10 9 7 5 3 1

Library of Congress Cataloging-in-Publication Data

Westerfeld, Scott.

Afterworlds / by Scott Westerfeld. — First Simon Pulse hardcover edition.

p. cm.

Summary: In alternating chapters, eighteen-year-old Darcy Patel navigates the
New York City publishing world and Lizzie, the heroine of Darcy's novel, slips into
the "Afterworld" to survive a terrorist attack and becomes a spirit guide,
as both face many challenges and both fall in love.

[1. Authorship—Fiction. 2. Future life—Fiction. 3. Dead—Fiction. 4. Ghosts—Fiction.
5. Love—Fiction. 6. East Indian Americans—Fiction. 7. Lesbians—Fiction.
8. New York (N.Y.)—Fiction.] I. Title.

PZ7.W5197Aft 2014

[Fic]—dc23

2014006852

ISBN 978-1-4814-2234-5 (hardcover)

ISBN 978-1-4814-2236-9 (eBook)

ISBN 978-1-4814-3851-3 (Barnes & Noble proprietary hardcover)

ISBN 978-1-4814-3717-2 (signed Barnes & Noble proprietary hardcover)

TO ALL YOU WORDSMITHS, YOU SCRIBBLERS,
YOU WRIMOS IN YOUR VAST NUMBERS,
FOR MAKING WRITING A PART OF YOUR READING

We tell ourselves stories
in order to live.
   —Joan Didion

Education is the path from
cocky ignorance to miserable uncertainty.
   —Mark Twain

CHAPTER 1

THE MOST IMPORTANT EMAIL THAT DARCY PATEL EVER WROTE was three paragraphs long.

The first was about Darcy herself. It skipped the trifling details, her dyed blue-black hair and the slim gold ring in her left nostril, and began instead with a grim secret that her parents had never told her. When Darcy's mother was eleven years old, her best friend was murdered by a stranger. This discovery, chanced upon during an idle web search, both shocked Darcy and made certain things about her mother clearer. It also inspired her to write.

The second paragraph of the email was about the novel Darcy had just finished. She didn't mention, of course, that all sixty thousand words of *Afterworlds* had been written in thirty days. The Underbridge Literary Agency hardly needed to know *that*. Instead, this paragraph described a terrorist attack, a girl who wills herself to die, and the bewitching boy she meets in the afterworld. It promised skulking ghosts and the traumas that haunt families, and little sisters who are more clever than they appear. Using the present tense and short sentences, Darcy set the scene, thumbnailed the characters and their motivations, and teased the conclusion. This was the best of the three paragraphs, she was later told.

The third paragraph was pure flattery, because Darcy wanted very much for the Underbridge Literary Agency to say yes to her. She praised the breadth of their vision and paid tribute to their clients' genius, even while daring to compare herself to those illustrious names. She explained how her novel was different from the other paranormals of the last few years (none of which had a smoldering Vedic psychopomp as its love interest).

This email was not a perfect query letter. But it did its job. Seventeen days after pressing Send, Darcy was signed to Underbridge, a flourishing and respected literary agency, and not long after that she had a two-book deal for an astonishing amount of money.

Only a handful of challenges remained—high school graduation, a perilous decision, and parental approval—before Darcy Patel would be packing her bags for New York City.

CHAPTER 2

I MET THE MAN OF MY DREAMS IN AN AIRPORT, JUST BEFORE midnight a few days into the New Year. I was changing planes in Dallas, and I almost died.

What saved me was texting my mother.

I text her a lot when I'm traveling—when I get to the airport, when the flight's called, and when they make us put our phones away. I know, it sounds like something you'd do with your boyfriend, not your mom. But traveling alone made me nervous even before I could see ghosts.

And trust me, my mother needs to hear from me. A lot. She's always been kind of clingy, but even more so since my father ran off to New York.

So I was walking alone through the mostly vacant airport, looking for better reception. This late at night most of the shops were shuttered and dark, and I'd wandered until reaching another wing of the airport, which was closed off by a metal gate that hung from the ceiling. Through the steel mesh I could see a pair of moving walkways gliding past, empty.

I didn't see the attack begin. My eyes were focused on my phone, watching as autocorrect made war on my spelling. Mom was asking about my dad's new girlfriend, whom I'd just met during my winter break visit. Rachel was lovely, always well dressed, and had the same size feet as me, but I couldn't tell Mom all that. *She has awesome shoes and I get to borrow them* wasn't the right place to start.

My father's new apartment was also amazing, twenty stories up, with floor-to-ceiling windows looking down on Astor Place. His walk-in closet was as big as my bedroom back home, and full of drawers that slid open with a sound like spinning skateboard wheels. I wouldn't want to live there. All that chrome and white leather furniture was cool to the touch and didn't feel like home. But Mom had been right—my father had made a metric fuck-ton of money since leaving us. He was wealthy now, with a doorman building and his own driver and a glittery black credit card that made shop assistants straighten up. (Calling people who worked in stores "shop assistants" was a thing I'd learned from Rachel.)

I was wearing jeans and a hoodie, like always when I fly, but my suitcase was full of shiny new clothes that I'd have to hide when I got back to California. Dad's wealth pissed Mom off for good reason: she supported him through law school and then he bailed on us. I got worked up about it sometimes, but then he'd send some of that wealth my way and I'd get over it.

Sounds pretty shallow, right? Being bought off with money that should've been my mother's? Trust me, I know. Almost dying makes you realize how shallow you are.

Mom had just texted me: *Tell me she's older than the last one. And not a Libra again!*

Didn't ask her bitch day.

Um, what?

BIRTHDAY. Autocorrect fail.

Mom was mostly desensitized to my bad typing. The night before, she hadn't even noticed when I'd texted that my father and I were eating raw cock dough for dessert. But when it came to Rachel, no typo went unremarked.

Ha! Wish you'd asked her THAT!

I decided to ignore that, and answered: *She says hi, by the way.*

How sweet.

If you're being ironing, I can't tell. We are TEXTING, mom.

I'm too old for irony. That was sarcasm.

I heard shouts behind me now, back by the security checkpoint. I turned around and headed back toward my gate, but didn't look up from the phone.

I think my planet's about to leave.

OK. See you in three hours, kiddo! Miss you.

You too, I began to type, but then the world fell into sharp little pieces.

I'd never heard an automatic weapon in real life before. It was somehow too loud for my ears to register, not so much a sound as the air ripping around me, a shudder I could feel in my bones and in the liquid of my eyes. I looked up from my phone and stared.

The gunmen didn't look human. They wore horror movie masks, and smoke flowered around them as they swung their aim across the crowd. At first everyone was frozen with shock. No one ran or tried to hide behind the rows of plastic chairs, and the terrorists seemed in no hurry.

I didn't hear the screams until the terrorists paused to reload.

Then everyone was running, some in my direction, some the other way. A guy my age in a football jersey—Travis Brinkman, as everyone learned later—tackled two gunmen, wrapping his arms around them and spinning with them across the blood-slick floor. If there had only been two terrorists he might have won that fight and spent his life a hero, telling his grandkids the story till they got bored of it. But there were four gunmen in all, and the others still had plenty of bullets.

As Travis Brinkman fell, the first running people reached me. Smoke roiled in their wake, bringing a smell like burning plastic. I'd been just standing there, but the acrid scent snapped my panic and I turned and started running with the crowd.

My phone lit up in my hand, and I stared stupidly at it. There was something I was supposed to do with this glowing, buzzing object, but I'd forgotten what. I still hadn't grasped what was happening, but I knew that to stop running was to die.

But then death was right in front of me—that steel gate stretched across the entire hallway, floor to ceiling, side to side. The closed section of the airport stood behind it, the walkways still flowing. The terrorists had waited for midnight, when we were all trapped in the smallest possible space.

A tall man in a leather biker jacket threw his shoulder against the gate, and the metal rippled. He knelt to claw at the bottom, lifting it a few inches. Others joined him.

I stared at my phone. A text from my mother:

Try to sleep on the plane.

I stabbed at the screen to bring up a number pad. Some part of my brain realized that I'd never called 911 before. As it rang, I turned around to face the gunfire.

People were scattered on the floor, a trail of them. The terrorists had been gunning us down as we ran.

One of them was walking toward me, still a hundred feet away. He looked at the floor, stepping carefully among the fallen bodies, as if he couldn't see well through the mask.

There was a tiny voice in my hand, dulled by my battered ears. "What is the location of your emergency?"

"Airport."

"We're aware of that situation. Security is responding from on-site and they will be there soon. Are you in a safe location?"

The woman was so calm. Looking back, it always makes me cry to think how calm she was, how brave. I might've been screaming if I were her, knowing what was happening at the other end of the line. But I wasn't screaming. I was watching the gunman walk slowly toward us.

He was shooting the wounded people with a pistol, one by one.

"I'm not safe."

"Can you get to a safe location?"

I turned back to the gate. A dozen of us were pulling at it now, trying to lift it up. The metal rattled and swayed, but was catching against some kind of lock. The gate wouldn't rise more than a few inches.

I looked for a door, a hallway, a drink machine to hide behind. But the walls stretched away bare and flat.

"I can't, and he's shooting everyone." We were so calm, just talking to each other.

"Well, honey, maybe you should pretend to be dead."

"What?"

The gunman looked up from the wounded on the floor, and I could see the glitter of eyes through the two holes in the mask. He was staring straight at me.

"If there's no way to get to safety," she said carefully, "maybe you should lie down and not move."

He holstered his pistol and raised the automatic rifle again.

"Thank you," I said, and let myself fall as the gun roared smoke and noise.

My knees struck the floor with a burst of pain, but I let every muscle go, flopping over onto my face, a dropped rag doll. My forehead hit the tiles so hard that light flashed across my vision, and I felt a sticky warmth on my brow.

My eyelids fluttered once—blood was running into my eyes.

In a stunned heap I lay there, the gun firing again and again, the bullets hissing over me. The screams made me want to curl into a ball, but I forced myself to stay still. I tried to squeeze my own breathing to a halt.

I'm dead. I'm dead.

My body shuddered once, fighting me, demanding deeper breaths.

I don't need to breathe—I'm dead.

The shooting finally stopped again, but worse sounds filled the ringing silence. A woman crying for mercy, someone trying to breathe with torn lungs. In the distance, I heard the pop and crack of pistols.

Then the worst noise of all: tennis shoes squeaking on wet tiles, taking slow, careful steps. I remembered him shooting the wounded, making sure that no one would escape this nightmare.

Don't look at me. I'm dead.

My heartbeat thudded, hard enough to shake the whole airport. But somehow I kept myself from breathing.

The squeak of tennis shoes began to fade, crowded out by a soft roar in my head. My lungs were still now, not fighting anymore, and I felt myself falling softly away from my body, straight through the floor and down toward someplace dark and silent and cold.

It didn't matter if the world was crumbling. I couldn't breathe or move or think, except to remind myself . . .

I'm dead.

Behind my eyelids, vision went from red to black, like spilled ink spreading across my mind. Cold filled me, and my dizziness became a slow swaying, a feeling of stillness.

A long time seemed to pass with nothing happening.

And then I woke up somewhere else.

CHAPTER 3

THE MANILA ENVELOPE FROM THE UNDERBRIDGE LITERARY Agency was as thick as a college acceptance package. But instead of forms, booklets, and brochures, it contained four copies of the same document—a publishing contract—and a return envelope that was already addressed and stamped.

Darcy Patel had learned all this from an email a week ago, and had read the contract at various stages of its drafting. There was no mystery about the envelope's contents at all. But the act of slicing it open still seemed momentous. She had appropriated her father's Princeton letter opener for the occasion.

"It's here," she said at her sister's door. Nisha threw her book aside, sprang out of bed, and followed Darcy to her room.

They were quiet going down the hall. Darcy didn't want her father reading through the contract again and offering more legal advice. (For one thing, he was an engineer, not a lawyer. For another, Darcy had an agent already.) But Nisha had to be here. She'd read *Afterworlds* last November, as it was being written, sometimes aloud over Darcy's shoulder.

"Close the door." Darcy sat at her desk. Her hands trembled a little.

Nisha obeyed and padded in. "Took long enough. When did Paradox say they wanted to buy it? Three months ago?"

"My agent says some contracts take a year."

"That's seven today, and it's not even noon!"

By mutual agreement, Darcy was allowed to use the phrase "my agent" no more than ten times a day in front of her little sister; any overages cost a dollar each. This seemed generous to everyone concerned.

Darcy faced the envelope, hefting the letter opener in one hand.

"Okay. Here we go."

The blade cut smoothly at first, but halfway through it caught on something inside, a staple or a butterfly clip perhaps. It began to stutter, tearing instead of slicing.

Then it was stuck.

"Crap." Darcy pushed a little harder.

The opener moved again, but in its wake a ragged little filigree of white paper emerged from the slit.

"Smooth, Patel," Nisha said, now standing directly behind her.

Darcy slid the contracts out. She had torn the top of the first page.

"Great. My agent's going to think I'm a dipshit."

"That's eight," Nisha said. "Why do they need all those copies, anyway?"

"I guess it's more official that way." Darcy checked the rest of the envelope's contents. She hadn't destroyed anything else. "Do you think this one counts, now that it's ripped?"

"With a massive tear like that? Frankly, Patel, I think your whole career is canceled."

Something sharp levered itself between two of Darcy's ribs, as if the errant letter opener had slipped again. "Don't even say that. And stop calling me by my last name. *Our* last name. It's weird."

"Pfft," Nisha said to this. She developed new verbal tics about once a week, which was often useful. The protagonist of *Afterworlds* had borrowed a lot of her eccentric cursing. "Just put some tape on it."

Darcy sighed, sliding open her desk drawer. A moment later, the contract was taped together, but somehow it looked even more pathetic now. Like a fifth grader's art project: My PubLisHing ContRact.

"It doesn't even seem real anymore."

"It's a disaster!" Nisha fell backward on Darcy's bed, bouncing in her death throes and pulling the blankets askew. People were always saying how much older Nisha seemed than her fourteen years. If only they knew the truth.

"*None* of this seems real," Darcy said softly, staring at the torn contract.

Nisha sat up. "You know why that is, Patel? Because you haven't told them yet."

"I will. After graduation next week." Or maybe later, whenever Oberlin's deferral deadline was.

"No, *now*. Right after you drop those contracts in the mail."

"Today?" The thought of her parents' reaction sent a cold trickle down Darcy's spine.

"Yes. Telling them is what makes all of this real. Until then, you're just some little kid daydreaming about being a famous writer."

Darcy stared at her sister. "You remember I'm older than you, right?"

"So act like it."

"But they might say no."

"They can't. You're eighteen. That's, like, an adult."

A laugh erupted out of Darcy, and Nisha joined in. The idea of the elder Patels recognizing their children's independence at eighteen—or any age—was hilarious.

"Don't worry about them," Nisha said once they'd recovered. "I have a plan."

"Which is?"

"Secret." A crafty smile settled onto Nisha's face, which was about as reassuring as the shredded contract.

It wasn't only her parents' reaction that was making Darcy nervous. There was something terrifying about her plans, something absurd, as if she'd decided to become an astronaut or a rock star.

"Do you think I'm crazy, wanting to do this?"

Nisha shrugged. "If you want to be a writer, you should do it now. Like you keep saying, *Afterworlds* could tank and no one will ever publish you again."

"I only said that once." Darcy sighed. "But thanks for reminding me."

"You're welcome, Patel. But look—that's a binding legal contract. Until your book officially bombs, you're a real novelist! So would you rather blow all that money as a writer in New York City? Or as some freshman churning out essays about dead white guys?"

Darcy dropped her gaze to the torn contract. Maybe it had ripped because she wanted this too much. Maybe her hand would always slip at the last moment, tearing what she desired most. But somehow the contract was beautiful, even in its damaged state. Right there on the first page, it defined her, Darcy Patel, as "The Author." You couldn't get much realer than that.

"I'd rather be a writer than a freshman," she said.

"Then you have to tell the elder Patels—*after* those are in the mailbox."

Darcy looked at the return envelope and wondered if the Underbridge Literary Agency provided stamps for all its authors, or only the teenage ones. But at least it made sending off the contract as easy as walking to the corner, which took less effort than resisting Nisha. If her little sister had a plan, there would be no respite without compliance.

"Okay. At lunch."

Darcy lifted her favorite pen, and signed her name four times.

"I've got something to tell you guys," she said. "But don't get upset."

The expressions around the table—including Nisha's—made Darcy wonder if she should have started differently. Her father had paused in midbite, and Annika Patel was staring wide-eyed.

Lunch was leftovers from takeout the night before—fried red peppers, chickpeas cooked with tamarind, all of it swimming in garam masala and served straight from the styrofoam containers. Not an auspicious setting for important announcements.

"The thing is, I want to defer college for a year."

"What?" her mother asked. "Why on earth?"

"Because I have responsibilities." This line had sounded better in her head. "I need to do the rewrites for *Afterworlds*, and write a sequel."

"But . . ." Her mother paused, and the elder Patels shared a look.

"Working on books isn't going to take *all* your time," her father said. "You wrote your first one in a month, didn't you? And that didn't interfere with your studies."

"It almost killed me!" Darcy said. She'd dreaded coming home some days last November, because she knew that two thousand words of novel awaited her, on top of homework, college application essays, and studying for the SATs. "Besides, I didn't write a book in a month. I wrote a *draft*."

Her parents just stared at her.

"There's no good writing, only good *re*writing," she quoted, not quite certain who'd said it first. "Everyone says *this* is the hard part, turning my draft into a real novel. According to the contract, I have until September to turn in a final draft. That's four whole months, so they must think revisions are pretty important."

"I'm sure they are. But September is when college starts," Annika Patel said, all smiles. "So there's no conflict, is there?"

"Right," Darcy sighed. "Except once I finish *Afterworlds*, I have to write the sequel, and then revise that. And my agent says that I should be promoting myself already!"

Nisha held up both hands, her fingers silently indicating nine "my agents."

"Darcy," her father said. "You know we've always supported your creativity. But wasn't the main reason for writing the novel so you could put it on your college applications?"

"No!" Darcy cried. "Where did you get that idea?"

Annika Patel placed her palms together, as if praying for quiet. When she had everyone's attention, her look of long suffering softened into a sly smile.

"Is this because you're afraid of leaving home? I know that Ohio seems a long way away, but you can call us anytime."

"Oh," Darcy said, realizing that her announcement was incomplete. "I'm not staying *here*. I'm moving to New York."

In the silence that followed, all Darcy could hear was Nisha chewing on a samosa. She wished that her little sister would at least *try* not to look so amused.

"New York *City*?" their mother finally asked.

"I want to be a writer, and that's where publishing is."

Annika Patel let out a slow, exasperated sigh. "You haven't even let us read this book, Darcy. And now you want to give up college for this . . . *dream*."

"I'm not giving it up, Mom, just deferring it for a year." The right words finally came to her. "A year of studying the publishing industry. Learning all about it from the inside! Can you imagine what *that* would look like on a college application?" Darcy waved her hands. "I mean, except I won't need to apply again, because I'm only deferring."

Her voice took on a guilty quaver at the end. According to the Oberlin student manual, deferment was allowed only under "exceptional circumstances," and the definition of "exceptional" was up to the school. They could say no, and then she'd have to start all over.

But being under contract to write a novel was pretty exceptional, wasn't it?

"I don't know about this, Darcy." Her father shook his head. "First you don't apply to any universities in India, and then—"

"I'd never get into a good school in India! Even Sagan couldn't, and he's a math genius." Darcy turned to her mother, who actually read novels. "You guys thought it was awesome when my book sold."

"Of course it's wonderful." Annika Patel shook her head. "Even if you won't let us read it."

"Just until I do the rewrites."

"That's up to you," her mother said. "But you can't expect every novel you write to make this tremendous amount of money. You have to be practical. You've never lived alone, or paid your own bills, or made your own food. . . ."

Darcy didn't trust herself to speak. Her eyes stung, and her throat was tight. Nisha had been right—now that she'd uttered her dream aloud to her parents, it had become real. Too real to lose.

But at the same time countless other things had become real, all the nuts and bolts of food and shelter. Darcy had never even done her own laundry.

She looked pleadingly at her little sister. Nisha placed her fork down with a little tap, just loud enough.

"I was thinking," she said as everyone turned to her. "Moneywise, it might be better if Darcy takes a year off."

No one said anything, and Nisha played the silence for a moment.

"I was looking at Oberlin's financial aid forms. And of course the main thing they ask is what the parents earn. But there's another place where they ask for *the student's* income. Turns out, whatever Darcy makes comes straight off the top of any aid they offer."

Still no one spoke, and Nisha nodded slowly to herself, as if she were realizing all this just now.

"Darcy's going to make more than a hundred grand this year, just by signing that contract. So if she starts college now, she won't get any financial aid at all."

"Oh," Darcy said. Her two-book advance was about the size of a four-year education. By the time she'd finished college, every penny would be gone.

"Well, *that* doesn't seem fair," her father said. "I mean, maybe there's a way to change the contract and delay the—"

"Too late," Darcy said, marveling at her little sister's deviousness. "Already signed and mailed it."

Her parents were staring at each other now, communing in some unspoken parental way, which meant that they would discuss the matter in private, later. Which meant that Nisha had opened the door a tiny crack.

Now was the time to seal the deal.

"New York's a lot closer than Oberlin," Darcy said. "I'll only be a train ride away, and Aunt Lalana lives there, and there's a much bigger Gujarati community than in—"

Annika Patel raised her hand, and Darcy stammered to a halt on the word "Ohio." Maybe it was best to save a few arguments for later, in case this battle went to round two.

But already something momentous had happened here at this table. Darcy could feel her course in life, which had been set so determinedly since she was a little girl, bending toward a new trajectory. She had changed the arc of her own story, merely by typing a couple of thousand words each day for thirty days.

And the taste of that power, the power of her own words, made her hungrier.

Darcy didn't want this interruption to last only a year. She wanted to see how long she could stretch this feeling out. To be dizzy with words again, like in that glorious week at the end of last November when everything had fallen into place. Darcy wanted that feeling not just for a year.

She wanted it forever.

CHAPTER 4

WHEN MY EYES OPENED, EVERYTHING WAS WRONG.

My head hurt from having fallen to the floor. I touched my hand to my brow and felt the stickiness of blood. I was too dizzy to stand, but managed to sit up.

Beneath me was an expanse of gray tile, just like the airport floor, but everything else had disappeared. I seemed to be sitting in the midst of a formless gray cloud. All I could see were shadows, wisps of motion in the fog.

Hitting my head had done something to my senses. The light filtering through the mist was cold and hard, and there were no colors, only grays. A roaring sound echoed in my ears, like rain on a metal roof. The air tasted flat and metallic. My body felt numb, as if the darkness I'd fallen through had left me chilled.

Where the hell was I?

A dark shape flickered in the corner of my vision. But when

I turned my head, it vanished back into the mist.

"Hello?" I tried to call, but could barely squeeze the word out. Then I realized why—I hadn't taken a single breath since waking up. My lungs were like the rest of my body, filled with cold black ink.

I sucked in a startled gasp, my body starting up like an old car, in jerks and shudders. A few shallow breaths forced themselves into me. I shut my eyes, concentrating on breathing . . . on being alive.

When I opened them again, a girl stood in front of me.

She was about thirteen, with large, curious eyes that met my gaze. She wore a skirt that fell to the floor, a sleeveless top, and a scarf across one shoulder—all of it gray. Her face was gray too, as if she were a pencil drawing come to life.

I drew a careful breath before speaking.

"Where am I?"

She raised an eyebrow. "You can see me?"

I didn't answer. In that billowing cloud, she was the only thing I *could* see.

"You've crossed over," the girl said, stepping a little closer. Her eyes focused on my forehead. "But you're still bleeding."

My fingers went to my brow. "I hit my head."

"So you'd look dead to them. Clever girl." She spoke with an accent that I couldn't recognize at first. And though I could understand her words, what the girl was saying made no sense. "You're shiny. You *thought* your way here, didn't you?"

"Here? Where am I?"

She frowned. "Maybe not so clever after all. You're in the afterworld, my dear."

For a moment it was like falling again, the floor dropping

out from under me. The distant rumbling sound grew louder in my ears.

"Are you saying . . . I'm *dead*?"

She glanced up at my forehead again. "The dead don't bleed."

I blinked, not knowing what to say.

"It's very simple." She spoke carefully, as if explaining something to a child. "You willed your way here. My brother is just like you."

I shook my head. Anger was rising up in me, along with the certainty that she was *trying* to be confusing.

But before I could say something rude, an awful sound came through the mist.

Squeak, squeak . . . tennis shoes on the tile floor.

I spun around, staring into the formless gray. "It's him!"

"Stay calm." The girl stepped forward to take my hand. Her fingers were cold, and their iciness flowed into me, stilling my panic. "It isn't safe yet."

"But he's . . ." *Squeak, squeak.*

I faced the sound as he emerged from the cloud—the gunman who'd shot at me. He looked even more hideous now, with a gas mask hiding his face. He was coming straight toward us.

"No," I said.

The girl took my shoulder. "Don't move."

Frozen by her command, I expected the terrorist to raise his gun and fire. But he walked past us—*through* us, as if we were smoke and mist.

I turned and watched him recede into the cloud. His passage swirled the gray behind him, clearing a column of air. I saw plastic chairs and television screens and bodies lying on the floor.

"This is the airport," I murmured.

The girl frowned. "Of course it is."

"But why—"

Inside the swirling clouds something flashed, a metal cylinder clattering along the floor toward us. The size of a soft drink can, it rolled to a stop a few yards away, spinning and hissing, spraying more smoke into the air. In seconds the clear passage that the gunman had created filled with mist again.

"Tear gas," I murmured. This wasn't heaven. It was a battle zone.

Security is responding, the woman on the phone had said. I finally realized that the roaring sound was gunfire, muted by distance or whatever had gone wrong with my senses.

"Don't worry," the girl said. "Nothing can hurt you here."

I turned to her. "Where's *here*? None of this makes sense!"

"Try to pay attention," she said, exasperated now. "You've thought your way into the afterworld, and if you go back to reality, you'll be shot. So stay *calm*!"

I stared at her, unable to speak or move or think. It was all too much.

She sighed. "Just wait here. I'll get my brother."

I was afraid to move after she left.

The mist—or tear gas, I suppose—would clear now and then, and I could see bodies around me. Their clothes and faces were gray, like the rest of the world. Everything was leached of color, except for my own hands and the red blood I'd wiped away from my eyes.

Wherever this was, I didn't belong here. I was too alive.

It was long minutes of waiting before another shape loomed out of the mist—a boy my age. I could see the resemblance to his sister, except that his skin wasn't gray like hers. It was as brown as mine at the end of a long summer at the beach, and jet-black hair fell just above his shoulders. He wore a silk shirt that rippled like a dark liquid across his skin.

Even in that awful moment, I could see that he was beautiful. He shone somehow, as if sunlight were breaking through the mist, just for him. He was one of those boys with a perfect jaw, who looks stunning when he's clean shaven, but just that little bit more handsome with the barest shadow of stubble.

"Don't be afraid," he said.

I tried to answer, but my mouth was dry.

"My name is Yamaraj," he said. "I can help you."

He had the same accent as his sister—from India, I thought, with a touch of England. His words came out precisely, like someone who'd learned English in a classroom.

"I'm Lizzie," I managed.

He looked puzzled a moment. "Short for Elizabeth?"

I just stared at him. It was such a strange thing to say.

Something flashed in the corner of my eye—another man, running fast, ducking and weaving as he went. He wore a gas mask, a black uniform, and a bulletproof vest. He must have been one of the good guys, but at that moment he looked like a monster.

Yamaraj put his hand on my arm. "This is almost over. I'll take you someplace safe."

"Please," I said as he turned me away from the muted roar of gunfire.

But then I saw what was ahead of us—the metal gate that had doomed us all. A dozen bodies lay at its foot, still and silent. One woman had her arm flung across a child. Another man's fingers were bloody from clawing at the unyielding steel.

I froze. "This is where they caught us!"

"Close your eyes, Elizabeth." His voice had a quiet intensity that forced me to obey, and he led me gently forward. "Don't worry," he kept saying. "The overworld can't hurt you if you stay calm."

I wasn't calm at all. But my panic was like a poisonous snake at a zoo, staring at me from the other side of thick glass. Only Yamaraj's touch on my arm kept the glass from shattering. His skin seemed to burn against mine.

With every blind step forward I expected to feel a body underfoot, or to slip on blood, but there was only a slight tugging on my clothes, as if we were walking through brambles.

"We're safe now," Yamaraj finally said, and I opened my eyes again.

We were in another part of the airport, where rows of plastic chairs faced the sealed-up doors of boarding gates. Televisions were mounted on the walls, their screens blank. Sliding walkways moved between glass barriers, empty.

The light was just as hard and cold here, and everything still gray, except for Yamaraj, shining and brown. But the tear gas was only wisps and haze around us.

I turned to stare back the way we'd come. The gate was in the distance, the fallen bodies on the other side.

"We walked through that?" I asked.

"Don't look back. It's important that you stay—"

"Calm. *I get it!*" Nothing makes me more annoyed than some-one telling me to stay calm. But the fact that I could snap at him meant that I was coming out of shock.

My anger sputtered when I turned to face Yamaraj. His gaze was so steady, and the glint in his brown eyes softened the hard light around us. He was the only thing in this world that wasn't gray and cold.

"You're still bleeding." He grasped the tail of his shirt with both hands, and with a sharp movement ripped a piece away. When he pressed it against my forehead, I could feel the warmth of his hand through the silk.

My mind steadied a little. *The dead don't bleed.* I wasn't dead.

"That girl who found me, she's your sister?"

"Yes. Her name is Yami."

"She said some weird stuff."

A smile touched his lips. "Yami is unhelpful sometimes. You must have questions."

I had a hundred, but they all boiled down to one.

"What's happening?"

Yamaraj looked past me. "A war, perhaps?"

I frowned. This boy wasn't from around here. "Um, this isn't a war. It's some kind of terrorist attack. But what I meant was . . . I'm not dead, am I?"

His eyes met mine. "You're alive, Lizzie. Just hurt and scared."

"But those other people, they shot them all."

He nodded. "You're the only one left. I'm sorry."

I pulled away from him, stumbling a few steps back and sinking into one of the plastic chairs.

"Were you traveling with someone?" he asked softly.

I shook my head, thinking how my best friend Jamie had almost come to New York with me. She might have been lying there with the rest. . . .

Yamaraj settled on the arm of the chair next to mine, pressing the torn piece of shirt against my forehead again. My sanity was clinging to the simple fact that someone was taking care of me.

My hand clasped his.

"Do you remember what happened?" he asked softly. "How you crossed over?"

"We tried to run away." My voice faltered, and it took a few slow breaths to continue. "But the gate was locked, and one of those men was coming toward us, shooting everyone. I called 911, and the woman on the phone said I should play dead."

"Ah. You played too well."

I closed my eyes and opened them again—same airport, same plastic chairs and blank televisions. But everything looked wrong, like when a hotel elevator opens on a new floor, and the carpet and furniture and potted plants are the same, but different.

"This isn't really the airport, is it?"

"Not quite. This is where the dead walk—beneath the surface of things. You thought your way here."

I remembered lying there playing dead, that feeling of falling through the floor. "A man walked through me and your sister. Because we're . . . ghosts."

"Yami is. She died a long time ago." Yamaraj lowered the cloth and peered at my forehead. "But you and I are something else."

"What do you mean?"

"We're . . ." He stared at me a moment, an expression of longing on his face, and I was transfixed again at how beautiful he was. But then he shook his head. "You should forget this ever happened."

I didn't answer, looking down at my hands, at the familiar whorls on my palms and fingertips. My skin had the same shine as Yamaraj's, but it was still me. I felt the way my tongue slid along my teeth, and swallowed the taste of my own mouth. Everything was perfect in detail, even the way my feet felt in my sneakers.

I looked up into his brown eyes. "But this is real."

"Some part of you knows that, for now. But once you're safe in your own home, you can put it out of your mind, like a dream." He said it softly, with a kind of knowing sadness, but to me it sounded like a challenge.

"Are you saying I'll be too afraid to believe this happened?"

Yamaraj shook his head. "It's not about courage, Lizzie. It's about the world making sense. You may not even remember the attack, much less me and Yami."

"You think I'll forget *this*?"

"I hope so."

Part of me wanted to agree with this beautiful boy, to let everything I'd seen fall into some dark hole of memory. But for a moment my mind went back to when my father left home. My mother lied to me for the first few months, saying he was just working in New York, that he was coming back soon. And when she finally told me the truth, I was angrier at myself than at my parents, because I should have figured it out on my own.

Hiding from the truth was worse than being lied to.

"I'm not very good at fooling myself," I said.

"Believing won't be easy either."

Something like a laugh pushed its way out of me. "You think things are going to be easy? After *this*?"

The look of longing crossed his face again, but then he shook his head. "I hope you're wrong, Lizzie. Believing isn't just hard, it's dangerous. Doing what you've done, crossing over, can change you in ways you don't want."

"What does that even—" I began, but Yamaraj was staring past me, beyond the metal gate. I turned, and saw something that made the inky cold rise up in me again.

Walking through the mist were dozens of people—eighty-seven, as the news kept repeating later—their faces gray, their clothing torn by bullets. They shuffled together in a mass, crowding around Yami, as if they all wanted to be close to her. They didn't touch one another, except for one little girl holding both her parents' hands. She was staring at me, her expression clearly wondering, *Why does that girl get to stay?*

Yami knelt and touched the tile floor, and a darkness began to spread out from her, as if some slow black liquid were bubbling out of her hand. The dead people looked down at their feet. And then they began to sink. . . .

A bitter taste rose in my mouth. "This isn't fair."

"Close your eyes," Yamaraj said.

My heartbeat pounded in my wounded head, and the world started to shift around me, normal colors shimmering through soft gray. The mass of ghosts flickered for a moment, transparent, and through them I could see the flash of gunfire. The hideous roar grew sharper in my ears.

Yamaraj grasped my hand. "Stay with me here. Just a little longer."

I shut my eyes, but only for a moment, willing my heartbeat slower. When I looked again, the gray world had steadied, and I could see the crowd of ghosts perfectly, Yami at its center.

"Where's she taking them?"

"Somewhere safe." He squeezed my hand again. "We're here to guide the dead. It's okay."

"It's *not* okay!" I pulled my hand from his, my voice breaking. A single teardrop squeezed from my left eye. "Those men with guns . . . they had *no right*."

Suddenly the thick glass between me and my panic was gone, shattered by anger. I could smell blood and gun smoke, and an acid scent that made the back of my throat tickle. The real colors of the airport were bleeding into the grays around us.

"Something's happening," I tried to say, but my throat closed on the words. The air itself had begun to burn my eyes and skin. As my grasp on the afterworld failed, the gas was leaking through to me. I could feel my cheek burning where the single tear had squeezed out.

Yamaraj stood up. "I have to take you back."

He took my hands in his, which suddenly weren't warm and living anymore. I felt a coldness rushing into me. I realized that he wasn't taking me back to the real world, but to the dark place I'd passed through while playing dead.

"Wait," I tried to say.

"It isn't safe here, Lizzie."

I tried to protest, but my lungs stilled once more. My eyelids fluttered closed, and I felt myself falling away, spiraling back down toward the silence.

I'm dead again. I'm dead.

I had a vague sense of Yamaraj lifting me from the airport chair and carrying me back the way we'd come. I could see and hear nothing, but felt him watching over me.

Finally, a long time later, he whispered in my ear.

"Believing is dangerous, Lizzie. But if you need me, call me. I'll be there."

His lips pressed against mine, and a wave of heat flooded into me. Not only warmth, but energy, a force that stirred every muscle in my body. The cold inside me turned sharp and buzzing. Electricity coursed through my nerves and across my skin.

The heat built, pushing against my heart and lungs, the power of it coiling around me and squeezing tight. My eyes sprang open, but there was only darkness rushing past me, and then something sharp and jagged burst from my lungs . . .

I was *breathing*, coughing and sputtering, spasming on cold hard ground. There were spinning lights in all directions—the metal flash of badges, the dull glint of body armor.

I was lying on the sidewalk outside the airport. Fluttering yellow tape marked off the sidewalk around me, a corral of motionless bodies under white plastic sheets. Red and blue lights pulsed from every vehicle, sending shadows swinging, as if the bodies were twitching beneath their covers.

There was so much *color* in the world, everything bright and alive. The crackle and hiss of radios electrified the air.

I became aware of people suddenly gaping at me—two paramedics, a police officer with a hand on his holstered gun and terror in his eyes. A plastic sheet was wrapped tight around me, its edges fluttering in the freezing wind, and I wanted to yell at them to set me free. But it was all I could do to keep breathing, to keep that fire that Yamaraj had relit inside me burning.

I was alive.

CHAPTER 5

MOXIE UNDERBRIDGE LIVED IN A TALL AND CURVACEOUS TOWER on the south side of Astor Place. The neighborhood was full of weathered colonnades and arched windows, but Moxie's building was shiny-new and wrapped in sinuous reflective glass. The mirrored checkerboard of its windows divided the sky overhead into a pack of blue-and-white playing cards.

"This looks fancy," Nisha said to Darcy.

"It should be fancy," said their mother. "If that woman is putting my daughter here."

"Moxie isn't *putting* me here. She's letting me borrow it." Darcy muttered this softly enough that a passing taxi swept her words away. In two weeks she would be moving into her own apartment, which would no way be this fancy—or secure. Best not to start her mother thinking about that.

The lobby was even more impressive, with an arched marble

ceiling and a chandelier with electric bulbs that flickered like tiny gas lamps. Before Darcy could open her mouth, the uniformed doorman said, "You must be Miss Patel."

Moxie had told the building management Darcy was coming, of course, and how many young Indian girls strolled into this building every day? But it was still intimidatingly efficient.

"Yes, she is," her mother said when Darcy was too slow answering.

The doorman nodded. "I understand you already have the keys, Miss Patel?"

Darcy nodded back at him, her fingers dipping into the outside pocket of her laptop case. The arrival of Moxie's keys a week ago had reignited the whole college deferment battle with her parents, and Darcy had hidden them beneath her mattress, half fearing that her mother would steal them.

"You two go ahead." Annika Patel flicked a hand at the elevators. "I'll wait here. Who knows how long it'll take your father to find a parking spot!"

Darcy blinked. Were they actually being allowed to go up alone?

Nisha grabbed her hand and pulled her forward.

At Darcy's first hesitation with the keys, Nisha snatched them away and made short work of Moxie's two dead bolt locks. She strode through the door, kicking off her shoes with a victorious smirk. Darcy followed, slightly miffed that her little sister had crossed the threshold first.

The foyer spilled down a few steps into the living room, where sunlight filtered through a curtain that snaked along the floor-to-ceiling windows. Nisha took hold of one end and slid the curtain along its runners, the nineteenth-story view spilling open in her wake.

"Be careful with . . ." Darcy swallowed the rest of her warning. This would be her apartment for two whole weeks, but Nisha was driving back to Philly with their parents in a couple of hours. It was only fair to let her enjoy it. It was strange to think that tonight, her little sister wouldn't be a few footsteps or a shout away.

As the serpentine expanse of glass drew open, the city seemed to wrap around them: rooftop gardens with stunted trees in pots, water towers like chunky flying saucers, the spires of distant sky-scrapers.

Nisha stared wide-eyed at the view. "Holy crapstick. Your agent must be *loaded.*"

"My agent is kick-ass," Darcy said softly, slipping off her shoes and setting her laptop case on the couch.

"That's number eleven!" Nisha didn't turn from the view. "You owe me a dollar, Patel."

Darcy smiled. "Money well spent."

"Why the hell does your agent go on vacation? It's so awesome *here.*"

"It's probably nice on the French Riviera too." Darcy was fairly certain of that, but Nisha's point stood. How could Moxie stand to leave this view behind?

"The French Riviera," Nisha said slowly, as if all three words were new to her. "Agents make more than authors, don't they?"

"Um, I think that depends."

"Well, she gets fifteen percent of your money, right?"

"Yes," Darcy sighed. She'd already had this discussion with Dad, who'd offered to negotiate the contract himself for a mere 2 percent of the advance. He was good at missing the point that way.

"And how many clients does she have?"

"Maybe thirty?" While writing her query letter, Darcy had dutifully googled them all. "Thirty-five?"

"Damn!" Nisha turned from the window, triumphant. "Fifteen percent is a seventh of a hundred percent, and a seventh of thirty-five is five. So Moxie makes about five times as much as her average author."

"I guess." Darcy was pretty sure that Nisha was missing something too. "But I think most writers make, like, zero dollars most years. Not that you should tell the parentals that."

"My lips are sealed." Nisha smiled. "But forget writing. When I grow up I'm going to be an agent."

A squawk came from another room, and Nisha jumped up onto the big living room couch. "What the hell!"

"Relax," Darcy said, remembering the email from Max, Moxie's personal assistant. "That's Sodapop. He's a parrot."

"Your agent has a parrot?"

The squawk had come from an open door, which led into a room crowded with a huge bed, a duo of oak valets heaped with clothes, and a covered birdcage the size of a gas station pump.

Max usually fed Sodapop while Moxie was away, but it would be Darcy's job for the next two weeks. She approached the cage, and heard a feathery shuffling from inside.

She reached up and pulled the cover off. A brilliant blue bird with streaks of yellow and red in its tail gave her a cockeyed stare.

"Hello?" Darcy said.

"Want a cracker?" Nisha said from the doorway.

"Let's try to avoid clichés." Darcy held the bird's stare. "Do you talk?"

"Birds don't talk," the parrot said.

Nisha shook her head. "That's fucked-up."

"Don't teach my agent's parrot to swear."

"*Two* dollars."

"Whatever." Darcy turned to survey the rest of the room. A half-open sliding door revealed a large black marble tub, and another door stood closed. She crossed to open it and peeked inside. "Oh, my god."

"What is it, Patel?" Nisha was headed across the room. "Porn stash? Author dungeon?"

"No. It's a . . ." Darcy tried to wrap her head around the space. "I think it's a closet."

It was as large as her parents' bedroom at home. Two poles stretched from wall to wall on either side, bowed under the weight of dresses in plastic covers and suit jackets with tissue paper stuffed into their sleeves. Directly across from the door were ranks of glass-fronted drawers, with a bank of cubbyholes along the bottom stuffed full of shoes.

Darcy walked into the closet, peering through the little glass windows into the drawers. Each held exactly three shirts, neatly folded and with a white curl of cardboard keeping their collars stiff.

"Whoa," came Nisha's voice from the closet door.

"Look at these drawers," Darcy said, close enough to fog the glass. "You can see what's inside *before you open them!*"

She pulled on a handle, and the shirts rolled out with the shush of hidden little wheels. When she pushed, the drawer drifted slowly closed, pausing for a moment before shutting, as if an invisible hand guided its passage.

Darcy opened and closed the drawer again. The sound had the metal fizzle of ball bearings, like a bicycle wheel turning free, but less clicky.

The flattest part of her first chapter was Lizzie's father's super-fabulous apartment in New York City. Darcy had assembled it from images in catalogs and movies, but now she had a real-life model.

How would she describe a closet like this in a single sentence?

"Rewrites are going to be fun," she murmured.

"So where are you going to put *your* clothes?" Nisha asked. "Looks pretty crowded in there."

"Doesn't matter. I only brought T-shirts."

"Seriously, Patel?"

"That's what Mom did when she came over. No clothes from India except jeans and T-shirts, not a single sari. She waited till she saw what Americans wore, so she could fit in."

Nisha rolled her eyes. "New flash: New York isn't a foreign country. Plus it's on TV all the time, if you wanted to find out how people dress here."

"Those are actors. I want to dress like real people," Darcy said, but what she really meant was *writers*. There were swarms of them here in New York. From what she could tell, the population of Brooklyn was at least 10 percent writers. With so many in one spot, there had to be a certain look they shared, a way of dressing and standing and moving. And once her agent (*my agent*, she repeated to herself, because thoughts didn't count against her total) had introduced Darcy around, she would know that look. Until then, she wasn't going to walk around dressed like some girl from Philadelphia.

So jeans and T-shirts it was, even if the plan had appalled her mother.

"So you have to pay rent, buy furniture, *and* get all new clothes. Good financial planning, Patel."

"Yeah, I was wondering." Darcy turned to face her sister. "Maybe you could make me a budget? I mean, you're so good at that stuff."

"Flatterer," Nisha said. "Twenty bucks."

A knock came from the living room.

"You let them in." Darcy pulled out her phone. "I want to take some notes about this closet."

"No way." Nisha yanked Darcy out and shut the closet door. "If they see all those clothes, they'll know where your fifteen percent went. And Dad'll want to do all your contracts from now on."

"Seriously," Darcy had to agree.

As Nisha opened the apartment door, she extended a hand toward the living room windows with a proprietorial air. Darcy was pleased to see her parents' dumbstruck expressions.

"My agent lives in the sky," she murmured, too softly to cost herself another dollar.

Her father had Darcy's suitcase in hand, and her mother was carrying something else—a garment bag.

Darcy took a step forward, blocking her way. "Wait. What's that?"

"I thought you might need something other than T-shirts." The words came out in a rush, over-rehearsed.

Darcy groaned, but her mother kept talking.

"Really, Darcy. I should never have told you that story about coming from India with nothing to wear. It wasn't by choice. We simply didn't have *money* for proper clothes. And the first thing I bought here was a cocktail dress." Annika Patel smoothed the garment bag. "I thought you would want one just like it."

"You thought I would want a cocktail dress from 1979?"

Nisha laughed aloud at this, and even Dad cracked a smile.

"Hush, girl." Her mother unzipped the bag and held up the dress on its hanger. It was classic, short, and black. It was kind of perfect.

Darcy stared, admitting nothing.

"What do you think?" Her mother's eyes were alight.

"Well . . . I *do* have this sort of party tonight."

CHAPTER 6

THE PARAMEDICS WRAPPED ME IN SHINY SILVER MYLAR, LIKE the weightless blankets my dad used to bring on camping trips. They knelt to shelter me from the wind, and one gave me a hot thermos to hold.

But I couldn't stop shivering. The cold had crawled too far inside.

My lips were cracked, my muscles brittle. I couldn't feel my feet at all. When I tried to speak, all that came out was a dry rasp. My eyes watered with the sting of tear gas.

How long had I been lying dead in that sidewalk morgue?

One of the paramedics was shouting into a radio on her shoulder, another wrapping a blood pressure cuff around my arm. As it began to inflate, I thought the pressure would shatter me into splinters. I was made of ice.

An ambulance came to a skidding halt beside us. The rear doors opened, and a gurney hit the pavement, bouncing on dirty white rubber wheels.

"Can you lie flat?" someone asked.

I was in a fetal position, curled around the thermos. My muscles refused to thaw.

"Forty over forty?" shouted the paramedic taking my blood pressure. She shook her head, starting to inflate the cuff again. "Prep an adrenaline injection."

I tried to say no. The heat inside me was building, my body coming back to life.

On a three count, the paramedics hoisted me onto the gurney. The world spun for a moment, and then I was inside the ambulance. It was crowded and swaying as we sped out of the airport. A needle glimmered among the blinding lights, as long as an ice pick.

"In her heart," someone said.

They peeled the mylar blankets off me. Hands grabbed my wrists, prying my arms open. I tried to roll into a ball again to protect myself. My body was full of heat now, life flooding back. My lips still burned where Yamaraj had kissed me, and I didn't need their spike in my chest.

But the medics were stronger, and forced me flat. Someone unzipped my hoodie, and scissors pulsed cold along my belly, slicing open my T-shirt. A fist raised up over my bare chest, clutching the long needle like a knife.

"*Wait!*" A plastic-gloved hand slapped down over my heart. "She's at ninety!"

"Up from forty?"

"Don't touch me," I managed to say.

The three paramedics in the ambulance were silent for a moment. I heard the sigh of the blood pressure cuff deflating, and felt my pulse flowing back into my arm.

"Ninety over sixty," the woman said. "Can you understand me?"

I nodded, and tried to speak again. She leaned closer to listen.

"What time is it?" I managed.

She pulled away, frowning, but glanced at her watch. "Just after two a.m."

"Thank you," I said, and closed my eyes.

Two hours since the attack had started. I'd been in the afterworld for only, what, twenty minutes? The rest of that time I must have been lying outside in that makeshift morgue, my body freezing.

More than all I'd seen and heard, it was coming back to life that made me believe in the afterworld. I could *feel* that I'd been somewhere else. The scent of a faraway place lay on my skin. I could see Yamaraj perfectly in my mind, and his taste lingered on my lips.

On the way to the hospital, one of the paramedics kept saying he was sorry, over and over. A strange calm had wrapped itself around me, but the paramedic sounded like a man in shock.

"What are you sorry for?" I finally croaked. My mouth was so dry.

"I'm the one who called you."

I just stared at him.

"I couldn't find a pulse. Your head wound didn't look bad, but you had no respiration, no pupil response. You were so cold!" His voice grew ragged. "You looked too young for cardiac arrest, but I thought maybe you'd passed out on your back and the tear gas had made you vomit and . . ."

I finally understood. He was the one who had proclaimed me dead.

"Where did you find me?"

He blinked. "In the airport, with the other bodies. Everyone thought you were dead."

"It's okay," I told him softly. "I think you were right."

He stared at me, terror in his eyes. Maybe he thought I was going to sue him, or that someone would revoke his license over this.

Or maybe he believed me.

At the hospital there were beds lined up, a squad of doctors and interns waiting for the flood of wounded. But, as everyone soon realized, there was only one survivor. Just me, out of all those people.

By the time they rolled me into an examining room, I could sit up. My blood pressure and body temperature were normal, my pulse steady, and the blue tinge of hypothermia had faded from my skin.

Shudders kept rolling through me, but after the doctor put six stitches in my forehead, he declared that I didn't need anything but fluids. He was most confused by how little the tear gas had affected me. Nothing but an inflammation on one cheek, where that single tear had somehow burned my skin.

The paramedic who'd pronounced me dead brought a cup of hot water and lemon to me. Then there was a call that casualties were coming in, and for a few minutes I was left alone. It was a car accident, I think, nothing to do with the airport, but the staff was keyed up by the news blaring from a radio. People in scrubs hurried past my door.

I blew on my hot water, blinking at the antiseptic whiteness of everything. It was so noisy back here in reality, buzzing and chaotic. The paper cover on the bed crinkled. A black plastic widget clipped to my fingertip transmitted my vitals to a small screen, where they pulsed in colored lights.

Exhaustion was creeping over me, but I was too wired to sleep. Besides, on this narrow bed with its slippery paper cover, I'd probably roll off onto the floor.

I wondered if anyone had called my mother and told her I was alive. They hadn't even asked my full name yet.

My hand went to my pocket. But my phone was gone. Of course, I'd dropped it. I sighed and zipped my hoodie closed over my sliced T-shirt. At least no one had put me in a hospital robe. Maybe they would just let me leave.

I had no ride, of course, or much cash, and my luggage was back on the plane. . . . My mind spun away from everything that had happened back at the airport, and focused on how annoying it was to have no phone.

"Fucking terrorists," I said softly.

"You shouldn't say that word."

I looked up. There was a young boy in the doorway, maybe ten years old. He wore a red plastic raincoat, glossy and wet.

"Sorry," I said.

"It's okay." He took my apology as permission to step into the room. "I'm not supposed to tell grown-ups what not to say. Even if they use bad words. Are you a grown-up?"

"Only sort of. But compared to you, yeah."

"Okay." He nodded once. "I'm Tom."

"I'm Lizzie." My head felt heavy again. Terrorists, the after-world, doctors, and now this little kid. No one wanted to let me sleep.

His raincoat was dripping water on the floor.

"Is it raining?"

"No. But it was."

"Right," I said. But it hadn't been, and it was freezing out, too cold for anything but snow. Tom's bare legs showed beneath the hem of his raincoat.

"When was it raining?" I asked.

"When the car hit me," Tom said.

I felt a sliver of the cold that Yamaraj's kiss had forced out of me, like a cool finger sliding down the middle of my back. The hospital seemed to go still outside my room, as if the sound had been sucked up by something thirsty for noise and clatter and life.

I closed my eyes, but opened them again instantly. Tom was still there, looking at me funny.

"Are you okay, Lizzie?"

"I don't know. I died tonight, I think."

"Don't worry. It only hurts at first." He frowned at me. "But you look shiny, like the nice lady who comes."

"The nice lady?"

"The one who's not dead. She's my friend."

"Oh." My own voice was distant in my ears, as if I'd already fallen asleep and this was someone else's conversation leaking into my dreams.

"She comes every week to talk to me." Tom reached into his pocket and pulled out something soggy. "Want some gum?"

"No thanks." I could hear my heart beating a little faster, thanks to the machines by my bed.

I was shiny, like Yamaraj. And this woman who visited ghosts.

"Listen, Tom. Tonight was really weird. I'm kind of tired."

"Okay," he said. "I'm going to go now. But get well soon!"

"Thanks. You too . . . I guess."

Tom turned and walked back out into the hall, turning to wave at me.

"Bye, Lizzie."

"Bye, Tom." I let my eyes close again, counting out ten long breaths until the beep that was tracking my heartbeat steadied a little.

When I looked again, he was gone, and the bustle of the hospital had returned. People in blue and green scrubs went past the doorway, no one looking in on me.

I pulled the black plastic clip from my finger, slipped from the bed, and took a few steps to the door. I sank to my knees to place a palm flat on the spot where Tom had stood.

The hospital floor was cool and gleaming, but completely dry.

"Oh dear. What are we up to in here?" came a voice from the hall.

I looked up. It was one of the nurses who'd brought me to the room. He knelt and took my wrist gently, feeling for my pulse.

"Did you get dizzy?"

"No," I said. "I was just checking something."

"Down here on the floor?" His big hands took my shoulders. "What say we get you back to bed?"

I stood up on my own, and he gave me an encouraging smile.

"I just thought it was wet there, and someone would slip."

He looked at the floor. "Looks okay to me. Why don't you lie down, sweetie?"

"Of course." I lay back obediently, but his hand stayed on my elbow.

"I'm going to get Dr. Gavaskar now. Are you going to stay here in bed?"

"I don't think anyone called my mom," I said. "She must have heard on the news. She must be freaking out!"

"I think the airline and TSA are contacting relatives. But how old are you?"

"Seventeen."

His eyes widened a little. "I'll get you a phone. Just sit tight."

"Thank you."

He disappeared into the corridor, and I was left alone with the beeping of my heartbeat again. I decided that there was no need to tell him—or anyone—about Tom. My resolve to stay quiet on the subject of ghosts and afterworlds remained firm that night, through conversations with Dr. Gavaskar, a relentlessly nice woman from the airline, and two field agents from the FBI.

My mother arrived four hours later, and I didn't have to say anything to her at all. She just held me while I cried.

CHAPTER 7

MAX, MOXIE UNDERBRIDGE'S ASSISTANT, CAME TO COLLECT Darcy for YA Drinks Night at exactly six that evening.

Darcy had been ready since five, which wasn't like her. But the little black dress demanded makeup, which she'd never worn often enough to get any good at. Usually after her first attempt, Darcy had to start over completely. But today's ventures at the mirror had gone perfectly, leaving her fidgeting for a solid hour, afraid to touch her own face.

It would have been easier to wear jeans and her fancy black silk T-shirt, with no makeup, like she'd planned. When Max arrived, he was in chinos and a *Thundercats* pullover.

"Am I too dressed up?" Darcy asked as they rode the elevator down.

"You look great!" Max eyed her up and down. "But Drinks Night isn't what you'd call a party. It's just a thing Oscar does every month."

"And I'm really invited?"

"Anyone with a published YA novel is."

"Oh," Darcy said, wondering if *Afterworlds* really counted as published. It wouldn't come out until late next September, almost two years after she'd finished it. Didn't "published" mean your book was actually in stores? Or did it just mean you'd sold it to a publisher? What if you'd signed a contract but hadn't written a word?

The elevator doors opened, and a moment later they were outside, Max leading the way. The sky had turned a watery blue overhead. The sun was low and the streets in shadow. The heat of late afternoon was cooking up a thickish smell from the sidewalks, as if the city had worked hard all day and needed a shower.

Darcy tried to memorize the storefronts passing by, so she'd know the way home. An organic coffee place, a small theater, a bicycle repair shop.

"Are you online yet?" Max asked.

"Um, I have this Tumblr. But I don't update it enough. I don't know what to say, really."

He laughed. "I meant, did you get online at Moxie's?"

"Oh, sorry. Not yet."

"It's You_Suck_at_Writing."

Something twisted inside Darcy. "Pardon me?"

"Moxie's wifi network is You_Suck_at_Writing, with underscores. The password's 'DearGenius,' no space. You found the note on her desk, right?"

"Yeah, I guess." Darcy took a few slow breaths while the echoes of alarm faded. She'd seen a handwritten page pinned beneath a flickering white blobject on Moxie's desk, but Darcy hadn't even cracked open her laptop yet. After the family's tearful farewells, she'd sat in Moxie's bedroom, staring into the fabulous closet and arguing with Sodapop about whether birds could talk or not.

Living here in New York felt somehow fragile, breakable if Darcy moved too quickly. She wanted to wait until more realness had settled over her before daring to email her friends with photos of the apartment. Putting on the little black dress and daring Drinks Night seemed positively foolhardy, but she'd promised Moxie that she would go.

She felt a strange moment of jealousy for her friends Carla and Sagan back home, who had the whole summer to read novels and relax beside Carla's pool before heading off to college. Darcy had an apartment to find, a city to learn, and rewrites to finish in the next few months.

Without looking up from his phone, Max stepped over the stripped frame of a bicycle chained to a NO PARKING sign. "Did you get your ed letter yet?"

"Nan said it's coming this week," Darcy said, feeling new jitters. The editorial letter would be the official list of everything wrong with *Afterworlds*. It seemed perverse for her editor to go into detail, when Darcy herself had spent the last six months wallowing in the novel's shortcomings. But at least she had an excuse to procrastinate before the rewrites.

"And one last thing she wants me to ask . . ." Max was still reading from his phone, an email from Moxie, apparently. "How's *Untitled Patel* going?"

That was the contractual term for the sequel to *Afterworlds*.

But said out loud, the words sounded wrong, like one of Nisha's verbal tics.

"Um." A tiny dog tied to the stanchions around a sidewalk café skittered and yipped as Darcy went past. "I'm still outlining, I guess?"

"Still outlining," Max repeated in a neutral tone, typing with one thumb as they walked.

Darcy wondered why she'd just lied. *Afterworlds* had simply poured from her fingers, and she had no intention of outlining *Untitled Patel*. Darcy was fairly certain she didn't know *how* to outline.

It was possible she didn't know how to write novels either, and that last November's efforts had been some sort of statistical fluke. If a hundred thousand novels were written all at once, surely one would be good *purely by accident*, like passages of Shakespeare typed by a monkey. But that lucky primate would never write another sonnet, even if someone gave it a publishing contract.

Why was Moxie asking about *Untitled Patel* already? The first draft wasn't due for a whole year. Did agents yell at you when you were late? Or were they more like the teachers at Darcy and Nisha's school, quietly but *deeply* disappointed when you fell short of your full potential?

Max came to a halt, at last looking up from his phone. "And here we are."

Candy Ruthless looked like a quaint Irish pub, with its odd name painted in a kelly-green Celtic font on the picture windows. There were loading docks to either side and the faint smell of a fish market in the air. Over the ten-minute walk the neighborhood had changed from refined old edifices to working warehouses. Darcy had no idea of how to get home.

Max paused, his hand on the pub door. "How old are you again?"

"I've been to bars before."

Max only shrugged at this vaguery. Darcy was a published author, after all, and had a reasonably convincing Pennsylvania driver's license saying she was twenty-three if it came to that. Even so, she found herself grateful to her mother for the little black dress. In the mirror, it had made Darcy look positively adult, and fit perfectly.

"Okay," Max said. "I'm just going to introduce you to Oscar and leave. I'm not allowed in there."

"You aren't twenty-one?"

"I'm twenty-six." Max gave her an indulgent smile. "But Drinks Night is no agents, no editors, no whatevers. Unless they're published too, of course."

"Ah. Of course." Darcy took a steadying breath as she followed Max inside.

Darcy had expected Drinks Night to have taken over all of Candy Ruthless. She'd imagined a guest list on a clipboard at the door, or at least a private room separated by bloodred velvet curtains. But now, at ten minutes after six, the reality was a lone wooden table with a drink-ringed, battered surface and three people sitting at it.

Max ushered her forward. "Oscar, this is Darcy Patel."

Oscar Lassiter rose a little and offered his hand, beaming a class-president smile. "Nice to finally meet you!"

As she took his hand, Darcy realized that the other faces at the table were familiar. She'd seen them in videos, as Twitter avatars, on book jackets.

"Oh," she said to the less famous of the two, a man with red horn-rimmed glasses and a tweed jacket. "I follow you."

The man smiled at this, and Darcy felt foolish. The last time she'd checked, two hundred thousand people followed Coleman Gayle. Most of them didn't read the Sword Singer books, he always complained, and were only there for his profane political commentary and profound knowledge of vintage sock monkeys.

"Good to meet you, Darcy. You know Kiralee?"

"Um, of course." Darcy turned to face the woman at the table, but her gaze shied away. She could hear the tremor in her own voice. "I mean, we haven't met. But I totally loved *Bunyip*."

"Oh dear, Coleman. She's got it all wrong!" Kiralee cried. "Save her from herself!"

The others all laughed, but Darcy was perplexed and slightly terrified.

Oscar softly sat her down. "We were just discussing Coleman's theory about the proper way to meet famous authors."

"You check their sales on BookScan the day before," Coleman Gayle explained. "And whichever novel of theirs has sold the *least* copies, you say that one's your favorite. Because that's the one they think is criminally underappreciated."

"Easy for me, since *all* of mine sold the least." Kiralee tipped back her glass until ice rattled. "Except bloody *Bunyip*, of course."

"*Dirawong*'s my favorite," Darcy said, though really it was second to *Bunyip*.

"Excellent choice," Coleman said. "Given the criteria."

"BookScanning bastard!" Kiralee said to him while toasting Darcy with her empty glass.

Darcy finally managed to meet the woman's eye. In a gray hoodie, with twin white earbuds draped across her shoulders, Kiralee Taylor was dressed like a jogger. But she had the bearing of a dark faerie queen, her expression arch, her face framed by gray-streaked curly black hair.

"Though I'm afraid I haven't read your books," she said to Darcy. "So I can hardly be picky about which you like of mine."

"No one's read my books. Book."

"Darcy's a deb," Oscar supplied. "Paradox publishes her next fall."

"Congratulations," Kiralee said, and all their drinks went up in salute.

Heat crept across Darcy's face. She realized that Max had disappeared without even a good-bye, but she was allowed to stay. Here, among these writers.

She wondered how long before someone figured out she was an impostor and asked her to leave. Sitting here, she felt as though her little black dress didn't fit anymore. It felt too big on her, as if Darcy were a child playing dress-up in her mother's clothes.

"Welcome to the longest year and a half of your life," Oscar said. "Published but not printed."

"Like when you've kissed a boy but haven't shagged him yet," Kiralee said wistfully.

"Like you would know." Coleman turned to Darcy. "So what's your book called?"

"*Afterworlds*," Darcy said.

The three of them waited for her to go on, but a familiar paralysis crept over Darcy. It was always like this when someone asked about her novel. She knew from experience that whatever she said now would sound awkward, like listening to a recording of her own voice. How was she supposed to compress sixty thousand words into a few sentences?

"It's quite good," Oscar finally offered. "I'm blurbing it."

"So it's one of these tedious realistic novels?" Coleman asked. "All the rage now, aren't they?"

Oscar made a *pfft* noise. "My tastes are wider than yours. It's a paranormal romance."

"Are those still being written?" Kiralee was flagging a waiter down. "I thought vampires were dead."

Coleman grunted. "They're exceedingly hard to kill."

They ordered—Manhattans for Coleman and Oscar, a gin and tonic for Kiralee, and Darcy asked for a Guinness. She found herself glad for the interruption, which gave her time to marshal an argument.

Once the waiter was gone, she spoke, her voice only trembling a little. "I think paranormals will always be around. You can tell a million different stories about love. Especially when it's love with someone who's different."

"You mean a monster?" Coleman said.

"Well, that's what you think at first. But it's like, um, *Beauty and the Beast*. When you find out that the monster is actually . . . nice."

Darcy swallowed. She'd had this conversation a hundred times with Carla, and had never once resorted to the word "nice" before.

"But doesn't real love work the other way round?" Kiralee

asked. "You start by thinking someone's fabulous, and by the end of the piece you realize he's a monster!"

"Or that you're the monster yourself," Oscar said.

Darcy just stared at the pockmarked table. She had fewer opinions about real-life love than she did about the paranormal kind.

"So what's the love interest in *Afterworlds*?" Coleman asked. "Not a vampire, I trust."

"Maybe a werewolf?" Kiralee was smiling. "Or a ninja, or some sort of werewolf-ninja?"

Darcy shook her head, relieved that Yamaraj wasn't a vampire, werewolf, or ninja of any kind. "I don't think anyone's done this before, exactly. He's a—"

"Wait!" Kiralee grabbed her arm. "I'm keen to guess. Is he a golem?"

Darcy laughed, dazzled all over again that Kiralee Taylor was sitting close enough to touch her. "No. Golems are too muddy."

"What about a selkie?" Coleman suggested. "YA hasn't had any male selkies."

"What the hell is a selkie?" Oscar asked. He wrote realistic fiction: coming of age and drunken mothers, no monsters at all. Moxie had wanted a blurb from him to give *Afterworlds* what she called "a literary sheen."

"It's a magicked seal you fall in love with," Darcy explained.

"Just think of it as a portmanteau," Coleman said. "Combining 'seal' and 'sexy.'"

Oscar raised an eyebrow. "I don't see the appeal."

"In any case," Darcy said, not wanting the conversation to stray too far, "my hottie's not a selkie."

"A basilisk, then?" Coleman asked.

Darcy shook her head.

"Best to avoid horny lizards as love interests," Kiralee said. "And stick with something more cuddly. Is it a drop bear?"

Darcy wondered for a moment if this was a test. Perhaps if she proved her knowledge of mythical beasts, they would take her through a hidden velvet curtain to the *real* YA Drinks Night.

"Aren't drop bears more your territory?" she said to Kiralee.

"Indeed." Kiralee smiled, and Darcy knew she'd gotten a gold star on that one. Or perhaps a gold koala bear sticker. The drinks arrived, and Kiralee paid for them. "A troll? No one's done them yet."

"Too many on the internet," Coleman said. "Maybe a garuda?"

Darcy frowned. A garuda was half eagle and half something else, but what?

"Be nice, you two," said Oscar.

Darcy looked at him, wondering what he meant, exactly. Were Kiralee and Coleman gently mocking her, or all paranormal romances? But the Sword Singer books were full of romance. Maybe Oscar was simply bored with the mythical bestiary game.

"Darcy's love interest is really quite original," he said. "He's a sort of a . . . psychopomp. Is that the right word?"

"More or less," Darcy said. "But in the Vedas, the Hindu scriptures I was using for inspiration, Yamaraj is the god of death."

"Emo girls love death gods." Kiralee took a long drink. "License to print money!"

"How do you hook up with a death god, anyway?" Coleman asked. "Near-death experience?"

Darcy almost coughed out her mouthful of beer. Lizzie's brush with death was the book's unique selling point, the singular idea that had carried Darcy through last November, and Coleman had just come up with it off the top of his head.

"Um, not exactly. But . . . kind of?"

Coleman nodded. "Sounds pleasingly dark."

"The first chapter is megadark," Oscar said. "There's this awful terrorist attack, and you think the protag's going to get killed. But she winds up . . ." He waved his hand. "No spoilers—just read it. Much better than your average paranormal."

"Thank you," Darcy said, smiling, though suddenly she wondered how good Oscar Lassiter thought the average paranormal was.

CHAPTER 8

I COULDN'T TELL THE FBI ANYTHING NEW, AND THE DOCTORS had found nothing wrong with me that stitches couldn't cure, so two mornings after the attack, we left Dallas in a rental car.

Mom hated road trips, because highways in the hinterlands scared her. But she was worried I'd start screaming if I saw DFW airport again, or any airport. What she didn't realize was that I was too numb for anything so dramatic.

It wasn't just exhaustion. There was a sliver of cold still inside me, a souvenir of the darkness I'd passed through. A gift from the other side. Whenever I remembered the faces of the other passengers, or when a clatter in the hospital corridors sounded like distant gunfire, I closed my eyes and retreated to that cool place, safe again.

We left the hospital in secret. One of the administrators led us through basement corridors to a service exit, a squeaky metal door that opened onto a staff parking lot. No reporters waited there, unlike the front entrance.

There were pictures of me in the news already. Lizzie Scofield, the Sole Survivor, the girl who'd sputtered back to life. My story was uplifting, I suppose, the only bright spot in all that horror. But I didn't much feel like a symbol of hope. The stitches in my forehead itched, loud noises made me jump, and I'd been wearing the same socks for three days in a row.

Everyone kept saying how lucky I was. But wouldn't good luck have been taking a different flight?

I hadn't read any newspapers, and the nurses had kindly shut my door whenever radios and TVs were blaring near my room, but the headlines had leaked into my brain anyway. All those stories about the other passengers, all those people who'd been strangers to me, just passersby in an airport. Suddenly the details of their lives—where they'd been headed, the kids they'd left behind, their interrupted plans—were news. Travis Brinkman, the boy who'd fought back, was already a hero, thanks to security camera footage.

The rest of the world was hungry to know everything about the dead, but I wasn't even ready to hear their names yet.

No one seemed to know much about the terrorists. They had ties to a cult somewhere in the Rocky Mountains, but the cult's leaders were denying any knowledge or responsibility. The gunmen themselves had all been killed in the battle—no notes left behind, no manifestos, no clues.

Wasn't the point of terrorism to send a message of some kind?

It was as if they'd simply been in love with death.

*   *   *

We drove all afternoon, eating in the car, stopping only to use gas pumps and restrooms. We passed Abilene, Midland, and Odessa, and then the cities faded into a scrubby wilderness dyed brown by winter. Oil derricks pulsed on the horizon, and dust devils swirled across our path, carrying road trash with them. The highway sliced through outcrops of gray rock that had been dynamited open. The clear blue sky grew huge above our heads.

Mostly we were silent, and I thought about Yamaraj—his eyes, the way he moved, his voice telling me that I was safe. Those details were fast in my memory, while the rest of what had happened at the airport was an awful blur. The only part of that night that had seemed real was the part that no one would ever believe.

When Mom and I did talk, our conversation matched the landscape—brittle and withered. She asked about Dad's new apartment, what I thought of Rachel, and the fancy restaurants where we'd eaten. She asked me what classes I would be starting soon, and even delivered a little speech about keeping up the grades in my final semester of high school.

I could see that Mom was trying to be kind, talking about trivia instead of terrorism. But as the hours passed, her avoidance of reality started driving me crazy. Like she was gaslighting me, trying to make me think I'd imagined the whole attack. Every time her eyes drifted up to the stitches on my forehead, or the little tear gas scar on my cheek, an expression of confusion crossed her face.

But nothing that night had been imaginary. I'd gone to another world. Yamaraj was real. I could still taste his kiss, and when I touched my lips, his heat still lingered there.

Plus, he'd practically *dared* me to believe in him, which is a pretty good way to get me to do anything.

Mom just kept talking about nothing, driving us farther away from Dallas, her hands tight on the wheel. The closest she got to mentioning the attack was to say that my luggage would arrive in San Diego soon after we did.

"They said a few days."

No mention of who "they" were. The FBI? The airline? She spoke as if my bag were simply lost, not sitting in a pile of evidence for the biggest Homeland Security investigation in a decade. No big deal.

"Doesn't matter," I said. "I've got plenty of clothes at home."

"Yeah. It's much better to lose your luggage on your way home than going away!"

As if that was the big takeaway from surviving a terrorist attack.

"All I need is a new phone," I said.

"Well . . . maybe we can stop somewhere and get you one." She hunched forward, scanning a cluster of passing signs, as if one might lead her to an Apple store out here in the West Texas desert.

Didn't she understand that I needed things to make sense right now? I needed my mother here in reality with me, not off in make-believe land.

We kept driving. Long pauses were easy in this terrain, and it was a while before I spoke up again. "I feel weird without it. That phone saved my life, kind of."

Her grip on the steering wheel grew tighter, and her foot must have tensed on the gas pedal, because the car shuddered beneath us.

"What do you mean, Lizzie?"

I took a slow breath, drawing calm from the cold place inside me.

"I was running away, we all were, and I called 911. The woman on the phone said . . ." My voice gave out, not with any emotion that I could feel, but like a ballpoint pen running dry. I'd already told this story, I realized—to Yamaraj.

My mother waited, staring at the road ahead, the muscles in her shoulders tight, and I heard that calm voice from my phone: *Can you get to a safe location?*

"She told me to play dead," I finally said. "That's why they didn't kill me. They thought I was dead."

My mother's voice was tight. "The doctors told me about that paramedic, the one who thought you . . ."

"He was really sorry about that." I shrugged against my seat belt. "Guess I fooled him, too. But it wasn't even my idea. The woman at 911 told me what to do."

Well, not quite. She hadn't told me to think my way to the afterworld, meet a boy, and then come back. And she hadn't mentioned anything about seeing ghosts, either.

Tom hadn't reappeared once they'd given me my own room, so it was possible I'd imagined him. Or maybe he only haunted the ER.

Mom made a soft sound. She was trying to say something, but couldn't. The hairbreadth narrowness of my escape was more reality than she could take.

That was when I realized the weird truth: my mother was more freaked out than I was. And the fact that I was so cool and calm, not sobbing and shuddering, only made it worse for her.

She didn't know about my dark place inside, where I could escape anytime. She didn't know that I'd walked the afterworld.

I was going to have to take care of her. But at that moment the best I could manage was, "It's weird not having a phone."

"We'll get you another one," she said firmly. "Exactly like the old one, so everything feels normal."

"I'll get Dad to pay for it."

Her knuckles went white again, and I waited through another long pause, staring out the passenger window at the pulsing highway lines.

At last she said, "Your father really wanted to come, he told me to tell you."

I frowned, because it hadn't even crossed my mind that Dad would fly down to Dallas. I was used to him bailing when things got crazy. Once when I was twelve, one of our cooking pots had exploded, a grease fire flowering across the kitchen ceiling, and he'd beat the flames down with a towel like a total hero. He probably saved the whole house from going up. But the moment the fire was under control, he'd driven away to spend two nights in a hotel, leaving me and Mom to call the fire department, clean up, and air out the house.

That was just Dad being normal.

"I'm glad he didn't come," I said.

My mother let out a half-stifled laugh. "Really?"

"He's tough to handle when he's freaked out. And you've taken care of him enough for one lifetime."

She turned her head and stared at me. I'd never said anything like that to her before, even though it was totally true.

When her eyes started to glisten, I pointed ahead. "Um, Mom? Road?"

Her attention went back to the highway. "He called this morning. But I was kind of bitchy and wouldn't let him talk to you, since he wasn't flying down. Sorry."

"That's okay." I smiled. "He can call me when he buys me a new phone."

I don't know how late we drove that night. I fell asleep just as the sun was setting, the sky turning red and swollen overhead.

We were at a motel when the car stopped next, and I woke up just enough to stumble to our room. I remember that the bed smelled wrong—not bad, but wrong, because it wasn't mine and I wanted to be home. And then I was asleep again.

It was still dark when my brain switched back on, all at once.

There was an energy running through my body. Not the panic I'd felt at every sudden noise for the last two days, but something dark and warm. My fingers went to my lips, which were buzzing.

I sat up and looked around the room, taking a moment to remember where I was. Light from the ice machine outside was creeping around the blackout shades, revealing my mother asleep on the other bed. The darkness felt close, like something physical pushing in on me.

I'd fallen into bed in dirty clothes, but on the dresser were the T-shirts and underwear we'd bought at the hospital gift shop. I took a shower, which didn't wake Mom up, and dressed quietly. The hospital shop hadn't sold socks, so I slipped my sneakers over bare feet, grabbed my hoodie, and went outside.

The sky was streaked with shredded clouds, slowly turning burnt orange as dawn approached. A few spots of broken glass in the motel parking lot glittered like frost in the still, cold air. I pulled on my hoodie and crossed my arms against the chill.

A neon sign read WHITE SANDS MOTEL, and across the highway loomed the silhouettes of sand dunes. We'd made it all the way to New Mexico.

My father had taken me to White Sands for a camping trip when I was ten or so. I wondered if Mom even remembered that I'd been here before.

With no cars in sight, I strolled across the empty highway, brazenly stopping in the middle to close my eyes and listen. The warm energy that had awakened me was still playing on my lips. In the silence I could almost hear it crackle.

When I opened my eyes again the desert looked as blank as fresh paper. White Sands is a desert like little kids draw, the dunes featureless humps receding into the distance. The scrubby deserts of California had looked wrong to me ever since that camping trip with Dad.

The dunes were low by the highway, but after half an hour of walking they'd grown high enough that I was climbing with hands and feet, shedding little avalanches with every step.

From the dune tops, the desert lay spread out before me, ripples in a vast white sheet. The sky had lightened, erasing all but a few stars, and the eastern horizon was blossoming with dawn. Down among the dunes were metal picnic tables bolted to blocks of concrete. Forty-foot poles shot up from them, little plastic flags at their tips.

I remembered those flagpoles from our camping trip. They were to help picnickers find their way back to the tables. The sands were so featureless that you could get lost a hundred yards from your picnic and wander straight out into the desert, thinking that your table was just over the next dune, or maybe the next. . . .

I wondered if there were any ghosts out there, tourists who'd gotten lost in the desert.

That's when I felt it strengthen, the energy that had awakened me, a tingle on my lips and a heat in my veins. And I recalled something that Yamaraj had said . . . *Believing is dangerous.*

But I didn't have a choice in what I believed. I wasn't going to forget what had happened in Dallas. I'd seen firsthand what philosophers had been arguing about forever, that there was *something* after death. Whether it was good or bad, I didn't know, but at that moment the metaphysical issues didn't seem as important as one simple question:

Could I do it again?

Not only because it was something amazing, going to the land of the dead. But because Yamaraj had thrown me a challenge, saying that if I called him, he'd be there.

Did I believe in him enough to see him again? Did I believe in the afterworld at all?

I climbed the highest dune in sight and stood there, letting my breathing slow. I closed my eyes, focusing on the cold place that lived inside me now, my souvenir from the other side.

Was there some spell that could take me across? The first thing to try was obvious. . . .

"I'm dead." A shiver went through me as I spoke the words, but when I opened my eyes nothing had changed out in the desert. Of course, I wasn't lying in a pool of my own blood, with bullets whizzing overhead and panic in my veins. Plus, I was wearing a T-shirt with a picture of a stuffed bear holding a box of chocolates. (That's hospital gift shops for you.)

I closed my eyes again, letting myself remember the details I'd spent the last two days shutting out—the cold terror of running for my life, the squeak of tennis shoes on tile. And then, out of nowhere, gun smoke stung my nostrils, and a shudder went through my body. My heart beat harder, but I kept my breathing slow.

"I'm dead."

As the words came out, I imagined myself sliding down into the cool sand beneath my feet, down into darkness, through ink black and cold. It seemed like a long time later that I opened my eyes again.

But nothing had changed, except that dawn was a little brighter in the sky.

I sat down in the sand. This might be pointless, trying to think my way into the afterworld again. Maybe nothing short of a full-fledged terrorist attack would work. It wasn't magic words that had changed me that day, but an unlucky plane reservation, seeing people die, a call to 911.

With a little shiver, I remembered the woman's voice coming from my phone. She'd been so calm, almost mesmerizing in all that chaos. In a way, *that* had been the moment when I'd started to leave the real world behind.

For a third time, I closed my eyes and waited for quiet to settle over me. Then I said the words burned into my mind that day. . . .

"Security is responding."

A shudder went through the sand beneath me, but I didn't startle. I calmly breathed in the smell of gun smoke, and let the squeak of running shoes on tile pass over me. The tear-shaped scar on my cheek began to pulse.

I knew what to say next: "Can you get to a safe location?"

The changes came fast—the flat and metallic taste in the air, the silence of the wind, the sudden cold wrapped around my heart.

When I opened my eyes again, color had been sucked out of the world. The sky was huge overhead, as gray as polished gunmetal. There was no sun, only a scattering of red stars, like eyes peering down. Flowing rivers of black oil snaked among the dunes, the air above them wavering with heat. A sugary smell washed over me, sweeter than boiling maple syrup. The dark rivers below were rippling and shivering like a live thing, and my hands and arms were shining.

"Yamaraj," I whispered. It was the first time I'd said his name out loud, but it felt natural in my mouth. Like a word from a language I'd learned a long time ago and only half forgotten.

A shiver went through me, and my grip on this gray place slipped a little. Back in the airport, panic had almost thrown me out. But this time it was excitement, a current that ran along my skin.

I closed my eyes again, shutting out the huge gray sky. I wasn't sure what I was waiting for, but then another shift passed through the air. The scents of blood and gun smoke changed to something sharper, like a burning field of black pepper. And then a wave of heat . . .

"Elizabeth," came his voice, and the cold inside me began to fade a little.

I opened my eyes and Yamaraj stood there, halfway up the dune, a dark figure against the white sand.

I didn't know what to say at first. "Hello" seemed insufficient, ridiculous.

"It worked, didn't it?" I managed. "This is real."

He took a long, careful look at me, until a smile crossed his lips. "Very real, Lizzie."

Him saying my nickname—my *real* name—made the edges of my vision pulse again with color, as if the daylight world were trying to break through.

Yamaraj was as beautiful as I remembered. He still shone, as if lit by the missing sun. He climbed the dune and knelt a few steps from where I sat.

"I'm impressed." His voice was soft, serious.

"What do you mean?"

He spread his hands at the desert around us, the gray sky. "You crossed over on your own. You called me, and so soon."

I shrugged, trying to look casual. But at my sides, my palms had closed around cool fistfuls of sand. "You said I could."

"I said it would be better not to believe, Lizzie. Safer too."

"It's not like I had a choice." With Yamaraj this close to me, the sharp, cold place inside had softened, and the words came easier. "There was a ghost in the hospital, a little boy. Which means I can see spirits now. Did you know that was going to happen to me?"

"I knew it might, but . . . How did you know it was a boy?"

I blinked. The question made no sense. "Um, because he just *was*?"

"You could see him that well?"

"Sure. I didn't even know he was dead at first. He just looked like . . . a kid. He said his name was Tom."

Yamaraj sat a little straighter, as if I were suddenly something dangerous.

"What's the matter?" I asked.

"It never happens this fast. At first, you should only see wisps of light, or hear stray noises. You *talked* to him?"

I'd been so proud of myself for crossing over to the afterworld, for calling Yamaraj. But now it felt like I'd done something wrong.

I tried to smile. "Quick learner. That's what my Spanish teacher always says."

"This is serious, Lizzie."

"I know that." My mouth went dry, the taste of anger sudden and bitter. "Did you think I missed the *serious* part of watching eighty-seven people die?"

"No," he said simply, looking away across the desert. "But I hoped you'd forget. The changes fade, like scars, if you don't believe."

I took a few slow breaths. I wasn't angry at Yamaraj, but at the four men who'd broken my reality. "That's *not* going to happen. If I curl up and pretend none of this is real, then I'll always be scared. Because I'll still *know*."

"I see," Yamaraj said, still watching me carefully. "Then you're going to become one of us, and very soon."

I stared back at him, my skin restless and tight. The numbness

I'd felt since the attack was melting, like when you put your ice-cold hands under running hot water, and the cold turns into itches and sparks.

"What the hell *are* we?" I looked down at the glimmer that lay on my pale hands, a fainter version of Yamaraj's shine.

"There are many words," he said. "Soul guides. Reapers. Psychopomps."

I looked up. "Um, did you just say 'psychopomps'?"

"Some names are more graceful than others. I don't like 'reaper,' myself."

"Too grim?" I asked.

As he smiled, I noticed that his eyebrows had a natural arch in them, a crook in their curve. It made him look like he was teasing me, despite the topic of conversation.

"You can give yourself any name you want," he said. "What matters is, when we're brushed by death, we change. Some of us can see the dead and walk among them. Some of us even live in the underworld. But most of us take longer than a few days to see ghosts clearly."

I didn't know what to say. I had seen Tom only hours after the attack.

"Unless . . ." He paused. "Has anything like this ever happened to you before?"

"Are you serious? Not a chance. But you said *guides*. So where did your sister take all those people?"

"To our home." Yamaraj looked down at the rivers of black oil that coursed among the dunes. "Down to the underworld, where they'll be safe."

"Safe from what? They're *dead*."

He hesitated, then said softly, "There are predators."

The last word sent a trickle down my spine. Suddenly this all felt vast and paralyzing, like realizing for the first time that death was real, and scarier and more complicated than I'd ever imagined.

Yamaraj leaned closer. "You'll be okay, Lizzie. I can help you understand."

"Thank you." I reached out to take his hand.

At the spark of our fingers brushing, something went through my body, an ache, a longing. My heart beat sideways, and sudden colors wheeled across the sky, cutting the gray into tatters. For a moment I was back in reality, the rivers of black oil and red stars gone, like ghosts chased away by morning.

I pulled my hand away from him, and the gray world all came rushing back.

"Maybe this is too soon." He looked down at his own fingers, which had sent that surge through me. "I should go."

I swallowed, trying to speak. I wanted him to stay and tell me everything, but I also felt defenseless before all these changes—like the scar on my cheek, I was raw and new.

In the end all I could do was nod, and a moment later I was sitting alone on that tall sand dune, gasping fresh air, the sunrise pink and brilliant and warm on my skin.

"Shit a brick," I said, staring at my hand. One touch had been enough to throw me back into reality.

My fingers went to my lips, and I sat there for a while, feeling alive for the first time in two days. Only a little piece of the afterworld's cold remained, like a sliver of ice on my tongue.

My mother was stirring by the time I made it back to the room. My shoes and hair were full of sand, and sweat slicked my back inside my hoodie. But a shower could wait.

"Breakfast?" I asked as her eyes opened.

Mom nodded. "You must be starving. You hardly ate yesterday."

She got up and ran a brush through her hair, and a minute later we were headed toward the motel diner. As we crossed the parking lot, an eighteen-wheeler rolled to a stop in one of the truck-sized spaces. I could feel its rumble through my feet and the heat of its engine against my skin, as if it were a monster beside us.

"You look kind of spacey," my mother said.

"Not enough sleep." Then I did the math. "Make that too much sleep."

"Poor kiddo," she said softly.

We went inside and studied the place mat menus, Mom smiling at how much I ordered. My body was really waking up now, wanting food and coffee and for the world to make sense again.

After the waitress had left us, I caught my mother staring at the stitches on my forehead. Then her eyes lingered on the place where the single tear I'd cried in the afterworld had left a tear gas burn on my left cheek.

I doubted she knew how often she did that. Would she keep doing it for the rest of her life?

But finally she turned from me to look out the window. "It's so beautiful here. We should stop and see some of the sights."

"Um, like the sand dunes?"

"Well, they're kind of hard to miss. But there's a ghost town up north of here. It's called Chloride, because of a mining boom way back. There was a brochure in the room. Looked interesting."

For a moment I thought of Tom's face, and a shudder went through me. "No ghost towns, okay?"

She turned back from the window and saw my expression, then reached to take my hand.

"Of course not." She was talking just above a whisper, like she didn't want anyone else to hear. "Sorry I even mentioned that."

"No, I'm fine, Mom. It's just that . . ." These terrorists had tried to kill me but I'd gone to the land of the dead and now could see ghosts and apparently had acquired dangerous new powers and this boy, this boy had touched my fingertips—and they still tingled.

Plus, I really needed some better clothes.

"It's okay," my mother said. "We'll just get you home."

CHAPTER 9

AN HOUR LATER SOME TWO DOZEN AUTHORS HAD ARRIVED.
YA Drinks Night had taken over several tables, though these were
populated only by handbags and empty glasses, as everyone was
standing now.

Oscar had introduced Darcy around, as a writer whose debut
novel featured a hot Vedic death god. Everyone smiled when
they heard that phrase, or joked that they were *dying* to read it.
Somehow reducing her book to a single phrase made talking about
it less paralyzing. It gave Darcy a feeling of control, like knowing
Rumpelstiltskin's name.

Everyone was talking about their own work as well, and
about the superpowers of their agents, the bloody-mindedness of
copyeditors, and the perfidies of marketing departments. Darcy
was swimming in a sea of publication, and all she wanted was to
drown.

My first day in New York, she thought, a little giddy from her second Guinness.

"Are you Darcy Patel?" asked a young woman in a bright red fifties cocktail dress. "You signed with Paradox a couple of months ago, right?"

Darcy smiled. "That's me. *Afterworlds.*"

"Sister debs!" the woman cried, and gathered Darcy into a breath-stopping hug.

When she let go, Darcy stumbled back a step. "Um, sorry?"

"I'm Class of Fourteen too! We're sister debs!"

"Right." Darcy wasn't sure if "deb" was short for "debutante" or "debut author," but they meant the same thing. "It's nice to meet you."

"I'm Annie Barber. Pretty stupid, right? I should have gone with a pen name." She looked fearful, as if Darcy were going to revoke her publishing deal on the spot.

"I've always liked the name Annie," Darcy said.

"Yeah, but 'Barber' sounds like . . . a barber. But at least I'm at the beginning of the alphabet, so I'll get shelved at eye level. I've heard the end is okay too, because some people sit down and start at the end. It's just the middle letters that everyone ignores."

"Oh," Darcy said, wondering if her middling last name had doomed her to shelving oblivion. "What's your book called?"

"*A Parliament of Secrets.* Does that sound boring?"

"No, I love collective nouns. Like a parliament of owls, right?"

"Yes!" Annie's face broke into a smile, and her phone came up. "I'm tweeting this."

"Congratulations," Darcy said. "On your book deal, I mean. Not on tweeting this."

"I'm so glad I found you! We've been looking for more sister debs."

"We?"

In answer, Annie propelled Darcy across the room to meet three more debutantes from the Class of 2014. They were all as bubbly as Annie, most of them meeting each other for the first time in person. They'd been on an email list together for months, exchanging advice and gossip and ironclad rules of publishing, none of which Darcy had ever heard before.

"If you don't make a bestseller list in your first week, you're doomed!" was one.

"Blurbs don't work anymore!" was another.

"You should make sure that the quotable lines of dialogue in your book never exceed a hundred and forty characters!" seemed at best debatable.

"Your website should get at least a thousand hits a day *before* your book comes out!" was the scariest.

The strange thing was that the four of them seemed to be in awe of Darcy. They'd read about her deal in *Publisher's Brunch*, and had gleaned how much Paradox had paid.

"Do they, like, roll out a red carpet when you come to the office?" one of her new sisters asked. Her name was Ashley, and her novel was a dystopian set on Mars.

"Not exactly," Darcy said, laughing. When she'd come to New York in March to meet Nan and Moxie, all the carpets at Paradox had been industrial gray.

"Maybe you can blurb me!" another of them joked, and Darcy didn't know what to say to that. She was suddenly glad that

Publisher's Brunch hadn't given her age. Her sister debs were all in their midtwenties at least.

Again, the little black dress was feeling too big, as if Darcy were shrinking inside it.

"Isn't this fun?" Annie asked as she handed Darcy her third beer.

"Sure," Darcy said, staring at the drink warily. "But you guys all know so much. I haven't really figured out anything yet. Like, what should I do to promote myself?"

"Everything."

As that word twisted itself into Darcy, she drank carefully, casting her eyes around for Kiralee Taylor. Being teased by Kiralee and Coleman had been frightening, but it had filled Darcy with a prickly, shivery joy. Her sister debs' zealousness was generating only formless terror.

"Everything? As in . . ."

"As in do you have a blog at least?"

"Just a Tumblr. But I never know what to post. I mean, should I just talk about myself?"

"We could interview each other!" Annie exclaimed.

"Okay." Darcy tried to smile. "First question: Do you really think it matters where my name falls in the alphabet?"

"*Everything* matters," Annie said.

There was that word again. As Darcy took another long drink to consider it, she spotted Kiralee, who was in the corner with a tall young woman who Darcy hadn't met, both of them laughing as if *nothing* mattered. Maybe they would let her stand near them.

"How old are you, anyway?" Annie was asking.

Darcy hesitated, and the silence stretched until it was impossible not to make a joke of it. "My agent and I are keeping that a secret," she whispered.

Annie's eyes widened. "Good idea! You can do a big reveal of your age. Like a cover reveal, but years!"

Darcy could only nod. With her third beer under way, her feet seemed disconnected from the floor, as if gravity were sputtering a little. She'd always wanted to try Guinness, which contained something called "isinglass," which sounded magical to Darcy, even if it was made from fish bladders.

She realized that lunch had been hours ago, and dinner lay in a distant and uncertain future.

"Excuse me a second," Darcy said, and made her way across the room.

Kiralee was in a corner of the bar by the jukebox, an old-fashioned one, almost as large as Sodapop's birdcage and alight with red and yellow neon tubes. Some sort of liquid pulsed inside them, as if the jukebox were a living creature. Kiralee's friend looked only a few years older than Darcy, and wore a crisp white button-down shirt under a black linen jacket.

"Mine's only two-fifty a month," Kiralee was saying. "And it's very secure."

"I could almost afford that," the younger woman said.

Darcy moved closer, testing the bubble of the conversation. The two didn't seem to notice her at first, but she had to be brave. Like Nisha kept saying, she was an adult now.

Kiralee shrugged. "Everything's cheaper out in Brooklyn."

"I know," her friend said with a sigh. "There's nothing in

Chinatown for less than four hundred a month." She glanced at Darcy and smiled, which seemed like an invitation.

"Are these those rent-controlled places?" Darcy asked. "All the apartments I've seen online are at least two thousand."

They both stared at her for a long moment, and then Kiralee's face broke into a smile. "We're talking about parking spaces, darling. Not flats."

"Oh. Right." Darcy drank from her beer, hoping that it was too dark to see the blush galloping across her face. "Parking spaces."

A hearty laugh was bubbling out of the younger woman. "That's one way to save money. Just live in a parking lot!"

Darcy laughed along, wondering if she should head back toward Annie and the others, where she belonged.

But then Kiralee placed a kindly hand on her shoulder. "Have you two met? This is Imogen Gray, another of you endless debutantes."

Imogen smiled, extending a hand. "Darcy, right? Hindu paranormal?"

"That's me." They shook hands. "Seems like everybody here knows who I am."

"Oh," Imogen said. "I guess I just assumed, because you look . . ."

Darcy stared at her, taking a beery moment to understand. "Hindu?"

"Um, yes?" Imogen's eyes had widened a little.

Darcy smiled, trying to look reassuring. All the other writers she'd met tonight were white except Johari Valentine, a science fiction writer from Saint Kitts. "No worries. What I meant was, it's weird how everyone knows about *Afterworlds*."

"Death gods are the new selkies," Kiralee said.

Imogen rolled her eyes. "What she means is, it's nice to see some new mythologies explored. So your book's set in India?"

"No, mostly in San Diego, where my protag lives. And in the underworld, of course."

"Of *course*." Kiralee clinked glasses with them both, toasting the underworld. "So here's a tricky question for you. Does your Vedic death god speak English? Or does this girl from San Diego speak Hindi? Or Sanskrit, I suppose?"

"No. She's white." For a moment, they both looked at her, as if this needed explanation, and Darcy added, "Is that weird?"

Kiralee spread her hands. "Not at all."

"It's just, I wanted to have an Indian guy as the love interest, a guy who looks like Muzammil Ibrahim." They both gave her another questioning look, and Darcy felt embarrassed and young. "He's a Bollywood actor, a model, really. He's the hot guy who was never in the paranormals I read when I was little, you know? But I didn't want it to be about *me* wanting him."

"You wanted every girl to want him." Kiralee was smiling again. "So you chose a white girl from California."

Darcy suddenly wished she had drunk less, even as she took another drink. "Pretty much?"

"Makes perfect sense." Kiralee swirled her ice. "In a problematic way. But life is problematic, so novels must be too."

"That's really deep, Kiralee," Imogen said.

"But yeah, Yamaraj speaks English," Darcy said, because she wanted to show that she'd thought about this. "It's called *Afterworlds*, plural, because there's lots of them. And each afterworld has a raja or a rani in charge, a living person who can cross into the spirit realm."

"Is that from the . . . ?" Imogen frowned at her drink.

"The Vedas? Not really. It's just a thing I made up."

"That's what we novelists do," Kiralee said. "Make things up."

"That's for sure," Darcy said. In the chaos of last November, she'd never kept straight what she'd made up and what she'd lifted from scripture. "Anyway, Yamaraj's afterworld has lots of people from India, who speak languages from all over the subcontinent— Gujarati, Bengali, Hindi. English gets used as the common tongue down there, just like in real-life India."

"Ah, the language of the colonizer." Kiralee's expression brightened. "There are some interesting things you could do with that."

"Right," Darcy said, though she suspected she hadn't done any of them. She'd made Yamaraj speak English for the most practical of reasons, so that he and Lizzie didn't have to mime their undying love. "The hardest thing is making him sound old-fashioned; it just makes him sound unsexy."

"Old-fashioned?" Imogen asked.

"He was born, like, three thousand years ago."

"And hooks up with a teenager?" Kiralee tsked a few times. "Such a thing has never been done!"

Imogen laughed at this. "Except all the vampires ever."

"Well, he's still seventeen, really." Darcy took a sip of beer to marshal her thoughts. "Because time passes differently in the . . . crap. Is it creepy?"

Kiralee waved a hand. "As long as he *looks* seventeen, nobody gets squicked. And as for English, everyone speaks English on TV, even the bloody Klingons. Why shouldn't Hindu death gods?"

"You're babbling, Kiralee," Imogen said. "Klingons speak fucking *Klingon*. There's a language institute and everything. They're translating the plays of Shakespeare!"

"Right, I forgot. You can obliterate the cultures that told the first stories, but Elvish and Klingon must be maintained at all costs!"

Imogen turned to Darcy. "Just ignore her. Kiralee hassles everyone about this stuff. But it's only because she's always in trouble herself."

Kiralee shrugged. "As a whitefella who plunders indigenous mythos, I've had my share of squabble, all of it richly deserved. But at least I pass on my wisdom by hassling you young people."

"You get in trouble for your books? But they're so . . . inspiring!" After reading *Dirawong*, Darcy had done her sixth-grade final project on the Bundjalung people. "I mean, it feels like you *believe* everything you write. You're a lot more respectful than I am about the Vedas."

Kiralee laughed. "Well, I never used anyone's god for purposes of YA hotness."

Darcy stared at her.

"Not that I've read your book." Kiralee put her hands up in surrender.

Imogen rolled her eyes. "It's different when it's your own god, Kiralee."

"I guess so," Darcy said, but that was a tricky one. The only statue of Ganesha in her parents' house sat on her dad's computer, and had magnetic feet, and she'd rejected her family's vegetarianism when she turned thirteen. "Anyway, Yamaraj isn't really a *god*.

He's the first mortal to discover the afterworld, which gives him special powers. He's more like a superhero!"

Darcy was cheating here too. In the earliest scriptures, Yamaraj was mortal, but later he became a deity. That was the thing about the Vedas. They weren't one book but hundreds of stories and hymns and meditations. They had everything—many gods or one, heaven and hell or reincarnation.

But in *Afterworlds,* Yamaraj was just a normal guy who'd discovered, more or less by accident, that he could walk among ghosts. Wasn't that what mattered? Or had the words "hot Vedic death god" magically replaced the novel itself?

Imogen was smiling. "He's only a superhero if he has an origin story."

"He does! With lightning and everything!"

"Radioactive spider?"

"More like a donkey," Darcy said. "That's not from the Vedas, though. I ignored a lot of stuff, like the hymn where Yamaraj's sister is trying to sleep with him."

"That's *so* YA!" Imogen said.

"I'm *so* not going there." Darcy stared at the bottom of her glass, where there was nothing but foam. "Do you think I'm going to get in trouble?"

Kiralee placed her own drink on the jukebox and put a heavy arm around Darcy. "It's not as if you're some whitefella, plundering away."

"That would be your specialty," Imogen said.

"Look who's throwing stones!" Kiralee cried. "Your work is hardly free of scandal."

Imogen let out a sigh. "Right now my work's free of everything, including a plot. I can't find a decent mancy to use."

"What's a mancy?" Darcy asked, relieved that the conversation was finally moving past the plundering of religions. It had opened up questions that her drunken brain wasn't fit to consider.

"Imogen's debut is about a teenager who sets things on fire," Kiralee said. "Pyromancy! And she thinks *I'm* bad."

"Hey, I just glamorize burning shit down. That's way better than cultural appropriation." Imogen turned to Darcy. "My protag starts out as a pyromaniac, a kid who plays with matches. But then she develops gnarly fire powers, and it turns out she's from a long line of pyromancers."

"I knew a kid like that in middle school," Darcy said. "No superpowers, but he was always lighting toilet paper on fire."

Imogen smiled. "My first girlfriend was a pyro, too. In my trilogy, all the magic systems are based on impulse control disorders."

"Right." Darcy had thought that Imogen was her own age, perhaps a little older. But she was already thinking in trilogies, while Darcy had seen only glimmers of *Untitled Patel*.

The thought struck Darcy again: What if there had been only one novel out there for her madly typing fingers to stumble upon?

"The first one's called *Pyromancer*, of course," Imogen said. "But my publisher hates the title for book two."

"Can you blame them?" Kiralee cried. *"Ailuromancer!"*

"What the hell does that mean?" Darcy asked.

"Cats." Kiralee laughed. "Cat-lady powers!"

"Get us drinks." Imogen pulled an old leather wallet from her hip pocket and slipped out two twenties. Kiralee plucked them away and headed toward the bar, and Imogen turned back to Darcy. "It means precognition with felines. Like reading chicken innards."

Darcy's eyes widened. "Your hero chops up cats?"

"Eww, no. Ailuromancy is about reading the way they move, the twitches of their tails." Imogen's hand swept through the air in a graceful curve, as if stroking the back of a sleeping feline. "My protag can listen to a cat's purr and *know* things, like when you hear random words in the crashing of waves."

Darcy's eyes followed Imogen's hand. Sliver rings crowded her fingers, a skull-and-crossbones decorating her pinkie. "That's pretty awesome."

"The magic works fine, but everyone at Paradox hates *Ailuromancer* as a title. They want to call it *Cat-o-mancer.*"

"That's even worse than *Ailuromancer.*" Darcy's three Guinnesses made a mess of the word. "But hey, we have the same publisher."

"Who's your editor?"

"Nan Eliot."

"Me too!"

Darcy frowned. "But how do cats fit in with pyromania? Pets aren't a disorder."

"Are you kidding? My protag's mother is a full-blown cat lady. He's growing up in a cat-filled garbage house. His clothes smell like cat piss, and nobody talks to him at school. Social services is closing in. . . ."

Darcy was nodding. "And then he gets gnarly powers?"

"Precognition, and a bunch of other catty stuff as well—balance, climbing, hearing. He goes from shoplifting to being a legit cat burglar."

"Did you know cats don't have taste buds for sweetness?"

"Really? Cool." Imogen pulled out her phone and began to type. "They also don't get jet lag, because they sleep so much."

"Makes sense. In my book, they can see ghosts!"

Imogen smiled. "Don't think ghosts exist in my world. But maybe. I'm starting rewrites this week."

"Me too." Darcy felt a smile on her face. Had she just had some slight influence on Imogen's novel, just by being here and half knowing something about cats?

Maybe that made up for the fact that she was plundering her parents' religion for purposes of YA hotness. Darcy took a slow breath, letting that thought slide away again.

"But I have to come up with a mancy for book three." Imogen swiped her phone a few times, then read from the screen. "There's hundreds of them: austromancy, spheromancy, nephelomancy. The only hitch is, they're all crappy powers. But I guess it's not fun if it's not tricky."

Darcy contemplated these words. In her experience, *tricky* was mostly hard, not fun. If she'd known how tricky it would be to write a character traumatized by a terrorist attack, who had to process the horror of a massacre across four slow-moving and depressing chapters, she would've chosen a more peaceful way for Lizzie to think her way into the afterworld.

Everyone loved that first chapter, but it had made all the ones after it a lot trickier.

Kiralee returned, a trio of drinks clustered between her hands. "I was just having a think at the bar, and I may have solved your mancy problem!"

"Oh, great. Another one." Imogen lifted two of the glasses from Kiralee's grasp and handed the Guinness to Darcy. "Let's hear it."

"Why not have book three be about a flatumancer?"

No one said anything for a moment.

"Does that word mean what I think it means?" Darcy asked.

"From the Latin, *flatus*." Kiralee's eyes were sparkling. "It's a license to print money!"

"So you're suggesting," Imogen said carefully, "that the finale of my impulse-control-disorder-based dark fantasy trilogy should be about a character whose *farts* are magic?"

"Well, her farts wouldn't have to be *inherently* magic. But couldn't one control magical forces by farting? It's an act of will-power, after all. And it requires a certain purity of spirit."

"I hate you," Imogen said.

Kiralee turned to Darcy. "What's a better name: Fiona the Flatumancer or Freddie the Flatumancer?"

Darcy, trying not to laugh, was unable to reply.

"I think they're both equally good," said Imogen. "In that neither is good."

"But wait," Darcy managed. "What do you *do* with flatumancy? I mean, besides the obvious?"

"Well, I haven't worked out the *entire* magic system yet." Kiralee waved her drink vaguely. "But the spells will all have evocative names: the Cushion Creeper, the Air Biscuit, the Brown Zephyr, and of course the dreaded Secretary of the Interior!"

Even Imogen was laughing now. "Sounds like those spells all do pretty much *the same thing*."

"Only because I haven't mentioned the Flaming Flabbergaster!"

"You plagiarizing cow!" Imogen cried. "The Flaming Flabber-gaster is clearly *pyro*mancy!"

"Pyro-*flatu*mancy, yes," Kiralee said, maintaining an air of absolute dignity. "But let's not be pedantic."

"No, let's not," Darcy said, and the three of them clinked and drank.

The night went on like this, a mix of serious talk, utter bullshit, self-promotion, and slumber-party giddiness. It seemed to last all night, and yet it was still before ten when Darcy looked around and realized that YA Drinks Night was ending. The bar had grown crowded, but now it overflowed with random nonwriters who had wandered in. She recognized only a handful of faces.

Her new friends began to congregate in a last cluster.

"Anyone fancy sharing a cab to Brooklyn?" Kiralee asked.

Someone did, a writer of gothic gay romances who lived in Mississippi and was staying with friends. Darcy's quartet of sister debs was organizing dinner at a pizza place nearby, but she felt too dizzy from her four beers (or was it five?) to go anywhere but home.

"Do you know the way back to Moxie's?" Imogen asked her.

Darcy found herself short on bluster, and told the truth. "No idea. But it's across from Astor Place. A cabdriver will know where that is, right?"

"That's only ten minutes from here. I'll walk you."

"Sorry to be clueless." Darcy had reached the stage of drunken-ness when apologies and promises were frequent. But Imogen only smiled.

They said long, gushing good-byes to everyone and walked out into the night.

The warehouses seemed to have grown larger since sunset, and the streets felt empty and dramatic, like a film set through which they had been permitted to wander after hours. The air was cool against Darcy's skin, which felt fevered from hours of writerly blather.

Imogen pointed. "Ghost building."

Darcy looked up and saw the discoloration on a high expanse of brick before her, a silhouette of a building torn down decades ago. The angle of the roofline was visible, and the jutting shape of a chimney. Above was a ghost billboard—a faded ad for a car repair shop, ancient enough that the phone number had letters at the start.

"My protag can see ghosts," Darcy said.

"Of course. He's a death god."

"Not him. The other one—Lizzie."

"Seriously?" Imogen asked.

"Seriously what?"

"Your protag's name is Lizzie . . . and yours is Darcy?" Imogen began to laugh. "Jane Austen much?"

Darcy came to a halt. "Oh, fuck."

"You didn't *realize*?"

"I didn't mean to. Seriously! It's my *mom* who's the Austen fan!"

Still laughing, Imogen pulled her forward again. "No one's going to notice. Well, except everyone who reads Jane Austen, which is everyone who reads."

They headed toward Astor Place again, Darcy still in tow.

Was it too late to change Lizzie's name? A search-and-replace could effect the switch in seconds, a silent shifting of zeroes and ones. Only a few friends and editors would ever know. But for Darcy it would be like reading a different book, as if some shape-shifter had taken the place of her protagonist. An impostor who might look and act like Lizzie, but whose resemblance only made the impersonation more uncanny.

"I can't change it. It wouldn't be real."

"You could use a pen name," Imogen said. "Change your name instead of hers."

Darcy thought of Annie Barber and the unlucky alphabetic placement of "Patel." "Do people really do that?"

"More than you'd think," Imogen said, squeezing her hand. "But worry about it tomorrow."

Darcy nodded. She had lots of things to worry about tomorrow. Finding an apartment, opening a bank account, and figuring out how to live alone in New York City.

As they walked, she began to read the passing street signs—she needed to learn the city. But it was good to have Imogen beside her.

"How did you meet Kiralee?" Darcy asked.

"She blurbed *Pyromancer*, right after Paradox bought it. And when I wrote to thank her, she invited me to lunch. We've been friends for a year now, I guess, since I moved here from college."

Darcy frowned. Imogen might be a debutante, but she was at least five years older, with college and a whole year in New York behind her. And she'd already written two books, not just one lucky fluke typed in November.

"When does *Pyromancer* come out?"

"This September." Imogen breathed out through her teeth. "Finally."

"You're lucky. Mine's not out till *next* fall."

"Being an author sucks, doesn't it? It's like telling a joke and nobody laughs for two years."

Darcy nodded. Nisha had sent her a text today from the car ride home . . .

Only 462 days till publication!

Darcy suspected that she would get tired of that joke before Nisha did.

They walked without talking for a while, Imogen silently pointing out the shadows of vanished buildings. Darcy began to wonder if things other than people might have ghosts—not just cats and dogs, but motorcycles, typewriters, and school yards. Or even the careers of novelists who'd peaked too early, or had never peaked at all . . .

Darcy was still holding Imogen's hand, and she squeezed it a little tighter. She looked up—the sky was too swollen with the glow of the city to leave any room for stars.

CHAPTER 10

IN THE END WE DID A LITTLE SIGHTSEEING, AND THE TRIP HOME to San Diego took that whole day and most of the third.

Mom let me take the wheel every now and then, but only after a long talk about how post-traumatic stress can affect driving skills. Because that's what people need after traumas, apparently—lots of long conversations about the effects of trauma.

To make things worse, my mother used the trip home to indulge her own road-trip phobias. She commented on the gothic weirdness of the roadside diners we passed, how they looked like they had dead bodies in the freezers out back. And anytime a car stayed within sight for more than a few miles, she thought we were being followed. Driving with Mom was about as fun as it sounds.

Of course, she'd always been a nervous mother. When I was little, I was only allowed to play in our backyard, never at other kids' houses. She got me a phone when I was only ten, which was cool at first, till I found out it was basically a tracking device. And now four terrorists had confirmed all her fears. I wondered if she would ever stop worrying about me now.

But when we crossed the California border just past Yuma, her mood brightened, and she made me play a stupid highway game of spotting palm trees (five points), hybrid cars (ten points), and roof-racked surfboards (twenty!). I quickly got bored of this and shut my eyes in protest, falling asleep until the crunch of tires over driveway gravel told me that we were home at last.

Rubbing sleep from my eyes, I got out and came around to the trunk, ready to unload luggage. But of course there wasn't any. Mom had packed in a hurry, and I only had my hospital gift shop bags full of dirties.

"I'm so tired. We can return this car tomorrow." Mom pulled her overnight case from the backseat and shut the door. "You mind following me over to the rental place in the morning, early?"

"Early's no problem." I'd been waking up at six a.m. every day. Maybe I was still on New York time, or maybe sleep didn't stand much chance against a terrorist attack and a three-day road trip.

Inside the front door there was an awkward moment of parting, my mother gathering me into a long hug.

"Thanks for coming to get me," I said.

"I always will." She stepped back, still holding my shoulders. "I'm so glad you're home."

"Yeah, me too."

We stood there another moment, then wordlessly retreated to the luxury of separate bedrooms.

I dropped the plastic bags on my bed and opened my computer, but when a progress bar showed hundreds of emails downloading, I shut it again.

My face had been on TV, hadn't it? In a sad, awful way I was famous now.

Sitting on my bed, I tried to imagine recounting the attack to all my friends. Would telling the story become something automatic and detached from me, like the time I'd broken my arm in fifth grade?

That was a depressing thought. What had happened in Dallas was about a thousand times more horrible than falling from a tire swing, and also more private. I'd gone to another world, and had brought back pieces of it inside me. That wasn't going to fade, even if Yamaraj said that would be safer. But at the same time, it wasn't something I wanted to share aloud so many times that I'd *memorized* it rather than truly remembering.

I stood and went to my closet, wondering what to wear now that I was a soul guide, a psychopomp, a reaper. Presumably black was appropriate. I didn't have many black clothes, except for a few things I'd just bought in New York. But my suitcase wasn't here yet.

The main thing was to avoid hospital gift store T-shirts with love bears on them. I pulled off the one I was wearing and stuffed it in the trash can by my bed. Then I took a long post-road-trip shower. The water at home was hotter than at any of the motels we'd stayed at, and seemed to thaw the cool place inside me a little. But the cold never went completely away, even the afternoon before in Tucson when I'd stood in the sun on hot black asphalt, willing myself warm. The only time the cold had really gone away was in the desert with Yamaraj.

I wondered if he'd known what his touch would do to me, make my heart shudder so hard that I was thrown back into reality. Or was it something he'd be embarrassed about the next time we saw each other?

There were so many things I wanted to ask him, about the black oil, the underworld, and if he cared whether people had been good or bad in life. But most of all, I wanted to know how Yamaraj had become one of us. What awful thing had happened to send him over to the afterworld that first time?

His face was so serene and flawless, not like someone who'd been through a reality-shattering trauma. Of course, as I stared into the bathroom mirror, I expected my own face to be different, to show what I'd gone through. But the only changes were the scars on my cheek and forehead, as if I'd only fallen off a bike.

I was back in my bedroom drying myself when a noise came from behind the door.

"Yeah, Mom?" I wrapped the towel around me.

The door didn't swing open. It didn't move at all. But it slipped somehow ajar for a moment, like a piece of the world gone missing, and I could see through it into the hallway behind. A little girl stepped through the gap. She wore red corduroys with a brown plaid shirt tucked tightly in, and two fat braids of blond hair hung across her shoulders.

I took a step back. "Um, hello?"

She looked timid and uncertain for a moment, but then she placed her hands on her hips and lifted her chin. "I know this is going to be a little weird at first, Lizzie. But the thing is, I've been in this house just as long as you have."

Her name was Mindy Petrovic, and she was a friend of my mother's from way back.

"We grew up across the street from each other," Mindy began. We were both sitting on my bed, me still in my damp towel. "Your mother had a dog called Marty who ran all over the neighborhood, and he used to chase me on my bike. I made friends with Marty first, then with Anna." Mindy's eyes got a faraway look for a moment. "And I went to the vet with Anna when he died, which was only about a week before I did."

I didn't know what to say. I'd never heard of Marty or Mindy before, but I vaguely remembered pictures of a collie in my mom's old photo albums.

"That's when Mom was how old?"

"Eleven, like me." She smiled. "I'm only two months older than Anna, but she was always in the grade below me. She got born with bad timing."

"But she grew up in Palo Alto."

"Duh," said Mindy. "Me too."

I frowned. "That's hundreds of miles away. And you're . . . here."

"Ghosts can walk, you know. And we have other ways to get around." She looked down at where her fingers were picking at the bedspread, an old quilt my grandmother had made. "But yeah, it's kind of dorky. Like that Disney movie where the pets get stranded on vacation and have to get home. Ghosts are really loyal, like dogs. Except dogs can't see us, only cats."

I shook my head. Mindy kept skipping around, as if she'd never told her story out loud before.

"After I died, my parents started to hate each other. There was a lot of yelling, and it was all my fault, so I moved across the street to Anna's. Her room was always my favorite place. Especially her closet. I would hide in there with her for fun."

"And you've been following her around for . . ." I did the math. "Thirty-five years?"

"I don't know exactly." Mindy looked up from playing with the bedspread. "But I feel more real when I'm around her. Like I'm not fading. It helps to be with people who remember you, and who still think about you."

"Okay," I said, wondering why Mom had never mentioned her. I was also curious about how Mindy had died, but it seemed rude to ask.

"Then you got born!" Mindy said happily. "When you got to be my age, I used to pretend we were best friends."

My reaction must have shown on my face.

"Sorry to be creepy," she said, staring down at the bedspread again. "I never lived in your closet, only hers."

"Right. And *that's* not at all creepy." I was way too claustrophobic to have ever hidden in a closet when I was little.

Mindy shrugged. "It's just, I don't have any friends like me."

"You mean dead people?"

"Yeah. Ghosts are scary. And mostly kind of weird."

She paused for a moment, like someone who's just said they hate their new haircut and you're supposed to disagree. And it was true that Mindy didn't scare me. Somehow it wasn't creepy sitting here and talking to her. She'd been around my whole life, so I'd gotten used to her without realizing it.

But all I said was, "It must suck, being dead."

"I guess. But now that you can see me, we can be *real* friends, right?" She looked up with a timid smile.

I didn't know how to answer that. Maybe my mom had been close to Mindy, but it's not like I was looking for an eleven-year-old invisible best friend.

Then I realized something. "When you walked in here you *knew* I'd be able to see you."

"Of course." Mindy's stare softened, as if she were looking through me. "When you came in, you had that shiny look, like pomps have. That's why I hid at first, because I thought you were one of them." She smiled. "But then I realized that it was just you, Lizzie, and that you'd never do anything bad to me."

"Okay. But why are you afraid of . . . pomps?"

"They come looking for ghosts sometimes," Mindy said. "They take them away. But I always hide."

"Do they take them someplace bad?"

"I think so." Mindy stared down at the pattern of the quilt again. "I met a boy once, who'd gone down to the underworld. But he ran away because he didn't like it. He said it was better to stay up here and fade away."

My skin was crawling with questions now. I'd assumed that Yamaraj was telling the truth, that he and Yami were taking all those people to safety. But what did I really know? All I had to go on was his pretty face.

"What happened to you, Lizzie?" Mindy said, reaching out to run her hand down my naked arm. Though I could hardly feel her touch, goose pimples sprang up beneath her fingertips. "How'd you get so shiny?"

I pulled the towel tighter. The cloth was still damp, though my skin had dried. I didn't feel like telling Mindy about the airport—I wasn't ready to tell anybody about that yet—and I didn't want to mention Yamaraj either. She might tell me not to trust him, and he was the only thing I had to hang on to.

"I should get dressed." When I stood up and went to my dresser, Mindy didn't look away. "Um, do you mind?"

She only laughed. "Lizzie! I've seen you naked, like, a zillion times. Since you were a little baby!"

"Yeah, that's awesome. But it's kind of different now that I can see *you*."

"Pfft," she said, but turned around.

I dressed quickly, in a T-shirt and cargo pants that were both dark gray, the closest thing I had to black. If my trip to the after-world had changed me, I could at least look the part.

Was this what my life would be like from now on? Having ghosts watch my every move? I hadn't seen any on the trip home, at least not that I'd recognized. But Mindy looked pretty normal except for wearing out-of-date clothes and walking through solid doors. Maybe I'd passed hundreds of wandering spirits and hadn't even noticed.

"So how many of you ghosts are there? I mean, is the whole world haunted?"

Mindy shrugged. "Most places, not so much. In this suburb I'm mostly alone, because no one remembers their neighbors. But little towns . . ." Her voice dropped a little. "They're crawling with whispers."

A knock came at the door, and I jumped a little.

"It's just Anna," Mindy said.

I tried to keep my voice steady. "Yeah, Mom?"

She opened the door, her eyes scanning the room. "Um, were you talking to someone?"

"I wish. No phone." I tried not to look at Mindy. "I was just singing along with something."

Mom looked at my laptop, which was shut. Other than my phone, it was the only thing I ever played music on.

"Something in my head," I clarified, pushing wet hair behind my ears.

"Okay." She gave me a nervous look. "I thought we might make pasta tonight. From scratch, with squid ink. I've got the island all cleaned off so we can make a mess."

"Perfect time to make a mess. I just took a shower."

My mother hesitated, so I smiled again to show I was kidding, still managing not to look at Mindy. After what I'd been through, it wouldn't take much to convince my mom that I was going crazy.

"Great! I'll go start the sauce," she said, and shut the door.

"Mmmm . . . spaghetti," Mindy said.

I looked at her. "Ghosts can eat?"

"We can smell," she said.

"Oh, right." I was whispering now, convinced that my mother was outside with her ear pressed against the door. "But you have to stay in here while we cook. I'm not used to this invisible friend thing yet, and I don't want to look insane in front of Mom."

Mindy pouted, running a palm across the bedspread as if she were smoothing it out. But the wrinkles stayed. It had to be frustrating, being shut off from the world of objects and people, unable to connect.

"That's not very nice of you," she said. "Now that you're a pomp, we should be *friends*."

"But Mom's going to want to talk about stuff. She always gets deep and meaningful when we cook. And I won't be able to concentrate if you're hanging around. So please?"

"I'll sit in the corner and not say anything. Promise!"

I hesitated, wondering how reliable Mindy's promises were. She might be two months older than my mother, but she still talked like an eleven-year-old. I wondered if ghost children never grew up.

"If you let me hang out, I'll tell you a secret," she offered.

"Awkward details from my mother's childhood? No thanks."

Mindy shook her head. "It's something really important. Something you need to know."

"Okay, I guess." Mindy knew more about the afterlife than I did. And given Yamaraj's warnings about dangers and predators, it wouldn't hurt to learn more. "What's your big secret?"

"There's a man watching our house," she said. "He's been there for three days."

I took the backyard path, the recycling bin trundling behind me. My mother had seemed a little surprised when I'd volunteered to take it out, but she hadn't argued.

Mindy was walking ahead, checking that the way was clear, but my nerves were jumping. I had no reason to trust Mindy. My mother had never even mentioned her. What if there wasn't anybody watching the house, and this was some kind of . . . ghost trap?

But what else could I do? Pretend Mindy hadn't said anything?

"He's not in the back lane," Mindy said from the other side of the gate. "He usually parks his car in front of the Andersons' house."

"Who are the Andersons?"

"You don't know our neighbors very well, do you?"

I didn't answer, pulling open the gate and rattling the bin into its usual spot in the back lane. Ghosts had plenty of free time on their hands, I supposed, and spying on the neighbors was probably more interesting than staring at the walls of my mother's closet.

With a glance at the house to make sure Mom wasn't watching, I headed up the lane, staying a good distance behind my ghostly escort. Out here in the daylight, Mindy looked more out of place than she had in my bedroom. It wasn't just her bold checked shirt and wide 1970s belt. The way the late-afternoon sun played on her looked wrong.

And then I realized it—she had no shadows. Not just the big shadow that should have been rippling along the ground beneath her, but all the little ones in the wrinkles of her clothes were missing. The sunlight didn't texture her the way it would have a living person.

I'd found a way to spot ghosts, at least in daylight.

From the end of the back lane we could see the car, a black sedan with California plates.

A young man with dark hair sat in the driver's seat, a tablet computer of some kind propped on the steering wheel. He was reading from it, tapping on the screen, but then his eyes lifted to peer at my house. After a long moment, his gaze fell back to his tablet.

"Crapstick," I whispered. "You weren't kidding."

"I don't kid about scary men," Mindy said.

I stood there, willing my heart to slow down. "Can you go see what's on his screen?"

Mindy looked at the ground, kicking without effect at a dry leaf blowing past. "I'm kind of scared of him. Can you come with me?"

"Um, not invisible. Remember?"

"But you're a pomp." She frowned. "Can't you cross over?"

"You mean, into the afterworld?"

She giggled. "Just call it the flipside. Dork. That's what you say when you're walking around up here, and not down in the underworld."

"Okay, the flipside." I wondered if I could manage right here in the alley, or if I even wanted to. That meant remembering what had happened at the airport, replaying it all in my mind again. "Maybe."

Mindy cocked her head at me, wondering if I was kidding. When my expression didn't change, she held out a hand.

I took it a little hesitantly, and felt the distant tingle of her palm in mine. The cold place inside me responded to her touch, swelling into icy fingers that stretched around my heart. The earth seemed to sink beneath my feet, like when an elevator begins its descent.

It was happening again, right here in my back lane.

I almost dropped Mindy's hand, but she squeezed tighter—suddenly her small fingers felt real and solid. The cold inside me pulsed and surged, sweeping through my body. It flooded my head and fell across my senses, turning everything gray and quiet.

The afterworld air had its familiar taste, like I was holding a rusty nail under my tongue. The dead leaves stirring around our feet were silent.

"Huh." My own voice sounded distant in my ears. "It's not usually that easy."

"Maybe because you're new." Mindy had turned gray, like the rest of the world. "But the man can't see you now. You're just like a ghost."

I looked around, breathing hard. It was strange seeing my own neighborhood turned colorless and flat, like the airport. I realized that Mindy was the opposite of Yamaraj. Her touch had pulled me over to this dead, gray place, while his had sent me back to the world of the living.

I took a few cautious steps. My feet felt numb, as if they'd fallen asleep. When I stamped my bare soles against the asphalt, I felt only a dull ringing in my feet.

I hadn't noticed any of this the first times I'd crossed over. Maybe I'd been in shock. Or maybe it was different when Yamaraj was there beside me.

"This is weird," I said.

"Sucks to be dead," Mindy agreed. Then she saw my expression and added, "Not that *you're* dead. You're just a psychopomp."

"I think maybe I'm going to use another word. One that's less . . . psycho."

She shrugged. "That's what everyone calls them."

I looked at the black sedan again. My shaky first steps had taken me out into the road a little, but the man hadn't looked my way. Of course, the terrorists hadn't been able to see me at the airport. One had walked straight through me.

But Mindy's touch had made it seem too easy. "You're *sure* I'm invisible?"

Mindy nodded. "Does he look shiny to you? No way can he see the flipside."

I looked at my own hand. The shine wasn't as radiant as on Yamaraj's brown skin, but it was definitely there. My shadow had disappeared completely.

"Okay, invisible," I murmured. "Sweet."

I walked out from the back lane and toward the black sedan. The man's gaze stayed on his tablet, even when I stood right in front of his car.

Finally his eyes flicked up at me, but they registered nothing, peering straight through me to my house beyond.

Mindy came up timidly beside me. "He's scary, right?"

"He's stalking my house. What do you think?"

I went to the driver's side and knelt, looking straight at the guy. It was almost intimate, being this close without him seeing me, like spying on someone through a one-way mirror. I could hear him breathing through the open window, and could smell his coffee in the cup holder below the car window. He looked younger than I'd thought at first, in his midtwenties, maybe. He wore a dark suit and tie, and thick-framed nerdy glasses.

"What's he doing with that computer thing?" asked Mindy.

I looked at her. "You mean his tablet?"

She gave me a shrug, and I wondered how much of her understanding of the world was stuck in the 1970s.

I leaned in closer, my lips only inches from his ear.

"Hey, dipwit!"

His long eyelashes blinked once, but otherwise he didn't respond. I let out a nervous laugh, then leaned farther into the car, trying to read from his tablet.

On his screen was a list of emails. My eyes darted through the subject lines. Nothing weird—a reminder about a party, someone asking for a missing file, and the usual smattering of spam. He tapped at one of the emails, and it expanded to fill the screen. I leaned in closer to read, my cheek almost pressing against his.

Maybe I brushed against him then, or maybe it was just a coincidence, but at that exact moment he decided to scratch his ear. The back of his hand slid across my cheek, leaving sparks and tingles in its wake. I startled, pulling away, and banged my head on the top of the car window.

"Crap!" Anger surged through me.

Mindy stumbled back from the car. "We should run!"

"Run? What do you . . . ," I began, but already it was happening—the world brightened around me, the gray wash over my vision peeling away. Warmth flooded into my body, and I sank to one knee, dizzied by the onrush of light and color, gulping in the air that suddenly tasted fresh and real.

"Come on, Lizzie!" Mindy shouted, already running away.

A moment later I was sitting there by the stalker's car, blinking in the bright, all-too-normal sunshine, and he was staring down at me with his eyes wide open.

CHAPTER 11

THE MORNING AFTER YA DRINKS NIGHT, DARCY SAT UP IN BED to discover that she had a hangover. She was still wearing the little black dress, to which clung an inescapable whiff of beer. Her first instinct was to lie back down again, but by then the bed was spinning.

Her first few minutes upright were difficult, but once Darcy had a bathrobe on and coffee in hand, her condition began to shift from dizzy to quietly philosophical. The churning of the world outside Moxie's ten-foot-high windows proved soothing. Airplanes drew stately contrails across the sky, and a steady flow of cars and taxis headed northward toward the spires of Empire and Chrysler. Darcy watched the people sifting through Astor Place from a writerly remove, telling stories about them for her own amusement.

The refrigerator contained only batteries, mustard, and makeup and the pantry held even stranger things, like canned truffles and pickled quail eggs. But while starting up the house wifi to search for nearby food, Darcy found a sheaf of menus on Moxie's desk. These offered breakfast, lunch, and dinner all delivered to the door, which was exactly what Darcy needed.

After ordering breakfast, she had an intense conversation with Sodapop about how birds couldn't talk, then connected to You_Suck_at_Writing. There were emails from Carla, Sagan, and Nisha, and she replied to them all with the story of having met Kiralee Taylor, Coleman Gayle, and Oscar Lassiter in the flesh. Indeed, she hadn't just met these writers, but had discussed superpowers and book titles and cultural hijacking with them. Darcy tried to convey how intoxicating it all had been, while only hinting at how terrifying.

Her mother had also sent an email, making sure that Darcy hadn't been mugged or murdered overnight. Darcy thanked her for the little black dress, and managed to mention that she'd gotten home before eleven the night before. Then she replied to Aunt Lalana's welcome to New York City, cc'ing her mother so that the whole family knew that all was well.

Thankfully her in-box held nothing from Paradox. Darcy felt far too fragile for the long-awaited editorial letter. It was all she could do to reassure herself that last night had been real, that no one had questioned her right to be here in this city.

It felt safe, holing up here in Moxie's tower for her first full day in Manhattan. Everyone she'd met at YA Drinks Night had seemed so poised, so sure that they were really writers. Not melting into a puddle in the face of their certainty had left Darcy emptied of all her aplomb. She needed to recharge.

*   *   *

The next day she made sorties out of the apartment, noting cafés and bank machines, buying two reams of paper at an office supply store, and dropping off the indispensable little black dress at a dry cleaner's. Her confidence grew with every transaction, and Darcy wondered if she should limit her apartment search to Moxie's neighborhood, now that she had a beachhead here.

Or was that cowardly, like those limpet girls who became best friends with whoever they met on the first day of school?

New York had dozens of neighborhoods, after all, whose inhabitants swore by them with a kind of tribal loyalty. But Darcy didn't know much past what she'd gleaned from movies and TV, and she had only twelve days before Moxie returned. Her cluelessness gave her the same empty feeling as unfinished homework. Maybe she should have spent the last month researching the city instead of going to senior parties.

So on the third morning after YA Drinks Night, she decided to call for help.

"Um, would you want to look at apartments with me?"

"Sure, I guess." Imogen sounded amused. "Where were you thinking?"

"Um, the East or West Village. Or maybe Tribeca, Chelsea, or Chinatown?" These were all the neighborhoods Darcy could name off the top of her head.

"So . . . Manhattan. Do you have a list of places to see?"

Darcy did, printed out on the first sheets of those reams of paper that would one day hold rewrites and sequels. She and Imogen agreed on a place nearby and a time between breakfast and lunch.

* * *

"You have to accept that the first places will suck." Imogen was staring down at her phone, using it to guide them through the grid-addled streets of the West Village. "But that's just to soften you up."

"Right. So the realtors show you the crappy places first, to get you to pay more."

"No, I don't mean them. It's the city itself, fucking with you." Imogen looked up from her phone, dead serious. She was dressed in a rust-colored sundress, worn over jeans that she'd obviously worn while painting. The flecks of paint were the same ruddy color as the dress, which Darcy found rather artful. "You have to prove to New York that you really want to live here."

"But I totally do." Darcy was already certain there was nowhere else, that she would crawl over glass to live here. "Can't the city just *know* that?"

"It's a ritual. Embrace it."

Darcy nodded and took a steadying breath, one of many that day.

The first apartment was situated in a basement from whose cold floors arose the smell of wet concrete. The only sunlight entered through a high sliver of window in the very back, which looked as though the ceiling and the rear wall hadn't quite met during construction, and the rift had been plugged with glass.

"Okay. This is weird." Darcy was trying vainly to catch a glimpse of sky, hoping to dispel the claustrophobia the apartment was giving her. It was like peering up through the lid of a giant coffin slid slightly ajar. "What's this window thing called?"

"In a bomb shelter," Imogen said quietly, "it would be the viewing slit."

"It's a loge," supplied the agent, but he had lost Darcy's confidence by trying fourteen keys before finding the right one for the front door. "Very whimsical."

"Very." Imogen was staring at the matte-black claw-footed bathtub in the kitchen. "And it's all this one room?"

"Yes," the agent said. "Basement lofts are very popular now."

"Basement lofts," Darcy repeated, and she and Imogen smiled at each other, sharing amusement at the contradiction in terms. But then her claustrophobia started to come on stronger, and Darcy had to leave.

The next apartment was equally whimsical, though the real estate agent here was better with keys. It spanned the top floor of an old freestanding servants' quarters, which occupied a courtyard behind a West Village row house. This apartment smelled fresher than the basement loft had, and was blessed with views in all directions. But every window looked straight into the tenements surrounding it, which were only yards away.

"Panopticon," Imogen said, engaged in a staring contest with an orange tabby in a neighbor's window.

Darcy didn't know the word, but it had a lovely sound and its meaning was clear enough. She wondered if there was any way to fit "panopticon" into *Afterworlds*, and if Imogen would remember today and suspect she'd inspired its use.

As they descended the stairs, Darcy said, "So is the city done with me yet? Can we see the *good* apartments now?"

Imogen shook her head. "After only two? You're not very steadfast."

"I'm steadfast. I'm the fucking steadfast tin soldier. But Moxie's coming back in eleven days!" Darcy pulled out her list. "Maybe we should skip to the more expensive ones."

They were out on the street now, and the sky had darkened. All of Darcy's weather apps had warned her of rain today, but she had no umbrella of her own, and Moxie's was huge and covered with vintage images of naked men.

Imogen held out a palm to check for drops. "Those last two places looked pretty pricey already, even if they were whimsical. What's your budget?"

"Three thousand a month."

Imogen's eyes widened a little. "Seriously?"

"That's what my little sister says."

"Your little sister's coming to live with you?"

"No way! I mean, she's only fourteen." This might have been an apt time for Darcy to tell Imogen her own age, but she didn't. "Nisha's the math brain in the family. She made me a budget for the next three years, because *Afterworlds* comes out next year, and the sequel a year later. So I figure by the year after *that*, I'll know if I'm a real writer or not."

"You mean, you'll know how you're selling?"

Darcy nodded, wondering if her words had been a false step. "That's a habit Nisha got me into. She keeps saying I'm a *real* writer now, but I might not always be."

"You wrote a book," said Imogen. "That's real, whether it's a bestseller or not."

Darcy stared down at the black fossils of chewing gum on the sidewalk. "But it's not just sales. It's getting to say 'my agent' and being allowed in at Drinks Night. I know it's kind of pathetic, but all that stuff makes me feel more real."

"Don't apologize. Money and status are pretty real."

"It's not that I need to be super-rich and famous," Darcy went on. "It's just . . . it feels like someone's going to ask me for ID. Like, writer ID."

The sky let out a rumble, and they both stopped in the middle of the sidewalk. As the first drops fell a man went past them in a hurry, walking a beautiful black greyhound. The metal dog chain slid for a moment against the knee of Darcy's jeans.

Imogen pulled Darcy beneath an awning, and they stood together against the glass front of a shop that sold pipes and cigars. The sweet, heavy smell of tobacco mixed with the fresh scent of rain.

"I know what you mean," Imogen said. "Remember back in high school, when you were at a party, and if you weren't talking to *that one* person you had a crush on, it was pointless being there? Like everyone else wasn't real. Which is a crappy thing to think about other people, but that's what it felt like, you know?"

Darcy knew very well, but she nodded vaguely, as if those days were a distant memory.

"Or sometimes it's food," Imogen said, the rain coming on harder as she spoke. "Like when a big pile of french fries is the only real thing to eat, and you have to go out at midnight and find some or you'll die." Imogen's hands were in fists now. "For me, writing's the only thing that's *always* real. I've never regretted a day I wrote a good scene, whatever else I screwed up that day. *That's* what's fucking real."

Darcy had stopped breathing, because she agreed so much. She wished she could spin time backward and steal Imogen's words, just to hear them in her own voice.

"I know," she managed. "But it only happened once. . . ."

Last November, she meant, when that billionth random monkey had taken up residence in her head and helped her type *Afterworlds*.

"Right. Sophomore slump." Imogen waved a hand, her intensity fading. "I was like that after *Pyromancer*. Because my first girlfriend was a pyromaniac, so maybe that was the only thing I could ever write about. Like it was all an accident. But books don't happen by accident."

Darcy nodded. Imogen's certainty was contagious, and Darcy felt more real just standing here with her, the rain building to a roar and clearing the air around them. "So I just need to write another book, and I'll be cured."

"For a while. There's one little hitch: I felt the same way again after finishing *Ailuromancy*. And Kiralee says that every book she's ever written feels like an accident. We can all look forward to an endless sophomore slump."

"That's okay, kind of," Darcy said. The slumps would be worth it, as long as there were more Novembers.

Imogen was smiling now. "So you can suffer a lifetime of angst, but you can't deal with a few more whimsical apartments?"

"I remain steadfast." Darcy looked at her list, but the addresses had begun to swim before her eyes. "Where do *you* live, anyway?"

"Chinatown."

"Is that good for writers?"

Imogen laughed. "I live there for the food."

"Oh, right," Darcy said. "I like noodles."

This made Imogen laugh as well, though it had sounded feeble in Darcy's ears.

"If you hate everything up here, we can go look near my place. Got anything on your list?"

"A few, I think." Uncertain of where Chinatown began and ended, Darcy handed over the printouts. "I'm not keeping you from writing a good scene, am I?"

"I don't write when the sun's up. Too unromantic."

"Well, if we've got all day . . ." Darcy waited to be contradicted, to be told that Imogen only had another hour or two to spare, but Imogen said nothing. "Let me buy you lunch, then we can keep looking?"

"Great." Imogen handed back the printouts and pulled Darcy into motion, despite the rain. "I know a place with noodles."

Darcy's budget, which was really Nisha's budget, went like this:

Afterworlds and *Untitled Patel* had sold in a two-book deal to Paradox Publishing for the princely sum of one hundred and fifty thousand dollars each. Of that three-hundred-thousand-dollar total, fifteen percent (forty-five thousand) belonged to the Underbridge Literary Agency, and another hundred thousand or so to the government, depending on how much Darcy let Nisha finagle her taxes.

After a new laptop and some furniture, that left her with about fifty thousand a year for three years.

At this point, Darcy could do the math herself. Fifty thousand divided by twelve was a little over four thousand a month, which meant a maximum of three for rent. And a thousand divided by thirty was thirty-three dollars a day.

Neither she nor Nisha knew if that was enough to eat, clothe, and entertain oneself in New York City, but it sounded reasonable. And there were always noodles.

Though at this exact moment the noodles that Darcy and Imogen were eating—ramen with Tuscan kale, pork shoulder, and white miso reduction—had exceeded that amount already.

"Whoa," Imogen said when Darcy was done explaining the budget. "You're rich!"

"I know. Crazy lucky, right?" Even as she spoke, Darcy realized that when her mother used that word—how *lucky* Darcy was to have published a book—it made her unspeakably angry. But between Imogen and herself, *lucky* was okay. "I know everything I write won't sell for that much."

"Yeah, you never know," Imogen said. "Kiralee's books haven't done well since *Bunyip*."

Darcy looked up from her noodles. "Really? I thought Coleman was kidding the other night."

"Nope. He says Kiralee's books only sell about ten thousand copies each," Imogen said.

"That sucks." Darcy wasn't sure exactly what that number meant, but it sounded low compared to her own advance. "And it's scary. If a writer like Kiralee can't sell books, how am I supposed to? I mean, everyone I know has read all her books."

"The people you know read books." Imogen gave a shrug. "But *Bunyip* broke into a much bigger demographic—people who *don't* read books. Or, they read maybe one a year. Coleman says that's where the money is in publishing—people who don't read."

"Whoa. That explains a lot about the bestseller lists."

Darcy had spent every spare minute of the last four years in her high school library, surrounded by the Reading Zealots, who all had widgets on their blogs counting down to the next Sword Singer or Secret Coterie pub date, and who sent each other photoshopped YA covers with lolcat captions for Valentine's Day.

But now that Darcy thought about it, that was only about twenty kids out of a thousand in her school—2 percent. What if the rest of the world's readers shared those slim proportions?

"Now I feel guilty," she said.

"You should. One-fifty times two? Crap."

Darcy wondered what Imogen had been paid for *Pyromancer*, but Imogen hadn't volunteered the number, so she felt weird asking. "Well, minus taxes . . . and Moxie's cut. *And* the twenty bucks Nisha charged me to make that budget!"

Imogen grinned at this, and her eyes blinked in a slow, catlike way. Darcy wondered if that always happened when she smiled.

"Speaking of Kiralee," Imogen said. "She wants to read *Afterworlds.*"

Darcy froze. "But it . . . it's not even edited."

"Yeah, she hates reading edited novels. There's not enough to complain about. If you send me the draft, I'll forward it to her. Maybe she'll give you a blurb."

"Um, sure." Darcy recalled the mix of elation and anxiety at having her book analyzed by Kiralee, and wondered how gut-churning the examination would be once she'd actually *read* it. "So how serious was she the other night? You know, about my hijacking a god for purposes of YA hotness?"

"Pretty serious," Imogen said. "But it's got more to do with

Bunyip than you. It's her book that everybody loves, but it's the one she has the most regrets about."

Darcy frowned. "What do you mean, exactly?"

"Okay, so it takes the mythology of an ancient culture, and uses it to frame a colonist girl's angst about her first kiss. Which is tricky enough. But then all the aboriginal characters, who are actually *from* that culture, don't really appear in the last half of the book."

Darcy thought for a second. "Whoa. I didn't even notice."

"Yeah. Because it's all about that first kiss."

"Which is such a great kiss," Darcy said. "And the funny thing is, if Kiralee hadn't stolen that myth, I wouldn't know about bunyips at all."

"That's the power of Story. And with great power . . ." Imogen spread her hands. "Kiralee doesn't want you to feel the same way about *Afterworlds* in fifteen years."

"Or sooner." Darcy was already nervous about her mother reading the book, and now she had another eight hundred million people to worry about.

"But you're a Hindu," Imogen said. "Isn't it your culture?"

"I modeled Yamaraj on a Bollywood star, which shows how much I know about Hinduism. I'm worried he turned out more hot than serious. For a lord of the dead, I mean."

Imogen shrugged. "Well, you've still got rewrites."

"There's only good *rewriting*," Darcy murmured. She still couldn't remember who'd said that first.

The waitress brought the check then, and Darcy waved away Imogen's battered wallet and paid with cash. With a tip, the bill was more than twice her Nisha-approved daily allotment, but the noodles had been very good indeed.

"Do you want to read it too?" Darcy asked as they headed for the door.

"Of course. I'll send you *Pyromancer*." Imogen scooped up a handful of matchbooks with the noodle shop's logo on them and shoved them in her pocket. "Ready for more whimsical apartments?"

"Sure," Darcy said. "Thanks for showing me this place."

"The best way to know a city is to eat it."

"I'm a tin soldier. Steadfast," Darcy said tiredly. But the word had lost all meaning. Maybe she would use it somewhere in her rewrites, just to remind her of this endless day.

They were approaching their sixth apartment since eating. The first two had been in the Meatpacking District, one across from a FedEx garage, whose rumbling trucks Darcy could feel when she pressed a palm against the walls, the other on a street that smelled like meat. The next three had been soulless white boxes in the glass towers surrounding Union Square. It was the sort of neighborhood that Annika Patel would approve of, but Imogen had warned that nothing written in such a sterile place would ring true.

So they'd headed down to Chinatown in the clearing rain. They were met in front of a corner building by an Israeli man named Lev, who had a Russian accent and wore a three-piece suit. He led them up a wide staircase that, instead of doubling back at the landings, just kept climbing in the same direction, like the steps of a Mayan temple. Without any key fumbling, Lev opened the door of apartment 4E.

It was the largest Darcy had seen yet, occupying half the floor of the building. The ceilings were at least twelve feet high, and two walls had rows of windows looking down onto the street corner below. A glimmer of pale sunshine had appeared in the sky, a glaring leak in the clouds. It angled through the windows to ignite a galaxy of dust suspended in the air.

"You could roller-skate in here," Imogen said with quiet awe.

"It was dance studio." Lev gestured at the mirrors along one wall. "But you can take those down."

Darcy stared at herself in the mirrors; she looked tiny with all this open space around her. She went to the nearest window—the glass was mottled with age, bulging in the bottoms of the panes like a slow liquid. The buildings across the street were garlanded with fire escapes covered in leftover raindrops, dripping and sparkling. The floor creaked as Darcy walked from window to window, looking out at Chinatown.

"Where does that hall go?" Imogen asked. It was beside the apartment's front door, in the corner opposite the two walls of windows.

"There are two changing rooms for dancers." Lev wiggled his finger for them to follow. "And a kitchen, not very big."

The two changing rooms weren't big either. Each had a row of lockers along one wall, and between the two rooms was a bathroom with a shower.

Imogen stood in the hallway. "You could make one a bedroom, the other a closet. You'll be the only person in Manhattan with a shower connecting to your closet."

"No," said Lev. "I have seen this before."

"I didn't bring that many clothes," Darcy said. Though, of

course, she could always ask her parents to drive up with more. And she planned to buy clothes here in New York, of course, once she'd decided what writers wore. She'd forgotten to take notes at Drinks Night, too overwhelmed with everything else.

Lev showed them the kitchen last. It was the smallest room in the apartment, but Darcy didn't see herself cooking much. She wanted to go out and eat the city until she knew it in detail.

"How far is this from your place?" she asked Imogen when they were back in the big room.

"Five minutes' walk? We'd be neighbors if you lived here."

Darcy smiled back at her, then looked at her printout of apartments. Her heart squeezed a little when she saw that this was one of the places with no listed price.

"Is this lease even legal?" Imogen was asking Lev. "I mean, a dance studio would be zoned for business, not residential."

"It was illegal as dance studio," he said with a shrug. "Now is legal again."

Darcy didn't care. The very fact that she could live in New York, in this apartment, hardly seemed real. Legality was an afterthought.

She took a slow breath. "How much?"

Lev opened a green leather binder, the spine of which crackled. "Thirty-five hundred. Utilities included."

"Crap," Darcy said, and two things clicked inside her. One was a hopeless feeling of falling through the floor, the other was the certainty that she could write here. That she *had* to write here.

"Can you give us a moment, Lev?" Imogen asked quietly. He bowed, a knowing smile on his face, and drifted away into the tiny kitchen.

"I have to ask my sister," Darcy said, already texting: *What does $3500/month do to budget?*

"So you want it?"

"I *need* it. I don't even know why." Darcy stared down at the street. It had the same bustle as the view from Moxie's, but the streets were more crowded here in Chinatown. And from only five stories up instead of fifteen, the rippling current of bodies was more intimate, more personal. An open-air stall selling fresh fish bathed in a shaft of sunlight, white ice and silver scales glittering. "This room's so big, I'd have to tell myself stories just to fill it up."

Imogen smiled. "Where would you write?"

"My desk goes there." Darcy gestured at the corner where the two walls with windows met. She would orient the desk outward and diagonally, taking in the whole view. The rest of the room would stay empty.

"You can pay that rent and still eat?"

"Maybe. Or maybe I'll just write and not eat." Darcy realized that the desk she was imagining was from her school, square and wooden, with a scooped plastic chair. Was that the best her imagination could do? Some writer.

Her phone dinged with Nisha's answer:

$3500/mth = 2 yrs, 8 mths #mymathisyourgod

She groaned and showed the message to Imogen. "This means I lose four months!"

"Um, you *could* get a job, you know."

Darcy almost started to explain that her parents would surely make her go to college if it came to that. But Imogen probably thought that Darcy had already graduated. She promised herself to tell Imogen how old she was very soon, even if it meant feeling young and, frankly, a bit less real.

But not right now, while her future was being decided.

The phone dinged, Nisha again.

Alternate plan: 3 whole yrs but eat only $17/day

HAHA RAMEN GIRL! #weightgain

Darcy sighed. Nisha didn't realize how expensive ramen could be here in New York. Of course, there were noodles with Tuscan kale, pork shoulder, and white miso reduction, and there were noodles pressed into bricks and priced at three for a dollar. Darcy liked them, too, as long as she could add Tabasco, turmeric, and a soft-boiled egg. She could write on seventeen dollars a day, especially in this magnificent room.

"I'm going to take it," she whispered, and Imogen gave her a smile and a satisfied cat's-eye blink, as if she had never doubted Darcy's steadfastness at all.

CHAPTER 12

"WHAT THE HELL ARE YOU DOING?" SAID THE MAN IN THE BLACK sedan.

I scrambled away from him, across the sidewalk and onto the Andersons' lawn. My heart was pounding and the world felt sharp and real.

"What am *I* doing?" I yelled. "You're the one stalking my house!"

"*Your* house?" He glanced up at the stitches in my forehead. "You're Elizabeth Scofield, aren't you?"

"I'm the person who's calling the police unless you get the hell out of here!" My hand went to my pocket, where there was no phone.

"No need, Miss Scofield." He reached into his jacket and pulled out a large wallet, which he flipped open to reveal a badge and photo ID. "Agent Elian Reyes, Federal Bureau of Investigation."

I stared at his ID, then at him again. It definitely was his picture, nerdy glasses and all, and the badge looked very real. A metal eagle splayed its wings across the top, fiery gold in the bright sun of the living world.

Agent Reyes flipped the badge case shut and opened his car door. But he paused a moment, waiting for my approval before stepping out onto the sidewalk.

I nodded, but took another half step backward.

"Sorry to upset you, Miss Scofield." He pocketed the wallet as he stood, then leaned back against his car, arms crossed. "It wasn't my objective to frighten anyone."

"Then why the hell are you stalking my house?"

He paused a moment, drumming his fingers on his arms. "I'm authorized to tell you why I'm here, to avoid any misunderstanding. It's because of the attention you've received since the attack."

"Right. But there aren't any reporters here."

"There were, but they gave up yesterday. That was smart, taking your time getting back from Dallas."

"Uh, thanks." I wondered if Mom had thought that part through.

"But I'm not here to protect you from reporters." His voice dropped a little. "My agent in charge is concerned about the group who committed the attack."

I kept my breathing steady. "But they're all dead."

"The attackers are, but they were members of a larger cult." He paused again, as if wondering whether to continue.

"Please tell me what's going on, Agent Reyes."

"You're only seventeen."

"Old enough to sneak up on FBI agents, apparently."

All I got for that remark was a raised eyebrow, and then the words, "Perhaps I should talk to your mother."

"I wish you wouldn't do that. My mother scares easy. Like, she's afraid of cars on highways."

"That must make driving interesting."

"You have no idea." I took a step toward him. "Just tell me what's going on, Agent Reyes. I survived machine guns this week. I can probably handle whatever you have to say."

He glanced back at my house, then sighed. "Fair enough. The gunmen belonged to an organization called the Movement for the Resurrection, which has an Armageddon mentality, an isolationist dogma, and a charismatic leader. In other words, all characteristic of a destructive cult—what is sometimes called a death cult."

"Crap," I said. "But everyone says those four guys did it on their own."

"That's what the cult leaders say. But we're still looking at the group as a whole." He raised his hands. "Not that you should be concerned. It's just that you've been on the news a lot."

"As a symbol of hope," I said softly.

"Yes, Miss Scofield. A symbol of life, even."

"And they're a death cult." I let out a slow sigh. "Crap. I hate death cults."

"I also dislike them. But, again, this is purely precautionary." He turned to glance at my house again, as he'd done every thirty seconds or so while we'd been talking, even though I was standing right in front of him. My mother was still inside, of course.

That thought, that as we stood here he was still doing his job, calmed me a little.

"Thank you," I said.

"It was only fair to tell you." He nodded, a firm little motion of his chin.

"No, I mean thank you for doing this." My gaze dropped to his beautifully shined shoes, and I suddenly wished I wasn't barefoot. "For protecting people."

My mind went back to the airport. The TSA agents there, the guys my dad always complains about when they search his luggage, had fought back against the attackers, pistols against machine guns. . . .

"You're very kind, Miss Scofield," Agent Reyes said. "But rest assured that the Movement will be under surveillance for the foreseeable future. There's no reason for you to be scared."

"I'm not." I had powers now, after all, and I'd walked on the flipside. Some of my best friends were ghosts.

Not that Mindy was anywhere in sight. Had she vaporized in a fit of fear? Or just run off?

"I should go. My mom's waiting. Thanks for not telling her."

"That's your call." Agent Reyes reached into his jacket and pulled out a business card. "But if you change your mind, I'm happy to explain everything." With a hint of a smile, he added, "Hopefully not in a scary way."

"Okay. Maybe." I looked down at the card. "'Special Agent Elian Reyes'? You didn't say you were a *special* agent."

He gave me a shrug as he got back into his car. "Little-known fact about the FBI: we're all special agents."

He didn't sound like he was kidding, but I had to laugh. Then I felt dorky, and waved as I turned and walked away, trying not to consider the fact that his glasses were kind of cute.

*   *   *

Mindy wasn't in the back lane, or in the backyard. She wasn't going to be much help if I ever got in trouble in the afterworld, I realized. Not that it was fair to blame her for running away. Whatever year she'd been born in, she was basically an eleven-year-old.

"Lizzie?" My mom stood in the back doorway, rubbing her hands on a dish towel. "Where'd you go?"

"Oh, sorry." I looked over my shoulder. "I was just looking around."

"For what?"

I shrugged, and squeezed past her into the house. Mindy wasn't in the kitchen either.

On the kitchen counter was a pile of dough, stained black with squid ink. It had my mother's handprints in it, and the uneven look of dough that wants more kneading. I went to the sink to wash my hands.

"Are you okay?" my mother said.

"I'm fine. I just wanted some fresh air." If Mom demanded a better excuse than that, I could always hand over Special Agent Reyes's business card and let him explain.

But all she said was, "Okay."

We split the dough in two and stood there awhile, kneading it to an even consistency. It felt good to have something squishing between my fingers, something pungent and fishy-smelling and undeniably corporeal.

I wondered where Mindy had run off to. Was she hiding in the house? Or was there some deeper level of reality that she could go to? Somewhere farther down than the flipside, where I couldn't see her at all?

Both she and Yamaraj had mentioned "the underworld," wherever that was.

My mother was staring at me, and I realized that she expected to hear more about my little wander outside.

So I changed the subject. "Did you ever have a dog?"

My mother's hands stopped moving. "When I was little, yeah. Do you want to get one?"

"Nine months before I go to college? That would be kind of random."

"Right, but maybe you'd feel safer with a dog around." She glanced out the open kitchen door, like she thought I'd been checking the backyard for terrorists.

"I feel totally safe, Mom. I was just wondering. You don't talk much about when you were little."

"I guess not." She stopped kneading again. "Where's this coming from?"

"Nowhere." That wasn't true, but I could hardly say it had come from the ghost of her best friend, the one she'd never mentioned. "I guess I'm asking . . . did you ever go through anything like this?"

"Like a terrorist attack?" Her eyes went wide. "Jesus, kiddo. You know they're really rare, right? A lot more people get hit by lightning than killed by terrorists."

She looked fragile saying that, so I smiled and reached out to take her hand. "Lightning? Good. That means I've had my lifetime quota."

We combined the two masses of dough and began to work together, standing shoulder to shoulder, our palms turning gray.

Squid ink takes a couple of days to fade completely from my skin, which always fascinated me.

This time it was extra weird seeing my hands turn gray, as if the flipside were breaking through into reality. Of course, Yamaraj and I looked normal in the afterworld, while everyone else, living or dead, was gray.

We psychopomps were special.

As Mom and I worked the dough, I realized that I'd told her the truth—I *wasn't* scared of the Movement of the Resurrection, or whatever they were called. What had Special Agent Reyes said about their "isolationist dogma"? That probably just meant they lived in the mountains with crappy toilets. They were small people with a small worldview, and I was learning how to enter a whole new reality. Forget them.

At the moment I was more worried about Mindy. I wondered again why my mother had never told me about her.

"What's the worst thing that ever happened to you, Mom?"

"The worst thing?" She drew in a long breath, dusting off her hands, then opened the big utensil drawer and began to rummage. "I suppose when your father told me that all our years together had been a waste of his time."

"Oh, right. Of course, sorry." I stopped kneading to give her a floury hug. "But I meant when you were young. Like, the most traumatic thing that ever happened to you."

She pulled out a rolling pin and turned it slowly against the palm of her left hand. "Maybe now's not the time."

"I think now pretty much *is* the time, Mom. Help me process this."

"But I don't want to scare you."

It was all I could do not to laugh at her then. Not to be mean, but because it was so funny. "Mom, the stuff that's going to scare me this week *already happened*. And I survived, so please tell me."

She looked at me closely for a moment, as if I had changed into something she didn't quite recognize. But, like Agent Reyes had, in the end she told me.

"It was when I was eleven."

I nodded to encourage her to keep going, and because I'd known that much already.

"My best friend," she said softly, "a little girl who lived across the street. She was abducted."

"Oh," I said.

"She was driving across the country on a trip with her parents, and they were at one of those big rest stops . . . and she just disappeared."

I stared at her, trying to keep track of all the things that were becoming clear at once. My mother's fear of highways. How nervous she'd always been about letting me play outside. "Did they ever find out who did it?"

She shook her head. "No, but they found her a few weeks later, and that was the scariest part."

"What was?"

"Mindy had been buried . . . in her own backyard. So whoever it was *knew where she lived*, maybe even knew her family. Even though she'd disappeared hundreds of miles away. That's why my parents moved down here. They couldn't live on that street anymore."

A shudder went through me, and I felt the cold place inside growing around my heart, like when I'd placed my hand in Mindy's. The taste of metal slivered across my tongue, and for a moment I thought I would cross over to the flipside, right there in front of my mother.

"Crap," I said, hugging myself with floury arms.

"Oh, I'm so sorry, Lizzie." Mom's eyes were wide. "I'm an idiot."

"No, you're not." I breathed hard, gathering deep lungfuls of the air of the living world. "You had to tell me. We both went through something bad. I *needed* you to tell me."

"Kiddo, you didn't need that horrible story. Not right now." Her hand reached out, her fingertips almost touching the teardrop scar on my cheek.

"It's okay. I'm fine." I turned and washed my hands. "Just give me a minute. That's all."

I hugged her again, hard enough that a ghostly mist of flour filled the air around us, and then walked toward my bedroom.

"Just a minute," I said, and shut the door behind me.

My heart was beating hard, life pushing back the cold inside me. I touched my lips where Yamaraj had kissed me in the airport, and felt his heat there. I wasn't going to cross over. It had just been a passing chill from my mother's story. From Mindy's story.

I looked around the room.

"Are you here?" I whispered.

There was no answer, but suddenly I knew where she was.

I stepped back out into the kitchen and gave my mother a happy smile. "Turns out I just needed to pee."

I went past her and down the hall to the other side of the house, pausing in the bathroom to splash cold water on my face. Then I went a little farther, into my mother's bedroom.

Her overnight bag lay open on the bed, still half full of clothes. That was weird. My mother usually unpacked everything the moment she got home. There was more mess than usual, clothes strewn on the floor and draped across the back of her dresser chair.

And there beside Mom's bed was a framed photo of her and her parents, posing on the front lawn of a northern California bungalow with a wide front porch. She looked about Mindy's age, and had the same long pigtails. The picture was familiar to me, something Mom always kept on her dresser, but I'd never thought much about it.

I crossed the soft carpet and opened the door of her closet.

It was dark inside, only the glimmer of shined shoes and dry cleaner's plastic catching the light from the bedroom windows.

When I was little, I'd always been afraid of closets. But now I could see the appeal of a private, cozy place to call your own.

I knelt on the carpet, keeping my voice low. "Don't be scared. It's just me."

There was no response.

"I talked to that man, and he wasn't scary. He's an agent from the FBI, a special agent. He's here to make sure we're safe."

Still nothing.

"So everything's okay," I whispered. "But I get why you're scared. My mom told me what happened to you, back when she was little."

I heard a tiny intake of breath, and a moment later she spoke.

"I told you she remembered me."

"She does. Like it was yesterday."

"Does it still make her sad?"

"Of course it does." There was no answer, so I added, "But that's not your fault, Mindy."

"No. It's the bad man's fault. He messed up everything. My mom and dad. My friends. Me." She sighed. "Max was the only one who got away, because he'd been put to sleep already. He had dog cancer."

"That's sad too." I swallowed. "But the bad man can't hurt you anymore. You know that, right?"

"I guess not," Mindy said, and her form began to emerge from among the shadows. She slipped out through the hanging dresses, which remained undisturbed by her passage.

"Do you want to come and watch us cook dinner?" I asked.

She looked at me, tears glistening in her eyes. "Are you sure? I don't want to bother you."

"It'll be fine. Just remember we can't talk to each other."

"I'll be quiet," Mindy said, then held out her hand.

I took it without thinking, but when the cool and distant tingle fluttered across my palm, I realized what she was doing.

"I can't cross over right now," I said. "My mom's waiting."

"Just for a second?" she asked, and I tasted metal on my tongue, and felt the floor falling away from me. The sunlight spilling into the bedroom turned hard and mean. "Please?"

I nodded and clutched Mindy's hand harder, and a moment later the world was colorless.

"Thank you," she said, gathering me into a hug. She felt small and cold, shivering like a little kid who'd just climbed out of a swimming pool. I was still kneeling, and her head rested on my shoulder.

"It's okay, Mindy," I said softly, and she hugged tighter. "The bad man can't hurt you now."

She pulled away, her hands still in mine, her eyes wide and glistening. "But what about when he dies, Lizzie?"

"When he dies . . ."

"Then he'll be a ghost too. And maybe he still remembers me. What if he can find me, even in the closet?"

I shook my head. My heart was thumping in my chest, and without Mindy pressed against me, the world began to shift again.

"I won't let him touch you." The gray was fading from the room.

"Promise?"

"I promise."

She smiled, which squeezed a single tear from her eye. I reached out, still enough of me on the flipside that I could feel it for a moment, wet against my fingertip.

I brushed her tear away, and then we were in different worlds again.

CHAPTER 13

"AND IT HAS THESE AMAZING WINDOWS," DARCY SAID. "YOU can see the rooftops of Chinatown. It's perfect."

Aunt Lalana smiled. "It sounds like an exciting place to live."

"I can't wait to move in." As Darcy took a bite from her burger, she felt a guilty trickle of juice run down her left wrist. She'd ordered without thinking. "Um, you don't mind that I'm eating a cow, do you?"

A laugh came from Lalana. "Darcy, I was there at dinner when you announced you were becoming a carnivore. You were, what, thirteen?"

"Right, but it still feels rude. Especially since I'm asking you for a huge favor."

They were in a café in the West Village, near Lalana's apartment, which was small and prim and elegant, like Lalana herself. She was as coordinated as always today, wearing a blue collared shirt under a bright yellow jacket, one dangling earring in each color.

"It's not your diet I'm worried about, Darcy. It's your rent." Lalana glanced at the lease, which lay on the table between them. The offending number was there on the first page. "Isn't it a *little* expensive?"

"It's more than I wanted to spend, but it's the perfect place to write."

"So that's why it's so much. Good writing vibes. Of course."

"My writer friend Imogen looked at it with me, and she agreed." Darcy imagined Nisha rolling her eyes at this conversation, and making up new rules about saying "my writer friend." "If it's a good place to work, it'll pay for itself."

"I suppose those publishers *are* giving you an awful lot of money. No offense, Darcy, but sometimes I can't quite believe it."

"Me either," Darcy said with a shrug. "My agent says it was the first chapter. She says the buyers from the big chains only have time to read one chapter. So if a book's got a killer opening and an awesome cover, it'll be in all the stores."

Lalana looked dubious. "But the people who buy it, don't they read all those *other* chapters? Shouldn't the rest be good too?"

Darcy felt a twist in her stomach, as she did every time she thought of a stranger (or thousands of strangers) reading her novel.

But she put on a smile. "Are you saying my book sucks?"

Lalana laughed. "How can I tell? You won't let us see it."

Darcy didn't answer. Of the family, only Nisha had been allowed to read *Afterworlds*, and she was sworn to secrecy.

After all, Annika Patel had never told her daughters about her murdered childhood friend. So in return, Darcy had never told her mother about discovering the story. Instead, she'd directed all her questions into her writing.

But it still felt strange to have borrowed her mother's childhood tragedy as a plot device.

"Like I keep saying, you can read it once it's officially published. I just want you guys to see it as a real novel, not just some story by, like, *me*."

"I can't wait, Darcy, and I'm sure you'll write many more." Lalana's eyes fell to the lease again. "But don't you want to have *some* of your advance left over?"

"The important thing right now isn't saving money. It's making my books as good as I can."

Lalana finally gave up, laughing. "You're just like your mother. Nothing in half measures, always so certain of herself."

Darcy wasn't sure what to make of this compliment, if that's what it was. Lalana was the glamorous sister, the one who lived in New York, had a job in fashion and a revolving cast of handsome boyfriends. To Darcy and Nisha, she was the more driven, the one who'd always done what she wanted.

Which was why she was the perfect choice to ask for this favor.

"I'm certain about some things," Darcy said. "Writing, and New York, and this apartment."

"I know you are. But certainty has a slippery side. You're sure I won't get in trouble if I cosign this lease?"

"Of course not. Paradox owes me a hundred grand, any day now. It's just that the building management company doesn't believe some eighteen-year-old is getting paid that much."

Her aunt laughed a little. "Listen to you: 'a hundred grand,' like a gangster."

"Sorry. That's the way Nisha always says it."

"I'm not worried about the money, Darcy. What I meant was, will I get in trouble with your parents? Why aren't *they* cosigning?"

"There's no time to get the lease to them. Other people want the apartment, like, yesterday." Darcy took another bite, which muffled her next words. "But yeah, they might freak out about the price. A little."

"More than a little." Lalana neatly speared a chickpea with her fork. "And if I'm the cosigner, Annika will blame *me* if you starve to death."

"Nisha says I'll have enough money."

"She does?" Lalana cocked an eyebrow. When it came to practical math, Nisha's word was gold. Even their engineer father had her check the family tax returns.

"Her budget says I've got seventeen dollars a day after rent." Darcy looked down at her burger, which would cost at least that much after tip and tax. "That means I'll be eating less meat. That's good, right?"

Lalana shook her head. "It takes more than food to cook, Darcy. Do you own any dishes? Any pots and pans?"

"Um . . ."

"Or anything to clean your house with? A mop? A broom? Rubber gloves?"

Darcy laughed at the thought of herself wearing rubber gloves. But it was true that she didn't have any of those things. Not a single scouring pad or frying pan.

"And what about chairs? A desk to write on? Pens and paper?"

"Nisha left room for start-up costs in my budget. Like furniture and . . . mops."

That last word came out flat. A mop seemed like such an uninspiring thing to buy. Darcy had only ever spent money on things she really wanted—clothes, food, music, beer, and books. But lately she'd started to realize how many *boring* things people owned—curtains, wastebaskets, laundry detergent, lightbulbs, extension cords, notepads, pillowcases. When she'd gone back to pick up the lease and take one last look, apartment 4E had contained nothing but dust bunnies and one old telephone wire sticking out of the wall.

It was so empty, so ready to be filled with stories.

"I only need a desk, a chair, and a laptop," she said.

"And cooking stuff. You *love* food."

Darcy couldn't argue. She and Lalana had spent the morning in Little Italy, where the store shelves glittered with shiny metal kitchen gadgets—pasta makers and coffee machines and pizza cutters—that seemed almost edible themselves. In one shop, wheels of cheese had been stacked from floor to ceiling, each as big as a car tire. The ones on the bottom had looked shinier, and when Darcy knelt to investigate, she realized that the combined weight of all the other cheese wheels was pressing down on them, squeezing out a glistening patina of oil. The store had smelled like heaven, as if all that cheese were leaking into the air.

But the wheels were five hundred dollars each. Or, as Darcy now had to think of it, a month's allowance.

"Of course, everyone has to learn to live on a budget sometime,"

Lalana was arguing with herself. "Might as well be now, before you go to college."

Darcy nodded in agreement, but something must have shown on her face.

Lalana looked closer. "Darcy. You *are* going to college once your second book gets written, right?"

"Um . . . sure," Darcy said. If her parents had been here, even that pause would have been fatal. "But that's more than a year from now. It all depends on how my career is going."

Her voice faltered a little on the word "career," which she felt silly saying, like a kid playing dress-up again. She'd worn her black silk T-shirt for Aunt Lalana, but her jeans were threadbare in the knees.

"Well, then," Lalana sighed. "I suppose it's my auntly duty to sign. I wouldn't want you in any other apartment."

"Thank you!" Darcy cried, then frowned. "Wait . . . why exactly?"

Lalana produced a tiny silver pen from her handbag. "Paying this rent, you won't be able to stay in the city forever."

"Oh." It was true, every dollar Darcy spent brought her closer to the day when she would have to leave New York and go away to college. But if all she'd wanted was to write as *long* as possible, she could have stayed at home or lived in a cardboard box somewhere.

The point was to be a writer forever. And apartment 4E was as essential as New York City itself to what Darcy wanted to become.

Aunt Lalana's pen hovered above the paper. "But if I sign this, you have to promise me two things, Darcy."

"Sure. Anything."

"Don't let yourself be distracted by the city. Get your writing done."

"Of course. That's all I want!"

"And don't keep secrets from me, even if you leave your parents out of certain things. I want updates, understand?"

"I'll tell you everything," Darcy promised, though Aunt Lalana was already applying her wide, looping signature to the document.

"There." The pen smacked against the table and Lalana lifted her glass of iced chai. "You have an apartment now. And it's all my fault."

Darcy felt a smile growing on her face, though at the same time the floor of the café seemed to tip dizzily beneath them. Apartment 4E was real.

Now nothing could go wrong.

"Now that we have a deal," Lalana said. "What's the first thing you haven't told your parents? Any boys you have a crush on?"

"You said no distractions! And I'm all about the writing." Darcy laughed. "But there is one thing, kind of. And you really can't tell my parents."

Lalana didn't promise, just waited.

"I missed the deferral deadline for Oberlin. It was first of June."

"Are you kidding, Darcy?"

"I didn't realize, and it was really hard to find on their website." Darcy didn't add that she hadn't looked until a week ago, which had already been too late. "But it's okay. I just have to apply again next year."

"This is *not* okay."

Darcy held up her hands. "I can use the same SAT scores, and

I'll whip up a whole new essay about writing novels in New York. Do you really think they won't want me anymore?"

Aunt Lalana turned her face to the window, then gave Darcy a sideways look. "I suppose any college would be glad to have a young novelist. But your parents aren't around to hold your hand anymore. You have to start being more responsible."

"I will. Starting now." Darcy raised her own glass. "Thanks for trusting me. I promise not to mess up again."

"I'm sure you'll surprise us all," Lalana said. "One way or another."

As their glasses clinked, Darcy wondered what exactly that meant.

CHAPTER 14

"YOU CAN SEE GHOST BUILDINGS EASIER IN A VACANT LOT,"
Mindy said. "And at night."

"Because it's dark?"

"No. Because there's not as many livers around."

I hunched my shoulders against the cold. "Is that really a thing? Calling us 'livers'? Because that sounds like chicken livers."

"Have you got a better word?" Mindy asked.

"Um . . . how about *people*?"

"Ghosts are people too."

"Okay," I said. "But dead people have their own word—'ghosts.' People who are alive are just *people*."

"You're being a bigot."

"Excuse me for living."

It wasn't the first time I'd made that joke, and her only response was to make a grumbly noise. A jogger was headed toward us from half a block away, and Mindy knew I didn't like her to talk unless we were alone.

The jogger huffed past with a little nod to me. It was past midnight, and we were at least a mile from my house. Normally a passing stranger would've given me a flutter of nerves, but nothing was normal anymore.

If anything, I was the one spreading jitters, dressed all in black, my hood up, hands deep in my pockets. It was the coldest night all winter, and steam curled from my mouth when I talked to my invisible friend.

"What was this place when it was . . . alive?"

"A school. It got torn down right after we moved here. Now it's a vacant lot full of broken trucks and rusty school buses. Like that box in Anna's closet where she throws stuff and forgets about it." Mindy came to a halt. "But a lot of livers must remember this school."

She was staring at the high fence that stretched along the opposite side of the street. Its chicken-wire pattern caught the streetlights, and a makeshift barrier of wooden planks leaned against the metal from the other side. Glittering thorns spiraled along the top.

"Do you see it?" Mindy asked.

"What? That shit-ton of razor wire I'm going to have to climb over?"

"No, behind that. Behind *everything*."

I squinted into the darkness, but couldn't see anything except the rusty yellow tops of school buses. "Sorry."

"Here." She took my hand, and a trickle of death traveled up my arm. Over the past week I'd gotten good at crossing over, with or without Mindy's touch. But there was always a shiver of reluctance just before, as if I were about to dive into cold water. Something inside me didn't want to cross over. My body knew the scent of death.

But I needed to practice using my powers, which meant getting over the whole death-is-scary thing.

I hadn't called Yamaraj again. I didn't want to be some floundering girl, needing him to show me the ropes. I wanted to demonstrate that he didn't have to be afraid for me, that I belonged in his world, even if I didn't know what to call myself yet. "Soul guide" sounded too wimpy. "Psychopomp" too psycho. "Reaper" too grim. I was still looking for something better.

As I crossed over, the moonlight shuddered around us, and the taste of metal filled the air. The sky above went from velvet black to flat gray dotted with red stars. Mindy's hand grew solid in mine.

"See it now?"

I nodded, still breathing hard. Rising up behind the fence was a terra-cotta roof against the gray sky. The building was much smaller than my high school a mile up the road. Parts of the roofline were sharp and clear, but other sections had faded into translucence, like old paint wearing away.

A ghost building.

Mindy had explained that a lot of things had ghosts, not just people. Animals, machines, even things as vast as a paved-over forest or as humble as the smell of good cooking could leave traces of themselves behind. The world was haunted by the past.

"Come on." I headed across the street. As we drew closer, the fence grew fainter, almost transparent. It hadn't stood there in the old days, I guess, so it was only a ghostly presence here on the flip-side. I walked up to the chicken wire and reached out. . . . My fingers passed through, then dipped into the wood behind.

"Sweet," I said.

This was my first time using the flipside to pass through something solid, at least since Yamaraj had led me through the metal gate at the airport. Mindy ran by me like it was nothing, straight through the fence and across the school grounds. The school buses and city trucks, parked so tight they were almost touching, offered no resistance to her.

As I followed, the fence tugged at me, like a thornbush catching my clothing. But then I was on the other side, the school yard growing clearer before me, the buses and trucks fading.

It was like going back in time. The parking lot was tiny—I guess kids didn't drive themselves to school back then—and there were no white lines, just hand-painted signs for a few teachers' spaces. The ghost playground looked dangerous, with its ten-foot-high jungle gym over hard asphalt. Mindy climbed to the top, hooked her knees over the highest bar, and hung there, upside down and facing me.

The building itself looked more like a mansion than a school, with its tiled roof, stucco walls, and long front porch. The windows just looked wrong. They were empty rectangles, black pits that didn't reflect the streetlights.

"Are there ghosts in there?" I asked.

Mindy swung her arms, her pigtails swaying. "Might be."

"Isn't that the point of ghost buildings? For ghosts to live in?"

"Don't be stupid." She reached up to grab the bar, unhooked

her knees, and swung down to land on her feet. "Ghosts live in normal places."

"Like my mom's closet?"

"Closets are nice." Mindy stared at the school in silence for a moment. "But a lot of ghost buildings aren't. I don't go inside them."

"You don't have to come with me." I took a slow breath, tasting rust in the air. The ghost building shimmered before me, as if uncertain of its own existence. "But I need to know how this flipside stuff works."

"It's okay." She took my hand and pulled me forward. "I'm not scared with you here. Just don't leave me in there."

"Trust me, I won't."

As we got closer, the school grew less shimmery. The front steps felt solid beneath my feet, and I knelt to place one palm flat against the painted concrete. It felt cold, just like stone on a cool night.

"It's so real," I said.

Mindy had stopped, unwilling to venture ahead without me. "That means everyone remembers this place. Maybe something bad happened here."

"*Or* maybe everyone totally loved it." I rose to my feet and climbed the stairs. "Whoa. How am I going up like this? I mean, these steps aren't here anymore. So does that mean I'm levitating?"

"The steps *are* here," Mindy said. "But the flipside is a here that livers don't see, except for pomps like you."

I sighed. "Pretty much every word of that answer was annoying."

"Well, maybe you're asking annoying questions!"

I bit back my reply. Mindy was gradually becoming my friend, even if she was a little odd. She was helping me learn about the afterworld, so I wouldn't be as clueless the next time Yamaraj and I met.

I still hadn't told Mindy about him, though. No point in scaring her off.

"Sorry," I said as we climbed the stairs. "I'm just nervous. Never been in a ghost building before."

"But you're a pomp! Ghosts should be afraid of *you*."

I smiled down at her and stood straighter, trying to conjure up some psychopompish bluster.

The front doors of the school were already open, as if welcoming us in. Locker-lined hallways stretched out, empty and dark, and a hand-painted sign pointed the way to the main office. There were no posters on the walls, no loose papers on the floor, not even dust in the air, as if the transient details had been worn away by time. But the murmur of children's voices lingered at the edge of my awareness.

"Do you hear that?" I whispered.

Mindy nodded, closing her eyes. "Those aren't ghosts. Not of people, anyway."

"Of what then?"

"Of this place. Of its sounds."

I looked at her, suddenly doubting whether "ghosts" was the right word for all this. "Memories. These are memories, aren't they?"

"That's what I keep saying! As long as people remember something, it never completely disappears."

I reached out to the nearest locker and ran a finger across the air vent. The *tick-tick-tick* of my fingernail against metal sounded real.

"So we're standing in memories?"

"I guess so," Mindy said.

"Maybe this isn't about ghosts at all. What if us pomps are, like, mind readers? We see other people's memories as if they were places and things and . . ."

Mindy was glaring at me. "And *people*? You think I'm just a figment of your mom's imagination?"

"I don't know." As the words came out, I could hear how unkind they sounded. Mindy wasn't a memory—she was a person whose existence depended on being remembered. There was a difference, maybe. "I was just thinking out loud. I don't understand any of this, really."

As we stood there in unhappy silence, a sound drifted down the hallway, a child's voice singing . . .

"Come down, come down, whoever you are."

"Um, okay," I said. "Is that, like, the ghost of a song?"

"No." Mindy reached up and took my hand, squeezing hard. "There's someone down there, Lizzie."

"Okay . . ." The song repeated, distant and forlorn, and sparks of fear kindled in my veins. "Are they going to come up?"

"I hope not," Mindy said.

We stood there, frozen for a moment, me trying to slow my breathing. The last time I'd panicked on the flipside, I'd popped back into the normal world right in front of Special Agent Elian Reyes. That wasn't something I wanted to repeat in the middle of a vacant lot surrounded by razor wire, especially with a creepy ghost-song leaking out of the ground.

The singing cut off. Mindy and I stared at each other in the awful silence.

"Okay," I said, taking a step backward. "Let's just try to—"

"Look," Mindy whispered, her eyes on the floor.

A darkness was spreading down the hallway, like spilled ink rolling toward us. It blotted out the tiles of the floor, pure black against the soft grays of the flipside. Like the rivers of oil I'd glimpsed in the desert, it moved with intent, a living thing, and it carried the same thick and sugary scent.

The singsong voice called out again.

"I can heeeear you up there. Why don't you come down and play?"

"Maybe we should just get out of here," I whispered.

"Yep." Mindy turned and ran.

"Wait for me!" I shouted, setting off after her, out the school door and down the stairs. As I ran across the playground, my heart galloped, pushing warmth outward into my arms and legs.

Life was surging through me, and the world began to shift. The playground faded, and stars shone through gaps in the flat gray sky, as if a vast fabric were tearing overhead. I wondered whether to stop and regather my grasp on the flipside, or try and run to the fence in time.

"Please don't go!" the voice sang from behind, which pretty much made the choice for me.

I ran harder, catching up with Mindy and passing her, my feet pounding the asphalt as hard as they could.

The fence in my path was looking more solid every second.

School buses loomed around me now, and I swerved to thread my way between two of them, not wanting to solidify inside a mass of metal and rubber.

The fence was right in front of me, and I launched myself at it, covering my face with both arms. The chicken wire pulled and sucked as I went through, like a thick spiderweb, sticky and reluctant to let me pass. But the tension broke with a *snap*, and suddenly I was on the other side, stumbling into the living world . . . and the street.

Headlights flashed as I skidded to a halt, the shriek of a swerving car screaming in my ears. I fell and dropped into a fetal position as the machine whooshed by, so close that I felt engine heat in the wind of its passage. But the scream of tires turned into the fading blare of a car horn, and the car flashed past and kept moving.

I uncurled myself and sat up, looking both ways down the street—no cars in sight except for the red taillights, accelerating now. I guess the driver hadn't been too keen on investigating black-clad figures popping out of thin air.

"Whoa." Mindy jogged up beside me. "That was close."

I stood up gingerly, swallowing when I saw skid marks curving around me. My right knee was throbbing and the heels of both hands were raw. The pain felt sharp and real after the gray flatness of the flipside. My scraped palms pulsed with my heartbeat, but it was wonderful, being back in the real world.

I limped as we crossed the road.

"Are you okay?" Mindy asked.

"Yeah, great. But next time, let's try a ghost building with no fence around it."

"Sure." Mindy looked back at the vacant lot, her eyes wide. "And maybe . . ."

I nodded. "Without anything scary in the basement."

"I don't know what that was. Sorry!"

"Going inside was my idea." I touched my right knee. My jeans were ripped, but not bloody. "Anyway, thanks for showing me how this works, Mindy."

She looked up at me. "Really?"

I nodded, still buzzing from the chase. Crossing the barrier between life and death was getting addictive.

We headed back to my house—*our* house, as Mindy kept reminding me.

On the way around to the back door, we checked in front of the Andersons' yard to see if Special Agent Reyes had reappeared, but he hadn't. His car had been gone the last few days, so I guess his boss wasn't worried about me anymore.

I'd looked up the Movement of the Resurrection online, and it seemed as though they had bigger things to worry about than me. After the Dallas massacre, all sorts of investigations had been opened up, from illegal weapons to tax avoidance. The Feds were closing in on them.

Not being a terrorist target was fine with me, but I kind of missed waving to the FBI on my way home.

Back in my bedroom, I pulled off my jeans, sat on the bed, and sprayed antiseptic on my palms and knee. The sting started my heart pounding again, but tomorrow I would be all bruises and aches, without the adrenaline of basement monsters and near car accidents to distract me.

When I looked up, Mindy was watching raptly.

"Never seen blood before?"

"I don't really feel pain anymore." She shrugged. "Everything is kind of soft over here. I'm mostly bored, and kind of restless."

"Sounds like school."

"It sucks. I never feel anything *real*."

"Except when you get afraid." I felt a smile on my lips. "I mean, you ran away much quicker than I did. And you should have seen your face when we heard that song!"

"Of course I get afraid." Her eyes flashed.

"Sorry." I'd almost forgotten how Mindy had become a ghost. Even if she was beyond suffering now, her last hours were something I could never imagine. "You know I won't let any bad men hurt you, right?"

"I know." But she didn't look convinced.

"Listen, Mindy. Maybe he died a long time ago. Maybe he's already faded into nothing."

She looked away from me, toward my mother's room and the closet, where she always went when she got scared.

No matter what promises I made, she remained certain that the bad man was out there, still alive. That he would die one day, and then wander the earth looking for her.

Maybe it was better to change the subject. "So what do you think that was, down in the school basement?"

She started tracing the pattern of the bedspread with one finger, not much happier. "I don't know."

"But it was the ghost of something, right?"

Mindy only shrugged.

"You must have *some* idea," I said. "Is there anything out there besides ghosts? I mean, what about vampires and werewolves?"

A laugh sputtered out of her. "Don't be a dummy. Those are just make-believe!"

"Are you sure? I mean, if ghosts are real, why not all the other creatures of legend? Golems? Garudas? Selkies?"

Mindy's smile faded. "I don't even know what those are, but I think some monsters never got legends. Some places are just *bad*."

"Okay," I said. "You don't have to know everything, I guess."

"Good, because I don't."

Mindy was an eleven-year-old girl, I reminded myself. To her, a monster wasn't something to be analyzed, it was something to be feared.

Not that I had the energy for monster analysis. The last dregs of my adrenaline were fading, and school was starting back up the day after tomorrow. The beginning of my last semester, and my first day in public as a national symbol of hope.

I'd avoided my friends since getting home, except for sending Jamie an email saying I wasn't ready to see anyone. My dad still hadn't bought me a new phone, despite promising to, so avoiding people had been easy enough. But I was going to have to face the real world soon.

I put the antiseptic away and slipped under the covers.

"Good night," I said, and turned off the bedside light.

Mindy, as always, sat on the end of my bed. Ghosts didn't sleep, which probably contributed to their boredom and restlessness. It was clear that Mindy wandered the neighborhood at night. She knew all the neighbors' names, and their secrets too.

"Sleep tight, Lizzie," she whispered.

"Thanks for taking me to ghost school."

She giggled, and we were silent for a while, my brain searching for sleep. But the pain of my injuries came and went like ants traveling around my body, first one scraped palm itching, and then the other.

The sting of the antiseptic slowly faded, though, and I was almost asleep when the scratching sound began.

It was like a fingernail running along the underside of the floorboards, almost too soft to hear, too quiet to believe in. But the sound persisted, refusing to disappear even as my brain tried to ignore it.

By the time I opened my eyes, Mindy was standing on the end of my bed, staring wide-eyed down at the floor.

I sat up slowly, carefully, but already my skin was damp with fear.

"What the hell is that, Mindy?"

"I think it followed us home."

"*What* did?"

The sound came again, scraping its way from my bedroom door toward me. My spine turned to water as it traveled beneath the bed.

It fell silent again, and Mindy whispered, "It's all connected."

"What are you talking about?"

"It's down there, Lizzie. That thing we heard singing."

"What do you—!" My voice rose almost to a shout, and I forced my mouth shut. Mom was a heavy sleeper, but I didn't dare wake her with a monster in the house.

"I'm sorry, Lizzie." Mindy's voice was shaking. "I didn't know it would follow us home!"

"Where is it?" I hissed. "This house *doesn't have a basement!*"

She looked at me with exasperation. "It's not in the basement. It's down in the river."

I shut my eyes, trying to make sense of Mindy's words. My body was wide awake, but my brain was still spinning up from being half-asleep.

"Come down, come down, whoever you are!" sang a voice from beneath my bedroom floor.

CHAPTER 15

THE INVITATIONS TO DARCY'S HOUSEWARMING PARTY HAD said seven, but at seven thirty not a single person had arrived.

"Crap." Darcy kicked the bucket of beer and ice waiting in the corner. A pool of condensation had collected beneath it, like an unloved and sweaty pet left by its owner on a country road.

It was awfully hot in here in the big room, and would only get worse if any guests ever arrived. Darcy pushed open another of the windows, letting in the roar of Chinatown traffic and a tired breeze that stirred the hem of her sundress. She'd bought the dress at a vintage shop that morning, only to realize moments out of the store how close it was to the one Imogen had worn the day they'd found apartment 4E.

It wasn't rust colored, at least, but the blue-gray of an overcast sky.

Darcy stared at her phone. Imogen had promised to arrive at six for moral support, but had texted an hour ago to say she'd be late. On top of that, Sagan and Carla had missed their intended train from Philly and wouldn't be showing up till after nine. Aunt Lalana was out of town on business.

The inevitable question was forming in Darcy's mind: What if no one came? It had been pure hubris, having a housewarming party in a city where she knew hardly anyone. Of course, a *few* people would show up, just enough to witness and ratify her humiliation.

The phone pinged in Darcy's hand, and she raised it eagerly.

Still nobody there? #Loserfest

Only 438 days till publication!

"Thanks a lot, Nisha," Darcy muttered, resolving never again to share doubts with her sister.

As she composed a suitably rude reply, the intercom sounded.

Darcy ran and buzzed open the downstairs door without asking who it was—party crashers were better than no one at all. She primped her hair in the wall of mirrors, opened the door, and stuck her head out. Climbing the stairs were Moxie Underbridge, her assistant, Max, and a young woman whom Darcy recognized from YA Drinks Night—Johari Valentine, a writer from Saint Kitts.

A moment later the three were inside, drifting past Darcy's greetings and toward the windows of the big room. Darcy felt a swell of pride as they exclaimed over the views. This was the best time for looking out, the hour before sunset, when the sky was rosy and the shadows long and sharp.

For the first time all day, Darcy felt that neither the party nor the apartment had been a terrible mistake.

"This'll be splendid in winter." Johari was staring down at the street. "The rest of us down in the darkness, you up here in sunshine!"

"Really now, Johari," Moxie said. "It's July. Are you still traumatized?"

Johari gave Darcy a mock shudder. "My next book's set on an ice planet. Dark and freezing, like winter up here."

"It's called *Heart of Ice*," said Max. "'Who holds the secret of fire, rules the world!'"

Johari shook her head. "Listen to you, Max. Peddling taglines for a book that isn't half-done. Might be about penguins by the time I'm finished."

"'Who holds the secret of penguins, rules the world'?" Max said. "See, it works with everything."

"Sounds awesome," Darcy said, but all the talk of fire made her think of Imogen, and wonder again where she was. She glanced at her phone—nothing.

"Sorry to arrive so early, my dear," Moxie said. "But we have a dinner at nine."

"I'm just glad someone's here!" Darcy put her phone away, praying that more people would arrive before they left. It would be inhumane of the universe to make her suffer *two* preparty freakouts in one night. "You guys want drinks?"

They did, and as Darcy set to work, Johari and Max poked their heads into the bedrooms.

"Great idea," Johari called, "having a party before moving in your furniture. Nothing broken if we get too lively!"

Darcy didn't explain that all her furniture was, in fact, moved in. Her new desk was in the corner of the big room, holding soft drinks, plastic cups, and two bowls of guacamole. It wasn't a real desk, just an unfinished door laid across two sawhorses. Page proofs and copyedits needed large surfaces, and doors were cheaper than desks.

Darcy was sleeping on her futon from home, which her father had driven up from Philly, along with a chair, some linens, and a few dozen indispensable books, which were now in the second bedroom on cinder-block shelves. Sagan and Carla had been warned to bring sleeping bags, but Darcy had forgotten to buy them pillows.

"And no TV?" Max was laughing. "The sign of a true writer."

"I'm all about the words," Darcy said, though she had yet to write a single sentence in apartment 4E.

She'd hardly noticed her lack of a television, given all the other things she didn't own. Aunt Lalana had been right. She had no extension cords, no vacuum cleaner, no umbrella, nor a vase if anyone brought flowers tonight. She had no bathroom curtains and hardly any real dishes, only two bowls and a tea mug, and exactly one pan for making masala chai and instant noodles, the only cooking she'd done so far. She had a spice rack, complete with cardamom and tamarind and even saffron, but that had been a housewarming present from her aunt.

As Darcy handed out red plastic cups, she wondered what else she was missing. She'd only remembered to buy a corkscrew this afternoon, and the tiny speakers connected to her computer were unlikely to get anyone dancing tonight.

"Thank you, darling." Moxie took her drink and swirled it thoughtfully. "Did you know Stanley David Anderson was in town?"

"Really? For an appearance?"

"Business. That's who we're dining with. You follow him, I presume?"

"Who doesn't follow Standerson?" Darcy asked. That was one of his internet nicknames. The other was the Sultan of Social Media. Standerson had a million followers, and there were a dozen YouTube channels *about* his YouTube channel. "But you don't represent him."

"Not at the moment." Moxie brushed an index finger across her lips. "But he's a bit unhappy over at Sadler Lit, and might be looking around."

"Whoa, that's great," Darcy said, though she was suffering a moment of petty jealousy. She wasn't invited to dinner with Moxie, Max, Johari, and Standerson, and her housewarming party wouldn't be the most glamorous YA event in New York tonight.

But this irrational moment passed when the buzzer sounded again, and Darcy sprang for the door.

As if the party's surface tension had been broken, the guests arrived quickly now. Soon the big room was pleasingly full. Darcy recognized a dozen writers from YA Drinks Night (thanks to Oscar Lassiter's email list), and Nan Eliot had come down from Paradox with a young assistant editor named Rhea. Carla had texted that she and Sagan were approaching Penn Station, but Imogen was still missing.

Darcy found herself poised between worry for Imogen and a sense of betrayal that she still wasn't here.

"I admire your monklike simplicity," Johari was saying. "A room for sleeping, one for books and clothes, one for food, and the biggest one for writing."

"Are you going to keep it like this?" Oscar asked. "Au naturel?"

"You mean empty?" Darcy shrugged. "Yeah, but it's not exactly a design choice. More of a money thing."

"Ah, yes," Oscar said. "I was a rent slave before I moved out to Hoboken. Had the best view of the Chrysler Building, but I had to suck my sheets for food."

"Enough about your personal life, Oscar." Johari patted his shoulder and asked Darcy, "How's your writing adjusting to a new space?"

"I haven't really tried yet." Nan's editorial letter still hadn't arrived, making revisions impossible to begin, and the thought of starting on *Untitled Patel* without guidance was too terrifying. "Should I be worried?"

"Writing fairies can get grumpy in a new house," Johari said. "Like cats. Mine pissed on the pillows every night for a week after I moved up to New York."

Oscar raised an eyebrow. "Your writing fairies pissed on your pillows?"

Johari ignored him. "I'd be worried about those mirrors. I couldn't write a single word if I had to watch myself at it."

Darcy turned to the mirrored wall and regarded the three of them. Oscar and Johari both towered over her, making Darcy in her blue sundress look very young.

"Those are left over from when it was a dance studio. But if I take them down, it'll be nothing but white."

"Like every other apartment in New York," Johari said sadly.

"I know!" Darcy said. Back in Philly, the rooms of her parents' house each had a signature color—pale yellow for the kitchen, forest green in the dining area, and dark purple for Nisha's bed-room walls, a leftover from her twelve-year-old goth phase. "What *is* it with all the white up here?"

"It's gallery space," Oscar said. "Neutral background for all the artists at work."

"Pfft," Johari said. "It's boring."

"I was in the hardware store yesterday," Darcy said. "And they had a whole section of white paints. But instead of 'white,' they all had names like Linen, Chalk, and Washed Rice."

Oscar laughed. "My walls are Dover, I think."

"Picket Fence," Johari admitted.

"Maybe I'll keep the mirrors," Darcy said.

"Good heavens! Are we all staring at ourselves?" It was Kiralee Taylor, whom Darcy hadn't seen come in. Other people were work-ing the intercom now, and even giving tours of the apartment to new arrivals. Moxie was making drinks, and Rhea collecting money for more beer and ice. The party had found its own momentum, its own heartbeat.

"Thanks for coming, Kiralee," Darcy said. They kissed each other's cheeks, like old friends.

"Lovely apartment. And what a handy wall of mirrors!"

"Dancers left it here," Darcy said. "Johari thinks my reflection will keep me from writing."

"One's own face is rarely as distracting as the internet," Kiralee said. "And you seem the industrious sort."

Darcy smiled at the compliment, but a tremor of nerves passed through her. Imogen had forwarded the first draft of *Afterworlds* to Kiralee two weeks ago. Enough time for her to have read it by now.

Darcy searched for some clue in the older woman's expression as to whether she had loved or hated it, or even started it at all. Was "industrious" some sort of damning faint praise?

"That said, I spent all day worrying about my face." Kiralee turned to the mirrors to adjust her tie, a pulvinate double Windsor. "Bloody photo shoot this afternoon."

"Ah, I hate authors' photos," Johari said. "I don't see why my looks are relevant to the story!"

"Indeed." Kiralee checked out her profile in the mirror. "I liked my old photo, but it's getting a bit long in the tooth. Or, rather, I am."

"And you *are* touching your face in it," Oscar said.

Kiralee punched him, and Darcy looked at them questioningly.

"Beware, my dear." Johari's arm encircled Darcy. "When you get your author's photo taken, be sure *not* to touch your face."

"Why would I do that?"

"It's a mystery, but quite common. You must have seen this one." Oscar struck a brooding pose, his fist beneath his chin. "For the author whose brain is too heavy to stay up on its own."

"Friend of mine got stuck with one of these for a whole trilogy." Johari stroked her cheek thoughtfully. "Like he was coming up with amazing ideas *right in front of the photographer!*"

"Yikes." Darcy turned to Kiralee. "You did that?"

"No, I went for the dreaded temple massage. It was a long time ago, and I had no wise elders to save me."

Darcy tried to recall the back of *Bunyip*. "But I totally had a crush on that picture. You look so smart in it."

"I look like a TV psychic."

Darcy glanced across the room at Nan and Rhea. "Paradox

won't make me get an author's photo, will they? I mean, lots of books don't have them."

"Pretty young thing like you?" Johari shook her head. "I should think it's unavoidable."

Darcy stared at herself in the mirror again, a familiar vulnerable feeling descending on her. Not only would her words be duplicated thousands of times for everyone to weigh and judge, but also her face.

She could see why it would be tempting to sneak a hand into the frame, just for a bit of protection.

Her phone pinged, and Darcy glanced down at it—Imogen.

"Pardon me, guys." She spun away and crossed to an empty corner, raising the phone to her ear. "Where the hell *are* you, Gen?"

"I'm on your roof."

"What? Why?"

"Someone buzzed me in, and I need to talk to you alone for a second. Come up."

"Um, my party . . . ," Darcy began, but as her eyes swept across the room, she saw Johari drawing Kiralee to the window, pointing out something below. Rhea was helping Moxie mix drinks, and Oscar was making faces in the mirror at Max.

The party could be left alone to find its own way, and Darcy still had a confession to make before Imogen met her high school friends.

"All right," she said. "See you in a minute."

Darcy hadn't been up to the roof before. But on the sixth-floor landing she found a smaller, separate staircase leading up to a metal door that was wedged open with a piece of concrete.

As she stepped out, the tar roof squished a little beneath her feet, like a bouncy playground surface. It had been a hot day, and the tar was giving up its scent.

"Gen?"

"Over here."

Imogen was sitting at the building's edge, her legs dangling off the side. Darcy sat next to her and leaned forward to stare down at the street. A shimmer of vertigo traveled from her toes to her fingertips.

"Don't fall," Imogen said. "I like that dress."

"If I decide to jump, I'll change." The words came out a little harshly.

"Look . . . sorry I was late."

"Me too, Gen." Darcy turned to her. "I spent all day shit-scared no one would come. My friends from Philly are late, and then you totally bailed!"

"It was a shitty thing to do." Imogen swung her legs, staring out at the skyline. "But I wanted to finish your book."

Darcy blinked. "What?"

"I've been putting off reading it, because I really like you. But then I realized that Oscar was here tonight and was going to ask me what I thought, and you might be standing there when I did. So I was like, fuck it, and started reading three hours ago. But yeah, my timing kind of sucked. I would have started sooner if I hadn't been scared to."

"Wait. Why were you scared?"

Imogen spread her hands. "Because what if it was crap? It would be really weird, me liking you this much if you were a shitty writer. I mean, would you want me to *tell* you if I thought it sucked? Or just politely never mention it? Because those would be your choices. I couldn't lie about it."

Darcy took a slow breath. The drop into space before them suddenly yawned, as if the roof were tipping, trying to spill her onto the street below.

"You didn't think I could write?"

"I had no idea. You're awesome, but a lot of awesome people can't write their way out of a wet sack."

"And . . . ?"

"And it makes things awkward! Everyone at Oscar's parties always talks about writing, so I'm all polite and everything, but inside me there's this tiny voice, like when you're at a wedding and you know the whole thing is doomed, and you get paranoid that when the preacher asks if anyone knows any reason why this wedding shouldn't happen, you'll shout, '*Marriage of fail!*'"

"Let me try again," Darcy said carefully. "You read my book, *and* . . . ?"

"Oh." Imogen smiled, taking Darcy's hand. "Well, I'm late, aren't I?"

"*Because* . . . ?"

"Because I couldn't stop. Because it was really fucking good."

Darcy still felt dizzy. "And you wouldn't be saying that right now if you hated it?"

"No." Imogen's voice was steady, undeceptive. "If it had sucked, I would have put it down and gotten here on time, and never mentioned it again."

"And I never would have known." A shudder went through

Darcy, relief mixed with the rattle of fear, as if the shadow of some monstrous bird of prey had passed over her. "You know, Gen, you could have *started* with the part where you liked it."

"Not liked. Loved." Imogen squeezed Darcy's hand. "I love *Afterworlds*."

Darcy felt a smile prying at her annoyed expression. "Why did you have to tell me on the roof?"

"I wanted to right away."

"Yeah, but you could have said it down there. I mean, feel free to make these thoughts public!"

"Even the part about liking you?"

Darcy blinked again, and for a second time said, "Wait. What?"

"I know this is a stupid way to tell you," Imogen said, taking both of Darcy's hands. "But it all got tangled up today, liking you and liking your book. So on the way over I decided to say both."

The roof was tipping again. "You mean . . . you *like* like me?"

"Yeah, a lot. Of course, it's possible you just regular like me, and if that's the way it is I'm not going to storm off and stop being your friend. But you should know that I'm hot for you, and for your book, too." Imogen was almost laughing, stumbling over her own words now. "I'm totally hot for *Afterworlds*."

"That's just weird." Darcy felt a blush creeping behind her cheeks.

"No it isn't. Your book is smart and beautiful. I want to have its sequels."

Darcy laughed. "Really?"

"You take all the right stuff seriously. Like, Mindy's backstory is *brutally* sad, and you never try to skim past it. And the way the terror of that first chapter never really fades out, Lizzie just learns to *use* it."

"It's her origin story," Darcy said softly.

"Exactly." Imogen took a strand of Darcy's hair between her fingers. Their eyes stayed locked. "And it's not just about the gnarly powers it gives her, it's how other people see her differently. Like, when anyone thinks Lizzie's still a kid, she's all, 'When's the last time *you* survived machine guns, dude?' And they have to respect her."

Darcy didn't answer. No one had said things like this about *Afterworlds* before. Those first letters of praise from Underbridge Literary and Paradox had been full of compliments, but nothing as specific as this. Being fathomed was even better than being flattered, it turned out. The words made her skin tingle and her lips burn.

"I like books where magic has a cost," Imogen went on. "The more powerful Lizzie gets, the more she loses." She leaned closer. "You've got the juice."

"The what?" Darcy asked.

"You don't just write well, you tell *stories*." Imogen's voice was a whisper now. "Beautiful sentences are fine, but the juice is what makes me turn pages."

Darcy closed her eyes. Their lips met, and she breathed in the scent of the sun-heated tar beneath them and the salt of Imogen's skin. She felt the rumble of the traffic below traveling up through the building and into her spine, her fingertips, her tongue. Her breathing slowed to match the pace of Imogen's, steady and deep.

Imogen's hand moved to the back of Darcy's neck, fingers interlacing with hair, holding her close even after the kiss was over.

Darcy whispered, her lips brushing Imogen's as she spoke: "Wow. You *are* hot for my book."

"Totally."

It meant everything, but Darcy wanted more. "No criticisms?"

"Well, you know. It's a first draft. And a first novel. And don't ask me if you're hijacking Hindu gods, because I don't have a clue."

Darcy opened her eyes. "Okay. But what did that second one mean?"

"About it being a first novel? Well, it might be a little bit innocent, for a book about death."

"Innocent?" Darcy pulled back. "Is *that* what you think I am?"

"Good question." Imogen drew closer, studying her. "Until ten seconds ago, I had no idea whether you were into me or not. Are you, like, incredibly smooth or just . . ." She blinked slowly. "Have you ever kissed a girl before?"

"I never kissed anyone before," Darcy said in a rush, so she wouldn't have time to chicken out and never say it at all. "Not really."

Imogen was silent for a moment—a little too long.

"Seriously?" she said at last.

Darcy nodded. There had been a sort of practice kiss with Carla once during a sleepover, and an attempt at real kissing with the boy who was cocaptain of the Reading Zealots. But neither of those had counted, and this did.

"Was I okay?" Darcy asked.

"Better than okay."

"If you hated it, would you be lying right now?"

"That's the second time you've asked me that." A smiled curled Imogen's lips. "Don't you trust me?"

Darcy had never seen anyone talk the way Imogen did about things that mattered to her. No one could lie that fiercely, could they?

"I trust you."

"Good." Imogen's eyes shone with the last band of pink in the sky before nightfall. She leaned closer, and they were kissing again. At first Darcy's hands clutched at the warm tar of the rooftop for balance. Then she reached up to take Imogen's shoulders, to feel the muscles flexing. She drew Imogen closer, tighter, and they stayed that way until Darcy's phone buzzed in her pocket.

"Sorry . . ." She pulled away, reaching for it. "My friends from Philly might be lost."

"Like I said, my timing sucks."

Darcy read the message. "Crap, they're already here! Someone let them in and they're down there looking for me!"

Imogen got to her feet and held out a hand. "Come on. Duty calls."

Darcy stood, guiltily wishing that Carla and Sagan had missed just one more train. But it would be cruel to leave them alone in a room full of authors they idolized.

At the roof stairway, Imogen kicked the piece of concrete aside, and the metal door slammed shut behind them. They descended quickly, and a moment later stood before the door to 4E. The sounds of a healthy party were leaking out into the hall.

Imogen took Darcy by the shoulders. "You okay? You look kind of dazed."

Darcy was very dazed and very okay, too much of both to discuss in the hallway. Instead, she rose a little onto her toes and they kissed again.

Then she straightened herself and, still holding Imogen's hand, opened up the door.

CHAPTER 16

I DRESSED QUICKLY IN JEANS AND A SWEATSHIRT, THEN CREPT
to the kitchen to get a knife.

I didn't know if metal blades worked on ghosts, or even if the
thing in the basement *was* a ghost, but any weapon was better than
bare hands. I chose a short, narrow knife with a fat metal handle.

Mindy was still standing on my bed, afraid to touch the floor.
Her eyes widened when she saw the knife. "We should just run
away, Lizzie."

"And hide in my mom's closet?" I slipped the knife into my
back pocket. "I live here, Mindy. I don't have anywhere to run. And
didn't you say that ghosts should be afraid of *me*?"

"Whatever's down there doesn't sound very afraid, does it?"

As if in answer, the voice beneath us started up again, close enough
to the floorboards that it could whisper. *"Come down and play. . . ."*

I shuddered, and slipped on the pair of sneakers beside my bed.

"Please, let's just run away," Mindy begged.

"No. I'm going to call someone."

She stared at me. *"Who?"*

"Someone I met when I started seeing ghosts. Someone I didn't tell you about."

"You mean a dead person?"

I shook my head. "Someone like me."

"A pomp?" Mindy turned away and jumped onto my desk, like a kid playing don't-touch-the-floor. She was headed for the bedroom door, and then my mother's room and the safety of her closet.

"It's okay, Mindy! He's nice."

She turned back to me, balanced on the dresser. "They always *say* they're nice. But then they take you away."

I shook my head. "He saved me."

Mindy looked at me like I was an idiot, and for a moment I wondered why I trusted Yamaraj so much. What if he took Mindy away from me?

But I'd seen enough horror movies to know that you didn't check out scary noises in the basement all alone. Especially if your house didn't have a basement.

"Trust me." I took a step closer and reached for her hand. "I need to cross over to call him."

"No way!" Mindy pulled away.

"Fine. I can do it on my own." I took a deep breath. "Security is responding. . . ."

The thing beneath us went quiet, as if listening, and my voice grew steadier in the silence.

"Can you get to a safe location?"

The words made me shiver, stirring the night chill in the room. My breathing began to slow. It was weird, saying both sides of the conversation, but I could feel the spell working.

"I can't, and he's shooting everyone."

The cold became a physical thing, pushing at me from all sides.

"Well, honey," I said softly. "Maybe you should pretend to be dead."

As the last word left my mouth, I felt myself cross over. It happened all at once, the shadows flattening to soft grays, the bright digits of my alarm clock going flickery and dim.

But this time the air didn't taste flat and metallic. A sugary scent, like I'd smelled out in the desert, lay heavy around me. I looked down and saw a pitch-black stain growing in the center of my floor.

It was like the ink flooding the ghost school, or the black rivers I'd seen in the desert—a pool of emptiness. It started no bigger than a spilled cup of coffee, but spread across the floor as I watched.

"Don't let it touch you," Mindy said.

I took a step back. "Yamaraj, I need you."

His name suddenly sounded like "mirage," and it seemed crazy to expect him to hear me. He could be a thousand miles away, or a thousand miles below. . . .

But he'd come the first time I called him.

"Yamaraj, please come to me." As I spoke his name again, heat flickered across my lips.

The pool of nothingness was drawing closer to my feet. I took another step away from it, and felt the wall at my back.

"What *is* this stuff, Mindy?"

"It's the river," she squeaked. "The stuff between up here and *down there.*"

The bed was close enough for me to jump to, but the blackness had reached the toes of my sneakers, and suddenly my feet were ice-cold. The muscles of my calves felt too weak to move.

A moment later my sneakers were sinking into the floor.

"How do I get out of this stuff?"

Mindy was too scared to answer, and only watched with wide, terrified eyes. I could feel the blackness creep up to my knees, as cold as winter mud. I reached out, trying to grab the edge of my bed, but it was too far away.

The iciness crawled up my body as I sank, every inch sending fresh waves of shudders through me. The sweet smell filled my lungs, almost too thick to breathe.

Just as it passed my waist, the door to my bedroom opened. It was my mother in a white nightgown. She must have heard me arguing with Mindy before I'd crossed over.

"Lizzie?" she called softly, squinting at my empty bed.

"Mom!" I yelled, but of course she couldn't hear me. I was on the flipside now, hidden from her. Suddenly, being invisible wasn't such a great superpower.

The black goo passed my shoulders.

"Yamaraj, I need you," I cried one last time, and felt heat kindle on my lips again.

I tried to scream, hoping that my panic would pop me back into the land of the living. But the cold ink slowed the pounding of my heart and pressed the air from my lungs. It covered my mouth, my eyes, my ears, like liquid midnight sliding over me.

A moment later I was down in the river.

*   *   *

It was cold down here, and dark.

The only sound was a low moan, a steady wind scouring a huge, empty space. The air felt almost solid, ruffling my hair and clothes and trying to push me off my feet. But I wasn't drowning, and at least I was standing on something solid; my feet had settled on a surface in the formless dark.

A glimmer of white appeared, not too far away—a man's face.

He looked older than his voice had sounded, as old as my grandfather, very pale with white hair. As my eyes adjusted to the darkness, the rest of him came into focus. He wore a long coat covered with patches, and his hands were plunged into its pockets. The hem of his coat rippled in the wind.

He was staring at me. "You're alive."

"No kidding."

His hand emerged to stroke his chin, pallid fingers shining in the darkness. His skin was pale, but not quite gray. It had a sweaty glow, like the gloss of a marble statue.

"What the hell are you doing under my bedroom?" My voice sounded thin against the constant wind.

"I smelled a little girl." He had the slightest accent. "Is she yours?"

"Mine?"

He raised one pale eyebrow. His eyes were colorless, almost transparent, like those pale fish that live in ocean trenches, too deep for light to reach.

"You don't collect?"

"Collect *ghosts*?"

"You must be new." The man's smile appeared gradually, like something controlled by a dial. It made the basement colder.

Then I realized that his skin glowed softly in the dark, just as mine did.

"You're like me," I said. He wasn't some monster of legend. He was another psychopomp.

"Well spotted." He was smirking at me. "But do you really know what we are?"

"Yes. And I don't collect ghosts."

"I could teach you how," he said, taking a step forward.

"Stay *right* where you are."

He smiled again. "Do I frighten you?"

"Terrorists with machine guns frighten me. You're just pissing me off. I was trying to *sleep*."

"My apologies." He made a little bow. "But sleep is not something you need anymore."

"What do you mean?"

"Sleep is a little slice of death. And you've already had a *big* slice, haven't you? All the cake you'll ever need."

"You kind of suck at metaphors," I said.

The old man's eyes flashed in the darkness. "English may not be my first language, but I'm good at many other things, and I've always wanted an apprentice. I can show you my tricks. All it will cost you is that little girl."

I wanted to scream at him then, but the anger I should have felt was missing. The cold had a firm grip on my muscles, and the constant wind seemed to strip my emotions away.

My lips were tingling, though, a flicker of heat in all that dark.

"No thanks," I said.

The old man's fingers tugged at the corners of his pockets,

which opened wider and wider. Somehow they were darker than the basement itself, depthless and hungry.

"Don't you want to see what's in my pockets?"

Finally I felt a trickle of fear, and my muscles jolted to life. I reached into my back pocket and pulled out the knife. "Not even slightly."

He looked disappointed. "A knife? How absurd. There's no need for violence, my dear. I have no interest in anyone as *lively* as you."

"Then leave me and my friend alone."

"That little ghost is not your friend. They aren't really people, you know."

I didn't want to hear this, and yet I asked, "Then what are they?"

"They're loose threads of memory, stories that tell themselves. And if you know how, you can weave the most beautiful things from them." He stroked his pockets with his palms. "Are you sure you don't want to see?"

The horrible thing is, part of me wanted to look. Part of me wanted to learn all the secrets of the afterworld, no matter how terrible they were. But even listening to him felt like a betrayal of Mindy. I shook my head.

"There are lots of other tricks I can teach you. Nothing to be squeamish about."

"Like what?" I asked.

His smile returned. He knew that my curiosity was hooked. "How to use a ghost's breath to keep yourself warm here in the river. How to make the pestering ones fade. How to slice out the finest memories for yourself. You can taste the best bite of birthday cake your little friend up there ever had. Or feel what it was like to listen to her favorite bedtime story, all snuggled up in warm covers."

"Are you serious? Those are your *nonsqueamish* tricks?"

"I'm as serious as death." He took another step toward me. "You don't know what you're missing, girl."

My hand tightened on the knife handle. Its metal flashed in the darkness. "Stay away from me."

"I'm offering you wonders." He was still drifting toward me. "Don't insult me in return."

"Stay away from me!" I took a step backward, and something cold and damp brushed against my spine, like wet leaves.

"What's that behind you?" asked the old man very gently.

I wanted to turn around, but I was frozen, my fingers tight around the knife handle. A breath of a whisper played across the back of my neck, as if the wind had spoken.

But then something shifted in the air, the darkness growing warm around us. My tingling lips began to burn, and whatever had been behind me was suddenly gone.

I smiled and let the knife slide back into my pocket. "You'd better go. My friend is coming."

"Your little friend?" The old man looked up greedily, smoothing his pockets with pale hands.

"This one's too old for you."

The man's smile faded.

"What's the matter?" I said. "I thought you *liked* cryptic bullshit."

"You're becoming annoying, my dear."

"Annoying? Like being woken up in the middle of the night?" My anger was bubbling up from where the cold had tamped it down.

"Like noises under your bed? Like old men who chase little girls?"

All false politeness had left his expression. His face was as cold as marble. "You should show some respect."

I just smiled and looked past him. A wave of heat was sweeping through the darkness, along with a sharp and smoky scent. From the darkness Yamaraj strode toward us, sparks coiling around his feet, like someone walking through embers. The pinpricks of light scattered in the wind.

It was a magnificent sight, but the old man didn't cower. He turned back to me a moment, his expression curious.

"You have interesting friends," he said, and shoved his hands back into his pockets and spat on the ground in front of him. Then he stepped forward and seemed to fall into the earth, disappearing like a snuffed candle.

I stood there, breathing hard.

Yamaraj raised a hand, which flared hot and white. The light scattered the darkness of the basement, confirming that the old man was gone. At last I saw where we were standing, on a gray plain that shone like damp earth, stretching away endless and empty. Above us, where my bedroom floor should have been, loomed an empty sky. A column of smoke rose up from Yamaraj's glowing hand, billowing wider as it climbed, bent into an arc by the constant wind.

He looked about carefully, and then dropped his hand. We were plunged again into a darkness that shimmered with shapes burned into my vision.

"Are you okay, Lizzie?" came his voice.

Even as I nodded, my hands began to shake. The other psychopomp might have looked like an old man in a patched suit, but something monstrous had lurked beneath his pale skin. I could still smell it in the sweet, heavy air around us.

"What did he want?" Yamaraj asked. I couldn't blink away the fiery afterimages in my vision, but I could feel him coming closer.

"He wasn't after me," I said. The words calmed me a little.

Yamaraj was close now, warming the air around us, which only reminded me how cold I'd been a minute before.

"Except he wanted to show me something," I said. "Something made from ghosts, I think."

"But you didn't look?" Yamaraj's gaze held mine. His brown eyes cut through the darkness, and through my fear.

"No. I didn't."

His gaze softened. "Good. Some of us collect things, pieces of lives. Things you can't unsee."

A shudder went through my body then, a mix of leftover anger and fear. A chill clung to me, something I couldn't shake. Part of me wanted to throw my arms around Yamaraj's warmth, but I didn't want to seem pathetic. Besides, last time just touching him had thrown me back into reality.

This wasn't at all how I'd imagined things going when we met again. I'd wanted to impress Yamaraj with everything I'd figured out on my own, but here I was, cold and scared and dressed like a slob.

"Thank you for coming," I said.

"Of course." He looked around. "But how did you get here?"

"You mean . . . down into the river? That old man followed me home, I guess, from this ghost building we were exploring. And he was under my floor, and driving me crazy. I had to face him."

"You were exploring." A half smile, unintended and beautiful, played on Yamaraj's lips. He was worried for me, but also impressed.

I couldn't take my eyes from him. I'd pictured Yamaraj a thousand times in the last week, and now my memories were fitting themselves into the sharper details of reality. That hitch in his eyebrows, like the bend of a boomerang. The hard line of his jaw, and the way his dark hair curled behind one ear, but had been tugged free from the other by the wind.

"Did you say *we*?" he asked.

"Yeah, my friend. She's this ghost that lives with me."

His smile faded now. "Your friend? Ghosts can be hard to get rid of, Lizzie, once you let them into your life."

"She was *already* in my life. She was my mom's best friend a long time ago, and she's been around me since I was born. She's teaching me things."

"What things, Lizzie?"

"How to see ghost buildings. How to walk inside them." I remembered the old man's voice singing in the school hallway, and shivered. "What *was* he? A psychopomp, like you and me, right?"

"He's not like you and me." Yamaraj turned away from me, his gaze scanning the darkness. "He's something heartless and empty."

"He said that ghosts aren't people."

"Some of us see the dead that way—as objects, as toys." Yamaraj sighed. "But some people see the living that way too."

"Great, psychopomps and psychopaths."

He didn't answer.

The heat Yamaraj had brought with him seemed to be fading,

and I crossed my arms over my chest against the cold. Suddenly the reality of everything I'd seen that night was crashing down on me.

At least now I knew why Mindy was so afraid of psychopomps. The afterlife had a food chain, and we were higher on it than ghosts.

"The old man wanted to teach me things," I said.

"There are things you don't want to know."

I held Yamaraj's eyes for a moment. The problem was, I wanted to know everything, the good and the bad. Maybe being the old man's apprentice wasn't for me, but this was a whole new world, and I needed to explore it.

"So *you* teach me," I said

"You're already changing so quickly, Lizzie. I don't want to make it happen faster."

I gestured out into the formless darkness. "Because that's worse than stumbling around down here, not knowing anything?"

There it was again, the look of longing I'd seen on his face in the airport. However worried he was about me, Yamaraj wanted to keep this connection between us. His lips parted once, then pressed together again.

Finally he said, "What do you want to know?"

It took a moment to answer. I wanted to know about ghosts, about the old man in the patched coat, about everything I'd seen. I wanted to know how Yamaraj had brought light and fire with him in the darkness, and why his touch threw me from the gray world back into reality.

But with that vast emptiness surrounding us, I asked a simpler question. "Where are we?"

"The River Vaitarna. It's the boundary between the world above and the one below."

"A river, like the Styx."

"Everything old has lots of names." He looked up at the empty sky. "The overworld is up there, full of the living and wandering ghosts. Below us is the underworld, where the dead reside. The river is the oil between the two."

I looked around. "It doesn't seem like a river. I mean, where's the water?"

"We're in it."

As if to reinforce Yamaraj's point, the wind whipped up, like an eddying current around us. It pressed his black silk shirt against his abdomen, and for a moment I could see every cord of muscles there.

I pushed my hair out of my eyes. "Okay, next question. Where are you from?"

"A small village, by a large sea."

I rolled my eyes. "That's a little vague, since you're supposed to be teaching me. You're from India, right?"

"I suppose. But that was before there was an India."

I nodded slowly, fairly certain that India had been around for a long, long time. "How old are you?"

"I was fourteen when I crossed over." His smile admitted that he was playing games with my questions.

"You look older than that. Maybe seventeen?"

"Maybe."

At first he didn't say anything more, and we had a little staring contest there in the darkness. But I liked staring at him, and I won.

"This is the afterworld, Lizzie. We're like ghosts, and ghosts don't get tired or hungry. They don't get older, either."

I stared at him. "You mean, I'm not going to age anymore?"

"You will in the overworld." He looked up at the empty sky. "Whenever other living people can see you and talk to you, you're getting older every second, just like a normal person."

"So you must never leave."

He shook his head. "I've spent a few years in the real world, since I crossed over that first time. A few days here and there, but that's all."

"Oh." My eyes dropped to the black expanse beneath our feet. "So you live down in the underworld? That's where Yami was taking all those people."

He nodded.

"What's it like down there?" My thoughts went to Mindy's fears. "Is it a good place, or a bad place?"

"It's quiet, mostly. Only the memories of the living stir the dead, and most of the dead have been forgotten. We do what we can."

"We?"

"There are many of us, living people who've found the underworld. We each have our own people. We learn their names, so they don't fade away."

I nodded, remembering what Mindy had said, that my mother's memories kept her from disappearing. "But millions of people must die every year. How can you remember them all?"

"We don't. Most wander lost until they're forgotten. Some are taken by people like that man you met, and used. The lucky ones find us." Yamaraj stood a little straighter. "My people are only a few thousand, but I know all of them."

"A few thousand, out of millions? That's kind of depressing."

"Death can be that way." For a moment, he looked older.

"So I've noticed," I sighed. "Is there anything you can teach me that's *not* depressing?"

Yamaraj thought a moment, then a smile played on his face again. "How about this: The river isn't just a boundary. It's also a way to travel."

He held out a hand, and I stared at it for a moment.

"Are we going somewhere?"

"Name a place you'd like to go."

"Seriously?" My eyes blinked a few times. "Like, the Eiffel Tower? The Great Pyramids?"

"That depends. You need a connection to the place you're going. Memories of having been there, some kind of bond. But yes, the River Vaitarna connects the entire world."

I stared at him, wondering what places I had a real connection to. I'd lived in the same house all my life. There were my elementary and high schools, of course, but the idea of going to another empty school building gave me the creeps. I couldn't exactly show up at my friend Jamie's house, or my father's apartment in New York.

But there was always the rest of New York City. I'd always had a soft spot for the Chrysler Building, since I was little and read a book about how the Empire State had cheated to become the tallest in the world. I'd made my father take me during my visit. But did that count as a bond?

I wanted to learn how to do this. If I could travel anywhere, being a psychopomp might be worth having ghosts in my life.

With the thought of Mindy, I suddenly knew where I wanted to go.

"What about a family connection, like the house my mother grew up in? She's never taken me there, but I've seen pictures."

Yamaraj frowned. "Out of the whole world, that's where you want to go?"

I hesitated a moment. I didn't want to lie to Yamaraj, but finding Mindy's bad man didn't sound like the sort of expedition he would be happy about. "It's part of my family history. Something happened to my mother there when she was little. Can we go there?"

"If the place is important to you, then yes."

"So teach me how."

"Of course. But one more warning."

I sighed. "What now?"

"If you feel something behind you, don't turn around."

"Um, okay." I remembered the cold, wet thing that had brushed against me just before Yamaraj had arrived. "What's going to be behind me?"

One crooked eyebrow lifted. "I thought you didn't want to learn any more depressing things."

"I guess not. So what do I do?"

Yamaraj reached out to take my hands, but I pulled away, afraid his touch would jolt me back into the real world.

"It's okay," he said gently. "This is the river."

"Which means what?"

"You're in too deep for panic to matter."

I stared into his eyes. "I don't *panic*. I think we established that in Dallas."

"What would you call it then?" Yamaraj was almost smiling.

I didn't tell him that his touch was electric. That it was sparks and heat and fire. That his one kiss in the airport had lingered on my lips for the last ten days.

What I said was, "Jitters."

"Sorry." He pressed his hands together, bowing a little in apology. Then he held them out for me to take.

I reached out for him, and as our fingers brushed, a trickle of current spilled across my skin. It made my heart flutter and jump, but there was no sudden burst of color in the sky, no pulse of the overworld breaking through.

This wasn't my bedroom. This was the River Vaitarna, the boundary between life and death. And Yamaraj's hands were warm and real.

"I'm ready to go," I said.

The reluctant smile finally spread across his face. "Hold on tight."

CHAPTER 17

THE PARTY HAD GROWN. THE BIG ROOM WAS MORE CROWDED and also more alive, or perhaps the buzzing of Darcy's lips just made it seem that way.

In the weeks they'd known each other, Darcy had never thought about kissing Imogen. Attraction wasn't something that burned inside her, not like the forest-fire crushes that Carla went through every few months. Darcy could still list the guys she'd thought were hot in high school, but none had ever made her heart beat sideways. And at the beginning of senior year when Sagan had asked her quite seriously if she preferred girls, Darcy hadn't been able to answer him.

But now she was certain—about Imogen at least, if not about girls and boys in general—and it was a relief and a revelation. She felt as though she'd leaped across a thousand pointless crushes and landed someplace real.

She also felt, now that Imogen had taught her the term, like she was more full of juice than ever. Darcy wanted to sweep the bowls of chips and guacamole from her desk and start on *Untitled Patel* right now, with Imogen at her side.

But a few steps into the room, Kiralee descended on them and swept Imogen away. There was the tiniest rip in Darcy's heart as her hand parted from Imogen's, but she didn't follow them off to the corner where Oscar was holding court. She had to find her friends.

Darcy scanned the crowd, recognizing more arrivals from YA Drinks, a pair of publicists she remembered from a meeting at Paradox, and then—

"Sister deb!" It was Annie Barber, with three more sister debs in tow.

"Oh. Hi, guys."

"Twenty-fourteen!" Annie said, and they all put up a hand.

"Right!" Darcy high-fived them all. "Listen, I'm looking for—"

"This is *such* a rock-star apartment!" Annie cried. "And in *Manhattan*."

"You are, like, our official idol now," said Ashley, whose book was a dystopian on Mars, Darcy remembered.

She found it hard to answer. Her lips were buzzing, her body still thrumming from the kiss with Imogen. She felt like a rock star, a little, but mostly she was dizzy.

"So we have a confession," Annie said. "We all have bets on how old you are."

"It's not really a—"

"No spoilers!" Annie interrupted. "We want to wait for the reveal, like everyone else. I've got seventeen."

"I've got nineteen," Ashley said. "I know, that's probably way too old."

"I can neither confirm nor deny," Darcy said. She'd finally spotted Carla and Sagan alone by the guacamole, looking wide-eyed and terrified. "And I kind of have to deal with something. Besides, a single word might reveal too much."

"Of course," Annie said, and the sister debs parted for her.

"Guys!" Darcy called to Sagan and Carla as she threaded her way across the room.

"*There* you are!" Carla gathered her into a hug, and they spun once in a circle.

"Sorry. I was up on the roof. There was . . . a situation." Darcy touched her own lips, and for a moment her first real kiss seemed imaginary.

"I'm just glad we made it." Carla's eyes swept across the room. "Look at your glamorous apartment, city girl!"

Sagan nodded at this, a corn chip in his hand. "Illustrious party is illustrious."

"Seriously illustrious." Carla's voice dropped to a whisper. "I mean, is that Kiralee Taylor over there?"

"Yep."

"She didn't even have to look," Sagan said to Carla. "You'd think someone would check on a claim like that, Kiralee Taylor being in their living room. But no, she just assumed it to be true."

"Because Darcy is, like, famous now," Carla said. "And there are frequently famous people in her living room."

Darcy rolled her eyes. "Come on, guys. I'll introduce you."

"Introduce us?" Sagan asked, sputtering on his corn chip. "But I didn't bring my copy of *Bunyip*."

"This isn't a signing, Sagan," said Carla. "It's, like, Darcy's living room, somehow full of famous authors."

"It's just my housewarming party," Darcy said, though suddenly none of it seemed believable to her either. She turned to confirm her own existence in the wall of mirrors.

"But what if I go all fanboy?" Sagan said. "Because *Bunyip*."

Darcy smiled. "You should fanboy her about *Dirawong* instead. Kiralee's pretty much over *Bunyip*, because everyone loves it so much, and because . . ."

She left the rest unspoken, but reminded herself to ask Sagan later about using Hindu gods for purposes of YA hotness.

"Right," Carla said. "Like John Christopher was totally bored of *Tripods*."

Sagan nodded. "Ravel hated *Boléro* by the end."

"Jimi Hendrix and 'Purple Haze,'" Darcy said, then waved her hand. "This game is already stupid. Come on over, guys. She's awesome."

Darcy took a step toward Kiralee, but her friends didn't move. "What?"

"I think we need a second," Carla said, her gaze drifting along the floor. "We haven't even unpacked yet."

Darcy saw the rolled sleeping bags shoved beneath the desk, along with two small suitcases. "Right. Sorry. You just got here, and I'm dragging you around my party. Hostess failure."

"We should have arrived before your party started," Sagan said. "The Amtrak timetable incident may have been my fault."

"Finally you admit this!" Carla said.

Darcy knelt to pick up the sleeping bags. "I'll put these in your room."

"We'll stay here," Sagan said. "Your party is nervous-making, but I don't want to miss anything."

"No problem." Darcy extended the handles of the suitcases and wedged a sleeping bag under each arm. She managed to wheel her way through the throng without knocking anyone over, and soon was alone in the guest bedroom.

"Crap, still no pillows," she muttered, letting the sleeping bags fall to the floor. She rolled the suitcases into a corner, wondering how illustrious Carla and Sagan would think she was when they saw their room.

The makeshift bookshelf was looking particularly lopsided this evening. Darcy knelt to adjust the cinder blocks, but instead found herself reaching for the familiar green-and-gold spine of *Bunyip*. There on the back cover was Kiralee, much younger and perhaps a little photoshopped, and not nearly as distinguished as she looked now. Worse, she had two fingertips pressed thoughtfully against her forehead, like the poster for a mind-reading act.

The door closed behind her, and Darcy turned.

It was Imogen, beer in hand.

"Hey," Darcy said, the word sounding loud in her ears. The closed door muffled the party to a rumble, and suddenly she could hear her own breathing. "What's up?"

"I missed you."

Darcy rose to her feet, her lips buzzing again. "Me too. Is that weird?"

"The absence of old friends one can endure with aplomb," Imogen said. "But even momentary separation after a first kiss is unbearable."

Darcy frowned. "Is that a quote?"

"Oscar Wilde, adapted." Imogen smiled at *Bunyip* in Darcy's hands. "I hear that's a good book."

"My friends say it's awesome."

Imogen knelt beside the bookshelf, sliding her finger across the spines. "That's the only book of Kiralee's you own? She'll *hate* that."

"I've got all of them!" Darcy exclaimed. "And extra reading copies for my first editions. This is, like, *one* percent of my library. Dad was driving up some stuff, so my little sister picked these out to send along."

Imogen turned to look up at Darcy, her eyes narrowing. "Your dad drove them up?"

"They were in my room . . . at home." Darcy knelt beside Imogen, not quite meeting her eye. "So there was this thing I was going to tell you before the party started. But you were late. And I was going to tell you up on the roof, but then we were kissing, and I forgot to."

Imogen barely nodded, waiting. Darcy took a steadying breath, her mind flashing through all the previous, *much* better moments she might have chosen to reveal her age. But as she'd felt more comfortable here, more real as a writer and a New Yorker, the urgency to confess had faded.

But now that they'd kissed . . .

"We went to high school together, Carla and Sagan and me."

"You told me," Imogen said. "But you didn't say when."

"No." Darcy's voice dropped. "We just graduated."

"As in, a *month* ago?"

"Pretty much."

Imogen nodded slowly. "And that explains why you've never..."

"I guess. Though many people kiss in high school, I've heard." Darcy found herself talking in Sagan's flat cadence. "I'm sorry, Gen."

"For what?"

"For not saying that I'd just got out of high school! For failing to mention that I'm a teenager!"

Imogen inspected her own fingernails. "I guess it didn't come up."

"I think it did, a couple of times," Darcy said. "You asked me what I'd majored in once, and I changed the subject."

"Yeah, I sort of noticed. So you're, what, eighteen?"

Darcy nodded.

"Well, that's just fucking ridiculous." Imogen stood up.

Darcy stayed kneeling by the bookshelf, her face burning. She couldn't make herself look up, and so stared at the back cover of *Bunyip*. A young Kiralee Taylor gazed back at her with an expression of profound contemplation.

"I mean, seriously," Imogen said. "You wrote a book that good at *eighteen*? That's just ... galling!"

"I was seventeen when I finished it," Darcy said softly.

"Fuck! I was writing *Sparkle Pony* fan fiction when I was seventeen!" Imogen sank to her haunches again, sighing. "Actually, I still do. Just not full-time. So you're blowing off college to write, like that's no big deal?"

"It is for my parents," Darcy said. "They're shitting themselves."

"That's funny. My dad still thinks my English degree was a waste of money."

"You're mad at me, right?"

"I'm amazed by you, actually." Imogen turned to face Darcy. "Blowing your whole advance to live here. That's pretty crazy. And brave, I guess."

"Really?"

"Yeah. But you might want to use that bravery more."

Darcy shook her head. "For what?"

"For *trusting me*, which means *telling me* about stuff." Imogen reached out to cup Darcy's chin with her fingers. Then she kissed her. It was less fierce than the first two times, softer and slower, but not in a way that left any doubt.

When their lips pulled apart, Darcy asked, "So you're not mad?"

"I'm five years older than you. Maybe I'm a little . . . hesitant."

"Hesitant? You just kissed me again!"

Imogen shrugged. "Yeah, I kind of suck at hesitating. But maybe we should go slow."

"Slow is okay, I guess. But you can ask me whatever you want, right now. Any question, no matter how embarrassing. I promise to tell you the truth!"

Imogen considered this a moment. "Okay. Do you really like me, or are you just excited because you've never kissed anyone before?"

"I really like you!" Darcy cried. "You make my hair stand up when you talk about writing."

Imogen raised an eyebrow.

"And also when you kiss me," Darcy added.

"Okay, good answer. Is there anything you need to ask me back? Just so we're all clear."

Darcy shook her head, but then found a question on the tip of her tongue, even if it wasn't exactly relevant to the conversation. "Do you know if Kiralee's read it?"

Imogen looked at the book in Darcy's hand. "Probably, seeing as how she wrote it."

Darcy shoved *Bunyip* back into its spot on the shelf. "I meant *my* book. As you know."

"Oh, that." Imogen was smirking now. "Not yet. Kiralee wanted me to read it first. You know, in case it sucked."

"Seriously? You were *checking me out* for her?"

"Sure. Don't you ever do that for your friends?"

Darcy frowned. Among the Reading Zealots, Darcy had been a relentless first adopter of books and movies and manga series. She was on the ARC list at her library, was immune to online spoilers, and had even sat through the notoriously crappy first season of *Danger Blonde* so she could explain the story to Carla, who was skipping straight to season two.

But this was different somehow. "You guys suck."

Imogen laughed. "Do we suck a little less if I just told Kiralee that you have the juice, and she should read your novel?"

"Pretty much." As she stood, Darcy felt dizzy with relief. Hiding her age had been stupid, but she'd been forgiven. No more pointless mistakes like that, she decided. "I promise to trust you, Gen, with everything."

"Good." Imogen opened the door. "Then I guess you should introduce me to your friends."

*   *   *

Sagan and Carla were rooted to the same spot, Sagan eating his way through the guacamole while Carla took surreptitious photos of the party with her phone.

"Your stuff's in the guest bedroom," Darcy said. "And I brought you a nonthreatening author to meet."

"As in, not famous." Imogen offered a hand.

As they introduced themselves, Darcy couldn't help but notice how young Carla and Sagan seemed beside Imogen—they were all fumbles and tics where she was graceful and assured. And Darcy knew that she shared her friends' foibles. How had she tricked everyone in New York into thinking she was an adult?

Right. By publishing a novel. Which meant her adulthood would vanish if she never managed that trick again.

"I'm surprised we haven't read your stuff, Imogen," Carla was saying. "Even if you're not famous, we read *everybody*."

"My first novel's not out till September."

"We get ARCs," Sagan said. "Our librarian is, like, connected."

"I see." Imogen was smiling. "It's called *Pyromancer*. Imogen Gray's my pen name."

"Isn't that your *real* name?" Darcy asked, but Imogen didn't answer.

"I don't think we got that one," Carla said. "So a pyromancer must be like a firestarter, right?"

"Pretty much," Imogen said. "My protag likes to play with matches. Then she finds out she doesn't need matches."

"I would totally TBR that," Sagan said.

"Darcy's got the file." Imogen rested a hand on Darcy's shoulder, sending the tiniest shiver through her. "She can send it to you guys if you want."

"That would be awesome," Carla said. "We promise not to forward it to all our friends."

Imogen shrugged. "I'll take piracy over obscurity."

Sagan turned to Darcy. "So you must get to read everything way early, now that you're a big-time author."

"Some stuff," Darcy said, though it occurred to her at this exact moment that she had not, in fact, read *Pyromancer* yet. Not because she was worried it would suck, but because her life in the last two weeks had been a whirl of packing and unpacking and improvised furniture and begging her parents to FedEx her bedsheets.

Darcy blushed a little. But she had to be brave, to trust the people she'd just kissed. "Actually, I haven't started it yet. I'm sure it's awesome, though."

But as she said the words, a fresh trickle of anxiety went through Darcy. What if passionate, brilliant Imogen, the first person who'd ever made her heart beat faster, *didn't have the fucking juice?*

"I mean, Kiralee blurbed it!" she added.

As the others wowed over this fact, Imogen squeezed Darcy's shoulder and leaned in closer. "Hope you like it," she whispered. "Might be tricky if you didn't."

At this moment Darcy decided that she was reading *Pyromancer* first thing tomorrow morning, regardless of the thousand other things on her to-do list. Brave or not, she needed to know.

"So I just realized," Sagan said. "Your book is all about fire,

Imogen, and Darcy's is all about a cold place inside. Funny, huh?"

Imogen and Darcy stared at each other for a moment, unsure what to say.

Then Carla spoke up. "Did you ever get that letter from your editor? The one that tells you what you have to change?"

Darcy shook her head. "Nan keeps promising, but it never comes. You think I should ask her about it, Gen?"

"At your own party? That's kind of tacky. But I bet Moxie would do it."

"Right," said Darcy. The great thing about agents was, they did 100 percent of the unwriterly parts of the job for 15 percent of the money. "But she had to leave early."

"Leave? She's right over there, talking to . . ." Imogen blinked. "Is that . . ?"

"It is," Sagan said. "Your party just got way more illustrious, Darcy."

"*Squee*," Carla added in a tiny voice.

Darcy turned, wondering if Coleman Gayle had finally arrived. But it wasn't Coleman headed straight toward her across the room. It was no less than the Sultan of Social Media, Stanley David Anderson.

"Hello," he said, extending a hand. "I understand you're the hostess of this affair."

"Yes," was the best Darcy could do. She took his hand and shook it, and then remembered to say, "Darcy Patel."

"Stanley Anderson."

"I know," Darcy said. "I mean, um, this is Imogen and Carla and Sagan."

"Carla and Sagan?" Standerson nodded. "That's quite funny, though you might be too young to know why."

"The odds against it are astronomical," Sagan said.

"Billions and billions to one." When Standerson giggled, his expression barely changed. "I hope you don't mind me crashing your party, Darcy."

"Of course not. But weren't you having dinner with Moxie?"

"I was. But I've had one of my frequent bouts of dyspepsia."

"Oh," Darcy said. "That sucks."

"The 'Frequent Bouts of Dyspepsia' episode was my favorite," Sagan said. "From season one, anyway."

"Mine too," Standerson said. "I wish I'd had a better camera back then. Is that guacamole?"

"Yes," Sagan said. "I find its consistency soothing."

"I concur." Standerson took a corn chip from the bowl and loaded it up. He turned to Imogen. "I think we're touring together this fall."

Darcy turned. "You *are*?"

"Paradox wants us to." Imogen looked a little stunned. "But it's not a done deal, so I didn't think . . ."

"Could be fun." Standerson nodded. "I'll talk to Nan."

"That would be amazing," Imogen said softly, but Standerson was helping himself to more guacamole.

It was strange to see Imogen struck silent, but not as strange as seeing Sagan making instant friends with Standerson. The two were in their own little world now, discussing the guacamole-carrying capacity of various shapes of corn chips.

"This alarms me," Carla said quietly as they watched. "And yet it also makes sense."

"I know, right?" Darcy said.

"I liked how you were in no way smooth with Standerson," Carla said. "That was reassuring, city girl."

"Thanks." Darcy turned to Imogen. "Since when are you touring with him?"

"Last time I heard, he wasn't sure if he wanted to. But I guess now that he's met me, the idea's more real, you know?"

Carla laughed. "Stuff always happens at Darcy's parties, ever since fifth grade. Breakups, hookups, big fights, all the craziest stuff. But the weird part is, it never happens to *her*."

Imogen and Darcy glanced at each other, and Darcy felt a little smile flash across her face. Her lips felt hot and dry.

"Well . . . so much for *that* theory," Carla said, and began to giggle to herself. She slipped an arm around Darcy, squeezing her old friend hard, and suddenly she was laughing aloud, and people were looking at them from across the room.

"Um, Carla?" Darcy asked. "Are you okay?"

"I'm great. But this party is giving me *all the feelings*."

CHAPTER 18

IT FELT JUST LIKE A RIVER, STRONG AND SWIFT AND BRUTISH. carrying us with the simple mindless power of fast-moving water.

It had been roaring past me since the moment I'd sunk beneath my bedroom floor. That constant wind really was a current, and once I let myself go it took me, suddenly and completely, as if someone had given me a giant kite to hold. Only Yamaraj's hands gripping mine made me feel as though we would ever stop moving again.

The river was full of cold, wet things like the one that had brushed against me. They always came from behind, soft and whispering, never quite forming words against my ear or the back of my neck. Yamaraj said they were harmless, unless you turned to look at them. So I learned to shudder and ignore. The trip felt endless, dizzying and wild, and it was all I could do to keep the image of my mother's old house in mind. But once we eddied to a halt, it seemed as if hardly any time at all had passed.

We came to rest on another dark expanse, just like one we'd left behind.

I looked up into the empty black sky. "How can you even tell where we are?"

"We're where you wanted to be, Lizzie. If you have a real connection to this place. Otherwise . . ." He shrugged. "We could be anywhere."

"Right," I said, wondering if the Chrysler Building might have been the safer choice.

Yamaraj knelt and placed his palm on the ground, and a moment later black oil began to bubble up. It spread quickly, and I skipped back to keep my sneakers out of it.

"What are you *doing*?"

"It's okay, Lizzie." He pulled me closer, my feet joining his in the black oil.

"Seriously?" We were already sinking.

"This is how it's done. You'll understand better if you keep your eyes open."

"Um, okay." I held Yamaraj tighter as we descended, hungry for his body heat, and not minding the feel of lean muscles through his silk shirt. The black oil wasn't much colder than the river's current, but shivers still fluttered through me as it climbed my spine.

I managed to keep my eyes open, and as the darkness rose past my vision a new reality fell into place around us—houses and trees and mailboxes, a whole suburban street.

I looked up, half expecting the black water's surface to be there just above my head. But there was only a starry night sky, with the same half-moon we'd left behind in San Diego. In front of us was a house just like the one in my mother's old photograph, except that at some point someone had added a picket fence.

We were in Palo Alto.

I took a breath, and the metallic smell of the flipside filled my lungs.

"This makes no sense." My voice sounded thin in my ears. "I sank through my bedroom floor to get to the river, and we just went down to get *out* of it too?"

"That's the afterworld for you. Down always works."

"Of course." I realized that I was still clinging to him and let go, stepping back.

Yamaraj was smiling. "The river isn't as depressing as the rest, is it?"

"No, it's more like a roller coaster. Except you wear a blindfold, and creepy wet things brush against you." I turned to the house before us. "But it takes you someplace, at least."

The little bungalow was older than the other houses on the street, with a wide front porch. The flipside had painted it gray instead of the sky blue in my mother's photograph, but this was definitely the right place.

Of course, this old house wasn't really why I'd wanted to come here.

"This is amazing, Yamaraj. But it's kind of weird, finally seeing this place. Do you mind if we walk around a little first?"

"Of course," he said, and took my hand again.

It felt bad making him think that this was some big emotional moment, when really I was playing Nancy Drew. But I swallowed my guilt and led him away, glad to have his hand in mine.

My mother's old street seemed normal enough, with tidy lawns and mailboxes decorated with seashells, a few palm trees swaying in the moonlight. Not the sort of neighborhood that looked like it was harboring a child killer. Though I guess that was the point of living here, if you happened to be one.

What I was looking for had to be somewhere nearby, though I didn't really know how to recognize it. Most likely, the bad man had died or moved away in the last thirty-five years, but maybe he'd left some sort of sign here on the flipside.

A small form shot from beneath a car right in front of us, streaking across the road. I jumped back, letting out a shriek.

But it was only a cat, a long and lean tabby that came to a skidding halt on the far sidewalk, staring straight at us. Its eyes glowed unearthly green against the gray background of the flipside.

"What the hell? Is it *looking* at us?"

"Cats see everything," Yamaraj said. His voice was soft, almost reverent. "Their eyes are in both worlds."

"Right. Mindy said something about that." My heart was pounding in my chest, and I realized that the gray world wasn't fading around me. "That scare didn't send me back. My grip on the flipside must be getting better."

Yamaraj shook his head. "You can't cross back to the real world here, only where you started. The river is carrying only your spirit, not your body."

"So this is like astral projection?" I pinched the flesh of my own arm, which was goose-pimpled and cold, and felt totally real.

"Only for now," Yamaraj said. "One day you'll be able to travel in body as well."

"So if my body isn't here, where is it? Back in my bedroom, where my mother's going to find it and freak out?"

"Don't worry." He paused, thoughtful for a moment. "This may sound strange, but it's in the ground beneath your house. Safe among the stones."

"Nothing creepy about that."

"The afterworld isn't comforting, Lizzie."

"You said that already. But still . . . this is pretty amazing." I stood and caught my breath, taking in the hilly landscape around us, so different from the flatness of San Diego. "I didn't even know the address, and we came straight here."

"Not bad for your first time."

"Thanks." Motion flickered at the corner of my eye, and I spun to face it. But it was only the tabby, following us from a distance.

Yamaraj was looking closely at me. "You're funny, Lizzie. In the airport, you were composed enough to play dead. And just now you were facing down that old man without any help from me. But this neighborhood has you jumping at shadows."

"I guess so." I didn't want to lie to Yamaraj, so I went for vague instead. "Like I said, something happened here when my mom was little."

"Something bad?"

I nodded. "Bad enough that she never talked about it. She only told me after what happened in Dallas."

"Nothing bad will happen now," he said, taking my hand again.

We walked in silence, taking in the moonlit empty streets. It was nice simply being with him, and basking in the fact that I had brought us here with my mystic powers. I didn't see any sign of the bad man, which was fine with me.

Yamaraj was too polite to ask any more about my mother, but after a while he said, "Every psychopomp has a story like that."

"Like what?"

"One that's hard to tell. We all cross over the hard way, the first time."

"So what's your story?" I asked softly. "How did you wind up playing dead?"

He shook his head. "There were no wars where I was born, no terrorists. My sister and I come from a small village. A quiet place."

"Sounds nice."

"It was beautiful, but to me and my sister it mostly seemed small. When we saw sails on the horizon, we'd rush down to the docks for glimpses from other places. The sailors were like people from another world. They wore cloth dyed in colors we'd never seen before, and used bronze knives that our village coppersmith couldn't dream of making."

"Bronze knives were high tech," I said. "Okay, so this was a while ago."

He shrugged. "It was, and our village was backward even then, I suppose. When the sailors showed us pressed flowers from other lands, and claimed they were warriors slain in a great fairy war, my sister and I believed them."

"That's sweet."

"They knew other languages too, and my sister would trade

them her prettiest seashells for foreign words. She had a fine collection of curses."

I felt a smile on my face. "Sounds like my Spanish."

He smiled back at me, but the expression faded. "It was a good place to grow up. But people didn't live long back then. My sister died younger than most."

"Yeah, she only looked about fourteen. Wait, were you . . . ?"

He nodded. "Twins. We still are, even if I'm a little older now."

"Right. Weird." Yami was stuck forever at the age she'd died, but her brother wasn't. "Is that why you stay in the underworld? So you don't leave her behind?"

"I live there to keep my people from fading away."

"And she's one of them. You're a good brother."

He didn't answer, and we walked a little farther. I'd always wondered what it would be like to have a brother or sister, especially a twin. I'd imagined making up our own language, and giving each other secret names.

Of course, I'd had an invisible sister all that time. Mindy had been there every day, watching me grow into an eleven-year-old, then aging past her. A shiver went through me.

"Are you okay?" Yamaraj asked. His eyes glinted brown against the gray world. He and I were still in color, as if we didn't belong behind this veil of death.

"I'm fine. So when your sister died, is that when you became . . . like us?"

He nodded. "I couldn't let her go alone."

"Whoa. So that whole twin-bonding thing is real."

Yamaraj thought for a moment, then shrugged. "It is for us."

"How did she die?" I asked, my voice small.

"She was betrayed by an ass."

"Um, pardon me?"

"A donkey," he said. "A beast that belonged to my family."

I was still confused, but my next question froze in my mouth. Past Yamaraj and down the street, the cat lurked in the shadows, green eyes glimmering.

But it wasn't watching us anymore.

It was staring at another bungalow, even older than the one my mother had grown up in. The house was set back from the road, with gnarled desert trees in the front yard. Around each was a planter box full of stones.

Standing on the lawn were five little girls, all Mindy's age, dressed in outfits that all looked out of date—plaid jumpers, shirts tucked into jeans, short dresses. They were all staring at the house.

"He's still here," I murmured.

Yamaraj turned to follow my gaze. "Who is, Lizzie?"

"The bad man. The man who killed Mindy."

He took my arm. "*This* is why you wanted to come here?"

"She needs to know."

"Be careful," Yamaraj whispered. "There are some ghosts you can't save."

"I don't want to save them, I just want to help Mindy. She's afraid all the time, even after all these years." I couldn't take my eyes from the *collection* of little girls. They just stood there staring at the house, silent and fidgeting, as if waiting for a performance to start.

"She needs to know if the man who killed her is still alive. Or if he's wandering the flipside, looking for her."

"Come away from here, Lizzie." Yamaraj pulled at my arm, but I shook him off.

"I have to make sure he's still alive."

"You don't want to go any closer to that house," he said.

As I opened my mouth to ask why, one of the little girls moved. Her head turned slowly, the rest of her body utterly still, until her gray eyes rested on us. She was a little younger than Mindy, wearing overalls and sneakers. Her gaze lingered, her expression blank except for the barest hint of puzzlement.

Yamaraj turned to face me. "Don't look at them."

"But they're just . . ." My words faded as the other girls, all in one motion, turned their heads to stare at us. Their five little gray faces regarded me with growing interest. "Okay, maybe this is kind of weird."

Yamaraj was already kneeling, his palm on the asphalt. He stood up as the bubbling oil began to expand beneath our feet, and put his arms around me, his muscles tense and hard.

"You don't want them in your memories," he whispered as we began to sink into the street. "Just think of home."

Our second journey in the river seemed faster, as trips home often do. It was easy to hold an image of my own house in my mind, because I wanted to be there so badly. But it was harder this time to ignore the wet, shivery things that brushed against us. Some part of me had realized what they were—loose memories, fragments of ghosts who had faded away.

I kept my eyes shut the whole way, head pressed against Yamaraj's chest, his warmth and solidity protection against the blank stares of the gray-faced little girls.

We came to a halt on another windy expanse under a blank sky, but somehow I could feel home just overhead. Or maybe it was beneath us—the afterworld had confused me on the concepts of up and down.

But before I returned to my bedroom, Yamaraj took me by the shoulders.

"You give this up, Lizzie. Don't go there again."

"I have to help Mindy. It's what I would do for a living person."

"But those ghosts are in your head now."

"That's for sure." I shuddered, seeing their gray faces. "But why is that such a bad thing, besides the potential for nightmares?"

"Ghosts go where they can for nourishment. Think about it. Mindy died in that house, didn't she? Hundreds of miles from here, but she lives with you now."

"Right. Because my mother remembers her."

"More than anyone else in the world. More than her own parents."

"That's kind of sad. And weird."

He shook his head. "It's not as strange as you'd think. Sometimes when children go missing, their parents can only stand to hold on to their memories for so long. When they let go, those children fade, unless someone else keeps them in mind."

My mouth was dry. "But that means those little girls are there . . . because the bad man remembers them better than anyone else?"

"Their last days, perfectly. But what if they had *you* to nourish them instead?"

I imagined the five little girls on my front lawn, waiting and wanting, and a shudder went through me. I could still see the face of the first one who'd turned to look at me—her worn overalls and the half-dozen sparkly barrettes in her short hair.

"How am I supposed to forget what I just saw?"

"You can't, Lizzie." His hands fell from my shoulders, and he sighed. "It was only a glance, not enough to bring them here."

"So you're just trying to scare me?"

"You *should* be scared." He was angry now, his brown eyes locked on mine. "Promise me you'll never go near that house again."

I turned away. I'd had enough of being afraid, and Mindy had been trapped with her fear for decades. I couldn't just leave her in limbo, now that I knew where the bad man lived.

I chose my words carefully. "I promise I won't ever see those little girls again."

Yamaraj stared at me a moment longer, but finally he nodded. "Thank you."

With the anger fallen from his voice, he sounded tired. He was probably starting to think that I was a lot of work, like a student driver who keeps crashing the car in her first lesson.

At least I knew that the bad man was still alive. Mindy was safe, for now. We had Yamaraj to thank for that.

"It was nice of you to come and save me."

The storm in his eyes lifted a little. "I'm not sure you needed saving."

"Maybe not. But it was fun seeing you chase that guy off."

Now a smile danced at the edges of his mouth. "I was wondering if you were going to call. My sister was certain you would."

"Oh? Does Yami have an opinion about me?"

"She thinks you might become a distraction."

"I hope she's right."

He nodded. "She's always right."

"Yamaraj . . ." I shivered a little, saying his name aloud again.

"Call me Yama. 'Raj' is only a title."

"Really? What does it mean?"

"*Prince*, or perhaps *lord*."

I raised an eyebrow. "You mean, I've been calling you *Lord Yama* all this time?"

He was fighting a smile. "You've only said it once or twice."

"Yeah, but I've been thinking it in my head!" I groaned, feeling like a ditz. "Anyway, now that I actually *know* your name, will that work? I can call you and you'll come?"

He nodded. "The name is important, but it's like traveling to a place. There also has to be a connection."

"You heard me tonight. So there's already a connection."

"There is." He took a step closer. "But it could be stronger, just to be safe."

"And how do we do that?" My eyes were drifting closed.

"Like this."

As his lips met mine, something keen and buzzing flowed into my body. It bloomed in my chest, making my breath skid and shudder, scattering the fear this long night had left inside me. The kiss grew hotter, fiercer as I pressed my mouth against his, hungry for more.

The wind of the river turned sharp and dry around us, filling with pinpricks that played across my skin. My eyes opened for a moment and I saw sparks swirling past, like when Yama had appeared to save me, the air burning around his feet.

"Did you make those?" I murmured.

"Not just me."

We didn't say much more.

An hour later I left him and descended into my bedroom, safe and welcoming and familiar. My skin still tingled. My body felt lighter. The cold place inside me was almost gone, burned away by Yama's lips.

There was just one little problem left. My mother was sitting there on my bed, staring at her phone.

After everything that had happened tonight, I'd forgotten her coming into my room just before I'd sunk into the river. She hadn't seen me, of course, and I was still on the flipside, but I couldn't stay here forever.

With Yama's body against mine, I had felt boundless, powerful. But now I felt like a little kid about to get grounded. If I went outside and came in through the front door, pretending to have been taking a walk, how would my mother respond? After this week, she might flip out. Or worse, start checking on me every night.

I didn't even know how long I'd been gone. And I couldn't let her sit here any longer, not knowing where I was. I had to think of a reasonable explanation why I wasn't in bed.

Mindy was gone, probably having scampered back to my mother's closet after I'd sunk through the floor. Which gave me an idea . . .

I wasn't an expert at walking through walls yet, but the door to my closet was open a little from when I'd changed into jeans. I slipped inside, and settled myself on some dirty clothes on the floor. My closet wasn't as spacious as my mother's, but it was big enough to huddle there and pretend to be asleep.

I took a few sharp breaths, making my heart beat faster, and soon my grasp on the flipside was fading. The slant of light coming though the closet door showed colors bleeding back into the world.

When I'd crossed over, I quietly slipped out of my jeans and hoodie, then let out a soft yawn.

After a long wait in nervous silence, I was about to yawn again when I heard my mother's voice.

"Lizzie?"

I pushed the closet door open. It swung with a plaintive creak, revealing my mother's astonished expression.

"Oh, hey," I said sleepily. "What're you doing in here?"

"I heard your voice, and I came in to see what was up. And you weren't . . ." She shook her head. "For heaven's sake, Lizzie. What are you doing *in your closet*?"

"Um, sleeping." I sat up, blinking my eyes and stretching. "I had this really scary dream. And after I woke up, it just felt safer in here."

The sorrow on her face made me feel awful. But a made-up nightmare was a better explanation than, *Got accosted by an evil psychopomp, then went to visit an old serial killer's house. Oh, and hooked up.*

"Lizzie, I'm so sorry. Do you need to talk about your dream?"

I shook my head. "No big deal, no airports or terrorists. It was just . . . my feet were stuck in this black goo. I was sinking."

"That sounds awful, kiddo."

"Sorry I woke you up." I crawled from the closet and stood.

My mother managed a smile, and rose from the bed to give me a long hug. When we parted, she looked down at my makeshift nest on the floor.

"It's funny," she said. "You used to be afraid of closets when you were little. But the house where I grew up had these huge walk-ins. I used to do sleepovers in there with . . ."

I waited for more, but Mom was still staring. She knelt and lifted something from the closet floor. It flashed in her hand—the kitchen knife I'd taken with me to the afterworld. It must have fallen from my pocket when I pulled off my jeans.

I tried to smile. "Oh, yeah. I was kind of scared."

The look on her face was so sad.

"I'm sorry, Mom. I know it seems weird."

She held the knife carefully with both hands. "I know what it's like to be scared all the time. After my friend disappeared, I was like that for months. You'll do anything to make yourself feel safer."

I nodded, an image of all those little girls flooding back into my head, and I knew for certain that, in a way, my mother understood. And I also knew that I would be going back to Palo Alto, to make sure that the bad man never hurt anyone again.

CHAPTER 19

HER FAVORITE PART OF SETTING FIRES HAD ALWAYS BEEN THE matches. She liked the way they rattled, stiff little wooden soldiers in a cardboard box, and the way they bloomed into hot flowers between cupped palms. She loved the ripping, fluttering noises they made as they fought the wind. Even their remains were beautiful—spindly, black, and bowed—after they'd burned all the way down to fire-calloused fingertips.

Ariel Flint never went to school without them.

She was early today, so she headed for the smokers' den, a hidden corner of the school grounds formed by two temps wedged against the backside of the gym. The temporary buildings had been classrooms years ago. Through their cloudy windows, you could still see blackboards on the walls. Now they were storage for the theater department, stuffed with old sets and props, racks of costumes with the tattered look of moth food. The temps were always locked, but they stood on cinder blocks and you could crawl away beneath them in a pinch.

This morning's pinch was already under way when Ariel came around the back of the gym. Peterson, the school's rent-a-cop, was on one knee in the corner, peering into the shadows beneath the temps. He was calling threats after some escaping student, the radio in his hand sputtering and angry.

Ariel spun around on one heel, ducking her head. Once a month or so Peterson busted the smokers' den, rounding up everyone for detentions and "community service," which meant slopping out food in the cafeteria. The thought of wearing a hairnet for a week of lunches sent Ariel into a run, heading toward the gymnasium's rear doors.

A moment later she burst onto the basketball court. The doors slammed behind her, filling the empty gym with echoes—booms mixing with the squeak of her boots on the pine floor. She froze for a moment, breathing hard and coming up with excuses, but Peterson hadn't followed her.

Ariel smiled and spun once at center court, miming a shot at the basket to the applause of an invisible crowd. Capture evaded!

The year before, she'd written a paper on gambling for psychology, about an experiment with caged pigeons who fed themselves by pulling a lever. If the lever always produced a single food pellet, the pigeons pulled it only when they were hungry. If the device stopped giving them food at all, the pigeons soon gave up on it. But when the lever worked like a slot machine, sometimes giving nothing, other times paying off big, the pigeons got addicted. Even when they already had plenty of food, they wanted to see what would happen with the next pull.

Pigeons, like people, loved to gamble.

While writing this paper, Ariel had realized that getting caught in the smokers' den worked the same way. Had Peterson shown up every day, everyone would've found another place to smoke, or maybe quit altogether. And if no one ever tried to bust them, smoking wouldn't have been nearly as much fun. But Peterson came along just often enough to keep things interesting.

Of course, the smokers at Reagan High were addicted to nicotine, not gambling, and would've been fine with being left alone. But Ariel had never been a smoker. She was there to light other people's cigarettes, to watch the smoke curl from their mouths, to glory in fiery tips flaring with every drawn breath. For her, the chance of getting caught was part of the thrill of starting fires, large or small.

"What the *hell*, Flint?" boomed a voice from across the gym.

Ariel turned from the empty bleachers, and found a pissed-off Erin Dale striding toward her.

"Um," Ariel said. "Just made the winning shot."

Coach Dale came to a halt a few yards away, crossing her arms. She wore her usual uniform, a tight sleeveless T-shirt and sweatpants, her hair tied in a long ponytail. On her left shoulder, three red claws extended out two inches from beneath the shirt. No one had ever seen the rest of the tattoo, but Ariel was somehow certain that it was a dragon curled between the coach's breasts.

"It's nice to see you take an interest in sports, Miss Flint. But you're wearing Doc Martens on my pinewood."

"Oh, right." Ariel looked down and saw a spiral of tiny black marks around her feet. "Whoa. Sorry."

Coach Dale regarded Ariel coolly. In gym class, Ariel only ever worked at running, jumping, and climbing—useful skills for getting away—and was hopeless at anything involving a ball or a score. But she had an old and smoldering crush on Coach Dale, and wouldn't have dreamed of smudging her basketball court.

In a show of contrition, Ariel lifted one offending boot from the floor and balanced there, untying its laces. Wobbling only a little, she wrangled it off, then did the same with the other.

"Good coordination and flexibility," Coach Dale said. "Wish we saw more of that from you in class."

Ariel didn't answer. The gym floor was cold beneath her stocking feet, and she felt small and penitent under the coach's gaze.

One of the rear doors swung open. It was Peterson, radio still in hand.

"Hey, Coach," he said, his eyes on Ariel. "Anyone come through here?"

Coach Dale's pissed-off expression didn't change. "Not that I've seen. Have you seen anyone, Miss Flint?"

Ariel shook her head.

Peterson didn't look like he bought it, but he flashed the coach a salute and went back through the gym doors to resume his hunt outside.

After another moment of silence, the coach uncrossed her arms. "It's pointless telling you how bad smoking is for your lungs and stamina. But you know it makes your lips thinner, right?"

"And gives you yellow teeth, puffy skin, and wrinkles around the eyes," Ariel recited. "That's why I don't smoke."

Coach narrowed her eyes and came closer, until they were face-to-face. Ariel tried to keep from staring at the red claws sneaking out from beneath the T-shirt.

The woman sniffed. "Is that smoke I smell?"

"Yeah, but it's not cigarette smoke. I built a fire this morning . . . to warm up."

The coach raised an eyebrow. But Ariel wasn't lying, and cigarette smoke didn't smell at all like an honest fire.

It had only been a small one. Ariel had indulged on the way to school, in an already burned-out oil barrel behind the Shop 'n' Save. Someone had left a bundle of three-foot cardboard tubes in a Dumpster, impossible to ignore. She'd arranged them into a pyramid balanced on the rim of the barrel, and it had taken only a few minutes before the burning structure had crumbled, spitting a galaxy of sparks into the air.

"Whatever you say, Flint. Follow me."

Ariel trailed her toward the girls' locker room, boots in hand.

The locker room smelled as it always did, like old sweat and cheap soap. Coach Dale opened the door to the Cage, which was what everyone called her office with its walls of metal grating. She slid open her desk and pulled out an eraser the size of a cigarette lighter, pink and new.

She tossed it to Ariel, who caught it with her free hand.

"That should do the trick. Use spit if you need to."

Ariel stared at the eraser for a moment, and Coach Dale sighed and reached across the desk. She plucked the boots from Ariel's hand, slid open a file drawer, and dropped them in. She shut the drawer and turned its lock.

"You get those back when I can't find a single mark on my court."

"Okay, but—" The blare of the first bell cut Ariel off.

Coach Dale sank into her desk chair, picked up a clipboard and pen, and kicked up her feet. "Fifteen minutes till first period. Better get erasing, Flint. Just remember to rub *with* the grain of the wood."

Ariel started to protest again, but tasted defeat before the words left her mouth. She sighed, turned, and walked out of the Cage, through the locker room, and back to the court. Her heart was no longer racing from her escape from Peterson, nor with the dying dregs of her crush on Coach Dale.

This sucked.

She knelt at center court, counting black smudges until her tally reached twenty. She rubbed at the smallest mark with the eraser, spitting on it once or twice, until it had completely disappeared.

Then Ariel looked up at the big sweep-hand clock over the door. Twelve minutes left till homeroom, more than nineteen marks to go. She doubted Coach Dale would be writing her a late pass.

That was the hitch with getting caught. One infraction led to another until you were certified a bad kid, unsalvageable. But all Ariel could do was keep erasing little black marks and ignoring how cold her feet were.

She was less than halfway done when the first-period late-bell rang. A moment later a crowd of girls surged from the locker rooms, already suited up in field hockey uniforms.

Coach Dale followed them out, yelling, "Four laps, ladies! No cutting corners!"

Ariel made the mistake of looking up, and caught the eyes of the first runners in the pack. She saw their expressions switch from momentary confusion to a mix of amusement and pity.

She stared at the floor again, at her pink eraser rubbing hopelessly at the black marks. Ariel was an expert at keeping her head down, but that didn't do much good here in the middle of the gym, a score of girls running circles around her with nothing else to stare at. Her face grew as hot as her feet were cold.

"Any time now, Flint," Coach Dale called from the sidelines. "I need my basketball court."

"Sorry," Ariel muttered, just to be saying something.

She heard her last name repeated by the runners, like a whisper traveling through the gym. She closed her mind to her surroundings, narrowing her focus to the black marks in front of her. . . .

Then she felt it happening—the friction kindling beneath the pink tongue of the eraser, the growing heat at her fingertips. Her awareness expanded, not outward to the titters of the girls around her, but down into the materials of the gym itself. She felt the pine under her hands and knees, sensed the oxygen trapped in the tiny spaces of the wood's grain, the resins and oils that gave it color. Then farther out to the dry wood of the bleachers, the banners hanging from the walls. She could smell the iron oxide in the half-disintegrated eraser, and the hot filaments of the lightbulbs overhead.

The school was full of volatiles, wood and plaster, cloth and plastic, cans of paint and stacks of paper.

All of it waiting for a single spark. . . .

*   *   *

Darcy heard a bang and looked up from her screen.

But it wasn't Carla and Sagan in the other bedroom, just a truck rattling over a manhole cover down on the street. Darcy stretched her arms. The laptop had grown hot against her thighs, and her shoulders were tight from reading.

She let them relax, breathing out the words, "Thank fuck."

Pyromancer didn't suck, not even remotely. And more important, she could feel Imogen in its diction, in the rhythm of its prose, even in its hesitations, the quirks of commas and ellipses.

Darcy knew that she should get up now, shower and dress and ready herself for a day of museums with Carla and Sagan, of prying questions about Imogen, and of blowing her budget for at least a week.

But she wanted more *Pyromancer*. Not just because the sentences tasted like Imogen, but because the story had pulled her in.

These were pages that she needed to turn.

"My girlfriend's got the juice," Darcy whispered, and bent her knees to read some more.

"So what's she like?" Carla asked out of nowhere.

The three of them were at the Metropolitan Museum, in a vast gallery built around the Temple of Dendur, an ancient shrine to Osiris that had been shipped from Egypt in pieces and put back together stone by stone. The room's northern wall was made entirely of glass, and late-morning sunlight filtered through it to bathe the ancient sandstone. Sagan was inside the temple, reading centuries-old graffiti carved by soldiers. Carla had stayed outside with Darcy, who found the temple's interior claustrophobic—too many millennia crammed into such a small space.

"You met her last night," Darcy said. "She's like that, mostly."

"She seemed pretty easygoing."

Darcy had to frown. True, Imogen never seemed nervous, and she had a physical grace that drew Darcy's eye from across a room. But "easygoing" was off the mark.

"She's pretty intense, actually. You should see her talk about writing, or books."

Carla's hands fluttered in the air, then grabbed each other. "It's so cool that you're both writers. I can't wait to read her novel!"

"It's really good." Darcy was whispering now. "I started it this morning."

"So do you two, like, *write* together? In the same room, I mean."

"Um, I haven't written much since coming up here."

"Oh." Carla's expression sent a stab of guilt through Darcy.

"There's been so much to do," she explained. "Finding an apartment, moving, buying new stuff."

"New friends, new girlfriends, fancy parties." Carla sighed. "I get it. But when I think of you up here, I imagine you writing furiously all the time. Why else would you move away from Philly and cheat us of our last summer together!"

Carla was grinning as she said all this, but the guilt in Darcy's stomach tangled a little. Every day since moving here, she'd thought of her friends back in Philly less and less.

But this weekend was her chance to fix that. She had to spill all the details.

"I didn't even know Gen liked me until last night," Darcy said.

Carla's eyes widened. "*That's* why you were missing when we got there!"

"We were up on the roof. Um, hooking up, I guess."

Carla made a soft *squee* that echoed among the footfalls and murmurs filling the temple room. "Rooftop New York kissing scene!"

Darcy laughed. "I guess so."

"Was there dancing?"

"Imogen and I aren't really a musical," Darcy said. "We're mostly about words. And noodles."

"Noodles? Is that some new thing I don't know about?"

"They're like the noodles you know, but way more expensive. Gen's really into food. She says that to know a city you have to eat it."

Carla's smile ratcheted up a little. "Does she say that about anything besides cities?"

This question paralyzed Darcy for a moment. Indeed, she might have been frozen much longer—minutes, hours—if Carla hadn't burst out laughing.

"I'm sorry!" Carla managed, her titters bouncing sharply from the marble and glass of the temple room. "But there are certain turns of phrase."

Darcy noticed other tourists staring, and put a shushing finger to her lips.

"This conversation looks promising," Sagan said from behind her. "I assume it's about Imogen."

"Of course," Darcy sighed. "Join in."

"You weren't supposed to have this talk without me," he said to Carla. "We explicitly agreed."

"Sorry!" Carla said. "But you didn't miss much yet. I swear."

"Any salacious details?" he asked.

Darcy let out a groan. Sagan's voice was always a bit too loud, but here in the hush of the temple room, discussing this particular subject, he was like a foghorn talking. It didn't help that his question had sent Carla back into hysterics.

Darcy took them both by the arms and marched them toward the American Wing. She kept moving until they had reached the relative privacy of the Frank Lloyd Wright Room. The reconstructed living space, with its stately geometries and stained glass ceiling, helped to squelch the sputtering noises Carla was making.

Darcy faced her two friends. "Could you guys be any *more* like little kids?"

"You're the one who's blushing," Sagan said. "Does blushing mean that there are salacious details?"

"Was there sex on the roof?" Carla asked.

"The roof?" Sagan turned to Carla. "So I *did* miss something."

"They hooked up for the first time last night!" Carla was clapping. "On the roof!"

"Sex on the roof," Sagan said. "That sounds like a drink."

Darcy groaned. "There was a party. We needed privacy. The roof was private. There was no singing or dancing. There was no sex on the roof. You're all caught up now, Sagan."

"Who made the first move?" he asked.

Carla giggle-snorted. "Duh. Who do you think?"

Darcy gave her friend a sideways look, but couldn't argue.

"Did you know she liked you?" Sagan asked.

"Did you know you liked *her*?" Carla asked.

"Did you know you liked girls?" Sagan added.

Darcy swallowed. She hadn't known anything, really. Last night had simply happened without any initiative on her part, or action, or even *desire*. Which seemed pretty pathetic, now that she thought about it. But it had also been magical how one rooftop kiss—almost out of nowhere—had transformed everything.

"We'll take your silence as *no, no,* and *no,*" Carla said. "Poor little Miss Darcy."

"How old is Imogen, anyway?" Sagan asked.

"She's . . . ," Darcy began, but no specific number came to mind. "Um, she graduated college a year ago. Is that twenty-three?"

Carla shook her head. "Whatever it is, she's totally an *adult*."

"And how does this age disparity make you feel?" Sagan asked, thrusting an invisible microphone into Darcy's face.

"It doesn't matter," she said, pushing his empty hand away. "When I got here, I didn't tell anyone my age. It never even came up till last night. I guess she just accepted me as another writer."

"Writing conquers all!" Carla said. "That's so sweet."

"Possibly too sweet," Sagan said. "I'm detecting a lack of salacious details."

"We're taking it slow."

Carla patted Darcy's shoulder. "We would expect nothing less of you."

"Hey! Going slow was her idea, not mine!" Darcy took a step back from them both. "Do you really think of me as Little Miss Innocent?"

Even as the question left her mouth, Darcy knew the answer. She was much worse than innocent; she was oblivious. And to make things worse, now they were both staring at her with *adoring expressions*.

"Here's what I don't get," Carla said. "How did someone as clueless as you manage to write a convincing romance?"

"Actually," Sagan jumped in, "until the early eighties romance heroines were always virgins. Write what you know." He frowned. "Although it's unclear what constitutes virginity when it's two girls. There is debate on the internet."

Carla stared at him. "Exactly *why* were you googling that?"

"It was from the *Sparkle Pony* forum. You know how in episode forty-one, it's strongly implied that Tensile-Toes has a unicorn girlfriend? Of course, unicorns allow only virgins to touch them, so either Tensile-Toes is an actual virgin, like Darcy here, or she's only technically—"

"Shush!" Darcy hissed. A pair of girls in school uniforms hovered at the entrance to the Frank Lloyd Wright Room, taking notes, hopefully on the architecture.

Carla's words were soft but intense. "Darcy, we both love you exactly the way you are. Also, unicorns avoiding nonvirgins clearly doesn't apply to other equines."

"Agreed," Sagan whispered. "On both points."

Darcy nodded meekly. "I know Imogen likes me, for now. But what if I mess this up? This feels really real, and dangerous. Like taking my first driving lesson in a Ferrari!"

"Ferraris are quiet safe, actually," Sagan said. "Their high fatality rate is due to a high percentage of their owners being douchebags."

"Exactly!" Carla said. "You'll be fine as long as you go slow."

"I'm glad everyone's agreed on that," Darcy said, intending sarcasm, but she sounded earnest in her own ears. Last night at her party, she'd felt so mature and connected, fully equipped to show off in front of her high school friends. But the truth was that Carla and Sagan knew her better than anyone in New York, and she was still Little Miss Innocent in their eyes.

Darcy turned away and slipped past the schoolgirls, who were muttering to each other in what sounded like French, presumably about Darcy's virginity. She kept walking, through the American galleries and up a random set of stairs, with Carla and Sagan trailing silently behind.

They entered a wing of the museum with rust-colored carpets and soft lighting, full of painted folding screens behind glass. It was almost empty here, and Darcy slowed, no longer feeling as though the schoolgirls were pursuing them, notebooks in hand.

"Sometimes it's like I'm only pretending to be an adult."

Carla smiled. "I think that's how it works. You pretend for a while, and eventually it's real."

"Like playing sick to get out of school," Sagan said. "You wind up with a stomachache."

"Then I'm all set. I'm *great* at pretending." Darcy forced herself to smile, willing her desultory feelings to fade. So what if she was romantically clueless? So what if she was young? What she had with Imogen was real, and as long as that was certain, her other worries were meaningless.

Well, except for her worries about rewriting a book, starting a sequel, and not spending more than seventeen dollars a day.

"Hey, check this out." Sagan was pointing at a huge painting on cloth. "This guy killed your romantic lead."

Darcy stared at the painting. It was taller than her, and featured a three-eyed, blue-skinned monster surrounded by a halo of flame, wearing a headdress of skulls.

"Yamantaka, slayer of Yama," Sagan said, reading from the plaque on the wall. "The dude who killed Death!"

"Pretty badass," Carla said. "You should use him in your sequel."

"I've never even heard of him." Darcy nudged Sagan aside to read the plaque. "Right, because this guy's Buddhist. I'm in enough trouble without throwing in stuff from other religions."

"You're in trouble?" Sagan asked.

"Kind of," Darcy sighed. She'd been meaning to talk to Sagan about this today, and she couldn't ask for a better setting. "You know the first night I was here? When I met Kiralee?"

"Darcy's on a first-name basis with Kiralee Taylor," Sagan said to Carla. "It still freaks me out."

"You shared guacamole with Standerson!"

"Guys, listen," Darcy said. "That night at Drinks, they were asking about how I used a real god as my romantic lead. And about all the stuff I borrowed from the Vedas. Did you find any of that offensive, Sagan? Like, as a Hindu?"

He shrugged. "It seemed weird at first, but then I figured that it wasn't a problem, because there's no Hinduism in your universe."

Darcy blinked. "What?"

"Well, you know when Lizzie's trying to find a word that's better than 'psychopomp,' and she googles all those death gods? At first I didn't get why she never ran into the concept of Yama."

"Because that would be weird," Darcy said. "I mean, she's been making out with him. And he's not a god in my world, he's a person."

"Exactly. So I figured that the Angelina Jolie Paradox applies."

Darcy glanced at Carla, who looked equally confused.

"The what now?"

Sagan cleared his throat. "You know when you're watching a movie starring Angelina Jolie? And the character she's playing looks just like Angelina Jolie, right?"

"Um, yes. Because that's who she is."

"No, she's a regular person in that world, not a movie star. But the other characters never mention that she looks exactly like Angelina Jolie. No one ever comes up to her on the street and says, 'Can I have your autograph?'"

"Because that would mess up the movie," Carla said.

"Exactly. So when you cast Angelina Jolie in a film, you're creating an alternate universe *in which actress Angelina Jolie does not exist.* Because otherwise people would be noticing the resemblance all the time. This is what I call the Angelina Jolie Paradox."

"You know, Sagan," Carla said. "You could have named that paradox after any movie star."

"True. But as the paradox's discoverer, I have chosen Angelina Jolie, as is my right."

"I accept your nomenclature," Darcy said. "But what does it have to do with my book?"

"Well, given that Lizzie's been researching death gods, and yet somehow never realizes that her boyfriend is an actual death god for, like, eight hundred million Hindus, I assume your book takes place in a universe in which Hinduism does not exist. There's no other explanation."

"Fuck. You're right," Darcy said. She stumbled backward, dropping onto a dark wooden bench in the center of the room.

"Dude." Carla laughed and sat beside her, punching Darcy on the arm. "You just erased your own religion. That's like going back in time and killing Buddha or something."

"Stop laughing!" Darcy returned the punch. "This is serious!"

"Are you going to get, like, excommunicated?"

"The question is moot," Sagan said. "We have no one in charge to do the excommunicating."

"It's still not okay!" Darcy cried, staring at Yamantaka on the wall and realizing that she and the blue-skinned monster had something in common—they'd both killed Yama, Lord of Death. "I mean, are you kidding with this?"

"Granted, the Angelina Jolie Paradox is not widely accepted," Sagan said. "It's more of a conjecture than a theory."

"Also, it's very silly," Carla pointed out.

"But it's in my head now," Darcy said, because however ludicrous Sagan's paradox was, she couldn't deny that it contained a grain of truth.

Whenever she began to type a story, Darcy felt an alternate universe inside her computer taking form. Some parts of it intersected with her own world, real places like San Diego and New York, but other parts were made up, like Lizzie Scofield or the Movement of the Resurrection. Those connections with reality gave stories their power, and when that realness began to fray and splinter, something broke inside Darcy as well.

She looked up at the painting. A character like Yama, someone borrowed from the Vedas, already had his own stories out here in the real world. And every day, Darcy grew more uncertain whether he was hers to play with anymore.

"You could change his name," Carla said. "Call him Steve, or something."

Darcy coughed out a small cry, as if she'd swallowed a bug. *"Steve?"*

"Okay, an Indian name. She could use yours, right, Sagan?"

"My name means 'Lord Shiva,' so not really." Sagan struck a Bollywood archer's pose. "But I'm available to play Yamaraj in the movie."

Darcy shook her head. She could no more change Yamaraj's name than she could Lizzie's, or any of the characters. It was too late for that. Besides, filing the serial numbers off a stolen car didn't mean you owned it.

"You guys are killing my brain."

"And I haven't even told you the paradoxical part," Sagan said. "The only way *not* to erase Angelina Jolie is to never cast her in a movie."

Carla's eyes went wide. "Which would *also* erase Angelina Jolie."

Darcy made a small and whimpering noise.

Carla sighed, and stroked her shoulder gently. "You really think a three-thousand-year-old death god cares what you write about him?"

"Yamaraj is who he is," Darcy said. "This is about who I am."

CHAPTER 20

JAMIE KEPT LOOKING AT MY SCAR. NOT THE ONE ON MY FORE-head, where the stitches had almost dissolved, but the oval of red-dened skin that descended from my left eye, tracing the shape of a single tear.

"Can I touch it?" She was already reaching out.

I leaned closer across the Formica table. We were eating break-fast at a diner before our first day back at school, a celebration to mark the start of our final semester.

"Does it hurt?" she asked.

"No. It's kind of like a chemical peel, a really small one." Her fingertip was a whisper against my cheek. "From the tear gas react-ing with water. That's my terrorism beauty tip: if you get sprayed with tear gas, don't wash your face!"

All yesterday I'd practiced this line in my head, going for comedy in the face of tragedy. But Jamie was wide-eyed and silent.

I cleared my throat. "Just kidding. I have no terrorism beauty tips."

"But it *is* kind of pretty." Jamie picked up her phone from the table. "You mind?"

I leaned forward, and she snapped a picture from inches away.

Now she was staring at her phone instead of my face. "It's like a tattoo of a teardrop."

"That's what it is. I cried a tear, which left its mark."

"Whoa, deep. But only one tear? That's some pretty crappy tear gas."

I didn't explain how I'd mostly avoided the gas by willing myself to an alternate reality, one inhabited by ghosts and psychopomps and threads of memory twisting cold and wet and hungry in the wind.

Instead I said, "Can I have the rest of your bagel?"

She pushed it forward, her gaze still riveted to her phone.

Jamie was the first person I'd called with my new phone, which had shown up the day before, arriving via overnight express. (That was classic Dad behavior: waiting for more than a week to do something, then paying extra to make it happen faster. When I left a message thanking him, he texted back, *Thank Rachel. She kept bugging me.* Also classic Dad.)

Jamie had announced that she was picking me up for school an hour early, because we had so much to catch up on, and we'd wound up heading to breakfast here at Abby's Diner.

This was much more fun than Mom driving me to school. Between Mindy and Yama and having a strange new reality to explore, I hadn't realized how much I'd missed my best friend.

"I think it's really cool how you never went on TV," Jamie was saying.

"Mom made that decision, I guess. I never even thought about doing an interview."

"Would you have wanted to?"

"It's not like I've had time." There'd been skills to learn, after all. Afterworlds to conquer. "I didn't even practice my Spanish over winter break. For once Mom didn't make me."

"Poor Anna," Jamie said. "She must still be freaking out."

"Pretty much." It didn't help that she'd found me sleeping in a closet two nights ago, with a knife as a teddy bear. "She's tired all the time these days. Like she never really recovered."

"Was it weird, her and your dad seeing each other in Dallas?"

"He didn't come."

Jamie froze for a second, then she placed her fork down firmly. "What the actual *fuck*?"

I shrugged. My dad's behavior was always freaking people out, but I was used to him. "He doesn't deal well with stuff like this."

"Who the hell *does*? I know he's weird, but that's beyond crazy. And after you got *this* close to getting . . . crap. I wasn't going to ever say that out loud. I suck."

"Hey, I *know* I almost died. It's okay."

"Sorry."

I shrugged. "We're all freaked out."

"Not just us. Air travel's down, like, eight percent. And when the Feds searched the houses of those gunmen, they found all kinds of explosives and other scary shit. Like they were planning something really big. Everyone says the FBI is going to raid the cult's big compound soon."

I raised an eyebrow. "Been keeping up with the news?"

"Obsessively!" Jamie cried, loud enough that heads turned. Her gaze dropped to the table, and she began to adjust her knife and fork. "I hope that's not weird. It's just that when you didn't answer my emails, I had to get my info from *somewhere*."

"I know. And you're really awesome to not be mad at me."

Jamie was still staring at her silverware, and I could see that she was feeling everything at once: relief that I was alive, anger that I'd taken so long to get in touch, horror that the world was so random and deadly.

"It's my fault you haven't had a chance to process," I said. "It was selfish of me, hiding like that."

"Don't be silly. You're the one who was terrorized," Jamie said to her half-finished omelet.

"I get to be silly. And I get to hide, too. But I choose to get over myself now." I handed her one of my french fries. "See? Selflessness."

She took the french fry and ate it solemnly. "You can talk to me about what happened, Lizzie. Or about anything. You know that, right?"

"Of course."

She reached for another of my french fries. "Your mouth just did that thing it does when you're lying. How come?"

I looked away from her, letting out a sigh. "Maybe because I just lied. There are things I can't talk to you about. But it's only because I can't talk about them with *anyone*. Okay?"

I realized why I'd waited so long to call Jamie. It had nothing to do with being traumatized by terrorists or hiding from my weird new fame. It was because of how badly I wanted to tell her everything.

She was my best friend, and I couldn't say a word about the scariest and most wonderful thing that had ever happened to me. I couldn't tell her about knowing what came after death, or the ghost that haunted my mother, or those five little girls in Palo Alto. And worst of all, I couldn't tell her about Yama.

Being with him had changed everything. There were energies inside me that I'd never felt before, a psychopomp shine on my skin and fire in my hands. I hadn't slept in two days. The old man under my bedroom floor was right—I didn't need to anymore.

I was becoming something else. Something powerful and dangerous.

"Do you hate me?" I asked.

Jamie shook her head. "I didn't say you *had* to talk to me, just that you could. But maybe you need some other kind of help."

"Like a shrink." Suddenly I was annoyed. Mom had also suggested seeing someone, but it seemed different when a friend said it. "I'm okay, Jamie. In some ways, I'm better than okay. Better than I was."

There was a glimmer of sadness in her face. "How are you *better*?"

"Well, some of what I can't talk to you about, it's not really bad. It's more like, um, positive developments."

Jamie leaned closer, her eyes interrogating mine. My fingers went unbidden to my lips. It felt as though Jamie could see Yama's heat lingering there.

"Holy crap, Lizzie. You *met* someone."

I should have denied it, but I was too surprised. We sat there staring at each other, every second of silence confirming what she'd said.

Jamie shook her head. "I *thought* you were being kind of perky."

Something about the way she said "perky" made me giggle.

"Jamie . . . ," I began, but had nowhere to go. I giggled again.

"*Lizzie*," she said back at me. "Did this happen in New York? No, because you would have told me about that already. So you met someone in Dallas?"

A soft moan slipped out of my mouth, as if she were dragging the truth from me. But what I really felt was relief at finally telling someone, along with a happy panic as I tried to figure out what to say. "Yeah. I did."

"That's so romantic." Her eyes were wide and glistening. "At the hospital?"

"No."

"So, not another patient, and you're being super cagey about it. You haven't told Anna about this, have you?"

"Hell no."

"Aha! So he's older than you. Or are you being cagey because he's not a he? Did you switch teams, Lizzie? You know I don't care if you did."

"I know, but he's a he. And yeah, older." It felt weird saying it that way. Yama might have been born a long time ago, but he hadn't changed much since he'd left the real world. If Mindy was still eleven, surely Yama was my age. "Kind of older."

"A hot young paramedic?"

"No," I said, smiling. Jamie's guesses would never get her to the truth, of course, but for some reason it felt good to have her trying. It felt normal. "He was just somebody who helped me. And we have . . . a connection."

"That's sweet, but 'just somebody who helped you'? You suck at hinting."

"Who says I'm hinting?"

She reached across the table and punched me. "I say you are! More hinting, now!"

"Okay," I said. But what could I tell her that would even make sense? "He knows how to deal with tragedies."

"Like a grief counselor?"

This was probably as close as she would ever get, so I nodded.

"Deep." But then she frowned. "Isn't that kind of unethical? Swooping in on someone who's totally traumatized?"

"It's not . . ." I groaned. "He's not an actual grief counselor, Jamie."

"You just said he was."

"Not officially or anything." This conversation was getting too specific, so I went for vague. "He's just someone who gave me what I needed to survive all this. When nothing else made sense, he saved me. *He's* why I'm not falling apart right now."

She nodded slowly. "Okay, I like him so far. But he must be in Dallas, right? You know long-distance relationships mostly suck."

"He's here sometimes. He travels a lot. Um, for his job."

"His job? Lizzie, what *is* he?"

I opened my mouth, then closed it again. Soul guide? Psychopomp? Guardian of the dead?

"It's a secret," I spluttered. "His job is a secret."

There was a long pause as Jamie considered this, while I contemplated the epic corner I had painted myself into. Maybe *this* was why I hadn't called Jamie, because she always made me tell her more than I wanted to.

"Wait," she said a moment later. "He's some kind of spook, isn't he?"

"Um, what?"

"It's obvious." Jamie started ticking off points on her fingers. "Secret job. Travels a lot. Was at terrorist attack. Good at dealing with tragedies. Age inappropriate."

"Not *that* inappropriate. He looks really young."

"You're hooking up with a government agent!" she cried. "And how *old he looks* is what you're focused on?"

I looked around, wondering if anyone in the diner had managed *not* to hear Jamie's outburst. Nobody I recognized was there, but my mom's friends came to Abby's all the time. Plus, my face had been on the news a lot lately.

"We should stop talking about this now," I whispered.

"Because you can neither confirm nor deny." Jamie checked her phone. "Plus, we should get to school. I'll pay."

A little later we were in the car, watching the road slip past in silence.

This was what I got for opening up. I was stuck with a lie, and a ridiculous one. But if I denied that my secret boyfriend was some sort of secret agent, Jamie would just start asking questions again. And there wasn't anything true I could tell her that would make as much sense.

For that matter, how much truth did I have to tell? What did I really know about Yama? I had only the vaguest notions about how old he was or where he was from. He'd never even had a chance to finish his story about becoming a psychopomp. Something about a donkey, was all I remembered.

I didn't know the answers to any of the questions Jamie probably wanted to ask. But I had to say something.

"I know this all seems weird."

"Yeah, it does." She drummed her fingers on the steering wheel. "Part of me wants to believe that you're just straight-up crazy. Like, you invented a secret-agent boyfriend to make yourself feel safer."

"Why would you want to believe *that*?"

"Because then no one's taking advantage of you," she said.

I stared at her, my breakfast twisting in my stomach. "He's not like that."

"I'm sure it doesn't *seem* that way, Lizzie. Because in every action movie the girl hooks up with the guy who saves her, like that's supposed to be normal. But in real life it'd be a pretty messed-up way to fall in love, because your emotions go all haywire when you're getting shot at. Isn't it called Stockholm syndrome or something?"

"Um, I think that's when you fall in love with the terrorist, not the good guy."

"Right. That *would* be worse. But you didn't just hook up with somebody because you were scared, did you?" She pulled her eyes from the road to stare at me.

I shook my head. "It's not like that at all. In fact, he kept saying it would be better if I forgot the whole attack, even if that meant forgetting him. But I couldn't. We're connected, since the first moment I saw him."

Her eyes were on the road again. "By which you mean, he's hot."

"Yeah, he is." For a moment, I didn't know where to start,

though my body was singing at the thought of describing him aloud. "Brown eyes. Brown skin, too. He's tall, kind of wiry." I could still feel the way his muscles moved beneath silk.

"Wiry? You mean he works out?"

"No. He's more like someone who grew up on a farm." As I said the words, it fell into place. There'd been lots of manual labor all those years ago.

"Wiry. Okay."

Suddenly I wanted to tell Jamie everything, or at least everything that would make sense to her. "He's got this twin sister who's really important to him. It's like they have a bond."

"That's weird, but cool." Jamie sighed. "So you hooked up in Dallas? Like, while you were in the hospital?"

"No. It was here, two nights ago. That's the first time we . . . the first time anything happened."

"He was here in San Diego? Not stalking you, I hope."

"*No.* He just happened to be here. And I'm the one who called *him.* Like I said, we have this connection. Just trust me on this."

She turned to stare at me, and it was a long moment before her eyes went back to the road. "Okay. I trust you, Lizzie. And I'm glad someone was there for you. Just be careful."

"I will be." Of course, that was a lie. Being careful would mean taking Yama's advice and forgetting all about the five little girls in Palo Alto. But I couldn't do that. Mindy needed to know for sure that she was safe from the bad man. And I needed to know that everyone else was too.

I reached out and put my hand gently on Jamie's, wanting to say something that wasn't a half-truth. "I'm really glad we talked about this. It all seems more real to me now, just from saying it out loud to you."

She gave me a smile, our hands parting as she turned the wheel to guide her car into the student parking lot. It was already swarming, groups of friends clumping together, excited to see each other again or mutually depressed about being back at school. It all looked so normal and of-this-world that it made my heart twist a little.

Like I didn't belong here anymore.

It was strange. When I was in the gray world, I looked out of place, shiny and full of color. But this school parking lot felt foreign as well, too full of life for a psychopomp like me.

That word sucked. I'd started searching online for something better to call myself, but had found only the old standbys like "soul guide" and "grim reaper," and lots of gods and goddesses with names like Oya, Xolotl, Pinga, and Muut, plus two from Chinese mythology called Ox-Head and Horse-Face.

For obvious reasons, I was still looking.

Jamie drove us carefully through the throng and pulled into an empty spot. The moment I stepped out of the car, people were eyeing me with furtive looks of recognition, a few of them pulling out their phones. But at least there were no TV cameras or reporters. The winter break had lasted just long enough for my survivor fame to recede.

But as Jamie and I headed for the school's front entrance, I saw a black sedan parked in the street, a lone figure inside watching the students file past.

"Hang on a second," I said to Jamie, and crossed the strip of lawn between parking lot and street.

The driver's-side window hummed down as I approached.

"Hey, Special Agent."

"Good to see you, Miss Scofield." Elian Reyes was wearing his usual dark suit and sunglasses, and his tie was bright red today.

"It's good to see you too. But, um . . ."

"To what do you owe the honor of this visit?" His smile gleamed for a moment in the morning sun. "Nothing serious. My agent in charge was concerned about your first day of school."

"Anything I should know about?"

He gave a little shake of his head. "No new intelligence, Miss Scofield. Simply an abundance of caution."

"That's nice of you guys. But my friend saw something about that death cult on the news. Like, the FBI is going to raid their headquarters or whatever."

"That's a rumor, Miss Scofield."

"Right." I smiled. "Which you can neither confirm nor deny."

"One I can't give you any inside information on. Down here in Southern Cal we mostly deal with drug trafficking. A little high-glamour terrorism is always exciting, though."

"Glad I could help with that." Behind me, the first bell rang. I turned to look back, and saw Jamie watching us with widened eyes. "Oh, crap."

"Friend of yours?" Agent Reyes asked.

"Yeah. And now she probably . . ." I groaned at my own stupidity. "She probably thinks that you're my new boyfriend."

He lowered his sunglasses a little, his brown eyes narrowing. "Your new boyfriend?"

"My secret boyfriend that I just told her about. Long story, highly awkward."

"I agree. Feel free to disabuse her of this notion, Miss Scofield."

"I'll get right on that." The beginnings of a blush were creeping across my cheeks. "Um, that was the bell. I have to go to school now."

He nodded. "Let me know if you see anything unusual today."

"I already put your number in my phone." I saluted and turned away.

As I started back toward the front door, I noticed that more people than just Jamie had watched me talk to Special Agent Reyes. Just perfect.

"Hot indeed," Jamie said as I reached the door, a leering smile on her face. "But you said you *hadn't* been practicing your Spanish."

"No way! I mean, maybe he is kind of hot. But he's not . . ."

"Hispanic?"

I groaned. "You've got this all wrong."

She hooked her arm through mine and led me inside. "Right. He's some *other* hot secret guy in a totally government car who happens to be following you around."

"Yes! That's it *exactly*."

"Sure, babe."

A clump of sophomores was watching a little too keenly as we walked past, and I heard my name whispered, but Jamie silenced them with a hard glance.

"Neophytes," she muttered.

I thought about trying to convince Jamie of the nonboyfriend status of Special Agent Reyes again, but there was no point. She'd seen him with her own eyes, after all, which beat an invisible psychopomp any day. At least now she wouldn't think I was crazy enough to make someone up.

"Thanks, Jamie."

"For what?"

"For listening to me. For trusting me."

She squeezed our linked arms tighter. "I repeat: just be careful."

I nodded, content to let Jamie guide me to our first-period acting class.

It was strange. Our conversation might have been littered with half-truths and misunderstandings, but talking to Jamie had helped me make sense of everything that had happened. I'd never understood why Yama had been so hesitant at first, saying that I should forget him. But maybe brand-new ghosts became attached to him all the time, like ducklings imprinting on their mother. And he'd been worried about those little girls imprinting on me. . . .

But that wasn't what had happened between *us*, was it?

From the first moment I'd seen him, Yama had been so beautiful, so necessary. Not because I was traumatized, but *in spite of* the awful things happening around us. From our first kiss in the airport, he'd become a part of me. I could still feel his lips against mine, and he'd heard me when I'd called his name.

Our connection was real, and talking about it with Jamie had only made it more real, no matter how many times I'd had to lie.

CHAPTER 21

IT WAS ONLY TEN DAYS AFTER HER FIRST REAL KISS THAT
Darcy Patel received her first real editorial letter. It seemed fitting
that she share both with the same person.

"It's here!" she shouted into her phone.

"Hang on," came Imogen's sleepy voice, then the sound of teeth
being brushed, then spitting. "You mean your ed letter? About time."

"I know, right? This book comes out in 428 days!"

"How do you even know that?

"Nisha texted me this morning."

Imogen laughed. "That's handy. What did Nan say?"

"I haven't read it yet. I need you here!" Saying this made Darcy
feel pathetic, and a little annoyed that she had to ask: "Can you
come over?"

"I might be able to squeeze you in," Imogen drawled, but then
added: "Forward the letter to me. See you in five."

* * *

Fifteen minutes later, they sat on the roof of Darcy's building, phones and muffins in hand. Darcy was still in pajama bottoms and a T-shirt, but Imogen wore a crisp white shirt and a full complement of rings on her fingers, having proclaimed that editorial letters were serious business. She'd brought two coffees and muffins from the Chinese-Italian café downstairs.

"So far, so good." Darcy was scanning the letter's opening paragraph. "She still loves the first chapter."

"Nan always starts with praise." Imogen flicked her thumb across the screen.

"Hey! That's my praise. Don't scroll past it!"

"Save the praise till you need it. Dessert goes last."

Darcy rolled her eyes. "Says the person eating a muffin for breakfast. Why are we doing this on the roof, anyway?"

"To maintain perspective," Imogen said, gesturing toward the skyline.

Darcy didn't even ask what that meant. She had eyes only for the email. The next paragraph was about chapters two and three, when Lizzie was in Yamaraj's underworld palace after the airport attack.

There was a distinct lack of praise.

"Crap. She hates it."

"No she doesn't."

"She says it's all exposition!"

"Well, that's kind of true." Imogen wadded up her empty muffin paper and placed it beside her coffee. "But I *like* Yamaraj's origin story. Revengeful donkeys are awesome!"

"Thanks," Darcy said softly. The donkey story was one of the few things in the book that she had come up with on her own. It had nothing to do with Yamaraj of the Vedas, or her mother's murdered friend. It had come out of nowhere, it seemed, a tale from another era.

But Nan had a point. For two whole chapters Yamaraj and Yami sat in their palace explaining the rules of the afterworld to Lizzie, a giant block of exposition, just like every writing how-to book told you not to do. How had Darcy not noticed it before now?

She felt a tremor in her hand, and a fight-or-flight reflex in her stomach. Suddenly she hated those two chapters.

"Maybe if they explain things later," she said slowly, keeping the quaver from her voice. "Then Lizzie has to figure the afterworld out on her own, and it makes Yamaraj more mysterious at first."

Imogen nodded. "Mysterious is good. He's a death god, after all."

"Yeah. About that . . ."

It took a moment to say more. Darcy wondered when exactly she'd decided to borrow a character from her religion. Maybe those stories from the Vedas had always been in her head. Maybe it hadn't even been conscious.

But at some point Yama had gotten mixed up with all the other stories in her head, and he had blended with Bollywood actors, manga boyfriends, paranormal romance hotties, and even the handsome princes from Disney movies. . . .

"Shit. That's it."

"What is?" Imogen asked.

"The fact that Yamaraj takes Lizzie to his palace. It's dorky. Dudes with castles are so *Disney*."

"He's a raja of the afterworld," Imogen said. "What else would he live in, a bungalow?"

Even in her anguish, Darcy made a note to herself that she liked the word "bungalow," even if she wasn't quite sure what it meant.

"Okay, he does have a palace," she admitted. "He's got a whole city. But Lizzie can't just hang out there and drink tea. Not till later, when everything's going wrong, and the underworld is serious and scary and weird. Yama has to be a proper death god."

Imogen looked up from her phone. "Does this have to with what Kiralee said?"

"Not just her. My friend Sagan kind of freaked me out." The Angelina Jolie Paradox seemed too silly to explain to Imogen, but Darcy had to try. "By making Yamaraj a character, it's like I'm erasing him from scripture. But getting rid of him would erase him too. So all that's left is making him real. I owe him that much."

"You owe every character that much," Imogen said simply.

"Right, sure." The strange thing was, from that first day of writing last November, Darcy had imagined Yamaraj's beautiful underworld palace. But she'd never been to India, and her vision had been cobbled together from movies, cartoons, and websites for fancy hotels in India. "I really loved that palace scene. But it's too dorky, isn't it?"

"Kill your darlings," Imogen said, reaching out to trace a line down Darcy's bare arm. It sent a shiver through her, a kind of relief, the feeling of a broken darling leaving her system.

She switched her phone to a notes app and typed with one thumb: *Exposition later. Palace scarier. Yama more mysterious.* Her hand still trembled a little, and her breath was short, but it was no longer a fight-or-flight reflex. It was the buzz of ideas burning in her head, and of being here with Imogen in the spot where they had first kissed.

Canal Street rumbled with authority below, and the city seemed huge and steadfast around Darcy.

She kept her voice even. "This was a good idea, working on the roof."

Imogen answered with her lips, brushing them lightly against the side of Darcy's neck. She smelled of coffee and ginger, and a touch of starch from her crisp white shirt.

The kiss set off another shiver in Darcy's stomach, which tangled with the flutter of anxiety and caffeine. She wanted to turn and kiss Imogen full on the lips, but there was a momentum in her thoughts, and in her body, that she couldn't squander.

"So I have to figure out where Yamaraj takes Lizzie. Where would they go, if not the underworld? Somewhere dark and scary."

For a long moment, neither of them said a word. Darcy thought of all the settings in the book—the ghost school, the windswept island, the mountaintop in Persia. Which was the bleakest and scariest, most befitting an introduction to a death god?

It was Imogen who broke the silence. "Why do they have to go anywhere?"

"You mean . . ." Darcy's voice faded. Everyone loved the airport scene, so maybe she didn't have to leave it behind. "But there's a terrorist attack going on."

"If you want scary, that's a good thing. And if Lizzie's thought herself over to the flipside, she's invisible, and bullets can't touch her."

Darcy closed her eyes for a moment, imagining the scene: Lizzie waking up with bloody bodies on the floor around her, the terrorists blazing away at TSA agents and SWAT teams. She'd panic and bounce back into the real world. And get shot.

Unless, of course, Yamaraj was there to keep her calm.

"Of course, Lizzie has to know she's in another world," Imogen said. "Otherwise there's no genre transition."

Darcy's eyes opened. "No *what?*"

"You know, that moment when Lizzie realizes she's not in Kansas anymore, and the reader does too. Your book starts as a terrorism thriller, but then Lizzie wills herself *into another genre.* For me, that was the first moment that had the juice."

Darcy felt herself relax a little, happy to be back in the land of praise.

"Give me a second," she said. She closed her eyes again and let herself sink down into the experimental theater in her brain, the place where she imagined scenes. She saw the airport attack again, with Lizzie right there in the middle of it, but this time in the gray of the flipside.

As the silence stretched out, Imogen remained quiet, long past when Nisha or Carla would have spoken up to offer advice. And gradually Darcy let the certainties of what she had already written fade into smoke and mist, until finally her eyes popped open and she said . . .

"Tear gas!"

Imogen kept her gaze level, staying silent.

"When the police get to the airport, they start by shooting in tear gas. So when Lizzie wakes up, she's in a cloud."

"So she's coughing?" Imogen asked carefully.

Darcy shook her head. "The flipside has its own air. So Lizzie thinks she's in heaven, until she sees Yami staring at her through the mist."

"Creepy little sister in heaven. Nice."

Darcy smiled, her mind's eye still in the scene. "But what looks like heaven is really hell—dead bodies all around her, half hidden by the mist."

"And before she sees them and freaks out, Yamaraj is there to help!"

"And he says exactly the right thing." Darcy took a drink of coffee to pull herself back into the real world, her mind ringing with possibilities. But what she'd envisioned wasn't just a fix, it was a *whole new chapter*. "Shit. So Nan points out this problem in one paragraph, and I have to write thousands of words to fix it? That's not fair!"

"All's fair in love and art."

"And this letter has five more pages!"

Imogen was laughing now. "Guess that's why you get paid the big bucks."

They kept going all afternoon, for another hour on the roof and then down in the big room, at the desk with both their laptops open. Thankfully, most of Nan's comments didn't demand as much work as the first one. Some were positively niggling.

"Do I really use the word 'veins' too much?" Darcy asked.

"Kind of."

Darcy frowned. "Where the fuck else is Lizzie's adrenaline

supposed to be? In her armpits? And why do you keep agreeing with Nan?"

"She's a good editor." Imogen held up her hands in surrender. "But it's your book. You get the final say."

"I asked Moxie about that once, and she said it depends."

"Only on how brave you are," Imogen said. "If you disagree on something big, Nan can threaten not to publish your book. And I guess she could *actually* not publish it. But remember: she can't make you write a different novel."

"That's reassuring. Kind of."

"Don't worry. No one's going to cancel your contract on the 'veins' issue." Imogen tapped at her laptop keyboard. "Here we go . . . search and replace 'veins' with 'penguins.' Oh, look: '187 replacements made.'"

"I used 'veins' 187 times? Are you serious?"

Imogen was laughing. "Yeah, I think my protag had anger coursing through his veins last night too. You got into my head, girl!"

"Sorry. I suck at writing." Darcy frowned. "Um, exactly why did you replace it with 'penguins'?"

"So when you do the rewrites, you won't miss it." Imogen tapped her trackpad, and the *swoosh* of sent mail sounded. "You're welcome."

Darcy reached across to take Imogen's hand, and felt the warmth of her skin, the cool metal of her rings. "Thanks. Not for the penguins, but for being here. You make up for bad writing humiliation that's coursing through my penguins."

"One more page to go." Imogen's eyes flashed. "Will it be a last dollop of admiration? Or a final devastating edit?"

Darcy groaned as she scrolled to the final page of the letter. It was half-full, containing a single paragraph that looked forbiddingly dense.

"This better be praise," she said, and began to read.

A moment later Imogen leaned back and sighed. "That figures."

"Don't tell me you agree with her!"

"No, I hate the idea." Imogen drummed her fingers on the desk. "But I was worried this might happen."

Darcy read the paragraph again. It was a long and rambling explanation, more about sales and sequels than storytelling. But there was a firmness to it, a certainty in Nan's convictions that made Darcy feel young and small and defenseless.

Her editor wanted a happy ending.

"Crap. I thought I nailed those last chapters."

"I thought so too." Imogen was staring at her laptop.

"Then why did you expect this?"

"Happy endings are popular. Do you not watch movies?"

"Yeah, but that's *movies*," Darcy groaned. "Books are above all that!"

"No business is above money."

"But I never thought I'd have to . . . Wait, hang on. The ending of *Pyromancer* is way darker than *Afterworlds*. Did Nan ask you to change it?"

"No. She loved it."

"Crap! Is this because I'm younger than you? So Nan thinks she can push me around?"

"I doubt it." Imogen pointed at her laptop screen. "See what she says here? 'We have very high expectations for this book, Darcy, but we won't be able to live up to them without Sales fully on board.'"

"What does that mean?"

"It means they're paying you three hundred thousand dollars, and now they want their happy ending."

They lay together on Darcy's futon, Imogen holding her from behind.

Their bodies fit perfectly like this, two continents pulled apart eons ago but now rejoined. Though her head still spun from the ed letter, Darcy could feel every detail of Imogen behind her—the leanness of her arms, the pulsing ghost of her breath. Lying here like this was new enough to be sublimely distracting.

But it was impossible for Darcy to surrender to her body, because her brain buzzed with strategies—arguments against Nan's dictates, a dozen possible happy endings, tragic speeches to give if her book were canceled. And under the rest, the hum of worry that this was all her fault.

"It's because I'm a hack, isn't it?"

Imogen shifted, tightening her arms around Darcy. "What'd you say?"

"*Pyromancer* is edgy right from the beginning. And Ariel just gets more gnarly and complicated as you go, all the way to the ending."

"So you read it?"

"Yes! Sorry!" Darcy cried, realizing that in her excitement this morning, she had forgotten to say so. "Finished it, right after Carla and Sagan left. It was amazing, and gritty, and real. And nobody randomly shows up to save Ariel when she gets in trouble. Especially not some dorky death lord who lives in a palace."

Imogen chuckled. "You're going to fix the palace."

"It's too late now. Nan sees this as a happy-ending book, and so does Sales." Darcy burrowed backward into Imogen's warmth. "You get to keep your messy ending, because your characters are messy and complicated, and you don't borrow death gods and make them dorky. Because you're a real writer."

"Seriously, *this* again?"

"You know what I mean. Nobody expects *Pyromancer* to have some big Disney ending."

"Because nobody expects it to sell a million copies, no matter how it ends. Sales doesn't worry about working-class pyromaniacs who lust after their gym teachers."

"Then they're stupid. You're going to sell millions."

"Shush," Imogen said, pulling Darcy closer.

"But it's so awesome."

"Thank you, but shush."

They were silent for a while, Darcy wondering what to do next. Call her agent? Fight to the death? (The death of her contract? Her career?) Or did she really have to start writing a happy ending for Lizzie and Yamaraj?

"Doesn't Nan understand that my book is about *death*?"

Imogen's sigh was warm against the back of Darcy's neck. "Maybe that's why. You start with so much tragedy, she wants it to end happily."

"That's stupid."

"All happy endings are kind of stupid." Imogen pulled down the collar of Darcy's T-shirt and kissed the top of her spine, sending a shiver through her.

Darcy squirmed in Imogen's arms till they were face-to-face. "Do you think we're going to have a happy ending? Or would that be stupid?"

"We as in us?" Imogen considered the question, a wary look on her face. "I think it might be too early to think about endings."

"I *wasn't* thinking about endings," Darcy said, which had been entirely true until a moment ago. But now that she'd started, it was hard to stop. What did a happy ending even mean in real life, anyway? In stories you simply said, "They lived happily ever after," and that was it. But in real life people had to keep on living, day after day, year after year.

What were her chances of spending her whole life with the first person she'd ever really kissed? Darcy rolled away and brought her knees close, wrapping her arms around them.

"Fetal position, huh?" Imogen said. "Thought this might happen, so I saved you some good news."

"Glad to hear I'm so predictable. What's the news?"

"When *Pyromancer* comes out, I'll be touring with Standerson."

"It's official?" Darcy sprang out of her ball and rolled over to face Imogen again. "He's going on tour with you?"

"Well, technically I'm going on tour with *him*." Imogen's smile was growing as she spoke. "Not all twenty cities, of course. But we'll be on the same stage every night for a week."

"That's amazing!" Darcy leaned forward and they kissed properly for the first time that day. The pressure of Imogen's lips, the play of her tongue, all of it soothed the tightness in Darcy's stomach. She wondered why they'd waited so long.

When their mouths parted, Imogen was still smiling.

"I can't believe you!" Darcy shook her head. "You kept that secret from me *all day*?"

"Like I said, thought you might need it. Dessert goes last."

"You do realize that dessert-goes-last and happy-endings-are-stupid contradict each other, right?"

Imogen shrugged. "One's a strategy. One's a philosophy. No contradiction."

"Whatever," Darcy sighed. "But you and Standerson! All because of my party!"

"Glad I showed up," Imogen said. "For that and other reasons."

As Darcy laughed at this, a fugitive memory crossed her mind. She'd been a little drunk, and so much had happened that night. But in the days since, one moment of the party kept popping back into her head.

"You said something weird that night."

"That I was hot for your book?"

"Weirder. You said that 'Imogen Gray' was your pen name. You were just kidding, right?"

Imogen's smile faded at last. "No. It's true."

"So that's not your real name?"

"Not the one I was born with."

Darcy frowned. "But it's something close, right? Like, Imogen Grayson?"

Imogen shook her head. "There's no point guessing. I don't tell people my real name."

Darcy sat up. "Why the hell not?"

"It's no big deal."

"Then tell me what it is!"

Imogen let out a slow groan. "Listen, Darcy. Back in college I wrote a lot of stuff for this indie blog. It was basically a diary: everything I was thinking, everything I was doing . . . every*one* I was doing. And after Paradox bought my book, they asked me if I wanted to use a pen name. When I googled myself that night, I didn't love what I saw. So I decided to keep all that separate from my novels."

"Okay, sure. But separate from me, too?"

"For the moment, yeah."

Darcy sat there, wide-eyed, until Imogen took her hand.

"That's not who I am right now, is all."

"But you didn't change your*self*," Darcy said. "You just changed your name."

"At first, maybe. But it's a chance to start over, without having to go into witness protection or whatever. Having a pen name gives me a new identity: novelist Imogen Gray. And now that identity is me. Why are you staring?"

"I don't know." Darcy dropped her stare to the futon cover, but had to look up again. It was as if Imogen had announced she was an alien, a shape-shifter, or a flat-out impostor. "This is so weird. I've been calling you the wrong name this whole time."

"No you haven't. Imogen Gray is my name."

"So you changed it legally?"

Imogen groaned. "No, but *it's my name*."

"If I promise not to google it, will you tell me what your real one is?"

"No. And it's not any more real than this one."

"I thought you wanted me to trust you!"

"You can trust me, even if I don't tell you my name."

"Can you hear how weird that sounds, *Imogen*? Or whatever your real name is!"

"Listen, Darcy." Imogen let out a slow, exasperated sigh. "You know how it hurts when characters die?"

This felt like a trick, so it took Darcy a moment to say, "Sure."

"That's because characters are real. Because *stories* are real, even if they're fictions. Which means pen names are real too, because novels make their writers into different people. So Imogen Gray is real. That's who I am. Okay?"

"It still feels like you're hiding something."

"Not any more than you are."

"Me?" A laugh bubbled up in Darcy. "I never even kissed anyone before you, Gen. There's nothing to hide!"

"Really? So how come when you showed up in New York, you didn't tell anyone your age? How come you didn't bring any stuff? At your party Johari asked why this apartment was so empty, and you let her think it's because you're some sort of mad author-monk. But it's because you want to *start over*."

Darcy had to turn away from Imogen's intensity, and her eyes fell on the select and perfect row of novels on her shelves. There were no books she'd been forced to read for school, no manga series she'd given up halfway through. The bedroom walls were bare of old selfies and boy band posters, shorn of all the flotsam of childhood. Every morning when she walked out into the big room, Darcy breathed the air of a life made from her own choices, without leftovers or hand-me-downs. Nothing here was someone else's idea.

Apartment 4E was a blank page.

"You wanted to rewrite yourself," Imogen said.

Darcy stared down at Imogen's hands. They were twitching, as they always did when she ranted about writing and books. It was crazy to fight with her about this stuff. It was like arguing with someone's religion.

"Okay, I get it." Darcy took a slow breath. "But will you tell me one day?"

"Of course," Imogen said. "But right now I need you not to know, because you're part of what's making me."

"Making you what?"

"Just making *me*." The faintest blush played across Imogen's cheeks. "I've only had this name a year. I'm still a work in progress. You're part of that now. Maybe the biggest part of that."

"Okay." Darcy took one of Imogen's tight fists in her hands, and stroked it until the fingers opened. This had been their first fight, she supposed, and now that it was over, something was left bubbling inside Darcy. Relief that the argument was finished, but also a hunger that its passage had opened up. "You're part of what's making me too, Gen."

"I hope so," Imogen said, and drew her closer for another kiss, deep and slow and fervent. Darcy felt something kindling inside her, and for the first time wished that they weren't taking things slow. But she didn't want to risk two arguments in one day, so she kept that thought to herself.

CHAPTER 22

"JUST DON'T THINK ABOUT THE WALL," MINDY SAID AGAIN.

"You know, that might be easier if you didn't keep *mentioning it*."

Mindy frowned. "How can I not mention it? You're trying to walk through it."

"Right," I said. "And how can I not *think* about it when I'm trying to walk through it?"

Mindy looked genuinely puzzled by this, and I was reminded again that she was only eleven years old. She'd never mastered the subtleties of psyching herself out. Though, at the moment, my own mental focus was nothing to brag about.

I stared at the graffiti-covered wall at the edge of the old playground near my house. I'd spent the last hour trying to walk through it the way Mindy could, as easily as strolling through an open door. But all I had to show for my efforts was a bruised knee and a short temper.

"Maybe if you close your eyes?" Mindy suggested.

"Tried it." I pointed at my knee.

She didn't answer, just sat there on the wall, deftly managing to look perplexed and smug at the same time.

Now that I'd spent the last hour trying to do it, ghosts walking through walls made no sense. If you could go through a wall, why wouldn't you fall through the ground beneath your feet? And then keep on falling through the water table, the earth's crust, and a few thousand miles of magma until you wound up at the center of the planet?

But there was Mindy, sitting on top of the same wall that she'd strolled through a moment before. She seemed to make unconscious decisions every second about which objects were solid and which weren't—the key word of which was "unconscious." Every time I thought about it, I wound up crashing into things.

And the problem was much bigger than my bruised knee. Here on the flipside, I was just like a ghost. I couldn't move anything in the real world, which meant no opening doors. Walking through walls was necessary simply to get around.

Even if Yama had offered to teach me the ways of the afterworld, I wanted to master some skills without his help. Besides, if I was ever going to find out more about the bad man, I needed to learn how to do this, or stand around waiting for him to open his door to me.

"Come on, Lizzie. You've done it before." Mindy was swinging her legs, bored now. "You ran through that fence around the scary school."

"But that school was from the old days, when there was no fence."

"So maybe you should think about the past."

"Like, I should imagine dinosaurs in the playground?"

"Not that far back, silly."

Mindy was right—T. rex didn't haunt. Ghosts emerged from the minds of the living, so only things in living memory could exist in the flipside.

I turned to face the wall again. It was covered with graffiti, mostly a long mural of a monster eating its own tail, impressive even in shades of flipside gray. The monster wasn't quite a dinosaur, but it gave me an idea. I took a step closer and placed my hand against the wall, trying to imagine its surface new and untouched.

For a long moment, nothing happened that I could see. But beneath my palm the texture of the brick seemed to change, the smooth coat of latex paint replaced by something grittier. I pulled away.

"Whoa," I said.

Through an outline in the shape of my hand, I could see an older layer of graffiti, worn and softened by time. As I stared at the hole I'd made, the entire surface of the wall began to simmer and seethe. The monster boiled away, replaced by other images—a glowing pyramid, a laughing clown face, a giant unreadable word in five-foot-high letters—each dissolving in turn, as if the old layers of paint were being peeled away. Across the images danced the tags of a hundred street artists, squiggled signatures piled one on top of another, all of them rewinding backward in time.

For a brief instant the wall was bare, the mortar still wet and shiny between the bricks. Then at last it faded, and I could see through it to the grassy vacant lot beyond.

"That actually worked," I murmured.

"Make sure not to look at me," Mindy said.

I glanced up—and there she was, floating in empty space. For a moment my brain tried to reconcile the realities of past and present, and the bricks shimmered halfway back into place, a mirage uncertain of its own existence.

"I said *don't* look at me!"

"Shush." I forced Mindy from my mind and strode ahead.

For a moment the wall pushed back at me, like a gust of wind tugging an umbrella, and then I was on the other side.

"You did it!" Mindy shouted.

I turned back to her with a cry of triumph in my mouth, but madness had erupted behind me. The whole playground was bubbling over into chaos. The poured rubber surface churned, shifting into asphalt and then sand, weeds rippling in its cracks and edges. I saw ghostly streaks of movement, heard peals of laughter and cries of pain. The history of the playground rushed past in a torrent, sounds and smells and emotions. Broken bones and childhood humiliations crackled in the air—everything at once, decades jammed together.

For a moment I felt something akin to Yama's electricity coming from inside me, like a battery pressed against my tongue, sparks dancing on my skin. My heart skidded in my chest, and I had to breathe slow and easy to keep myself on the flipside.

"You okay, Lizzie? You look weird."

"I'm fine." The vision was already fading, the afterworld returning to its usual flat, gray stillness. But the sparks were still there, glitter on my hands.

I wondered if the things I'd seen were actual scraps of buried history. Were we psychopomps like psychic gravediggers, exhuming memories and giving them form? Or had the vision been a hallucination?

It had been a week now since I'd slept. The old man had been right; I didn't need it anymore. Sleep was just a slice of death, and I'd already eaten my fill. But my dreams were piling up undreamt, sometimes spilling out in daylight. Old taunts and jealousies lurked in the corners and stairwells of my school. I never knew which noises came from the spirit world and which from my imagination.

For a moment I thought of going home, lying down, and closing my eyes. But I was still buzzing from my vision, too full of energy.

And I could walk through walls now.

"We should go somewhere, Mindy."

She hopped down from the wall. "Like where?"

"Someplace far away. Like the Chrysler Building!"

"But that means going down in the river. It's too scary."

"It doesn't have to be." I said. "You're always saying how bored you are. This would be fun!"

She shook her head.

I sighed. "The bad man's still alive, Mindy. He's not a ghost. He can't hurt you."

"So what?"

"So *what*? You were so happy when I told you!"

Mindy turned away. "I was. But maybe it would've been better if he'd died a long time ago. Because then he would have faded by now." She turned to stare up at me, her gray eyes glinting. "He must be old, right? Livers die all the time."

"He could also last another twenty years."

"You mean, he might still be doing bad things?" she asked softly.

I stood there, for a moment unable to answer. Mindy had died thirty-five years ago, so the bad man had to be middle-aged, at least. But that didn't mean he'd retired as a murderer.

"Look, I thought about calling the police," I said. "But what can I tell them? That I saw the ghosts of his victims in his yard?"

Mindy stared at the ground. She was only eleven, and didn't know about evidence and probable cause. She just knew she was afraid.

"The police didn't do anything back then, either," she said.

"I'm sure they tried."

She looked up at me, the usual sadness showing in her eyes. The echoes of what had happened thirty-five years ago were wound up inside her, as inescapable as death. The only way for Mindy to get over her fear was for someone to end the bad man.

And I could walk through walls.

The River Vaitarna was wild and angry later that night, full of cold wet things. But it knew exactly where to take me.

As my feet touched the ground, I dropped my gaze to the street, not wanting to see those five little girls standing among the gnarled trees. More important, I didn't want them seeing me, connecting with me. I was already breaking my promise to Yama to stay away.

This wasn't my first time taking the river without him by my side. I'd been practicing all week, midnight jaunts to my old middle school or Mom's work. But it was strange being here, a place that really made me nervous, without him.

I walked to the next corner and checked the street sign: Hillier Lane. My phone didn't work in the flipside, but I pulled a folded piece of paper from my back pocket. I hadn't told Mindy where I was going, but she'd watched me print out the street map.

Eyes on the paper, I made a left turn, walked another block, and turned left again, circling toward the bad man's backyard. But the streets weren't a neat grid, and the alleyways didn't have signs. I wandered for a few minutes, half-lost. It was after one a.m., and there were no people around, no cars . . .

Just a cat, its green eyes peering at me from down the street.

"Is that you?"

The cat blinked. I'd seen it a week ago, when Yama and I had first taken the river to my mother's old house.

It watched me approach with vague interest, then turned and trotted away. I broke into a jog, trying to keep pace without scaring it.

The cat turned from the main street into a small back lane, like the one behind our house in San Diego, but messier. There were garbage bins lining the path, a set of abandoned dining chairs. Grass sprouted from backyards, tall and wild.

The cat finally slipped away through a gap in a wooden fence, and I couldn't follow. But I had to be close. I walked along the alley, checking both sides until I was staring at a house that looked familiar. It had the same small A-frame as the bad man's bungalow, the same thick coat of stucco. There were no ghostly little girls in the backyard, but I was glad for that.

I stood there, letting my breathing slow. I'd learned tonight that to walk through solid objects, I had to stay focused. The last thing I wanted was to get trapped in a panic on the wrong side of the bad man's walls.

As I passed through his backyard fence, its chain links tugged at me, but gave way with little *pops*, like icicles breaking. The bad man's windows were all dark, and when I climbed the steps to the back door, I heard nothing from inside.

I didn't have a plan, just a vague idea of finding something to tell the police about. But I had no excuse not to try. Here on the flipside I was invisible, invulnerable to anything a living person could do.

I took another slow breath and passed through his back door, out of the moonlight and into the darkness inside.

It was dead silent in the house. The air seemed thick, the smell of rust growing until it was a taste in my mouth. I took slow steps forward, reaching my hands out in the blackness. Then I realized that the windows were covered with newspaper.

"Nothing creepy about that," I murmured, and stood still, willing my eyes to adjust. The thought of stumbling into something in those shadows made my skin crawl.

The flipside had its own glow, gray and soft. A utility room gradually came into focus around me, the sort of place where you'd change your shoes before going into the rest of the house. Shelves of paint cans and garden tools, a few bags of soil piled in one corner. Another door stood before me. After a calming breath, I passed through it without a hitch.

Here in the kitchen moonlight flooded through the windows, and it was cheery compared to the blacked-out room behind me. The sink was spotless, a row of water glasses sparkling in a drying rack. The tiled floor looked freshly mopped.

An ordinary kitchen, as far as I could see. Except for the freezer, which was too big.

White and shiny, long as a coffin, it took up a whole wall. As I stared at it, the compressor popped on, setting the floor rumbling beneath my feet. It would be no problem to fit an adult inside, much less a child.

But my body was back in San Diego, so I was stuck here on the flipside, unable to open the door. All I could do was pass through things.

I stepped closer, placed a hand on the freezer's cool metal skin. Its motor trembled beneath my palm. I closed my eyes, letting them adjust to darkness again, counting slowly to a hundred.

Eyes still closed, I bent over the gently humming machine, willing myself through solid metal. Cold air touched my nose, then spread across my cheeks and forehead, as if I were dipping my face into water.

The hardest part was opening my eyes again, not knowing what would be there, inches from my face. When finally I did, I saw something in the gray light of the flipside, lumpy and formless. . . .

Peas. Frozen peas in a bag.

There were also gray tubs of ice cream, plastic-wrapped steaks, and a pile of gel packs, the kind my father had used after his jogging injury a few years ago.

The bad man had bad knees, it seemed.

I pulled myself back out, and stood there shivering in the pale spotlessness of the kitchen. The freezer looked solid again in front of me, much less menacing now.

What if this wasn't even the right house?

Next to the kitchen was a living room dominated by a big TV. The couch was old and musty-looking, but very neat, the pillows plumped and fat. No pictures of family, no chairs for guests, just a folding tray for eating in front of the TV.

Past the living room was a hallway. The floorboards looked like they would creak when I stepped on them, but here on the flipside I was as weightless as a ghost. The hallway took me past a bathroom, a linen closet slightly ajar, and two closed doors, then finally to the bungalow's entrance.

I pressed my ear against the two interior doors. No sound from either.

I picked one, and passed into a study crowded with an old oak desk. A row of fancy pens lay on it, perfectly aligned with the edges. The whole house was obsessively tidy, nothing like the chamber of horrors I had imagined. No chains and hooks hanging from the ceiling, not a layer of grime in sight.

The desk had four drawers, and the shelves on the back wall were full of binders with neat labels. They didn't seem to be full of evidence of the bad man's murders, unless "State Taxes" meant more than it said. In any case, there was no way to open them. To do that, I would have to travel up here in the flesh.

My nerves were fading into annoyance. I'd been an idiot, thinking that he would leave evidence of his crimes lying around. This was a man who'd gotten away with murder for decades.

The desk faced out the front windows of the house, and I could glimpse the gnarled trees in the yard. Among them stood the little ghost girls, staring back at me. My gaze shied away, my breath catching.

Then I saw it on the desk—a phone bill. I stared at it, memorizing the bad man's name and phone number, trying not to think of the little girls outside.

There was only one more door to check out. I slipped back into the hallway and faced it.

It had to be his bedroom. Sleeping inside was the man who had killed Mindy and changed my mother's life, who was the reason she'd been afraid every minute of my childhood.

My nerves were back. But at least I could finally answer Mindy's question about how old he was, how close to death. I willed the door into transparency and stepped through.

It was darker in here, the heavy curtains drawn. A large bed sat nestled against the windows, full of a formless lump beneath gray blankets. When I listened, I could hear him breathing.

He didn't sound healthy. A rumble hid somewhere in his chest, something liquid fluttering with every exhalation. On a bedside table was a row of pill bottles, lined up as neatly as the rest of his possessions.

I knelt to read their labels: Pradaxa, Marplan, the made-up names of drugs.

Then I saw, inches from my face, a hand sticking out from beneath the blanket, motionless and pale. It was spotted, wrinkled. The hand of a very old man, or a very ill one.

I wondered what would happen if he died right now in his sleep. Would I see his spirit emerge into the flipside? Where would I guide him, grim reaper that I was?

I turned away from the protruding hand, stood up. The closet was open, full of neatly hanging shirts, shoes lined up on a rack.

There was nothing else to check in the room. Unless he kept something hidden under his bed . . .

I took a slow, shuddery breath. Beneath my own bed had always been the scariest place in any house for me, more claustrophobic than any closet.

But it was the last place I had to look for evidence. I knelt, my palms on the floor, and lowered myself, trying not to imagine anything peering back at me from the shadows.

At first I saw nothing but a smooth expanse of floorboards extending into dark gray shadows. No dust bunnies, no discarded tissues. Tidy as always. But then metal glinted deep in the gloom. The glimmer of reflected moonlight was curved, like a smile.

I reminded myself that I was invisible, invulnerable, that ghosts were afraid of *me*. I leaned on an elbow and reached into the shadows.

My fingers brushed a metal surface, cool and smooth. I stretched a little farther—my hand found a sharp edge, and followed it to a wooden cylinder mounted into the metal.

When I realized what the object was, I jerked my hand back.

A shovel. He slept with a shovel underneath his bed.

I lay there for a long moment, trying to remember exactly what I'd seen in his front yard. Five girls and five gnarled little trees?

Raising myself up to the window ledge, I peeked beneath the curtains. The five girls stood there in his front yard, next to six little trees. The numbers didn't match.

What if the extra tree was for Mindy? He'd buried her in her own backyard, my mother had said. But why had she been special?

I stared through the window, trying to imagine the front yard before those trees, before the new houses had been built across the street. And, just as it had in the playground, time began to ripple and rewind. The rest of the street was chaos, a churn of motion and construction, people moving in and out, but the old man's yard hardly changed, the grass pulsing with the seasons. Then suddenly one of the trees disappeared along with its ghost, then another, and another, the bad man's deadly career reversing before my eyes.

Finally only one tree remained, the one in the middle of the yard. No ghost stood next to it. The little girls were all gone.

Mindy had been his first. Because she had lived nearby.

I dropped my gaze to the floor, rubbing my eyes, blinking away the vision and trying not to hear the wheezy rattle of the bad man's breathing.

When I opened my eyes and looked out the window again, the present had returned. But the girls shifted a little under my gaze, as if they'd felt me dredging up the past. The one in overalls was staring back at me, her head cocked to one side like a puppy's.

I remembered Yama's warnings, and pulled away from the window. As I did, my shoulder brushed those motionless, outstretched fingers. The faintest spark passed between us, like when my cheek had touched Agent Reyes's.

The whistle of the bad man's breath sputtered for a moment, and a tremor passed through the gray bedclothes. I froze, staring at them, my heart pounding sideways in my chest. Even invisible, I felt as though any movement would wake him. I was afraid to breathe.

Though maybe it was the little girls outside troubling his slumber. They were here because of his memories, after all. What if the connection went both ways?

I almost took another look out the window, to see what they were doing. But what if they had come closer, and were peeking in through the curtains at me?

I crept backward across the floor, away from the window and the bad man's bed. I stood up and walked toward the door, needing to leave this house *now*.

But the door looked solid before me. I reached out, willing it away. . . .

My finger brushed the wood. I could feel the grain beneath the old paint.

"No," I breathed. "You're *gone*, stupid door."

It was still there. My slow-building panic had grown too strong.

I pulled back from the door, trying to slow my pounding heart-beat. If I tried to walk through and failed again, it might take me all night to regain my focus. So I sat down on the floor, cross-legged, trying to distract myself with everything I'd learned tonight.

I had the bad man's name and phone number. More important, I knew about the shovel under his bed, and the desk in the other room with its perfect view of the gnarled little trees, and the gardening supplies in back. . . .

Maybe the bad man hadn't been so cautious, after all. Maybe there was evidence to tell my FBI friend about, something buried right in the front yard. As I sat there, breathing hard, the rusty smell of death filled my lungs. How had I not noticed it before? I could *smell* what he had done.

Then I realized that the room had gone completely silent. The bad man wasn't wheezing anymore.

I stared up at the bed.

He was awake, his head risen from the bedclothes. He was almost bald—only a sparse fuzz of white hair glowed in the street-lights. With one hand parting the curtains, he was looking out the window at the gnarled trees.

Maybe he couldn't see the little girls, but what if he could feel them out there staring back at him, soaking in his memories? Need-ing him?

What if these moments late at night made him happy?

"Fuck this," I said. This was more than I could bear. More than I could live with. Not just for Mindy—this was for me now.

I stood up and walked away, my anger shredding the door like tissue paper, the walls and furniture rippling before me. I sliced my way out of his house and was in his backyard ten seconds later.

The moment my feet left the edge of his property, I let myself fall through the earth, out of the flipside, and down into the River Vaitarna. The current was wild and furious, as angry as I was. It flowed so fast that the shreds of lost memories were nothing but a cold spray against my skin.

As soon as I figured out how, I was going to give the police enough evidence to bust the bad man. And if that proved impos-sible, I'd make Yama help me, whether he wanted to or not. And if that didn't work, I was going to end the bad man myself and then tear his soul to pieces.

CHAPTER 23

DARCY AND IMOGEN CONSUMED THE CITY.

They waited for ramen until the day's writing was done, because a food blog had claimed that noodles tasted better after midnight. (It was true.) At a Southern restaurant near Imogen's apartment, they gorged on raw fluke that had been marinated in lime and blood orange juice. They bought unknown delicacies wrapped in lotus leaves and ate whatever was inside, no wimping out allowed. Once they waited an hour for fancy milk shakes, because the evening's sweltering heat demanded them.

Most days they left Nisha's budget in glorious tatters in their wake.

When Darcy was being more sensible, they went to art galleries instead. Imogen had worked at one for her first year here in New York, and knew the artists, the galleries, and best of all, the gossip.

But it was writing together that Darcy loved most. It was as demanding as anything she'd ever done, facing those clueless sentences she'd written as a high school student. They seemed to drip with everything she hadn't known back then, as embarrassing as old pictures of herself in middle school.

And yet there was something smooth and easy about writing with Imogen—a rightness, like arriving home. Mostly in the big room, surrounded by windows looking out across the sawtooth rooftops of Chinatown, but also on the familiar confines of Darcy's futon, or in Imogen's bedroom with her roommates on the other side of a thin wall. It didn't matter where, really. What mattered was the connection, the space formed between the two of them, a slice cut from the universe and made private and inviolable.

Sharing the act made it all entirely new, the difference between reality and a postcard, between cheap headphones and a live band in a packed house, between a cloudy day and a total solar eclipse.

Imogen changed everything.

"What's that thing where . . ." Darcy's words started as a murmur, and faded.

"More information needed." Imogen didn't look up from her screen, her fingers still tapping.

"When hostages fall in love. With the bad guys."

"Something syndrome. It rhymes."

"Stockholm!" Darcy cried, as triumphant as a cat coughing up a feather.

Rewriting could be huge and philosophical, a single sentence requiring a fundamental rethink of what stories were meant to do.

But sometimes it was more like completing a crossword, the right letters in the right order, fitting and clicking.

"That's the one." Imogen was still typing. She seemed never to stop, even on days when she claimed to have written only a dozen decent sentences. Every thought flowed directly from her brain onto the screen, if only to be excised a moment later. The delete key on Imogen's laptop was faded, worn in its center like the stairs in a monastery.

Darcy, on the other hand, preferred to gaze at her screen rather than fill it. She thought her sentences first, then murmured and mimed them before committing herself to keystrokes. Her hands acted out the gestures of conversation, her expressions mirroring her characters' emotions. She closed her eyes when the theater in her mind was populated by setting and characters, or when she was merely listening for a missing word.

"Sun's coming up," Imogen said, and closed her laptop.

Darcy kept typing, wanting to finish off the chapter that introduced Lizzie's best friend, Jamie. Nan had asked for longer scenes with Jamie, to give Lizzie more to hang on to in the real world. But Darcy's brain was wearying, and her gaze drifted out the window.

Down on the street, deliverymen unloaded fish in styrofoam boxes from a rumbling truck as dawn edged into the sky. True to her word, Imogen never wrote while the sun was up, which had turned Darcy's waking hours upside down. She was still amazed at the drama of sunrise, how quickly a hint of pink overhead jolted the streets of Chinatown into busyness.

Imogen was making tea. This was ritual now, three weeks into their writing together, eating together, everything together. Darcy should have closed her laptop at this point, or finally written a post for her dusty and windblown Tumblr. But another ritual had established itself in these few minutes while Imogen was away in the kitchen.

Darcy opened a search window and typed, *Changed her name to Imogen Gray.* This phrase was so simple and obvious, but she'd never tried it before.

There were no exact matches, just a scattering of hits about *Pyromancer*, less than two months away from publication.

"Crap," Darcy whispered, and salved her disappointment by looking at the images the search had found. A few unfamiliar photos appeared from a reading in Boston last year, when Imogen's hair had been longer.

When the teakettle began to sing, Darcy closed the window and cleared her search history. She'd never *promised* not to search the internet for Imogen's old name, but this was still a guilty business.

It was just so strange, not knowing her first girlfriend's name.

Some days Darcy felt as though she didn't know anything, not if she was a real writer, or a good Hindu, or even whether she was still a virgin. Annoyingly, Sagan had proven correct: the internet had more questions than answers. Was it a night together, fingers, a tongue, or something intangible? Or was "virgin" a word from a dead language whose categories no longer made sense, like some ancient philosopher, brought back to life, asking if electrons were earth, water, air, or fire?

Darcy's hypothesis was simpler than that: the real world worked differently than stories. In a novel you always knew the moment when something Happened, when someone Changed. But real life was full of gradual, piecemeal, continuous transformation. It was full of accidents and undefinables, and things that just happened on their own. The only certainty was "It's complicated," whether or not unicorns tolerated your touch.

It was hours later, in the early afternoon, that Darcy woke up.

It was still a surprise sometimes, finding Imogen beside her, and she stared at her girlfriend, noticing new things. Two cowlicks in Imogen's unkempt hair that reared up at each other, like crossed swords in a duel. The white marks left by her rings, growing gradually more pronounced as the summer tanned her hands. The freckles rising on Imogen's shoulders now that it was hot enough for sleeveless T-shirts.

Maybe it was certainty enough, knowing these things.

Darcy reached for her phone and checked her email.

"Hey, Gen," she said a moment later, nudging and prodding. "Kiralee wants to have dinner with us. Tonight!"

The reply was gummy with sleep. "Had to happen."

"What do you . . . ," Darcy began, then realized: "She's read my book."

Imogen rolled over, stretching her mousing wrist as she did every morning.

"Did she tell you anything?" Darcy asked. "Does she like it?"

All she got in answer was a shrug and a yawn, even as another dozen questions cascaded into her mind. How brutal were Kiralee's critiques? Why had *Afterworlds* taken her almost a whole month to read? Did she know that Darcy was already rewriting, that whole chapters had been replaced? Was it a good sign that they'd been invited to dinner?

But Darcy knew that these questions were all desperate sounding, so she boiled them down to the most important.

"Do you think she'll start with praise?"

Imogen groaned and rolled over, pulling Darcy's pillow over her head.

Kiralee Taylor had summoned them all the way out to Brooklyn, to a restaurant called Artisanal Toast. The walls were covered with paintings of toast, photographs of toast, and a giant mosaic of Jesus made from actual toast. The matchbooks that Imogen had scooped up at the entrance had pictures of toast on them.

After a few minutes of searching the menu, Darcy frowned. "Wait. They don't actually serve toast here?"

"Dude," Imogen said. "This is the dinner menu, not breakfast."

Kiralee nodded. "They aren't fanatics. Where do you think we are, Williamsburg?"

Darcy shook her head, because that wasn't what she'd been thinking. Mostly, she was nervous about what Kiralee thought of her book, and wondering whether she would be able to eat at all. A piece of toast sounded good about now.

Waiters arrived and effected a swift makeover of the table— copper chargers were removed, silverware adjusted, napkins unfolded and placed on laps. It seemed all very crisp and efficient to Darcy, as intimidating as waiting for a critique to begin.

But it was Imogen who Kiralee questioned first.

"How are the *Ailuromancer* rewrites?"

"At the spring-cleaning stage." Imogen's gaze drifted about the restaurant, unmoored and unhappy. "I've emptied all the closets out onto the floor. The rugs are hung and waiting to be beaten. In other words, a mess."

Kiralee patted her hand. "It has to get worse before it gets better. And what about that awful title?"

"Paradox is back to wanting the -mancer suffix for all three books, but they hate everything except *Cat-o-mancer*. Which *I* hate."

"There's felidomancy," Darcy said. "Which also means cats."

"But isn't much better, is it?" Kiralee said. "I'm sure you'll think of something, dear. Just keep pondering and the title fairy will show up one day. Have you started book three?"

Imogen shrugged. "No pages yet."

"Ideas? Notions? Inklings?"

"Well, I had this one . . . phobomancy."

"*Phobos* as in fear?" Kiralee leaned back into her chair and took a long, silent look at the Jesus made of toast. Finally she smiled. "You can make some serious magic out of fear. And it's easy to relate to. Everybody has a phobia or two."

Darcy nodded in agreement, a little surprised, a little confused.

Imogen leaned forward now, her hands moving as she spoke. "The setup is pretty straightforward. The protag starts off with a bunch of crippling phobias—crowds, dolls, spiders, and small spaces. Then one day she gets trapped in a closet, and has to face her claustrophobia head-on. Getting through that gives her the key to defeat her other fears, one by one. And as she does, she gains her magic. At first she can only *see* other people's phobias, like auras or something."

"But eventually she can control them." Kiralee's eyes were sparkling. "Could be a ripper."

"Really awesome," Darcy said. "And so *well thought out.*"

The last words came out sharper than she'd meant them to, and Imogen turned to her with a hint of apology in her eyes. "Yeah. I've been mulling it for a while."

Darcy looked down at the table, surprised at the sharp feeling in her stomach. First she'd spent all afternoon nervous about dinner, and now this. "It's a great idea, Gen."

And it was. But in their three weeks of writing together, Darcy had run every *Afterworlds* decision, every worry, every inspiration past Imogen, who in return had shared the details of her own rewrites. But Darcy hadn't heard a single word about phobomancy.

Kiralee Taylor's opinion was more *important* than her own, of course, because Kiralee had written a half-dozen nearly perfect novels. But why had Imogen kept this idea a secret until now?

Darcy felt her hand being squeezed beneath the table.

"Some things need to stay inside for a while," Imogen said softly. "I don't even realize I haven't told anyone about them, until they pop out."

"Sure." Darcy willed the sting of her jealousy to fade. Kiralee had to be thinking she was pathetic. "You should talk to my little sister. Nisha's got some great phobias."

"Like what?" Kiralee asked brightly.

"She's afraid of ice skates," Darcy said. "Raisins in cookies, and car batteries. She says it's unnatural for batteries to be square instead of round."

"Whoa," Imogen said, pulling out her phone to tap some notes.

"This could be the beginning of a whole new trilogy," Kiralee said. "With phobias instead of mancies."

"Don't tempt me." Imogen was still typing, her metal rings flashing.

"Nisha's also scared of dogs in sweaters," Darcy said. "And socks. Not dogs in socks, *all* socks." She smiled, happy to be contributing to this perfect idea. Even in her rush of jealousy, there had been something exciting, almost sensual, about having heard it direct from Imogen's lips.

At least the other two were pretending her hissy fit hadn't happened.

"You could combine both trilogies with a book called *Mancyphobia*," Kiralee said.

"I know you're just trying to be annoying, but that actually doesn't suck." Imogen put down her phone and raised her water glass. "To *Phobomancer*!"

Darcy followed suit, but Kiralee shook her head. "Toasting with water is bad luck, darlings. Wait for the wine."

As they obediently lowered their glasses, Imogen mumbled, "Talk about phobias."

"Superstitions are an entirely different trilogy, my dear." Kiralee opened her menu. "Now, let's eat family-style. I'll order, shall I?"

Just after the waiters had cleared the appetizers (barramundi risotto cakes with pickled red onions), Kiralee began out of the blue.

"I was intrigued by Anna."

It took Darcy a moment to realize that the long-awaited critique of *Afterworlds* had arrived, and her voice broke a little as she asked, "Lizzie's mom?"

Kiralee nodded. "I love how she hadn't told Lizzie about her murdered childhood friend. That she had a skeleton in the closet, literally."

"Not *literally*," Imogen groaned. "Mindy's not a skeleton, she's a ghost."

"She was literally in the closet, and surely ghosts have skeletons. Otherwise they'd be wobbly." Kiralee turned back to Darcy. "And Mindy is very sturdy indeed. I like that Lizzie doesn't simply realize that the world has ghosts, she finds out that *she* has ghosts. Or rather, that her mother does, which is more interesting. Well done."

"Thanks," Darcy said, relieved that Kiralee had begun with praise. "Actually, that's where I got the whole idea."

"How so?"

"From my mom. When she was little, her best friend was murdered. But she never told me about it." Darcy thought back to the fevered musings of last October, which seemed so long ago now. "I found out by accident, randomly googling my mom's family name. The case was a big deal in Gujarat."

Kiralee swirled her wine, watching it carefully. "And did your mother explain why she never told you about her friend?"

"I never brought it up with her. It was too weird. But I kept wondering about Rajani—that was the friend's name. Did my mother remember her? Because if she was haunting Mom, maybe she was also haunting me and Nisha. That started me wondering what a world with ghosts would be like, and the rest of *Afterworlds* kind of fell into place."

Darcy paused, realizing that she'd never said all this aloud before. She'd always been afraid to disturb the seed that had started everything.

She glanced at Imogen. "Sorry I never told you about this. I never told anyone but Nisha."

Imogen smiled. "Like I said, some ideas need to stay inside."

"What did your mother think after she read *Afterworlds*?" Kiralee asked.

"My parents haven't read it yet." Darcy stared at her hands, which were neatly folded on the table, like a little girl's. "I'm making them wait till it's published for real, with a cover and everything."

"Perhaps that's for the best," Kiralee said. "Until you're finished with that world, maybe you need to stay haunted."

Darcy looked up at her. "Haunted?"

"The fact that your mother's friend was a secret is what kept her ghost alive. When you talk about it with your mother, you'll put something to rest between you. So don't have that talk yet—stay haunted until you're done writing about Mindy."

Kiralee said this with a seriousness that sent a cool trickle through Darcy.

Which was strange. Even as a little kid, Darcy had never believed in ghosts or monsters. Her father, ever the engineer, had always been very clear about the difference between reality and make-believe. What Darcy liked about ghosts and vampires and werewolves were their traditions and rules: cold spots and holy water and silver bullets. The actual possibility of them was just silly.

"I don't think of Rajani that way. I'm not even superstitious. I toast with water all the time!"

Kiralee smiled. "I'm not talking about superstition. I'm talking about characters. How they die a little when you reach the last page. Try to keep Mindy out of your mother's sight until you finish writing about her. You sold two books, I recall?"

Darcy nodded, though she hadn't started *Untitled Patel*, and had no idea when it would be finished. The contract said she had another year to turn in the first draft, which seemed both too much time and too little. The contract didn't call for a third book, but so many fantasy series were like ghosts, rattling their chains forever, never fading.

"I can't stop my mom from reading *Afterworlds* once it's published. I mean, all her friends will be reading it."

"My dad still hasn't read *Pyromancer*," Imogen said. "Novels aren't his thing."

Darcy nodded. Her own father preferred old aircraft manuals, but novels were definitely Annika Patel's thing. She devoured prizewinning literary works, rubbishy bestsellers, the occasional YA series that Nisha and Darcy had raved about, on top of rereading the complete works of Jane Austen every other year. Extracting a promise from her to avoid *Afterworlds* until it was published had been almost as tricky as coming to New York.

"It'll be weird when she reads it," Darcy said. "But even weirder if she doesn't."

"That's publication in a nutshell," Kiralee said. "Both terrifying and necessary. As long as Rajani stays with you."

The chill came again, hearing Kiralee say the murdered girl's name. Darcy had never uttered it aloud before tonight. Rajani had always been more a concept than a person, but now a presence hung in the air around the table, like someone missing from an empty chair.

A moment later, though, three waiters swooped in with main courses in hand, breaking the spell and leaving only a few wisps behind.

Kiralee went on to dissect the book's opening chapters, pointing out the same problems that Nan Eliot had. With Imogen's help, Darcy explained the changes she was making, and Kiralee seemed appeased.

But then she said, "How old is your Agent Reyes? FBI agents have to be twenty-three, it turns out."

"Oh, I didn't know that," Darcy said.

"Is your Google broken?" Kiralee tutted. "There's a checklist for hiring on their site. You might also want to differentiate a bit more between the old man in the patched jacket and the bad man. Because the bad man is rather old, and the old man is definitely bad."

"But one's a normal human serial killer," Darcy said. "And the other has psychopomp powers. How would anyone get confused?"

"Because serial killers are the death gods of the modern world," Kiralee said. "That's why they always have superpowers. Perhaps you should give one of your bad old men a name."

"I have a name for the man in the patched coat," Darcy said. "But it's kind of obvious, so I didn't use it."

Kiralee raised her glass. "No one ever starved from being too obvious."

Imogen raised her own glass at this, and Darcy toasted with

them. Her anxiety was gradually fading into contentment mixed with a red wine buzz. Maybe Kiralee wasn't as scary as she liked to pretend.

So Darcy broached the issue she'd been dreading most: "I've been working on the whole religion thing, trying to make Yamaraj more serious. Less Disney."

Kiralee looked puzzled.

"At Drinks," Darcy said. "You said I was using someone's god for purposes of YA hotness."

"Ah. I think the key word there is 'drinks.' Sorry for descending on you like that. It sometimes happens when I've had a few." Kiralee gave her a sheepish smile. "You don't need some whitefella's permission to adapt your own culture."

"But what if it's not mine?" Darcy stared at her plate. "I eat meat. I don't pray. It feels weird, erasing a god and using him as a mortal."

"Maybe it is." Kiralee considered this a moment, pressing two fingertips against her forehead, for a moment like her old author photo. "But speaking as an atheist, raised Catholic, who finds her only succor in the stories of the Wemba-Wemba people, how the hell should I know?"

Darcy sighed. "So I have to figure this out for myself."

"You write as respectfully as you can, and then you publish. You uncover your mistakes by lobbing your books into the world."

"But people might yell at me!"

"Yes, it's a bit like learning French. When you open your mouth, you risk sounding like an idiot. But if you don't take that chance, you'll never speak at all."

"Yeah," Imogen said. "But bad grammar doesn't offend any-one's religion."

"Have you *met* the French?" Kiralee asked.

Darcy leaned back in her seat, letting them argue. She'd been silly, of course, coming to Kiralee for absolution. She would find her answers in the words she wrote, in the stories she told, not by asking for permission.

"What else did Nan suggest?" Kiralee asked as they began to eat again. "Nothing catastrophic, I trust."

Darcy shared a long look with Imogen, and neither spoke.

"Oh dear. What is it?"

When Darcy still didn't answer, Imogen spoke up. "Nan wants to change the ending. Less tragic. More marketable."

"Ah." Kiralee gave Darcy a look of boundless pity. "That's a tricky one."

"No kidding."

"Here's how I always look at it: you want to find an ending that you believe in, while keeping your publisher happy. That's not a moral crisis, it's a writing problem. One I have faith you'll solve."

"Thanks." Darcy tried to smile. "But won't *Afterworlds* suck with a happy ending? *Any* happy ending?"

"I doubt that. There are probably a dozen perfect happy end-ings you could write. And a thousand bittersweet ones, and at least a million that are gloriously tragic. Alas, you only get to pick one."

Darcy stared at Kiralee. She'd expected outrage, or at least indignation. But Kiralee was smiling, as if this was all some writing exercise or, worse, some sort of *learning experience*.

But this was Darcy's first novel, which for a whole year would be the only book in the world with her name on it. And it had always had the same ending in her mind.

"I seem to have paralyzed you, Miss Patel," Kiralee said.

"No, it's just . . . ," Darcy began, then steadied herself with a slow breath. "Don't you think the ending's good like it is?"

"It's very good. But there are other fine endings out there, some not quite so tragic. Maybe you can find one."

"But don't you think it's *annoying* that I have to?"

"Do you find it annoying that your publisher wants to sell heaps of your book?"

Darcy opened her mouth, but nothing came out. *Now* she was paralyzed.

"It's awesome that they want *Afterworlds* to sell," Imogen spoke up. "But less awesome that people only like happy endings."

"And not even true." Kiralee's gaze stayed locked on Darcy. "*Romeo and Juliet* has enjoyed some popularity. But perhaps killing Yamaraj limits your story going forward."

Darcy stared back, examining Kiralee's expression. Was this a test of some kind? Was she supposed to prove herself now, not just by standing up to Paradox Publishing but also by facing down Kiralee Taylor, author of *Bunyip*, as well?

"But Yamaraj was always supposed to die. He *has* to die. My book is *about death!*"

"And death is always tragic?"

"When terrorists are involved? Pretty much."

"Fair enough. But art can mix emotions as well as distill them."

Darcy looked at Imogen for help.

"Wait a second," Imogen said. "You're not saying Darcy should make her ending happy, you're saying she should make her *publisher* happy. Right?"

"Exactly." Kiralee was staring at the Jesus made of toast. "It's your story, Darcy. Which means you're allowed to change anything about it, especially the parts that are most precious to you."

"Kill your darlings," Imogen murmured.

"Indeed," said Kiralee. "Now, shall we have some dessert, darlings?"

"She was nicer than I thought," Darcy said as she and Imogen rode back to Manhattan in a mostly empty subway car.

Imogen was looming over her, holding onto the straphanger's metal bar and swaying with the motion of the train. "You thought she'd be mean?"

"Totally. The first time she heard about my book, she started making fun of paranormal romances."

"She was pretty harsh tonight. You're just tougher now."

"I am?"

Imogen let out a laugh. "Can you imagine if she'd read your book back then, and straight up told you that half of it was exposition?"

"Not *half*, just those two chapters. But yeah, I would have flipped out."

"You would've melted on the spot, then burst into flame." Imogen swung closer, her knees pressing against Darcy's. "But now you're an old pro with thick skin. 'Skip the praise and give it to me straight' is your motto."

"Very funny. Do you think she hates me and was just being nice?"

"Kiralee's never nice if she hates someone." Imogen stared out the window over Darcy's head. The tunnel walls were strung with construction lights that flashed with the train's passage. "Maybe she was thinking about her own career, and wondering if a few more happy endings might have been a good idea."

"Right. I keep repressing the fact that she doesn't have huge sales. I mean, if she can't make it, I'm doomed."

Darcy wondered what must Kiralee have thought, reading in *Publisher's Brunch* that some teenager was getting so much money. Some pipsqueak who had the gall to come out to Brooklyn to ask for guidance and advice. And at the end of the meal, Kiralee had even paid!

"She's never going to blurb me, is she?"

"Kiralee doesn't think that way. If she likes your rewrites, she'll give you a blurb."

"Really? Even though I'm hideously overpaid?"

Imogen shrugged. "She's seen debs like us come and go. Most careers don't last as long as hers."

"This is my favorite conversation ever," Darcy said.

"Hey, this was a good night!" Imogen swung down into the seat beside Darcy and put an arm around her. "Kiralee Taylor liked your book enough to talk to you about it, in person, over dinner! Tell *that* to your three-months-ago self."

"But every time I asked her what to do, she said it was up to me."

"So she thinks you can figure your own shit out. Boohoo."

Darcy sighed. She supposed that maybe it *was* a compliment, being told that you could find the answers yourself. But part of Darcy—maybe even most of her—wished that Kiralee had simply told her how to fix everything.

"Do you really think the book still makes sense if Yamaraj doesn't die?"

"If you *make* it make sense, sure. See what happens when you write it. Maybe he'll have to die anyway."

Darcy nodded. For the moment, that was enough. There were still hours of darkness ahead to write in, and two months left to pull apart *Afterworlds* and put it back together. And it was a year before the sequel's first draft was due. Publishing might move slowly, but in a way its stately pace was comforting. There was time to find the right ending, happy or not.

CHAPTER 24

IT WAS A FEW NIGHTS LATER THAT I CALLED SPECIAL AGENT Reyes. It was kind of late, but he didn't sound sleepy, only a little surprised when I asked him, "What if I knew someone who'd committed a crime?"

"That depends on what kind." He hesitated a moment. "And how well you know them."

"How well I *know* them?"

"Are you going to report your best friend for underage drinking? A good talking-to might work better."

I laughed. "Jamie doesn't drink, and I mean a stranger. And let's say it was a serious crime, like, say, murder. How would I get the FBI to look into it?"

"Oh." He sounded relieved, certain now that this was hypothetical. "You'd start with your local police. The FBI focuses on federal crimes."

"Murder's not a federal crime?"

"Not usually. Maybe if the victim were a federal official."

"Right. But in the movies, you guys are always looking for serial killers."

"We do." I thought I heard a sigh in the words. "What's this about, exactly?"

I looked at my bed, which was covered with printouts of my research on the bad man. A list of young girls who'd disappeared while their families were traveling, research on the habits of psychopaths, unsolved crimes in Palo Alto. Basically, a whole lot of nothing.

Knowing the bad man's name hadn't helped much. He wasn't in any news stories I could find, and searching online had only led to a hundred other men with the same name, all the wrong age or in the wrong city. It was as if he barely existed, or maybe his little bungalow didn't have an internet connection.

All I really had was his name, his phone number, and my own righteous anger, which seemed to be fading every day. So I told Agent Reyes the same thing I'd told my mom:

"It's, um, for a school project."

"You're a high school senior, Miss Scofield. Shouldn't your school projects be a little more . . . specific?"

"Right. I'm just getting to the specific part." I tried to collect my thoughts, but it had been more than a week since I'd managed to sleep. My body didn't seem to want it anymore, but my mind did. "Like, how many victims does it take to be a serial killer? Is there an FBI rule about that?"

"There are always rules, Miss Scofield. It takes three killings, at least one on US soil, to count as serial murder."

"Three? Great. I mean . . . this is more specific, right?"

"A little," he said. "Is there anything else you need to know?"

I hesitated. Agent Reyes was never going to believe me. Not about a quintet of little girls buried in an old man's front yard. So there was no point in hedging my words now. "Let's say no one had actually witnessed these murders, but I knew where the bodies were buried. What kind of evidence would I need to get the police to dig up someone's yard?"

There was a pause, but then he spoke with certainty. "The kind that convinces a judge to spend taxpayers' money to destroy private property. The very solid kind."

"Gotcha." I was pretty sure he thought I was an idiot now, which somehow compelled me to add, "Any news on the death cult front?"

"Only what's in the newspapers."

"Right. I haven't been keeping up, actually. You're moving in on the headquarters, right?"

"As of last night, Miss Scofield. The bad guys are surrounded by two hundred federal agents. It's nothing you have to worry about, of course, but given your recent experiences, have you considered changing your school project to something less . . . macabre?"

I stared at the mess on my bed. "I have, but I'm pretty far along with this one. Thanks for your help, Agent Reyes."

"Any time, Miss Scofield," he said.

I hung up and let out a sigh. I'd managed to sound demented without even getting to the weird parts of my not-so-hypothetical problem. Like the fact that at least some of these murders had been committed before I was born. And that the criminal lived in a city I'd never visited, except via undead astral projection. And that I didn't know most of the victims' names.

No judge in the world would send a bulldozer to the bad man's property based on my "evidence." No wonder Yama had simply turned away from the sight of the little girls. We were psychopomps, not the ghost police.

But I wasn't ready to give up yet. I wanted justice to be done, somehow. I wanted the world to make sense again, and I had to start by telling Yama what I'd learned.

It was our longest journey on the Vaitarna so far, the strangest and most varied. The river was angry at first, with touches of stray memories like a thousand cold fingertips brushing against us in the dark. But finally it settled, and for a long time we drifted on a current as slow and still as a flat sea.

Yama and I arrived on a crescent beach of white sand and small pebbles. The shoreline stretched away in both directions, curving in on itself in the distance to form a large circular lagoon. The roar of heavy surf was somewhere close, but the water before us lapped placidly at the sand. A warm wind played with my hair and rippled the silk of his shirt.

"Where are we?"

"On an island."

I looked at him. "Can you be more specific?"

"An atoll, specifically." He smiled at me, as if pleased about being his usual uninformative self.

I looked up into the night sky. There was no sign of dawn, so we couldn't be too far from California time. But the stars looked wrong. "The Pacific Ocean, right?"

Yama nodded. "About as far away from everything as it's possible to get."

"It's . . . nice," I said, though the atoll wasn't exactly a tropical paradise. There were no palm trees, no grass or flowers up from the beach, just stunted trees in rocky soil, their broad leaves shivering in the wind.

"It takes getting used to," Yama said, leading me away from the water and onto stony ground. There were seabirds huddled everywhere, and lizards as long as fingers skittered beneath our feet. The land climbed for a few minutes' walk, but as we crested a small ridge it fell away again before us, back down toward the sea. The whole island was like a squashed doughnut, with the still lagoon in its center and the wild ocean on the outside.

Huge waves tumbled out there, lumbering and dark. They looked big enough to roll across us and sweep the atoll away. It was a very lonely place indeed.

"Do you hear it?" Yama asked.

I listened. Even in the muffled air of the flipside, the roar of surf was loud enough to sink into my bones. Only a few sharp seabirds' cries slipped through its thunder.

"What am I listening for?"

"The silence. No voices at all."

I looked at Yama. His eyes were closed, and all the worry had lifted from his face. I reached out and traced the line of his eyebrow with my fingertip, and he smiled and took my hand.

"All I hear are waves and birds," I said.

"Exactly." He opened his eyes, as happy as I'd ever seen him. "No one has ever died on this island."

"Oh." I looked around at the rocky ground, the empty horizon. "But that's just because nobody's ever *lived* here either, right?"

"I would think not. But the result is the same—silence."

"Wait. You mean, you can hear the dead?"

"Always. Everywhere but here."

I remembered my vision on the playground. The history of the place flashing past in an instant, all its traumas and joys and aches. Was that what the world was like for Yama *all the time*? My own powers were growing every day, and he had been a psychopomp for thousands of years.

I could feel the ocean's roar with every part of my body. What would life be like with the voices of the dead as constant in my ears?

"Beautiful, isn't it?" he said.

I stood closer and linked our arms, needing his warmth. The wind was stronger up here on the ridge. It sifted the sand around our feet.

Standing there, I could see the island's desolate beauty. For me it wasn't about the silence of the dead, but about being here with him. It was like we'd been given our very own planet—a little bleak, but ours alone.

And there was something wonderful about the air, something I couldn't quite pin down.

I cupped my palm around the back of Yama's head and drew him closer for a kiss. It left me breathless, and the gray sky pulsed with color. For a moment this was the most beautiful place I'd ever seen.

Before we pulled apart, he kissed me once on my tear-shaped scar. A crackle of electricity stayed there, an itch for more.

"How did you find this place?" I asked, a little breathless.

"By searching for a thousand years."

"It took that long, just to find somewhere quiet?"

"I didn't know what I was looking for at first. But I wanted to explore the world, so I learned to travel on the river in body, not just spirit." His voice softened. "Everywhere I went, there were stories buried in the earth, voices in the stones."

My hand sought his again, and squeezed. "I'll hear them too, won't I?"

"I hope that's a long time from now." He spread his hands. "But when you need to get away, this island is yours, too, Lizzie."

I stared out at the gray and tumbling ocean, not sure what to say. I didn't want this splendid isolation yet, unless it was with Yama. The thought that this desolation could one day be beautiful for itself scared me a little.

How long did I have? I thought of the dead girls on the bad man's lawn, and wondered if I was more connected to them now, more joined to death itself. I needed to tell Yama that I'd been back there, and what I suspected about where the girls were buried.

But not yet. He looked too happy.

"Thanks for bringing me here. This is your favorite place, isn't it?"

"In a way," he said. "My city in the underworld is more beautiful. But this island is the only place I'm really alone."

"But now I'm here, so that's ruined."

Yama turned to me, his smile almost shy. "I can be alone with you."

"I guess that's a good thing?"

"More than I can say." He drew me closer, and the sky rippled with color again, my breath catching and shuddering in my lungs.

By the time our lips parted, I wanted to know every detail of this place. "How did you get here the first time? On a ship?"

"In the pages of a book." He pulled us back into motion, leading me along the windy ridge. "A Portuguese ship discovered it four centuries ago. It was forgotten, then found again, until naturalists came here and painted what they saw."

"So we can connect to places through books?" I asked, amazed. Of course, I'd traveled to my mother's old house using a photo. Suddenly being a psychopomp didn't seem so bad, if I could read my way around the world.

"Partly," Yama said. "But I also got to know a naturalist who'd come here. He said that only two kinds of plants grow on this island. Can you imagine?"

My eyes swept the bleak expanse. All the trees looked the same. "It's not *that* hard to believe. But you made friends with a liver—I mean, a living person? That means you left the afterworld."

"This was worth it." He closed his eyes again, breathing in the salt spray. "For the air alone."

That was when I realized what had been bugging me. "It doesn't smell rusty here. That metal scent the flipside usually has, it's gone."

He opened his eyes. "That's the smell of death. Of blood."

"Oh." A shiver went through me, and I drew us to a stop and pressed my face against his chest. Yama was always so warm, like something was on fire inside him, but still the shudders took a moment to subside. "It kind of sucks to be a . . ."

I still hated the word "psychopomp," but I didn't have a better one yet.

"Not always." He put his arms around me.

I held Yama tighter, needing the solidity of his muscles, the current of his skin. The sand beneath my feet felt slippery, the atoll so fragile in that endless gray ocean.

My geology teacher in tenth grade had always said that there were no islands, only mountaintops that brushed the ocean's surface. It made me dizzy for a moment, thinking of the coral reef beneath us, and beneath that a mountain reaching all the way to the lightless floor of the Pacific.

All those millions of tons of rock and coral, just to hold this lonely sliver of land a few yards above the water. I wondered how many times the sea had washed over it, erasing everything.

"How did you keep from going crazy, hearing voices all the time? I mean, before you found this place. It took so long."

His voice went softer, as if he were telling me a secret. "Looking for a thousand years is worth it, if in the end you find what you need."

I swallowed, taking a moment to answer. The words were clumsy in my mouth, like typing with hammers. "I'm glad you did."

His arms tightened around me, and for a moment the roar of the surf went silent in my ears. Or maybe it was inside my body now, all of me vibrating with that same huge sound.

We kissed there, the bell of the ocean ringing in my lips, until I needed to hear his voice again.

I pulled away and said, "You never finished your story about crossing over. You told me about where you and Yami grew up.

You said she died young, because she was betrayed by a donkey. Seriously?"

"That's how it seemed at the time." He turned, leading me along the rocky spine of the island, the ocean on one side, the lagoon on the other. "My father's brother had a farm, a couple of hours' walk away from our village. When Yami and I went there to play with our cousins, we brought along an old donkey. My sister could ride him when she was tired, and he knew his way home in the dark."

"The donkey knew the way home. Of course." I'd almost forgotten about the bronze knives in Yama's childhood, and now there was donkey GPS. The distant past sounded like a very strange place.

"One afternoon we stayed too late. There was a storm on the horizon, and my uncle said we should spend the night, but Yami refused. She said his house smelled of boiled onions."

"She hasn't changed much, has she?"

"Not really," Yama said with a sigh. "She wouldn't listen. We set off before dusk, but when the rain started it went as dark as night. There was lightning all around us."

I looked out across the sea, trying to imagine what a thunderstorm would look like from this empty, windswept island. "Sounds scary."

"It was, but the donkey led us through the darkness. He didn't complain."

"So how did it betray you?"

"We thought he was taking a different way home, along the sea instead of across the hills, to avoid the lightning. He was an old and sensible beast, and we'd always trusted him. But then he stopped in a place we didn't recognize. We could hear waves crashing, and the ground was sharp and crumbling underfoot. Something brittle was cutting my feet through the straps of my sandals. I knelt to see what it was."

He paused, and a shiver went through me.

"The ground was covered with bones."

I stared at him. "Holy crap. What the hell lived there?"

"Nothing at all." As we walked, Yama stared down at the rocks and shells beneath our feet. "It was the skeletons of dead animals. When the lightning flashed, we saw piles of bones broken and scattered all around us."

I shook my head, not understanding. Some little piece of my airport panic was returning, its cold tendrils creeping through my body. I pulled Yama closer.

"But then I remembered something," he said. "A few years before, when our donkey's mate had grown too old and sickly to work, my father led her to the top of a tall cliff near the sea. He brought me along to help."

"To help with what?"

He spread his hands. "To push her over the cliff."

"Whoa. That's cold-blooded."

"That was the way of our village," he said simply. "But it seemed awful to me, and that night, my sister and I thought the beast was getting his revenge. I suppose he was only visiting the burial place of his mate, his ancestors. There must have been centuries of bones there. Maybe he was paying his respects to death itself, and we were just along for the ride. But we were terrified."

"No kidding. So what happened?"

"A sheet of lightning came down around us, thunder booming right over our heads, and my sister startled and fell from the donkey's back. A shard of bone stabbed through her wrist." Yama's voice grew quieter, barely audible over the crash of surf. "She was bleeding. I held her wound, trying to keep the blood in. She wouldn't let herself cry, but I could tell it hurt. Dying is painful, if you fight it."

"Poor Yami." There was a tremor in my voice.

"She died at dawn, just as the storm was fading. I felt her growing cold, and I promised to stay with her, to protect her. So when I saw her leaving her body, I followed."

"And you've been taking care of her ever since."

He nodded. "That was my promise. If I forget Yami, she'll fade."

I drew him to a halt, and we kissed again. There was salt between our lips now. "You're a good brother."

"She helps me in return."

"With your people, you mean." The weight of it all struck me at last. Not just his sister, but thousands of ghosts depended on Yama's memories to keep them from disappearing. "You're taking care of all of them."

"All I can. Sometimes I wonder how many I've lost. It's hard to count the people you've forgotten."

The sadness on his face made me want to argue. "But doesn't every memory fade, sooner or later?"

"Everyone dies as well. That doesn't make murder okay."

I shook my head. "But ghosts are already dead. And that old man who followed me home, he said that ghosts are just stories that tell themselves."

"So are the living."

I stared out at the ocean, wondering if that were true. Some of us livers were made of the stories we *didn't* tell. I'd kept what had happened in Dallas to myself, spinning lies and half-truths to everyone I loved. And my mother hadn't told me about Mindy's death, even though it had haunted her for all those years.

Though maybe she had, just without words. Her fear of road trips, her need to hear from me every five minutes. She was telling the story of Mindy's disappearance every day of her life.

"Okay, sure," I said. "We're all made of stories. But you and me, we're flesh and blood in a way that ghosts aren't."

"It's not about what ghosts really are, Lizzie. It's about what you and I decide to make ourselves."

I looked at him. "What do you mean?"

"We choose whether to respect the dead or use them." Yama took a step back from me, and the cold wind slipped between us. "Think how easy it is for that old man, deciding that ghosts aren't people. It would be easier for you to think the same. You wouldn't have to worry about Mindy anymore, or any of them."

I stared at the ground. "I'm not like that."

"No. But it will always be a choice. You have to *decide* that ghosts are worth saving."

I looked up, daring the intensity of Yama's gaze. Thousands of people depended on his thinking they were real, including his own twin sister. Their need lay heavy on him, like guilt for a crime he hadn't committed yet—the crime of forgetting, of moving on.

"Okay," I said. "Ghosts are real. That's why I want to help Mindy. That's why I went back to that house."

Yama looked like I'd hit him.

"Her murderer still lives there," I explained. "He killed those little girls. Those trees are like . . . *trophies* in his front yard."

"You shouldn't have gone back there, Lizzie."

"But I had to do *something*. Mindy's scared all the time, worried he'll come for her again. She's been scared for longer than I've been alive."

He nodded, accepting all that. "But she's why you're changing so fast."

I stared at him. "What?"

"You've had death in your house since you were born. A dead girl was always there, in your mother's memories, close to your mother's heart. That's why you never doubted that the afterworld was real. That's why you could see ghosts that first night in Dallas. You were born to it, Lizzie."

I pulled my hands from his, took two steps backward. "Are you serious? You're saying I'm *cursed*."

"No. I'm saying the afterworld is second nature to you. Which means that you have to fight it, not go looking for it. You have to stay away from that house and those dead girls."

"That's crazy. Mindy wasn't a part of my growing up. Mom never even told me about her."

"She didn't have to. A ghost was right there in your house, wanting to be your friend, envying you for all those years of growing up that she never got. Her story was all around you. It's in your bones."

I couldn't even speak.

"You shouldn't talk to her anymore," he pleaded. "Just pretend you don't see her."

"Yama." I shook my head. "Mindy lives in my house. What am I supposed to do, move out?"

"As soon as you can, while she's still more connected to your mother than to you." He crossed his arms. "And you should probably stay away from me too."

"*Why?*"

"My people need me to protect them, to remember their names. You distract me from that." His voice was ragged. "And every time we touch, there's more death on your hands."

I reached for him, and he pulled away.

"This is crazy!" I cried. "My life was *normal* until two weeks ago!"

"The first time you took the river, I asked where you wanted to go. And of every place you'd ever known, where did you choose?"

I swallowed. "My mother's old house."

"Why?"

I didn't have to answer. Yama had figured it out already. Even that first night, I'd been curious about Mindy's story. "I wanted to look for clues."

His eyes flashed, his voice angrier with every word. "With your choice of anywhere on earth, you wanted to look for a murderer's house. And I thought that after you saw those girls, you'd never dream of going back. How many people would go to that house *twice*, Lizzie?"

"I had to. Because of Mindy."

"Exactly. Because her murder is inside you. It was a part of you before what happened in Dallas."

It was all I could do to keep standing. "You think I'm something awful."

"*No.* I think you're something wonderful. So you should be *fighting* this, not chasing it." He spread his arms, taking in the whole of the windswept island. "Imagine, feeling safer here than anywhere else in the world. Is that what you want?"

"That's why you . . ." My voice faltered. "Did you bring me here to *scare* me?"

He tried to say something, which came out broken. Then he turned away to face the ocean and tried again. "I brought you here because I've never brought anyone else here. And because you aren't like anyone else. But you have a life in the overworld—in the *real* world—which you shouldn't give up yet. Not for this desolation."

"I'm not giving anything up."

"You'll have to if you become like me. At least *try* to slow down, Lizzie."

I turned away from him. We had come to a halt at a wide inlet connecting lagoon and sea. The water was rushing out, pulled by the tides or maybe just the tumult of the ocean on all sides. The inlet made the whole place seem even more tenuous, as though the island were punctured and deflating, losing its battle to exist.

"Promise me you won't ever go back there."

I stared at Yama. This didn't make sense. He was supposed to fight the bad man with me. "So *your* people are worth protecting, but Mindy isn't?"

"I don't try to avenge their deaths. I don't judge the living."

"This isn't a *judgment* call. He's the worst kind of person who can possibly exist!"

Yama was silent. His gaze was still off in the distance, and I wondered if he was thinking of all the things he'd seen across thousands of years. Maybe to him, the bad man was just a blip.

But for me, the bad man was the fear in my mother's eyes every time I walked out the door.

"I'm not going to stop. I'm going to fix this for Mindy."

He shook his head. "It was a mistake, teaching you to use the river so soon. It was me being selfish."

Anger twisted in my gut, and I knew in a moment I was going to say something I'd regret. But after what I'd been through, he didn't get to treat me like a child. No one did.

My voice went cold. "Thank you for showing me this place, Yama, but I have to go. Mindy gets scared when I'm gone too long."

"Yami doesn't like it either. She thinks I'll forget them all, because of you."

My eyes stung, and I wondered if Yami knew what her brother really thought of me. That I was damaged, cursed from the moment I was born. I'd thought he was the person who understood me most, and all he saw in me was death.

But when he held out his hand to me, I took it. His skin was warm, full of heat and current.

I pulled him closer, rested my forehead against his shoulder, and breathed him in. There was no rust on Yama, no scent of blood. He was so *alive*, which made a lie of everything he'd said.

Or maybe it wasn't every psychopomp who was stained by death. Maybe it was just me.

"I have to go," I said again.

If Yama wasn't going to help me, I knew someone who would.

CHAPTER 25

"AND HOW'S YOUR BUDGET GOING?" AUNT LALANA ASKED.

"Not bad," Darcy said. "More like . . . terrible."

Lalana sat back in her chair, looking satisfied. "I suppose it's all the mops you've been buying."

Darcy rolled her eyes. She had, in fact, bought a mop. But it had been very cheap, and had broken in a week. Its replacement was on the long list of things she needed but couldn't afford.

"I've been exploring the city. To stimulate my creativity."

"That's very commendable. But isn't 'exploring' free?"

"Technically, yes." Darcy looked down at the thali in front of her, a half dozen different dishes in small bowls clustered on a steel tray. Lalana had brought her to the city's oldest Gujarati restaurant. The food was vegetarian, delicate and perfect, and the free refills were endless. "But not the way we do it, which involves lots of food research."

"I suppose I should be stern with you," Lalana said with half a smile. "But being right is too much fun. Who's *we*?"

"Oh, um, Imogen and me."

"You've mentioned her before. A writer friend, right?"

As Darcy nodded, she heard herself say, "She's more than a friend."

Aunt Lalana sat there, fork in hand, waiting for more.

Darcy had noticed lately that she'd stopped making decisions in the old-fashioned way: thinking first, then speaking. Maybe it was thanks to spending her days writing, which consisted of nothing *but* decisions—who dies? who lives? what happens next?—so by the time she got back to real life, she was done with deciding. Things just came out of her mouth.

Of course, she'd promised to keep her aunt informed.

"She's more like a girlfriend." Darcy cleared her throat. "In fact, she's pretty much exactly like a girlfriend."

"How interesting." Lalana took a bite of lentils and chewed thoughtfully. "Have you told . . ."

"Not yet." She hadn't even told Nisha, whose texts were too easy for their mother to stumble across. Darcy wasn't the only snoop in the family.

"But you will?"

"Of course. But face-to-face." That gave Darcy until Thanksgiving, at least.

"You know they won't be upset, right? At least, not Annika." Lalana shrugged, never quite sure about her sister's husband. "And Grandma P. might find it . . . challenging."

Darcy blinked. She'd forgotten all about Grandma P. and the

uncles, not to mention Mom's relatives back in India. Only a few of her cousins had ever visited America, but news about Darcy and Nisha seemed to scatter across the subcontinent like quicksilver dropped from a great height.

But all that was eight thousand miles away. What mattered was here.

"It's not that I'm worried about what Mom and Dad will think." This was true, but it was more complicated than that, and it took Darcy a moment to continue. "It's just, I never used to do things they didn't expect. And now that's pretty much all I do. They probably think I'm trying to rebel or something. That's not what this is. This is real."

Aunt Lalana gave her a smile. "There's that certainty again."

Darcy didn't know what to say to that. There were whole days when she wasn't certain of anything. Whether she was a real writer. If she would ever find the right ending for *Afterworlds*. How Imogen could stand to be with someone as prying, immature, and budget-challenged as her.

But . . . "I know who I love."

A wistful sigh escape Lalana. "That's such a big word, Darcy. And so distracting. I thought you were going to focus on writing."

"We write together, all the time. Imogen makes me better."

Lalana must have heard the certainty in her voice, because she only nodded.

"And you're not going to tell my parents? Really?"

"Darcy, that's for you to do." Lalana reached across the table and took her hand. "It's a big part of your growing up. I'd never steal it from you."

"Thanks," Darcy said. It was a nice sentiment, but it made her feel very young. "I'll find the right time."

"I'm sure you will. When do I get to meet her?"

"Anytime. You'll like her."

"I'm sure I will. But in the meantime, since your parents don't even know about this yet, it's my auntly duty to learn every detail." Lalana leaned back into her chair, interlacing her fingers. "Leave nothing out."

Darcy felt a smile settling on her face. She had plenty of details to share. The way Imogen's hands carved the air when she talked about writing. The way she collected scandalous gossip about artists, even ones who'd been dead two hundred years. How she never interrupted, no matter how long Darcy took to finish a sentence. The rings she wore on different days.

The conversation lasted all afternoon, and in the end there was only one thing that Darcy left out, because Aunt Lalana really wouldn't understand the fact that Darcy didn't know her girlfriend's real name.

Sometimes Imogen went out all night without Darcy.

Not that Imogen wanted to leave her behind—it was Darcy's idea. As much as she liked Imogen's friends, she worried that her fake Pennsylvania driver's license wouldn't stand up to scrutiny at a serious nightclub. And it was awkward, always being the youngest. There was still so much that Darcy didn't know, nuances of politics and gender and language that a certain kind of person learned about at college and talked about in bars. Darcy always found herself a step behind. Besides, she mostly wanted to talk about books and writing when she went out drinking, but Imogen's friends came from all corners of the city, not just publishing, thanks to the jobs in art galleries and small websites she'd worked at over the past fourteen months.

Also, Nisha's budget always came along and sat there in the corner of the bar like a noisy ghost, sometimes laughing at her, sometimes shrieking and rattling its chains.

So when Imogen headed out with her posse, Darcy usually stayed home. As their lives became more mixed and intermingled, she often found herself left behind not in apartment 4E, but at Imogen's, where she was free to snoop all she wanted. This was sometimes a bad thing.

Imogen, it turned out, collected matchbooks.

She collected lots of free and found objects—transit timetables, paint samples, discarded polaroids—but the matchbooks were her great obsession. Darcy had seen Imogen taking them from restaurants and coffee shops, and had heard Gen's laments about being too young for the glory days before smoking bans, when every sort of business had given matchbooks away as advertising. But until poking around in her girlfriend's closet, Darcy hadn't realized how deep the compulsion went.

Imogen kept her collection in clear plastic boxes. Each box was packed tight, carefully arranged so the commercial logos and phone numbers could be read from the outside, the interiors stuffed with duplicates and generics. There was a stack of these boxes in the closet, enough matches to burn down the whole city. Not that Imogen would ever *light* them, any more than a comic collector would cut up the pages of old issues.

As Darcy browsed the plastic boxes, she wondered what the story was behind this or that matchbook. When had Imogen eaten at a café out in Brighton Beach? Why had she visited a carwash in Queens? Why on earth would a dance academy have promotional matches?

Then, while snooping one night in late August, she found something even more intriguing at the bottom of the pile: a school yearbook from 2008.

Like any yearbook, it was full of thumbprint-size photos of the senior class, each with a name beneath it. Darcy did a quick calculation—2008 was Imogen's final year in high school.

Darcy slammed the book shut, breathing hard. Under one of those photos would be Imogen's real name. This wasn't just innocent snooping anymore.

For a moment, Darcy thought she was about to put the yearbook back into its spot beneath the pile of matches. She even felt a surge of virtuousness flow through her, the contented rush of having done the right thing. But then she opened up the book again and began to examine the student photos from the beginning, page by careful page.

The school was mostly white kids, the boys dressed in collared shirts for senior picture day, the girls wearing a little too much makeup. None of them looked like Imogen's younger self, or even like people who could be her friends and classmates. They seemed to be from a different universe than Imogen Gray. And there were no signatures on the photos, no inside jokes or inspirational sayings scrawled in the margins by friends.

Maybe this yearbook was simply a discarded object kept for research purposes, a source of character names and bad Midwestern haircuts. Or maybe it had been left here as a trap to torment a certain nosy girlfriend.

But Darcy kept reading, noting the names beneath the blank spaces labeled "No Photograph Available." It would be just like Imogen to skip senior picture day.

And then, on the very last page of photos, a familiar combination of letters arrested Darcy's eye—*Imogen.*

Imogen White.

"No way," Darcy whispered, staring at the picture.

The girl had a wide smile and big eyes, chunky glasses and black hair. Her face was too round to be Imogen's, her nose too small. It was a coincidence, nothing more. Imogen wasn't *that* rare a name.

But White and Gray . . .

Darcy kept searching, past the senior portraits and into the photos of activities and clubs and sports teams, looking for anyone who looked like *her* Imogen. Surely no one was friendless enough to escape the relentless cameras of a high school yearbook team.

Long minutes later she found the photo. It was in the Theatrical Arts section, a shot of a crowded stage with Imogen White and Imogen Gray next to each other in old-fashioned dresses. Beside the photo was the yearbook's only handwritten note:

> *Sorry to say it, babe, but you suck at accents*
> *and look stupid in a dress.*
> *Love forever,*
> *—Firecat*

Darcy blinked, remembering something her Imogen had said the first night they'd met. *My first girlfriend was a pyro.*

It was like being punched, and at first Darcy didn't even know why.

Of course Imogen had had girlfriends before Darcy. This girl in high school and a whole blogging career's worth in college. That fact had never bothered Darcy at all.

But this was something more. Imogen White was the original pyromancer, the spark of a whole trilogy, and when Gen had re-created herself as a novelist, she'd taken Firecat's first name. The jealousy she felt wasn't about sex or love, Darcy realized. It was about *writing*.

She lay back on the bed, suddenly exhausted.

If she were in a detective novel, Darcy knew, she would now go through the yearbook again, scribbling down all the names beneath "No Photo Available," then google them one by one with the appropriate search terms to find the answer.

But Imogen's old name didn't matter anymore. It was her new name—her *real* name, she always insisted—that told the story.

Darcy looked again at the picture of Imogen's girlfriend, muse, and namesake.

Where was she now? Was her love really forever? Had all those matchbooks been collected for *her*?

Darcy knew she should be wondering something else entirely, like how she had become such a seething bag of jealousy. This relationship was less than two months old, and already she'd managed to make herself envious of someone who'd been Imogen's girlfriend when Darcy was *twelve years old*.

She groaned aloud. Her body ached, as if her emotions were wired straight into her muscles. It hurt to breathe, to move, to think. How had everything gotten so intense?

She pulled herself from Imogen's bed and took a shower, hoping to wash away her jealousy. But the streams of water felt like ice-hot needles.

The thought of publishing—of the whole world reading *Afterworlds*—had always made Darcy feel naked and exposed, but loving had left her skinless.

Imogen got home, ruffled and drunken, an hour before the sun came up.

"You're awake," she said, her smile lighting the dark.

Darcy had been awake all night, thrashing and suffering, and by now was tangled in the sheets like a dreaming toddler. She'd put the yearbook back into the closet hours ago, beneath carefully restacked boxes of matchbooks.

"Couldn't sleep," she said. "Couldn't write either. I'm useless when you're not here."

"You're sweet." Imogen's voice was alluringly raw, as always after hours of fierce conversation over loud music. She smelled like the world outside, sweat and smoke, spilled drinks and dancing. She always smelled beautiful.

"Did you have a good time, babe?" Darcy asked.

Imogen hesitated, drunkenly wary for a moment. That last word had slipped out of Darcy, who'd never called anyone "babe" in her life. It had come from Firecat's note, of course. But this still wasn't some detective novel, in which a single clue revealed everything.

Imogen only nodded and sat down heavily on the bed. She leaned over Darcy for a kiss, which tasted of coffee and chocolate. On late drinking nights, she and her friends usually had dessert in an all-night diner before going home.

As Imogen pulled off her shirt, Darcy knew she had to speak up now, or she never would. She had to trust her girlfriend to understand.

"Um, I have a confession. I was snooping tonight."

The wary look again. "Snooping on who?"

"Who do you think?"

Imogen's eyes went to her laptop, which sat closed on her desk. "Tell me you didn't read my diary, Darcy."

"Don't be silly. I'd never do that!" A pause. "You keep a diary?"

Imogen groaned and flopped back on the bed, her legs flung across Darcy's. "Just the notes on my phone. They back up onto my computer, and they're *very* private."

"Of course." Even in her worst depths of snooping, it had never occurred to Darcy to pry open Imogen's laptop. "I wouldn't spy on your writing, Gen. You know that, right?"

Imogen tiredly turned her head, raised an eyebrow. "Are you sure?"

"Of course," Darcy said. "I was just looking at your match collection."

A laugh bubbled, low and sleepy, as Imogen turned to face the ceiling again, her eyes half closing. "*That's* your confession? You really need to get out more."

"Your old yearbook was in the closet."

A sigh left Imogen, and she pulled herself back up to sitting. "Okay, that *is* snooping. What'd you find out?"

"There was a picture of Imogen White."

"Oh." Imogen Gray rubbed one side of her face with an open palm.

"And one of you two onstage together. She wrote a note saying you look stupid in dresses, but I don't think that's true."

A half smile. "Me neither. But I think she meant frilly ones. We were in that ridiculous play."

"You both looked beautiful."

"So you must have figured out my real name."

Darcy shook her head. "You didn't have a picture, and Imogen's was the only note in the whole book." It was so strange, saying that name to mean someone else. "Didn't you have other friends?"

"Lots, but I wasn't there the week they handed out yearbooks. I skipped the last month of school, pretty much. Early admission to an Ivy, so I was untouchable."

Darcy breathed relief. For the last few hours, she'd kept imagining Gen spending her high school years friendless and downtrodden. But instead she'd been *untouchable.*

"Firecat brought that yearbook home for me. I didn't find what she'd written till a long time later. . . ." Imogen's voice faded, then she cleared her throat and said, "So that's what you needed to know? Whether I had friends in high school?"

"Why did you take her name?"

Imogen turned away and stared at the closet door. "Because she inspired my protagonist. She liked to light fires. I told you that."

"Sure. But that's different from naming yourself after her. Isn't 'Imogen Gray' your whole new identity? The one you're protecting by not telling me who you really are? Are you trying to *become* her, Gen?"

"No." Her voice had gone soft again. "Just to remember her."

For a long moment, Darcy listened to the sound of Imogen breathing. It was heavy with weariness and alcohol, and something else.

332

"Holy crap. Did she die?"

Imogen nodded, still staring at the open closet. "Suicide. We think."

"Shit." Darcy sat up. "I'm so sorry."

"It feels like a long time ago."

"It still totally sucks." Darcy wrapped her arms around Imogen.

"I was away at college and couldn't afford to fly back, which made it a lot worse. I kept forgetting, somehow. In the morning, I'd go five minutes before remembering she was gone."

"I didn't mean to bring all this up, I swear."

Imogen shook her head. "I don't mind you knowing. I wasn't hiding her, really. And I kind of love it that you want to know everything."

They drew each other closer and the room was silent for while, except for the rumble of traffic starting up below. The light was shifting as morning approached. Darcy felt her body shifting as well, fitting itself against Imogen's. The bite of alcohol and smoke softened into more familiar scents.

When they parted, Darcy said, "On a scale of one to ten, with ten being the most insecure, how shitty a girlfriend am I?"

"You're not a shitty girlfriend. You're hard work sometimes, is all."

Darcy looked away. "When I saw her picture, I was jealous. Not because you were in love with her. Because she made you want to write books."

"Lots of things make me want to write books. But yeah, she did." The hint of a smile crept into Imogen's expression. "And *that* made you jealous?"

"Of course."

Imogen keeled slowly backward onto the bed, like a drunken tree falling. Her laugh was throaty and raw. "Like that night with Kiralee, when you were jealous about my *Phobomancer* idea. You're hilarious."

"No, I'm not. I'm horrible!"

"Yeah, right. I just got home from six hours of drinking, dancing, and talking mostly about sex with a half-dozen beautiful, dauntless, smart-as-shit women. And what are you jealous about? Where I got my nom de plume!" At the sound of her own French accent, Imogen bubbled over with raspy laughter again. "And because you didn't get to hear my pitch before anyone else. That's just hilarious."

Darcy stared down at her girlfriend, wondering if she should have waited for sobriety to have this conversation. But when Imogen's laughter finally subsided and her eyes opened again, they held a look of absolute clarity.

She reached up to tuck a stray lock of hair behind Darcy's ear. "You're amazing."

"I'm a mess, Gen. I don't know how to stop being this way."

"At least you care about the right stuff." Imogen gave her a slow, catlike blink. "Do you really need to know my real name?"

"Do you want to tell me?"

"It won't kill me, I guess."

Darcy held Imogen's gaze for a moment. Was this the sort of thing that normal people argued about? Names and noms de plume and novel pitches? Surely not. "Keep it secret. You're Imogen to me."

The resulting smile was beautiful. "Okay, but just for now. Do you want to come on tour with me?"

Darcy only stared at first, because the words didn't parse. They were too far from this conversation to make sense. But then their meaning fell into place, and she smiled back. "That would be nice. Maybe someday we'll have a book out at the same time."

"I don't mean someday. I mean next month."

Darcy blinked.

"Hotel rooms don't cost more for two people," Imogen went on. "And Paradox is paying for them, and for the cars that pick us up and stuff like that. And food's cheaper outside of New York, so we'd save money there. All you'd have to pay for is your plane tickets, which I could help you with."

"Wait. You mean go on tour with you . . . and *Standerson*?"

"Right—we should ask him first, to be polite. But he likes you, and I already talked to Nan about it. She said that prepub tours are great, especially when they don't cost Paradox any money."

Darcy nodded, her mind focusing at last. She'd been unmoored since finding the picture of Imogen White, but solid ground had suddenly appeared beneath her feet. Imogen was talking about *publishing*, a subject that always cleared Darcy's head.

"A prepub tour? Is that a real thing?"

"Sure. You travel around meeting booksellers and librarians, and charm them so they're all excited when your book comes out." Imogen's smile grew. "And we'll be with Standerson, so his rockstar glow will rub off on us."

"And Nan really said it was okay?"

"She loved the idea. But like I said, we'll have to split your plane fare."

"I'll pay for my own planes, silly."

"What about your budget?"

"Fuck my budget." Darcy threw her arms around Imogen again. "I get to go on tour with you and Standerson? That's amazing!"

"You are kind of lucky, aren't you?"

Darcy pulled away, laughing. "This isn't about my luck, Gen. It's because you don't want to leave me alone for a week!"

"God only knows what you'd get up to."

"I promise I won't ever snoop again."

"Take it from a half-assed expert in obsessive-compulsive disorders: you can't stop yourself. But it's okay, as long as you don't look in my diary." Imogen's face went serious now, her voice suddenly sharp and ragged. "My mom used to read my notebooks when I was little, and I hated it more than anything. So don't do that."

"Never. I promise, Gen."

The hard look on Imogen's face turned swiftly back into a smile; her moods were oiled by the alcohol in her veins. "I'm glad you like my name."

"I love your name. Her name. I'm sorry you lost her."

"Me too." Imogen's eyes drifted toward the closet. "Even if she could be a total pain sometimes."

Darcy followed her gaze. "Are all those matches for her? For Firecat?"

"At first, but then I realized how useful they could be." Imogen reached for the half-full plastic box at her bedside. She turned it, looking at the matchbooks pressed up against the sides. "Whenever I need a location or a random job, I use them. See? I've got pawn shops and yarn stores and shoe repair places in here. Locksmiths and carpet cleaning and tattoo parlors, and look . . . roof restorations!"

"They're for writing?"

"All my collections are." Imogen reached toward the window-sill for more stuff, let it fall onto the bedcovers. "These paint samples are for colors. They have the best names: Candy Apple, Metal Smoke, Stone-Washed Surf."

"And the polaroids?"

"What people wear, what they look like. People who aren't in magazines." Imogen shrugged, staring down at the scattered pieces of her collection. The spark in her eyes was fading now, weariness taking over.

Darcy said softly, "I love you like crazy, Imogen Gray."

"Love you, too." Her smile was slow and soft, and then her eyes closed, and Imogen curled around herself, wrists pressed together beneath one cheek.

Darcy took the paint samples and matchbooks and placed them back on the windowsill. By the time the bed was clear, Imogen's breathing was slow and even, and Darcy reached carefully into the pockets of her jeans, sliding out keys and a crumpled wad of money . . .

. . . and Imogen's phone, a diary wrapped in black glass and slivers of titanium. When Darcy flipped the mute button to silent, the screen lit up expectantly.

"Never," she whispered to it, and placed the phone carefully beside the keys and cash. Then she curled up next to Imogen Gray, *her* Imogen, and closed her eyes to sleep at last.

CHAPTER 26

THE SCHOOLHOUSE WAS EASIER TO SEE TONIGHT. MY FLIPSIDE eyes had grown sharper. Every tile on the roof glimmered, clear and distinct in the gray moonlight.

I crossed the parking lot, hardly noticing the transparent hulks of school buses around me. I could see only the past, luminous and real. The first time I'd come here, the school's front steps had looked smooth and featureless, but now they were chipped and mottled with chewing gum stains.

Yama was right. Every time I crossed over, every time I traveled the river, the ghostly world laid a stronger claim on me.

But what did it matter? According to him, I'd been born to this. I wasn't even sure if he wanted me anymore, or if that fight on his ocean-swept island had been our last.

The front door of the schoolhouse was open, inviting me in.

"This isn't scary anymore," I murmured. "I belong here."

The hallways were silent tonight. The ghostly children's songs had faded or been frightened away, leaving my slow echoing steps the only sound. I walked carefully, because the squeak of sneakers on tile still paralyzed me. It took a few minutes' wandering to find the place where the voice had first taunted us.

"Are you still here?" My mouth went dry around the words.

No answer, just the fear in my own voice. The lockers wavered for a moment, as if desert heat were rising from the floor.

I pushed my dread down, letting the cold place inside me smother it.

"It's me, from the other night. You followed me home. You said you wanted an apprentice."

Nothing at first, but then motion flickered in the corners of my eyes, and the sound of laughter came from behind me.

I spun around, but found nothing but a sign on the wall: NO RUNNING.

It wasn't the old man in the patched coat, just the ghost of some ancient infraction.

I sighed. "You're *really* annoying, you know?"

That time I hadn't expected an answer, but one came—the sound of a fingernail against the floor, traveling down the hallway toward me. It clicked across the cracks between tiles, slow and patient. The sound was an icicle on my spine.

When it passed beneath my feet I jumped, feet dancing, a shiver rippling through me in its wake.

"For fuck's sake." I faced the empty hallway. "I'm here to ask you for help."

"You want a favor?" the response came, leaking up from the

floor. His voice sounded so pleased, so eager, that I almost ran for the exit. Color flitted in the corners of my vision.

I took a slow breath to keep myself on the flipside, and said, "I need to know some things."

In answer, black oil bubbled up, seeping from the cracks in the floor, the spaces between the lockers. It rolled hungrily toward my feet, and a moment later I was sinking down into the river, ready to face the old man in the patched coat again.

He was shinier than last time, his skin luminous in the dark. Maybe that was just my eyes again, more attuned now to the gleam we psychopomps gave off. These days, I could even see the cold, wet things in the river, like scraps of shadow floating against the darkness.

"What a nice surprise," the old man said. "I was starting to think you didn't like me."

"Feel free to keep thinking that." My hand went to my back pocket, where the knife I'd brought along was sheathed.

His eyes followed my motion. "A little rude, for someone asking a favor."

"Whatever." I let my hand fall back to my side. "You said you wanted to teach me things. I've got questions for you."

"Questions?" he said, amused. "You mean there are things your dark-skinned friend doesn't know?"

I decided to ignore that. "There's a man, a murderer. His victims are buried in his front yard, I think. They're haunting his house."

"Are you offering me some little ghosts? How sweet." He

smiled, but the expression didn't quite reach his pale eyes. "Alas, my tastes are very particular."

"I'm not *offering* you anything. I just need to know how to deal with him."

"Oh. You're talking about revenge."

"Not really. What I mean is . . ." My next words faltered in my mouth. To say that I wanted *justice* sounded pompous. I wouldn't mind if the bad man suffered, but mostly I just wanted to fix things. "I want my friend to stop being scared."

"Your ghost friend," the old man said. "The little one, who was with you when we met."

"Yeah, the one you wanted to *collect*." Saying that, I wondered why I'd come to the old man for help. But there was no one else to turn to. "He killed her, too. For all I know, he's still killing people, and I have to stop him."

"Interesting." The old man said the word like he meant it. As if none of this seemed evil or nightmarish to him, or even unusual. Just interesting.

I had to keep talking. "I have all these powers now. I can go places, see the past. I *know* what he did, but I can't prove it."

"You mean, you can't change it." He gave a little shrug. "People like us don't change the world. We just clean up its messes."

"There's no *people like us*. You and I aren't the same! But you said you wanted an apprentice, so teach me how to fix this."

He had a way of smiling—the expression surfacing slowly, like a bubble rising in a tar pit. "Your dark friend is keeping secrets from you, isn't he? That's why you've come crawling to me."

I was angry enough to have stabbed him then, but instead I

said, "He thinks I'm changing too fast. He wants to protect me."

"He's a fool then. There's no safety in ignorance. When you get called the first time, you'll need all the tricks."

"Called?" I shook my head. "By who?"

"Who do you think? By death."

I stared at him, the cold place inside me growing just a little. Every time I thought I had a grasp on the afterworld, it got more complicated.

"What does that even mean? Death isn't like . . . a person, is it?"

He laughed at that, hard enough that shiny little tears leaked from his translucent eyes. "A man with a scythe, you mean? Hardly. Or if he is, we aren't on speaking terms. Maybe death is just a force of nature, or maybe it has a flicker of intelligence. Either way, once its hooks are in, it will take you where it needs you."

I shook my head. "Which is . . . ?"

"The places you'd expect. A fire, a massacre. Perhaps a war. My first time was all three of those, an entire city dying. I was not entirely prepared."

"Oh." It struck me that Yama had appeared at the airport, just as eighty-seven people were being murdered. He probably hadn't been there to catch a flight. "So when lots of people die, psycho-pomps just show up?"

He shuddered a little. "Psychopomps. Such an ungainly word."

"Can't argue with that. Do you have a better one?"

"I think of myself as an artist." He patted the pockets of his patched jacket. "One day I'll show you what I mean."

"No thanks." But at least the old man was telling me things I didn't know. I would be *called* one day, it seemed. What else was Yama hiding from me?

"But maybe a different word for a pretty girl like you," he said. "Where I come from, we called them 'valkyrie.' It means 'chooser of the slain.'"

I didn't answer, but I liked the sound of it. It must have shown on my face, because the old man smiled again.

"I can help you with your murderer. I was a surgeon once." The old man took a step toward me, his slow smile fastened to his lips now. He opened his hands wide, coming closer through the darkness. "I'm very good with scissors and thread."

My hand went to the knife in my pocket. "What are you doing?"

"Showing you this." He straightened his patched jacket. He was only an arm's length away from me now, and I could feel him like a cold spot in the room. "I sewed it together from scraps. As you can see, it fits me very well."

"Why do I care?" My fingers clenched around the metal handle of the knife.

"Because I can cut his ghost to pieces."

"That's not what I . . ." My voice faded. I hadn't really known what I wanted him to do.

"Trust me," he said. "It's what you need to make your little friend happy again. I have only one condition."

I took a few steps back from him, and my shoulders brushed the cold things that had gathered around me in the darkness. I forced myself not to shudder.

"What?"

"Kill him yourself. Then I'll do the cutting."

I stared at the old man, trying to measure his smile. Was he kidding? "I can't do that."

He smoothed his jacket with a slow glide of his palms, as if it were of silk instead of scraps. "You can. You're a valkyrie. A warrior-maiden."

"No." It was true, the last time I'd been at the bad man's house, I'd wanted to end him. But really killing someone? "I don't even know how."

"He's just a man. All the usual ways apply."

"I can't travel with my real body, not yet. I'm just a ghost when I'm there." I shook my head. "This is a stupid conversation. I can't kill anyone."

"How disappointing," the old man sighed. "You're not the valkyrie I thought you were."

I stared at him. "So you're not going to help me?"

"I'm trying very hard to," he said carefully, then slipped his hands into his pockets. "But I see more work needs to be done."

A moment later he was gone.

I walked back toward home from the ghost school, hands in pockets, breathing in the cool fresh air of the overworld. Part of me was relieved that the old man had asked for something I couldn't give. Every moment with him was like standing in wet socks; all I'd wanted was for it to end.

Maybe Yama was right, and helping Mindy would only push me farther into the arms of the afterworld.

But then I saw something across the road. It glowed with bright fluorescent light, a garish white column in the darkness—an old roadside pay phone with scratched and battered plastic sides. There weren't a lot of pay phones around anymore, and for a moment I wondered if it was a ghost of some kind. If school buildings and sounds could have ghosts, why not phones?

This late there were no cars, no joggers, just the wind and the smell of the ocean. So I crossed the road, curious. The receiver felt hard and plastic in my hand—the phone was real. I half expected to hear nothing, but a dial tone buzzed in my ear.

I pressed zero, as if making a call was what I'd intended all along.

"Operator?" came a voice. It was small and tinny, like something heard from the flipside. For a moment, I expected it to ask what my emergency was.

"I'd like to make a collect call," I said. Before I could stop myself, I reeled off the bad man's phone number. It tasted acid in my mouth. But I had to do something, no matter how futile.

"Your name, please?" the operator asked.

"Sorry?"

"Who should I say is calling?"

It took me a second. "Mindy."

"Hold please while I connect, Mindy." Buzz and crackle, and the muffled sound of ringing. Then another distant voice said the word "hello."

Every muscle in my body flinched, and I jerked the phone away from my head. I was suddenly breathing hard, my sweat cold in the breeze. A bitter taste filled my mouth, and the phone felt slick in my hand. Hearing the bad man's voice had made him that little bit more real.

It took me a long time to bring the receiver back to my ear, so long that I was sure he'd hung up. But I heard breathing.

"Is this you?" I said.

"Who the hell is this?" His voice was ragged, like he'd just woken up.

My tongue was stuck. It was all I could do to breathe.

"I don't know any Mindy," came his voice. "Why are you calling me?"

"I know what you did," I managed. "I know what you are."

It was his turn to be silent.

"And I'm coming for you." The words were spreading a strange calm through me. "You can't stop me. I can walk through walls."

"Who *is* this?"

"Even your death can't stop me. I have a friend who cuts up souls." I didn't know where these words were coming from, what piece of me had made them. But they tasted sweet in my mouth. "I'm going to feed you to the cold things in the river. And those little girls in your front yard are going to watch."

He didn't answer, so I hung up on him. As I walked away, the pay phone's fluorescent lights flickered inside their plastic column, the darkness jittering around me. I'd just wanted to scare him, to make him pay a little bit for everything he'd done. At least the bad man knew there was someone looking for him now.

And then almost a minute later, at the edge of my hearing, the phone started to ring.

Mindy met me in my front yard, arms crossed. "You snuck away! That's not very nice."

"I'm sorry." I hadn't told her what I was trying to do. I didn't want her thinking about the bad man, or psychopomps, or any of this. "I had to do something important."

"Really?" Her expression softened. "You look sad."

"Just tired." I hadn't slept in almost two weeks now. Sleep wasn't a part of me anymore. When I lay on my bed, the darkness behind my eyelids was full of fluttering shadows, my brain full of undreamt dreams.

Mindy snorted. "Pomps don't sleep. You should play with me! I'm *super* bored."

I smiled down at her. At times when the fear lifted from her, you could see how happy a child she'd been before the bad man took her.

"Okay. What do you want to do?"

"Let's go to New York. Like you said."

I stared at her. "You want to go see the Chrysler Building? I thought you were afraid of the river."

"Well, *you* want to. And it's been really nice since you started . . . seeing me." Her voice went softer. "Like I said, it's boring around here."

I couldn't believe it. Maybe ghosts could change. Maybe Mindy had just needed to escape from her ghostly invisibility, and she could start to grow again. Maybe she'd just needed a friend.

"I won't be scared with you there," she added. "My own personal psycho-bodyguard. Just don't leave me alone."

"Of course not." I smiled as her cold little hand closed around mine. "I'll always bring you home."

*   *   *

The River Vaitarna was kind to Mindy on her first voyage. Only a few cold, wet scraps of memory brushed against us, and the trip to New York was swift and calm. Maybe I was getting better at this, or maybe my connection to the Chrysler Building was strong.

Or so I thought, until we left the river.

We were in New York City, but the neighborhood was all wrong. Instead of skyscrapers, we were surrounded by apartment buildings and a big department store. Only one tall, curvaceous tower stood before us, wrapped in reflective glass. It took me a moment to recognize it—my father's building.

"Whoa," Mindy said. "You were right. It's huge!"

"That isn't the Chrysler. I think I messed up."

She looked at me. "Are you sure? It's so *big*."

"The Chrysler Building's, like, five times taller. This is where my dad lives."

Mindy gave a disbelieving laugh. She'd never been to New York before, or much of anywhere, I supposed. She'd spent most of the last thirty-five years within a stone's throw of my mother's closet.

"Where are the houses?" she said, looking around. There were piles of gray snow everywhere. The winter up here was ten times colder than back in San Diego, but the flipside air was its usual indifferent cool.

"They don't have houses here. New Yorkers live in apartments." I took her hand. "Come on, I'll show you one."

She pulled me to a halt. "That whole building's full of people? And they live there?"

"Yeah. So?"

"That means they *die* there." She planted her feet. "There must be tons of ghosts inside!"

I sighed, wondering if we should just walk up to the Chrysler. But I was curious about why the river had brought us here. Did I have that strong a connection to my father's apartment? I'd never felt comfortable staying there.

"Don't worry, Mindy. They built this place a few years ago. My father only likes new and shiny things." She still didn't move, and I scented the air. It was rustier than San Diego, but nothing like the bad man's house. "Do you *see* any ghosts?"

She peered into the marble lobby, checking out the doorman, then swept her eyes along the streets around us. It was three hours later here in New York, not long before dawn, but there were still a few people strolling past.

"Just livers." Mindy's fingers tightened around mine. "But what if that's because there's lots of pomps to grab them?"

I sighed. "My dad said he likes New York because he doesn't have to talk to his neighbors. So ghosts probably fade, right? Or maybe they head back to their hometowns, where someone remembers them."

"Maybe. But stay close, okay, Lizzie?"

"Of course." I drew her gently across the street.

Here on the flipside I couldn't even press an elevator button, so we took the stairs. My dad lived on the fifteenth floor, but I wasn't breathless when we arrived. Walking around on the flipside didn't burn any calories, it seemed.

My nerves began to tingle as we stood before my father's door. I'd been a lot of places on the flipside, but this was the first time I'd used my invisibility to spy on someone I knew. It took a moment's concentration for me to pass through the solid wood.

Inside, the apartment was as I remembered it from a few weeks ago—chrome and leather furniture, floor-to-ceiling windows full of moonlit skyline. It sparkled like the icicles dangling from the veranda rail outside, as elegant and cold.

My father's giant TV was on, but I kept my gaze averted from the screen. From experiments at home, I knew that televisions looked very strange from the flipside. Turns out that cats, with their ghost-seeing eyes, are staring at TVs in abject horror. Or maybe cats are just weird.

"Who's that?" Mindy asked.

"Rachel, my father's girlfriend." The two were curled up together on the couch, focused on the screen.

"It's funny that he's here with someone else. I kind of miss him, even if he was a butthead."

"Me too," I said, surprising myself a little.

Mindy had never talked about my father before, though of course she'd known him for longer than I'd been alive. She probably knew more about my parents' breakup than I did, and yet she stared at the couple on the couch as if puzzled by the concept of divorce.

Sometimes I wondered if my mother also missed my father. She always seemed so tired these days, as if losing him had chopped some vital spark out of her. Or maybe it was just those extra shifts she had to work.

My hand went to my cheek, to my scar that was shaped like a tear. For a moment, I wanted to step from the flipside and show my father how badass it looked, and how I didn't cover it with makeup. And maybe ask him why he hadn't flown down to Dallas three weeks ago.

That was when I realized that anger had brought me here. Lately it seemed like I was anger's puppet, moving where it wanted. I'd lost patience with a lot of my friends, and everyone except Jamie was scared of me. Anger had made me call the bad man, in a feeble attempt to scare him.

I could still hear the pay phone ringing as I'd walked away. He probably knew where that pay phone was by now.

I sighed and turned away from my father to gaze at Rachel. I'd never mentioned to Mom how beautiful she was, and had expunged it from my memory out of loyalty. Her face glowed in the light of the TV, her large eyes drinking in the movie with the intensity of a child.

"He never tells her about that gun," my father said, pointing at the screen.

"Hush!" Rachel cried. "I told you, no spoilers!"

I rolled my eyes. This was my father's favorite form of entertainment: watching a movie he'd seen before with someone who hadn't. Like he was some kind of movie expert, and you were an idiot for not predicting what was going to happen.

"That's not really a spoiler," my dad said. "But it's something you should pay attention to, if you really want to understand his motivation."

Rachel groaned, and I wondered again why she was with him.

My father had lots of money, of course, and my friends at school used to say he was good-looking, for an old guy. But both of those reasons seemed too shallow for Rachel. She was smart, and fun to be with, and knew everything about art history. Visiting museums with her had been my favorite thing about my trip here. And she'd always known when I needed to get away from my father.

She must have found a side to him that I didn't know about. But spying on the two of them suddenly didn't seem like the best way to figure it out.

"Coming here wasn't such a great idea," I said.

"At least there aren't any ghosts." Mindy was wandering off toward the bedroom. "This place is teeny. I thought your dad was rich."

"Apartments are small compared to houses."

"Must make it hard to play hide-and-seek."

I laughed. "I don't think my dad's into hide-and-seek."

"But there must be kids in New York." Mindy frowned. "Right?"

"Of course." We were in my father's bedroom now, the only real one in the apartment. During my visit I'd slept in his study, on a pleasantly musty leather couch. "There's a playground near here."

It had been full of nannies and toddlers and dotted with splotches of chewing gum. I wondered what its history would look like flashing past in a vision.

"But there's nowhere to *hide*," Mindy said.

"You think? Check this out."

My father's closet door was closed, but I walked toward it. I didn't try to imagine the past, just kept walking until I passed through. The wooden door offered no more resistance than a dusty sunbeam.

As my eyes adjusted to the darkness, I saw that Mindy had followed. She stood there in the gray light of the flipside, gazing at the glass-fronted drawers and the gray suits hanging neatly in the darkness.

"Bet you wish my mom had a walk-in like this," I said. "Pretty luxurious for hiding in."

"No way," Mindy whispered. "Someone else could be hiding in here with you and you wouldn't even know it!"

I laughed, but Mindy was right. The closet was almost another bedroom in itself. Even in broad daylight the flipside was never bright, but in the deep corners of the closet were pools of shadow that could have held anything.

I held out my hand. "If you're scared, we can go."

"Course not," Mindy said, but she was standing close to me. "Still, I wouldn't want to live with your dad."

"Me neither." I remembered my uneasiness staying here. Maybe it hadn't been the sleek and uncomfortable furniture, or even the fact that I hadn't forgiven my father for running out on me and Mom. Maybe Mindy had spotted the important missing thing here—a place to hide, to disappear.

I let my fingers drift across the sleeves of my father's jackets, trying to feel the silks and tweeds and linens. But like colors and scents, textures were muted on the flipside. Money didn't matter much when you were dead, I guess. Even the best suits wound up gray and plain.

"I'm glad you brought me here," Mindy said. "My parents didn't like big cities. I never really saw a skyscraper before."

I looked down at her. "Let me show you a real one, then. We can walk up to the Chrysler Building in half an hour. It's five times taller, I swear."

"Really?"

"Much prettier, too. It has gargoyles! Come on."

But as I turned to leave, a whisper floated at the edge of my hearing, a half-formed word from the blackness of the closet's depths.

I froze. "Did you hear that?"

"Hear what?" Mindy asked.

I peered back into the darkness, listening for five slow breaths.

"Nothing, I guess." But a chill had settled on my skin, and as I turned to face the closet door again, it looked very solid.

I reached out and touched it. The wood felt hard and real.

"Oh, shit-stick."

Mindy's hand grasped mine. "What's wrong?"

I stared at the door. From the other side, it had seemed a trivial barrier. But from here inside the closet, it felt impenetrable, suffocating. How had I ever convinced myself that solid objects could be willed away?

A cold trickle of claustrophobia was rolling down my spine, a reminder of what it had felt like when I was little. "It's okay. Just . . ."

I heard the whisper again, wordless and soft from the back of the closet.

Slamming my eyes shut, I strode forward. But just as I'd expected, as I'd *known* would happen, my foot collided with the door.

"Crap." I took hold of the inside handle. I could feel the metal, sleek and cool, but of course my ghostly body was incapable of moving anything in the real world.

"It's okay, Lizzie. You know how to do this. Just don't *think* about it."

"Please don't say anything."

I took a deep, slow breath, and flattened my palm against the wood. I tried to push it through, but the door remained solid and unyielding.

My breath grew short and fast, but panic couldn't throw me back into the real world. My body was three thousand miles away.

A huge and awful thought came crashing down on me. What if I was stuck in here? My spirit cut off from my body forever . . .

Then we heard it, a noise from the darkness in the depths of the closet, from somewhere behind the back wall. It sounded like rusty scissors opening and closing, traveling along the smooth wooden floor beneath our feet.

It was the old man in the patchwork jacket. It had to be.

I made two fists and turned to face the darkness. "You again? Seriously?"

The darkness didn't answer. Not even a scratching noise. But Mindy's whimpering seemed to crowd the space around us.

"Please, Lizzie," she begged. "Let's just *leave*."

I didn't tell her that I couldn't leave. I didn't want to say aloud that the old man had trapped me here in a web of my own panic.

"It's okay. I'm not afraid of him." I was only afraid of the four walls, heavy and solid around me.

But fear only made me angrier. I hadn't brought a knife, but as I stared into the darkness, I was ready to punch and kick and bite. Mindy clung to me, shivering, and for a moment the only sound was our breathing.

Then a whisper came. "I want you in my pockets, little girl."

"Let's just *run*," Mindy said. "Please, Lizzie!"

"Just stay here beside me." I tried to keep my voice steady, but the air was thick in my lungs, the closet pressing in. My panic needed somewhere to go, and turned to a shudder traveling down my body.

"I want your secrets, little girl," came the old man's whisper.

Mindy's fingers were a vise around mine, her breathing as fast as a rabbit's.

"It's okay," I said. "I won't let him hurt you."

"I'm getting closer." The voice was almost in my ear.

"Lizzie!" Mindy cried, pulling me backward, away from the darkness. But the door stopped me, solid and unyielding, and Mindy did what was natural to her.

She ran.

The moment I felt her slip away, I turned and called her name. I beat my fists against the door, telling her to wait, to stay in here with me.

But she was gone, along with the presence that had occupied the closet with us. He wanted her, not me.

"Mindy!" I called again, my voice raw. No answer.

I had to escape this closet, so I threw my mind back to the first time I'd done this trick. Covering my eyes with shaking hands, I imagined the tower around me unbuilt, the walls unpainted, the apartments empty shells, the wiring and plumbing exposed . . .

When I let my hands drop, there was no closet door in front of me, no closet at all, not even a floor beneath my feet. Only the skeleton of a building, I-beams and girders in a grid, the cold gray city visible in all directions.

"Crap," I said as I began to fall.

But I wasn't tumbling down like someone thrown out a window. I was feather light, wafting slowly into the yawning pit of the building's foundation. And as its blackness surrounded me, I willed myself through the brittle surface of the world and down into the River Vaitarna.

A moment later my feet rested on its broad, empty plain. All my panic was gone, turned to anger, but I had no idea how to find the old man.

Except to say, "Yama, dammit. I need you."

CHAPTER 27

SUMMER FADED RELUCTANTLY, WAITING TILL MID-SEPTEMBER before the heat no longer made garbage bags sweat and leak. But finally cool tendrils of air crept in through Darcy's open windows at night, and the skies turned the deep blue of autumn.

The two of them kept at their rewrites, Imogen sending *Ailuromancer* to her publisher a few days before her tour. The book remained without a decent title, but Paradox had given her a deadline of early next year for that.

Darcy finished her *Afterworlds* rewrites, except for the new ending, the thought of which still paralyzed her. She tried writing an essay about her troubles, if only to have something to post on her empty Tumblr feed, but it just seemed like complaining. Finally she told Moxie, and a call to Nan Eliot won her an extension till late November.

November . . . the month when Darcy had written a whole

novel. Of course she could manage a new ending. And in the meantime, touring with Imogen and Stanley Anderson would surely clear her head.

Darcy and Imogen arrived at JFK almost two hours before departure time, dutifully wielding one carry-on bag and one backpack each. Standerson had warned that any checked baggage would be lost on their first flight and would never catch up. Disobeying Standerson didn't seem like a good idea.

The first flight was the longest of the tour, all the way to San Francisco. From there, they would wind their way across the Southwest and Midwest, ending up in Chicago. (Standerson, of course, would keep going for a whole month, with other hopeful young Paradox authors joining him along the way.)

Darcy waited for departure in a state of excitement, then demanded the window seat and stared down at the passing terrain, trying to read the giant glyphs of highway cloverleaves and radial irrigation. The country was so *big*. It was strange to think that tomorrow copies of *Pyromancer* would be emerging from cardboard boxes in stores all across it, along with electronic copies shooting down wires and scattering through the air. And in almost exactly a year, her own *Afterworlds* would do the same. . . .

Imogen was taking notes, as always, in case she ever needed to write a scene in a plane. She'd taken photographs of the emergency evacuation card, the layout of the cabin, even the texture of the seat fabric. Watching Imogen do research—especially for a book she wasn't even *writing yet*—only made Darcy twitchier.

"Have you never been on an airplane before?" Imogen finally asked.

"Of course. But not on *tour*."

Imogen smiled, prying Darcy's hand away from the armrest between them. As their fingers interlaced, she said, "Save some energy for tomorrow, and the six days after that."

Darcy played with her seat belt, feeling sheepish and young. "Are you still glad you asked me along?"

"Of course," Imogen said. "But this is just the first of many."

Stanley Anderson was waiting for them in San Francisco Airport, having arrived from Kentucky an hour before. He was sitting near their gate and reading a copy of *Pyromancer*.

Darcy found it odd to see him sitting there alone, with no one paying any attention to him. His humblest online remark generated a hundred responses in minutes, and at her party an expectant bubble of attention had formed around him, everyone glancing over their shoulders to check that he was real. But here in SFO he was just another traveler, dressed comfortably in sneakers, jeans, and a baggy army jacket.

He looked up as they approached. "You made it!"

"Sorry we're late," Darcy said.

"It's never the passengers' fault." He slipped *Pyromancer* into an oversize coat pocket and telescoped out the handle of his luggage, a rolling carry-on bag the color of a green highlighter pen. "Besides, I kind of like airports. All these signs telling us where to go."

He pointed to one above his head: TAXIS AND LIMOS.

As they followed him, Imogen made wide eyes at the top edge

of *Pyromancer* sticking up from Standerson's pocket. The book was dog-eared a third of the way in, roughly the point when Ariel Flint was gaining her fire-starting powers.

"You'll love our driver," Standerson said. "I get the same guy every tour. He's been a media escort for thirty years and knows *all the gossip*. Make sure he tells you about the time he set Jeffrey Archer's jacket on fire. Spoiler alert: it wasn't an accident."

"Whoa," Darcy said. She'd known that they would have drivers taking them around, but "media escorts"? It sounded very illustrious.

"But there's something you should know about Anton," Standerson continued. "He can't drive."

"As in drive a car?" Imogen said.

"Then how do we get around?" Darcy asked.

"In his car." Standerson shrugged. "I mean, he can drive, legally. He's just not very good at it anymore. He's sort of losing his eyesight, and coordination, and focus. But he's got so many awesome stories!"

"Like a realtor who can't use keys," Imogen said. "But more dangerous."

"He has had a couple of wrecks lately, which is kind of scary," Standerson said, then brightened. "But it's a well-known fact that if you die on tour, you go straight to YA heaven!"

Darcy looked at Imogen. "There's a YA heaven?"

"Of course," he said. They were passing down a long, tunnel-like hallway leading to the luggage area, and the lighting was slowly shifting colors around them. It was just some sort of software company ad, but it felt very mystical as Standerson's voice dropped low. "It's very nice up there. Every writer gets their own little bungalow, and they all lie around in hammocks swapping writing tips. There's a nightly discussion about world-building. Plus lots of drinking."

Imogen laughed. "I saw this thread on your forum. Doesn't everyone get their own research team, complete with historian, martial arts expert, and consulting surgeon?"

"That sounds nice," Darcy said as they reached an escalator headed down. "But what if you're not actually *in print* at the time of your grisly car accident? Do you still get into YA heaven?"

"That's a tricky one," Standerson said. "Do you have any blurbs yet?"

"One from Oscar Lassiter, and Kiralee Taylor is waiting for the rewrites to decide."

"Oscar and Kiralee? Goodness. Then heaven ye shall find!"

Darcy was oddly relieved at this news.

The baggage claim area opened up below them, hundreds of bags parading on a dozen carousels. It looked stressful and chaotic, and Darcy felt virtuous for having all her luggage already in hand. She made a mental note to follow all of Standerson's touring advice.

From the bottom of the escalator, a large man in a dark green suit was waving at them. He held a handwritten sign that said ANDERSON, and the two greeted each other with smiles and handshakes.

The man turned to Darcy and Imogen. "Welcome to San Francisco. Anton Jones at your service. My car's this way!"

They followed, and a few minutes later their luggage was in the trunk of a large gray sedan. Standerson sat in front with Jones, and Imogen and Darcy took the backseat. Their hands stretched out to find each other, squeezing tight. They were really here together, on tour.

As the car left the airport, Anton Jones told them all about his last client, a celebrity chef who ran his book signings like a restaurant during a dinner rush. The chef shouted orders to waiting bookstore staff behind him, who scurried forward with books that were butterfly clipped open to their title pages, while a team of publicists skulked about the edges of the room with trays of autographed photos and corkscrews.

It was a very funny story, but as Anton imitated the chef's shouts and gestures, it became clear that his bad driving was not one of Standerson's fantastical conceits. Jones thrust the sedan through the late-afternoon traffic, switching lanes with abandon and stomping alternately on the accelerator and brake, as if trying to crush a deadly ferret loose in the floorboards.

A cold sweat broke on Darcy's skin, and her stomach muttered the first rumblings of carsickness. She tried to swallow, but the dry air of the plane had left her cotton-mouthed.

As Jones swerved around a truck, the sedan's lateral momentum pressed Darcy into Imogen. Crushed in turn against the car door, Imogen let out a low groan. When the car steadied for a moment, she put an arm around Darcy.

"Tell me about YA heaven again?" Darcy pleaded.

The boys were still jabbering in front, heedless of danger, so Imogen answered softly. "There's a dress code. If you were a *New York Times* bestseller, you get to wear a black robe with red trim, like a don at a boarding school."

"That must annoy everyone else," Darcy said.

"Not really. The robes look fancy, but they're really hot, and everyone secretly covets the sparkly tiaras that only Printz winners are allowed to wear."

"The Printz Award's that big a deal?"

"Of course! It's basically a YA knighthood."

Standerson had heard her somehow, and said over his shoulder, "Actually, knighthoods are inferior, because they can be revoked for treason or other serious crimes. But even if you become a serial killer, they still don't take those Printz stickers away."

"Good point," Imogen said. "But awards don't matter in YA heaven, because you get to write all day. No bills, no cooking, no cleaning. Just writing and talking about writing, and everyone has cover approval."

Darcy closed her eyes and tried to imagine that the swaying of the sedan was a hammock beneath her. As silly as it was, the idea of YA heaven made her deeply happy. Often back at home, when the writing had gone well and they'd been out to dinner with Oscar or Coleman or Johari to argue plots and words all night, Darcy felt that she was already there.

With the tour beginning in earnest the next day, Darcy had expected not to sleep that night. But the giant and comfortable hotel bed, combined with three hours' jet lag, had her unconscious by midnight.

The next morning began with school visits. Anton Jones picked them up early for a drive out to the suburbs, where the auditorium of Avalon High awaited. Talking in front of student assemblies had always terrified Darcy, and she was happy that this was only her prepub tour. Her job was to schmooze with librarians and bookstore people, but otherwise keep herself from view.

The morning rush-hour traffic kept the sedan below lethal

speeds, and Standerson, who had suffered one of his frequent bouts of dyspepsia the night before, managed to fall asleep in the front seat. All went smoothly until the GPS announced that they had arrived at the school, which was only partly true. A tall wire fence stood between the sedan and a cluster of buildings glimpsed across a well-kept soccer field.

"Can never find the damn office," Jones said, and began to drive along the fence. The barrier seemed to stretch forever, without any hint of an entrance.

"Brilliant security concept," Imogen said. "Just one little hitch—nobody can get in."

Jones nodded. "Been this way since Columbine, which is ridiculous. That was students shooting up the place!"

"Didn't your schedule have a contact number?" Darcy asked.

"Right, the school librarian." Imogen started searching through the twenty-page fax of travel and event details that had been waiting at the hotel desk the night before. She pulled out her phone and tapped in digits. "Crap, it's going to a message. He's supposed to be waiting at the front."

"I don't see any front," Jones said. "This school's all backsides!"

"The suburban high school as impenetrable fortress," Imogen said grimly. "I was always so good at breaking *out* of these places."

Standerson stirred from his nap and opened one sleepy eye. "We there yet?"

"Sorry, Stan," Anton said. "It's one of those schools where you can't find the damn office."

"Flagpole," Standerson mumbled, then slumped back against the passenger-side window.

The other three leaned forward and, all at once, pointed ahead and to the left, at the stars and stripes whipping in a crisp wind.

Ten minutes later they were onstage, facing a thousand empty seats. Standerson seemed wide awake and not at all dyspeptic, Imogen paced nervously, and Darcy was mostly carsick.

"High school," Imogen said. "I thought I'd never be inside one of these again."

"I know, right?" Standerson inhaled deeply. "The smell of lockers and pheromones, the earnest panache of handmade posters. It's brilliant of our publishers to make us do school visits and remind us how all this really feels."

"I hadn't actually forgotten," Darcy said, though Standerson was right about the smells. High school was rushing back into her brain, like a memory from four days ago instead of four months. Her relief that she wasn't going up onstage was redoubling every minute.

"What if we never really left?" Imogen said. "What if we've always been here, and adulthood was just an illusion?"

"Nice concept," Standerson said. "But for a trilogy or a tweet?"

"I can't tell anymore," Imogen said.

Darcy was still wrestling with this question when the school librarian, who had left them for a quick trip to the office, reappeared. He was a tall man with red hair and a precision in his consonants that made Darcy wonder if he'd grown up speaking Spanish.

"Okay, they're about to call the classes down," he said. "I'm afraid there's some testing going on, so it'll only be about two hundred kids, grades nine and ten."

A nervous laugh spurted from Imogen. "Only two hundred?"

"I'll make sure they sit down front." The librarian turned to Darcy. "The publicist just emailed me last night to say you were coming. You're a novelist too?"

Darcy felt a blush forming. "Yeah. But not in print yet."

"And you're how old?"

"Eighteen," she said.

"That's great. I can't tell you how much my creative writing kids will *love* hearing your story."

Darcy blinked. "Wait. What? I'm not—"

"I'm sure they will too," Standerson cut in. "Darcy's an inspiration to us all."

"I'm not even supposed to—" Darcy began, but at that moment the school's loudspeakers crackled to life, and a call for all English classes to head to the auditorium was echoing through the hallways. By the time the announcement ended, the librarian had disappeared again, and a young student in a death metal T-shirt stood beside Darcy, clipping a lapel microphone onto her hoodie.

"So you wrote a book?" he said as he worked. "That's pretty cool."

"Um, thanks." She looked up at the entrance to the auditorium, where the first students were already arriving. The cold sweat produced by Anton's driving had returned.

Somehow she had no other choice than to go onstage, any more than the students trickling in had any choice but to watch. Imogen was right—Darcy was still in high school. She would always be in high school.

Moments later the three of them were led onstage, where three orange plastic chairs and a lectern waited.

Imogen covered her lapel mike with one hand. "You're lucky, Darcy. At least you didn't have time to get nervous."

"I think I'm catching up," Darcy whispered. The stream of arriving students had turned into a flood, and the volume built in the auditorium. The chatter didn't sound like it was made of voices, but of a primal and dangerous energy, directionless except for a posse of obvious Standerson fans gathered on the front row. They took countless pictures of him with their phones and emitted squees whenever he glanced in their direction.

Then a bell sounded, and as the crowd went silent, Darcy felt herself depart from her own body, as if watching everything from a thousand miles away. The librarian introduced the three of them, there was applause, and then Standerson began his presentation. He didn't talk about his book at all, but spoke of the people who had inspired him to write. F. Scott Fitzgerald, Jane Austen, his small-town librarian, and finally a cute and bookish girl he'd wanted to impress in tenth grade. He was effortless, charming, and seemed to know when every laugh would come, where every beat would fall.

When he was done, genuine applause swept the room.

Imogen stood up next. Her voice trembled at first, just barely, and her hands stayed locked in fists. But then she started talking about the obsessive-compulsive disorders she'd researched while writing *Pyromancer*—manic hoarders, chronic hand-washers, a woman who had to check her front door locks twenty-one times before going to bed—a host of bizarre details that held the audience rapt. Imogen's own hands finally started to move, and soon her passion was in full flight. Darcy found herself carried away by how beautiful her girlfriend was.

But then, far too soon and too suddenly, she was done.

It was Darcy's turn now.

She didn't stand up, as the others had, just sat on her orange chair with her hands tucked beneath her thighs. The lapel mike cast her voice into the auditorium's sound system, making it huge and unwieldy, as if she were typing the words with hammers.

"Hi, I'm Darcy Patel. Unlike these guys, I haven't written novels. I've only written one. Not novels. Novel; singular."

She sat there in the rich, deep silence for a moment, astonished that those words had sounded anything like a joke in her mind. But she had to go on, she had to keep talking. The hundreds of eyes gazing up at her would not accept silence.

"I guess that's because I'm only eighteen. A year ago, I was a senior in a high school kind of like this one, and I wondered what would happen if I wrote two thousand words a day for a month. Turns out, you wind up with sixty thousand words."

The weird thing was, people had actually laughed at this line before. Real, adult people who lived in New York City had found it humorous. Or at least, as Darcy realized now, far too late, those people had *pretended* to find it funny. Clearly they had done so as part of some misguided effort to be nice, but their generosity had left Darcy unprepared for the truth that the joke was *not* particularly amusing. And high school was all about the truth.

"Anyway," she managed to continue, "it turns out that sixty thousand words is pretty much a novel. So I sent my novel to an agent, who sent it to a publisher, and now I write novels for a living." As Darcy spoke, the term "novel" began to feel alien in her mouth, like a word that had echoed with meaning in a dream, but made no sense upon awakening. "But here's the thing: I didn't really have to write two thousand words a day. I mean, that's like six pages, which is a lot of work. But you can write just one page a day, and in a year you'll have a novel."

The last word reverberated in the auditorium, having lost every bit of meaning it had ever had.

"Anyway, people say a lot of stuff about books, and writing, and literature, most of which sounds really complicated. But in a weird way, it's very simple. You just type a little bit each day, and you get better and better at telling stories."

The strange thing was, the silence had deepened as she'd spoken. Almost as if they were listening.

"And that's how every book ever got made. Thank you."

Standerson was the first to applaud, with great swoops of his hands that started wider than his shoulders and swung together like cannon shots. The crowd followed him, and through some mysterious alchemy of teenage graciousness, there were even a few cheers mixed in. And at that moment, Darcy could see why a million people loved Standerson with all their hearts, and why so many people spent their whole lives trying to make other people clap for them.

But the applause faded, and it was time for questions.

The first was asked by a tiny girl with thick glasses. She pronounced each word distinctly, like a ten-year-old entrusted with two lines in a school play. "I have a question for all three writers. Which of the five elements of a story do you think is the most important? Plot, setting, character, conflict, or theme? Thank you."

Darcy looked across at the others. Standerson was stroking his chin, taking it all very seriously. He cleared his throat and said, "It's a well-known fact that plot is the most important element."

Imogen glanced at Darcy, shrugging a little.

"For example, check out this weird thing that happened to a friend of mine," Standerson went on. "A couple of months ago, his girlfriend got a new job. It was a normal job at first, nine-to-five, but after a few weeks she started working later and later. She kept saying she loved the job, but never told my friend much about it. And she was hardly ever home at all. So finally one day he got fed up and drove out to where she worked." Standerson leaned forward, his voice dropping just a little. "And there she was, coming out the door at five o'clock on the dot. So my friend ducked down in his seat, and when she drove away, he followed her, and found where she'd been spending all that time. . . ."

He stopped, letting the silence linger. There were a few squeaks of the chair hinges, a smattering of whispers, but the auditorium held its silence for second after endless second.

Finally Standerson said, "And that's why plot is the most important element of a story."

A confused burble broke out, breaking the silence that gripped the auditorium.

"But what *happened*?" one of the kids yelled.

Standerson shrugged. "I don't know. I just made that up."

A kind of roar erupted from the audience, half laughter and half annoyance. As the librarian tried to calm the students, Darcy heard them proposing theories to each other, finishing the story on their own, as if the narrative *demanded* its own completion.

When the room had finally settled, Standerson leaned back and said, "See? That story had no setting, no theme, hardly any conflict, and two characters called 'my friend' and 'his girlfriend.' And yet you all hate me right now because you will never, ever know what happens next. Plot rules."

Standerson pulled his sunglasses from his shirt pocket and dropped them on the stage.

Laughter came from the audience, still mixed with annoyance.

Darcy looked at Imogen, wondering how they were supposed to follow that answer. Obviously, Standerson had done this whole plot schtick before. But Imogen was smiling, already standing up.

She walked over to where Standerson's sunglasses lay on the stage, and looked down at them disdainfully. Then she knelt, picked them up, and put them on.

"He's totally wrong," she said. "Character rules."

The audience went silent at once, like a light switching off. This had become a competition.

"I'm going to give you a hundred million dollars," she began, which set off a few trickles of noise. She raised her hands. "And you're going to make a movie. With all that money, you can put in whatever you want, right? Dinosaurs, spaceships, hurricanes, cities blowing up. No matter what your story is, your movie is going to look totally real, because of all that money, and because computers can make anything look real. Except for one thing. You know what that is?"

She waited in silence, daring them not to answer. Finally a boy called up, "Actors?"

Imogen smiled as she took off the sunglasses. "That's right. You're going to need actors, because people never look right when you make them with computers. They look wrong. They look creepy. So why is that? How come special effects can make dinosaurs and spaceships, but not people?

"It's because everyone you love is a person, and everyone you hate is too. You look at people all day long. You can tell from the slightest twitch when they're angry or tired or jealous or guilty. You are all experts at people."

God, she was beautiful.

"And that's why character rules."

Imogen dropped the sunglasses back onto the floor. The reaction was less intense than what Standerson had produced, but the entire audience was engaged now. Like a pendulum, huge and sharp, their eyes swung to Darcy, whose brain began to race.

What was she supposed to do? Discuss the importance of theme? Of *setting*? She suddenly hated Standerson and Imogen with all her heart. How dare they make this a contest?

And with that thought, the answer was obvious.

Darcy stood up and crossed the stage to where the sunglasses lay. She rolled her eyes at them, and there was a smattering of laughter. This might work.

"How many of you woke up this morning worrying about which of the five elements of a story was most important?"

There was a little bit of laughter, and two or three hands went up.

"Right, no one cares. But for some reason you're all waiting to hear what I have to say. You know why? Because at some point this became a *competition*."

She turned to look at the other two. Standerson was leaning back in his chair, smiling. He'd figured her out already.

"You want to see who wins," Darcy continued. "It's like with reality shows. Millions of people watch contestants who can't sing, just to see who sings the least badly. Or those survival shows, where you watch total strangers competing over who can eat the most ants. You never cared about ant eating before. But suddenly it's important, because you want to know *who wins*."

She knelt and picked up the sunglasses, and handed them back to Standerson.

"Which is why conflict always wins," Darcy said. "Because conflict makes it a story."

She crossed back to her chair and sat down. Her heart was racing, her body electric with a full flight-or-fight response. But the audience didn't hate her. They weren't applauding or laughing, but they all wanted to know what would happened next, like readers who had to turn the page.

We've got the juice, Darcy thought.

"Well, okay then," the librarian said. "Three different answers, all very interesting. Who's got the next question?"

CHAPTER 28

HIS HEAT PRECEDED HIM, ALONG WITH THE SMELL OF BURNING grass. A swarm of sparks streamed from the darkness to whirl around me, dancing on the invisible eddies and currents of the river.

And then the beautiful sound of his voice. "Lizzie, what happened?"

He was coming toward me, fire and warmth in the darkness.

"The man in the patched coat, he came back." My voice still trembled from my panic in the closet. "He took Mindy away."

Yama came to a halt, close enough that I could feel his heat. "I'm sorry, Lizzie."

"We have to find her!"

He didn't answer at first, and for a moment I thought he would tell me it was for the best. That the last thing I needed was a little ghost dragging me into the arms of the afterworld.

But he said, "Do you know where he took her?"

I could only shake my head.

Yama turned, surveying the emptiness around us. "So they could be anywhere. Predators are hard to track."

"But there must be some way to follow him. He found us, and we were thousands of miles from home!"

"Then he has a bond with you."

I stared at him. "What do you mean?"

Yama took a step closer, his voice calm. "The river is made from memories of the dead, but the bonds of the living tie it together." He reached up and touched my tear-shaped scar. "That's why I can hear when you call me. We're connected."

I pulled back, needing to think. "But I didn't call that old man, and I'm *not* connected to him. I don't even know his name!"

"He must know yours," Yama said. "Names have power here, Lizzie."

I remembered the first time he'd followed me home. Mindy might have said my name in the schoolhouse, or in my room. "Maybe."

"But it's not just your name. He feels something for you."

"Are you serious?"

"He wants something, badly enough that the river carried him to you." Yama put his hands on my shoulders. "Tell me everything he said."

I looked into his eyes. We hadn't seen each other since the fight, and Yama didn't know I'd gone to see the old man again.

"He wanted me to kill someone."

"To *kill* someone? Who?"

"The bad man."

It took Yama a moment to figure it out. "When did he tell you this?"

My arms crossed, covering me. "I went to find him, to see if he could help with the bad man. This is all my fault."

"No, it isn't. This is his obsession, not yours. Which means he doesn't want Mindy. He wants you."

My breath caught, and the darkness of the river closed in around me, as if I were trapped in my father's closet again. A psychopomp stalker. Perfect.

But with that trickle of panic in my veins, I saw why the old man had taken Mindy in New York, and not in my home, where I felt strong and safe. He'd chosen that moment in the closet because he *wanted* me scared.

This wasn't about Mindy at all.

I pushed the thought away, let myself feel the warmth of Yama's hands on my shoulders, his current on my skin. *This* was a real connection. How did that crumpled old predator dare to think there was anything like this between me and him?

"He said he was going to put her in his pockets."

Yama's hands tightened. "It's only a threat. Taking her was a way to get your attention."

"He *has* it. So what do we do?"

"Nothing. He'll come for you when he wants to talk again."

"Can't the river take me to Mindy right now?" I closed my eyes and thought of her face, but Yama gently pulled me closer, breaking my concentration.

"You can't follow a ghost, Lizzie. The river is made of them."

I opened my eyes. "Then what am I supposed to do?"

"You have to wait. He'll test your will, maybe for a long time. But I'll stay here as long as you need."

"Thank you." My voice sounded so earnest in my ears, I had to make a joke of it. "You aren't afraid of getting death all over me?"

Yama tried to hide his smile. "I'm afraid for you sometimes. But that didn't stop me coming when you called."

A shudder of relief went through me. Since our fight, part of me had been afraid that he would stop answering.

I pulled him close, needing his heat on my lips, his body against mine. My palms slid down his back, searching for the ripple of muscle beneath silk. As his scent filled my lungs, the river's current surged around us, and my hair whipped and tangled.

When our lips parted, we were silent for a long time. I wondered if we could stand there forever in the River Vaitarna's embrace, never getting hungry, never tiring, never growing old. In the end forgetting ourselves and fading, becoming part of the river.

Even here in his arms, my thoughts were so grim.

"What if it's too scary?" I asked.

"Then we'll go to my island," he said simply.

"But what if it's *all* too much? Ghosts, predators, the dead in every stone. What if one little stretch of sand isn't enough?"

"Then we'll find somewhere else. Somewhere you feel safe."

My heart faltered a little as I realized what Yama had said. After a thousand years searching for his island, he'd just offered to set it aside and find another place for me.

Yama came closer, his voice a whisper. "This is all happening so quickly, Lizzie. I wish I could slow it down."

"I just wish I could fall asleep." The thin edge of panic was still in my voice. "The old man said I didn't have to anymore, because sleep is a slice of death. So I stopped, and now I *can't*."

"Ah. That happens sometimes." He put his arms around me. "Take me home, and I'll show you a little trick."

It was strange seeing Yama in my room. I'd been with him in a bloody terrorist attack, in a river made of dead memories and the places it had carried us, but never anywhere so mundane, so much a part of my real life.

Thankfully, I'd cleaned up the mess on my bed, not wanting my mother to see piles of research about serial killers and missing children.

"Here we are," I said, wishing I'd also shoved the school clothes hanging across my chair into the laundry hamper.

Yama was gazing at the pictures over my desk. "You have so many friends."

I sighed. "Not these days. Since Dallas, not everyone gets me anymore."

"Death shows you who's real," he said simply, and turned to me. "This works better in the overworld."

"What does?"

A smile flickered on his face. "Sleeping."

"Oh. Right." If you couldn't get tired or hungry on the flipside, then sleeping there would be pointless as well.

I was already nervous having him here, so a few quick breaths was all it took to throw myself back into the real world. The streetlights coming through the windows showed color spilling across the room.

Yama closed his eyes and took a slow breath, as if savoring the air.

I reached out and touched his face. He felt solid, not like a ghost.

"Wait," I whispered. "You're here too? I thought you never left the afterworld."

His eyes opened. "Call this an extravagance."

I looked at my bedroom door. "But my mother . . ."

Yama pressed close, until he was near enough to whisper, "Don't worry, Lizzie. We'll be very quiet."

His breath brushed my ear with fingertips of air, and a little shudder went through me. For a moment, nothing pierced the sound of the blood rushing in my veins.

A little dizzy, I sat down on my bed. Yama settled beside me, and I leaned against him. Here in the overworld he wasn't sparks and fire dancing on the wind, but he was still warmer than anyone I'd ever held.

I turned. "Okay. What now?"

"Do you usually sleep in a jacket?" His voice was still a whisper, sharpening every word.

"Oh." I unzipped it, let it fall from my shoulders.

Of course, I didn't sleep in sneakers either. I pulled off my shoes and socks. And I never slept in jeans. I stood up and let them slip onto the floor. Then I crossed the room and drew the curtains tighter.

In the darkness, the psychopomp shine on our skin seemed to grow stronger. The night air felt cool on my arms and legs.

I settled back onto the bed, stretching out beside where Yama sat, basking in his warmth.

"Somehow this doesn't feel very . . . *sleepy*." There was a quaver in my voice.

"There's no rush." He was looking down at me, his brown eyes glittering in the dark.

I reached up and touched his right eyebrow, the little crook of it warm beneath my fingertip. I traced the curve of his shoulder, the hardness of bone and muscle beneath silk. My fingers prized open his top button, widening the triangle of luminous brown skin.

In one supple motion, he slipped the still-buttoned shirt off over his head.

My breath caught. I'd never been with him in the real world before, without the soft gray light of the flipside, or the fire and spark of the river's currents. There was no light except the shine of our skin, as if nothing existed beyond the edges of us.

He leaned forward and held his lips against mine with an impossible stillness, as if the moment had frozen, time itself unraveling. The only thing moving in the world was the breath between our lips. Suspended in that perfect instant, I ached for more.

He brushed a fingertip feather-light against the side of my neck, and I felt my own pulse rise up to meet his heat. My heartbeat gradually steadied in that long, still kiss.

When finally our lips parted, my breath shuddered a little. He stayed close, his eyes locked with mine, and for a moment the spell was too intense. I had to break it with a whisper.

"Do you ever sleep, Yama?"

"Sometimes."

I swallowed. "What do you dream about?"

"This," he said.

A soft cry stuttered out of me. It felt as if his fingers had found a loose thread inside me, and were pulling, making me fray and unravel. The leftover nervous energy from all those sleepless nights went scattering across my skin.

My hands reached up, my fingers deep in the thick waves of his black hair. I held him there, his eyes meshed with mine, his gaze sinking deeper into me every time a sigh trembled in my lungs.

Soon the loose thread had tangled into a knot, which Yama drew slowly tighter and tighter. The fear that had wound itself into my muscles was burning away at last, turning to something bright and sharp and hungry. The weight of all those undreamt dreams pounded in my head, crashing and breaking apart, my whole body arching against him.

In the end I nearly came apart, and for a moment all of me was lost, shattering into countless pieces like the memories of a ghost on the river. And I didn't care if I'd been born cursed, sullied and marked by death, because it had brought me here into Yama's arms.

He showed me how to sleep again, like Prince Charming in reverse, though back in the airport he had woken me with a kiss as well.

Maybe his lips cured everything.

CHAPTER 29

THERE WAS ANOTHER PRESENTATION AT AVALON HIGH, AND then another at a different school ten miles away, the entrance of which was also tricky to find. So it was late afternoon when Anton drove the three of them back to the hotel for a rest before the bookstore event that night.

Perhaps it was jet lag, or the adulthood-lag of having been in high schools all day, but when Darcy reached the hotel room she fell onto the bed, fully clothed.

It was a solid hour later that she awoke to find Imogen beside her, stripped down to a tank top and boxers and banging away at her laptop.

"You didn't sleep?"

Imogen's fingers kept moving. "Are you kidding? Book birthday. Must blog. Must tweet."

"Oh, right." With all her morning's labors, Darcy had somehow forgotten that *Pyromancer* was sweeping into the world today. "You're in print, Gen! You are a legit published and printed author."

"I know, right? Can't quite believe it." At last Imogen's typing paused. "I mean, there were those copies at the schools today. But do you really think there are thousands of them sitting on bookstore shelves? What if there was some kind of glitch? What if it isn't really happening?"

Darcy put a hand on Imogen's bare shoulder. "It's real, Gen."

"But how do I *know*?"

"Um, because your publishing company told you? And they have this, like, huge building in Manhattan."

"Good point. That building *is* pretty big." Imogen pushed a stray strand of hair out of her face and looked up at Darcy. "It's probably just a passing case of impostor syndrome."

"Is that a real thing?"

"Of course." Imogen typed a few keystrokes and spun her screen around. Among the clutter of a dozen open windows was a Wikipedia article.

Darcy scanned the first few paragraphs. Impostor syndrome was pretty much what it sounded like—believing that everything you'd accomplished was luck, or cheating, or fraud. Dreading that it would all be taken away once your fakery had been revealed.

"Crap. This isn't you, Gen. It's *me*!"

"It's every writer." Imogen turned the laptop toward herself again and stared at the screen. "Okay, reading this was a bad idea. Can you get a syndrome just from looking it up?"

"This one, you can." Darcy reached out and gently pushed the laptop closed. "But the cure is to go onstage in front of a hundred rabid Stanley David Anderson fans. They don't let impostors do that."

Imogen nodded at this simple wisdom. "After all, how bad can a roomful of Standerson fans be?"

"Never bad." Darcy pulled Imogen closer to kiss her, and whispered in her ear, "Just intense."

"Oh, Stanley texted while you were asleep. He wants to meet for an early dinner downstairs."

Darcy looked at her own phone. Nisha had texted with the message: *Hope you're having a good tour—364 days till publication!*

She sighed and jumped up from the bed. Her clothes felt sticky from having been slept in. "I'll shower first."

They cleaned up and dressed, Imogen in a crisp white shirt and leather jacket, lots of metal on her fingers. Darcy lofted onto her toes to straighten the shirt's collar, which had crumpled in the suitcase. She wore her little black dress, the one she'd been given the night they'd met. Surely there was some good luck left in it still.

The hotel restaurant was decidedly nonillustrious. TVs hung from the ceiling, blaring sports in all directions. The vinyl seat of the booth squeaked like a baby seal as Darcy slid into it, and the menu was full of dishes grandiose and generic, like "the International Cheese Experience." This phrase, Standerson pointed out, was more than half a haiku.

After they'd ordered the least greasy food they could find, he asked, "Had either of you ever done a school visit before?"

Imogen laughed. "I never thought I'd be in a high school again, and Darcy's barely out of one."

"Well, I salute you both."

"Much as I love praise," Darcy said, "I'm still mad at you for volunteering me."

Standerson held up his hands. "That was your publicist! You think she emailed the librarian by accident?"

"I can be mad at you both equally," Darcy said. "But it was fun, kind of. I liked the battle of the story elements."

"Because you won," Standerson said.

Darcy made a *pfft* noise. "You got way more applause."

"Nobody won," Imogen said. "Because the victory didn't go to plot, or character, or conflict. It was all about *setting*."

The other two stared at her.

"High school," Imogen explained. "Where else would the interlocking, interdependent elements of narrative be reduced to adversarial comparisons, when in practice they rely on each other to make a coherent whole?"

Darcy shrugged. "In every love triangle ever?"

"Both your points are valid," Standerson said. "And you should keep doing the school events with us, Darcy. There's no better research than interacting with our constituency."

Imogen laughed. "Darcy *was* our constituency, like, five months ago."

Darcy ignored this and asked, "What's the worst question you ever got?"

Standerson gave this a moment's thought, then said in a theatrical voice of doom, "'Where do you get your ideas?'"

"That one's easy for Darcy," Imogen said. "She steals them."

"I do not!"

"What about my closet scene?"

Darcy looked down at the table, her cheeks heating up. "That was an accident."

"Trouble in YA heaven?" Standerson asked, his eyes lighting up. "Spill me the beans."

"Do we have to?" Darcy pleaded.

"Yes." Imogen turned to Standerson. "So *Pyromancer*'s the first book in a trilogy."

He nodded. "It's awesome so far."

"Thanks . . ." The compliment flustered Imogen for a moment, but she managed to continue. "The second one just went into copyediting, so I'm starting book three—*Phobomancer*. It's phobias instead of fires. The protag is claustrophobic, and it was supposed to open with her trapped in a closet. Great, right? So I tell my girlfriend here about the idea"—Imogen flicked Darcy's shoulder—"and she rewrites one of *her* scenes so that *her* protag gets trapped in a closet, complete with claustrophobic panic!"

"That was a coincidence!" Darcy cried.

"I thought you said it was an accident," Standerson said.

"It was both! A coincidence because I'd already made a big deal about Lizzie's father's closet being fancy, and Mindy sleeping in closets, so using a closet made perfect sense. And it was an accident because I didn't realize what I was doing. Plus, Gen, you admitted it was way better than my first version, where the old man just shows up and whisks Mindy away."

"Yes, it was better," Imogen said. "But it was *my scene!*"

"But *your* new scene is better too!" Darcy turned to Standerson. "Now her protag starts out trapped in the trunk of a car! Much scarier, right?"

Imogen didn't argue, just ripped a tiny piece from the corner of her placemat.

"We all steal," Standerson said. "The trick is to steal from regular people, not other novelists."

Imogen nodded. "My first girlfriend was a pyromaniac, and I can't remember half the lines I stole from her."

"Ariel was real?" Standerson leaned forward, his eyes alight. "Tell me about her."

Within moments, he and Imogen were in a deep discussion of Imogen White, *Pyromancer,* and the intersections between the real and the fictional. Soon they were arguing character and plot all over again, and planning what to say at tonight's bookstore event.

Darcy huddled in her corner of the booth, happy to listen. But the shame of her scene stealing lay hot on her skin. The closet idea had been so perfect for Mindy's kidnapping, and the writing of it so easy. Not until she'd read the words aloud to Imogen had she realized that the whole concept had been pilfered.

Maybe that was the price of loving someone: you lost your grasp of where they ended and you began.

The event that night was downtown, in a smallish bookstore with two levels. The place was already crowded by the time Darcy, Imogen, and Standerson arrived. The ground floor was full and there were more kids upstairs, looming over the small stage, their legs dangling between balcony rails.

Not wanting Standerson's arrival to start a riot, the store manager was waiting outside to take him around to the freight entrance. But Imogen insisted on coming in through the front door. Nobody recognized her or Darcy, of course, and they were free to wander and observe.

Of course, they went to see Imogen's books first. There was a pile near the door, the flame-red cover dazzling in quantity.

"See?" Darcy said, straightening the top of the pyramid. "You're not an impostor."

"I could still be a *really good* impostor." Imogen's fingers glided across one of the covers, reading the embossed letters of the title like braille. "But if so, these are excellent forgeries."

Darcy rolled her eyes and dragged Imogen away into the crowd.

Standerson's fans were abuzz—with anticipation and with each other. Most wore name tags with internet handles, so online buddies would recognize them in the flesh. Spontaneous friendships were popping up, lubricated by T-shirts decorated with Standerson's catchphrases and covers. A whole community was face-to-face with itself at last, and seemed dizzily happy about it.

"Aren't you nervous?" Darcy asked.

Imogen looked up from the photography book she'd been leafing through. "I always feel safe in bookstores."

Darcy laughed. "So it really *is* all about setting."

"That appears to be the theme of the day."

"Well, I'm nervous for you."

"As long as it's not contagious." There was the barest twitch in Imogen's eye.

"I won't say another word."

They mingled in silence, Darcy taking the measure of the crowd. They were almost all teenagers, and the adults looked more like Standerson fans than chauffeuring parents. They were maybe three-quarters female, and about as diverse as the students that day had been—a California mix of Hispanic, white, black, and Asian, including a few kids from the subcontinent. But all of them had decided to come *here*, to a bookstore, on a cold and drizzly Tuesday night, when they could be at home with a thousand channels or the whole internet at their fingertips. When Standerson had called them a "constituency," it had sounded odd to Darcy, but maybe it was the right word after all.

Ten minutes before seven, Anton appeared and took Darcy and Imogen to the break room. The bookstore owner introduced herself, and Anton delivered the smoothest pitch for *Afterworlds* that Darcy had ever heard, picked up from their random conversations in the car and polished to perfection. The owner listened raptly and asked Darcy a half-dozen questions, none of which were how old she was, and Darcy found herself forgiving all of Anton's erratic driving.

And then, quite suddenly, it was time for Standerson and Imogen to take the stage.

"Okay. Nervous now."

"You'll be great." Darcy hugged her, squeezing tight for luck.

A moment later, a cordon of bookstore staff was leading the three of them out into a rush of gasps, tears, screams, and squees. The crowd had transformed into a conduit, an engine pumping fannish fervor into the room. Darcy was placed to one side of the bookstore's stage, only an arm's length away from Imogen and Standerson. The stage was only two feet high and a few yards across, and the crowd pressed close.

Standerson waited patiently for the noise to subside, and when the crowd was finally settled, he nudged them back into raptures with nothing but a sheepish "Hello." They had been primed by a hundred videos to know every flick of his hair, every lopsided smile. And as Standerson began to talk, each delivery of his catchphrase—"Books are machines for completing human beings"—brought screams of recognition from the audience, even a kind of relief. He was exactly what they had expected him to be, but better.

The intensity of the crowd had settled a little by the time he introduced Imogen. He went about it casually, as if she were a friend he'd met on the way to the bookstore. But his praise was unchecked, and the audience loved her before she said a word. She was family now, like a long-lost cousin giving a speech at a wedding. And when she dropped a reference to frequent bouts of dyspepsia into her usual spiel about obsessive-compulsives, they loved her even more.

Darcy watched closely, struck with a kind of astonishment that this was the same man she'd had dinner with, the same woman she woke up with almost every morning. The spellbound audience made them shinier, more than real.

Darcy tried to absorb the performance, knowing that next year she would have to do this job herself. But she could hardly imagine any crowd so zealous for her, so full of love.

An hour after it had all started, the bookstore manager declared that it was time for the signing. The staff set to wrangling the crowd into some kind of line, and a folding table was hoisted onto the tiny stage.

Darcy managed to squeeze in beside Imogen. "You guys were amazing."

Imogen only nodded. She was breathing hard and shallow, like a fish on dry land.

"That was the easy part," Standerson said. "Face-to-face is when it gets tricky."

"Right. I guess I should leave you guys to it?"

"Stick around," he said. "You can be our flap monkey!"

"Um, okay." Darcy didn't know what a flap monkey was, but she was certain that she wanted to be here onstage with them.

The signing line was a long and winding beast. They brought Standerson cookies; they brought poems and fan art; they brought still more questions about his characters, his videos, his well-known love of the semicolon. And of course they brought books to sign. Some had his whole collection, some only a single tattered copy of his first novel. Oddly, a few brought editions of *The Great Gatsby* (which he was known to love) or *Moby-Dick* (which he famously despised).

A dozen or so of his fans bought Imogen's book that very night. A handful of them camped out at her end of the table, happy to chat about their own obsessive disorders, a little giddy at their proximity to Standerson. Imogen kept them entertained with her research on how to set things on fire.

All this time, Darcy was a busy little flap monkey, taking books from customers and tucking the flaps into the title pages, so that Standerson didn't have to scramble for the right place to sign.

Darcy had soon learned the difference between full- and half-title pages. (The latter didn't have the author's name, and was therefore unsignable.) Sometimes she swapped places with the bookstore staff working the line. There was something pleasantly third-grade-teacher-ish about making sure that everyone had sticky notes with their names on them, so that their precious moments in Standerson's presence weren't wasted distinguishing a Katelyn from a Kaitlin, Caitlin, or Caitlynne.

It was a long two and a half hours, and Standerson's patter began to cycle and repeat. His joke about hand cramps came every five minutes, his disquisition on smoked bacon every ten. Darcy's mind began to entertain the possibility that she had always been a flap monkey in this signing line. She would always be a flap monkey in this signing line. . . .

But eventually, finally, it was all over. The exhausted booksellers were stacking chairs and ushering the last fans out the door. A hundred stickies littered the signing table, square yellow leaves dead and fallen. Imogen went missing, but was soon discovered lying on the carpeted floor in the biography section. Anton guided Darcy in front of the store owner one more time, and the two shared weary anecdotes about the night, old friends now.

Everyone was exhausted on the way home. Standerson was silent, and Imogen lay in the backseat with her head in Darcy's lap. Even Anton's driving was pacific, the roads back to the hotel dark and empty.

"Are you seriously doing this for another whole month?" Imogen asked.

Standerson looked dazed by the question, and only shrugged.

"I mean, how you can stand so much adulation?"

"Adulation is like rain. You can only get so wet." Standerson turned to Darcy. "Was tonight useful for you? Did you learn anything?"

Darcy nodded, trying to find words. She felt smarter about readers, and was astonished anew at the power of the written word. Also, she knew the difference between full-title and half-title pages.

But something bigger had happened, a rearrangement in her brain. Since age twelve, Darcy had wanted unashamedly to become a *famous writer*. That pair of words had always called up certain fantasies for her: writing in longhand on a rooftop veranda, being interviewed by someone clever and adoring, a Manhattan skyline in the background. All these images had been calm, even stately, completely unlike that night's bookstore event. But now Darcy could feel her regal daydreams transforming into something louder, messier, and full of joyous pandemonium.

"I'll be your flap monkey anytime," she said. "The owner can't wait for *Afterworlds*. She asked for an advanced copy, signed to her personally. I should write her name down, I guess."

"Anton will make it happen." Standerson saluted Anton, who laughed. "Indispensable media escort is indispensable."

As she smiled at this, Darcy tried to recall her first rattling moments in Anton's car the afternoon before. That flutter of anxiety over a trifling thing like death seemed so long ago now, before her first school visit, her first stint as a flap monkey, her first glimmer of YA heaven.

CHAPTER 30

OVER THE NEXT DAYS, I WAITED FOR THE OLD MAN IN THE patched coat to come to me again. I hated not knowing where Mindy was, and I kept imagining her being unraveled into flailing threads of memory for the old man's amusement. The only thing that kept me sane was Yama, his presence in my room at night, his touch, and his certainty that she was okay.

Being able to sleep again helped a lot. School was much easier, no longer teeming with the phantoms of leftover crushes and humiliations. The echoes of the past were still there in the hallways, of course, but they were quieter now. My last semester in high school drifted toward normal life, almost boring after everything that had happened since Dallas.

But the best thing about sleep was that it washed me clear. Some mornings, I was awake for five minutes before the memories flooded back in.

*　*　*

"Any news on the secret agent front?" Jamie asked at lunch one day. "I haven't seen him lurking lately."

"He's been busy," I said, which was probably true. Agent Reyes had drugs to interdict, death cultists to surveil. I was thankful that the FBI had bigger worries than keeping watch over me.

"But you guys keep in touch, right?"

"Yeah, we talk most nights." This was also true, because I had decided that Jamie was asking about my actual boyfriend now, and not the secret agent from her last question. It was amazing how I never lied to my best friend, as long as I interpreted her questions flexibly.

"Most nights? That sounds serious."

I smiled at her, because it *was* serious. Not just the time spent in my room, but our conversations on his windswept atoll, and our long hikes in another of his places, a mountaintop that I guess was in Iran. (Yama called it Persia, because he was old-school like that.) And we'd made plans to travel farther, even to Bombay, once I was ready to face its excessive ghost population. And, of course, one day in the distant future he would take me to his home in the underworld.

"You still haven't told your mom about him, have you?" Jamie asked.

I shook my head. "I've thought about it, but she's always too tired for big news. She's had enough to deal with."

"Can't disagree with that." A pair of non-seniors hovered at the other end of our table for a moment, wondering if they could sit there, but Jamie sent them away with a glance. "You can't keep her in the dark forever, though. That's just being mean."

"Of course not." I'd already been wondering about how that was going to work. When *do* you explain to your mother that you're dating a millennia-old psychopomp? Do you spell out the rules of life after death? Or have him over for dinner with a cover story all prepared? "I was thinking of waiting until after graduation. Like, maybe when I'm away at . . ."

My voice faded, because college was up in the air as well. I'd finished my applications last semester, but did newbie valkyrie even go to college? What was the appropriate major?

"Are you okay?" Jamie asked.

"Yeah." I gathered myself, needing a moment of honesty between us. "It's just been hard to think about planning my life lately."

She didn't answer at first, her eyes glistening a little in the cafeteria fluorescents. Lunch was almost over, and the clatter of dishes rushed in to fill the silence between us. "You mean, you feel like something horrible might happen again. So what's the point in making plans?"

I nodded, though my problem wasn't that death could strike at any moment, but that death was all around me. In the walls, in the air. Leaking like black oil from the ground. I couldn't hear the afterworld's voices all the time, not yet. But I could feel its eyes out there, watching me.

"That's really common," Jamie was saying. "A lot of people who've had near-death experiences can't make plans."

I only smiled. The words "near death" seemed like an understatement. I was traveling on the River Vaitarna, waiting to rescue a kidnapped ghost, sleeping beside a lord of the dead.

I wasn't *near* death, I was swimming in it.

"Or maybe it's survivor's guilt," Jamie said. "Feeling bad that you made it and all those other passengers didn't."

I rolled my eyes. "Did you buy a psych textbook or something?"

"No, that's from *Les Misérables*." She leaned closer and sang a haunting line, barely audible above the buzz of the cafeteria.

"Okay," I said. "Maybe it's about that too."

"At least you don't have to worry about those Resurrection guys anymore."

It took me a moment. "The Movement for the Resurrection?"

"Um, yes. The guys who almost killed you. Did they slip your mind?"

Oh. I remembered what Agent Reyes had said on our phone call. "There's a big standoff at their headquarters, right?"

She stared at me. "You mean, the one that every FBI agent in the country is headed to? I assumed you knew about it, Lizzie! Don't you have a boyfriend who might be shipped there sometime soon?"

"He doesn't do that kind of thing," I said.

"Crap." Jamie frowned. "I keep imagining him in a bulletproof vest. Is that wrong of me? It wasn't in a lustful way, much."

I shrugged. Men with guns seemed so ordinary now.

"Okay," Jamie said. "I'm starting to think it's not near-death syndrome *or* survivor's guilt. You're showing classic signs of being in denial."

"I deny that completely," I said, which actually got a smile from her.

The bell rang then, and as I got up to leave, Jamie reached

across the table and took my hand. "It doesn't matter what you call it, Lizzie. Just as long as you know I'm still here. What happened last month doesn't go away just because it's not on TV anymore."

I squeezed her hand, trying to smile. She didn't know that what had happened to me would never, ever go away.

That night my mother announced that we were making ravioli.

It's not as tricky as it sounds. You have to roll the dough out really thin, but we had a machine with little rollers for that, and we used a cookie cutter to make the pieces all the same size. For the filling my mother had decided on ricotta cheese.

"If I'd gotten home earlier, I could have made some," she said as we got started, giving the tub of store-bought ricotta a suspect look. Even before my father left us, she thought that buying things was sinfully lazy if you knew how to make them yourself.

"We'll survive," I said.

Soon the dough was made, and I was sending the first wad through, turning the machine's little crank to spin the rollers. My mother took the end that came stretching out, as thin as a coin and marked with the flecks of black pepper we'd ground into the dough.

We worked in silence for a while. This was the first time we'd cooked together since the old man had taken Mindy from me. I missed her ghostly presence in the corner, the way she watched us, intent but dutifully silent.

My mother started with her usual conversational gambit: "How's school?"

"Better," I said.

She looked up from the bowl of ricotta, which she was crumbling with a fork. "Better?"

"My friends have stopped tiptoeing around me."

"That's great. What about everybody else? I mean, the kids who aren't your friends."

"Jamie keeps them in line."

My mother smiled. "How is she?"

It took a moment to realize that I didn't have a good answer. "We mostly talk about me. I've been a pretty crappy friend lately."

Mom reached up with a dishtowel and dusted flour from my chin. "I'm sure Jamie doesn't think you're a bad friend. She probably doesn't want to talk about herself. She wants to be there for you."

"Yeah, she's pretty good at making me spill my guts," I said, silently promising myself that the next time I saw Jamie, I'd listen to her problems too.

"So what have you been spilling your guts about with her?"

I gave Mom a look. She wasn't even *trying* to be subtle. "Whatever I've been thinking about that day."

She gave me a look back. "Such as?"

Apparently Mom wasn't letting me off the hook. But I could hardly tell her that we'd been discussing my secret boyfriend, and survivor's guilt, and how near-death experiences leave you unable to face the future. And I couldn't tell her that my other best friend, the ghost of Mindy, had been stolen from me.

But I had to say something. "Some mornings when I wake up, it takes a long time to remember who I am. Like, it takes a while for everything that's happened in the last month to download into my brain. It's nice, not knowing. Even if it's just for five minutes."

She didn't answer, probably because the expression on my face didn't match my words. I was thinking about how Yama's lips made sleep possible at all.

We started building the ravioli. We cut out round pieces of rolled-out pasta dough, plopped a spoonful of filling into each, folded them over, and sealed them with our fingers. Mom ruffled the sealed edges with the tines of a fork, so that the ravioli looked like miniature calzones.

It was slow going, and at some point in the process I always wondered if it was worth all the effort. It took about half a minute to make each piece, and only a few seconds to eat it. But there was something tiny and precious about them, like furniture in a dollhouse.

"Have you talked to your father lately?"

I looked up at Mom. She never brought up Dad if she could possibly avoid it. "Not since I texted him a thank-you for my phone."

"I don't mean texting him. I mean really talking."

This was definitely weird. "Mom, I haven't talked to Dad since I was in New York."

"He still hasn't called you?" Anger curled her lips. Directed at him, not me, but I still felt like I'd done something wrong. "You two have to stay in better touch."

"Where's this coming from?"

"He's your father. You'll need him one day."

I had stopped working by now, and was openly staring at my mother. Her hands trembled as she worked the edges of the ravioli, showing what it had cost her even to mention Dad.

"For heaven's sake," she said a moment later. "We haven't even started the water boiling!"

She turned away to wash the flour from her hands, and I watched her add a long pour of salt to our biggest pot, then fill it up with water. The stovetop's lighter popped a few times, followed by the *huff* of flame erupting.

Mom stared down at the water, her expression hidden from me.

"Can you finish up here?" she said brightly, then headed toward her end of the house. "I just need a minute!"

"Sure. I won't let the water burn," I said, repeating an old and stupid joke from my childhood. For a moment, I wondered if she'd been crying. But over what?

One of her friends had probably told her that I needed family right now, and to get over herself when it came to my dad. But did Mom really think I needed *his* help dealing with all this?

I had her, and Jamie, and Yama. Maybe Mom didn't know about the last of those, but still, I had enough. All I needed was to get Mindy back.

I folded the last piece of ravioli onto itself. It was a not-quite-circular cut, a leftover scrap that barely held a half portion of ricotta. I managed to squish it closed, then clapped flour dust from my hands.

"Done," I said.

"Very tasty-looking," came a cold voice from behind me.

I spun around. The old man in the patched coat stood there in my kitchen, his skin as pale as flour.

Without a word, I reached for the knife block, pulling out a sleek boning knife.

"Now, now, Lizzie." He spread his fingers, hands out wide. His colorless eyes glittered in the kitchen lights. "There's no need for that."

"Be quiet!" I hissed, looking over my shoulder toward my mom's room.

"I'm never visible, child. At my age, the overworld is bad for one's heart."

I glanced at the floor—he had no shadow. But he still didn't belong in my mother's kitchen.

"This is *my house*," I whispered. "Get the hell out of here."

"But we have business to conduct."

"Not here."

He curled his fingers toward himself. "Then come across."

I checked the hallway again. Still no sign of my mom. My heart was racing, though, and the knife trembled in my hand. There was too much panic in my system to slip across to the flipside.

Unless I used the words that had first sent me over . . .

"Security is responding," I whispered, and the knife steadied, my panic shifting into something sharper and cleaner—an alertness in my muscles, sparks on my skin.

"Well, honey," I murmured. "Maybe you should pretend to be dead."

The floury smell of uncooked pasta changed to rust in my nostrils, and the flame beneath the big pot of water turned a pale and lifeless gray.

I was on the flipside, the knife shining dully in my hand.

"Interesting technique," the old man said, as if it wasn't. But he'd been watching carefully.

I no longer had to keep quiet. "Where the hell is Mindy?"

"She's waiting for you."

"No cryptic bullshit!" I extended the knife. "*Where?*"

"Shall I take you to her?"

I took a slow breath, then nodded.

He reached a hand up to his mouth. Like a child giving up an illicit wad of chewing gum, the old man spat out a little blob of black into his palm. I took a step back.

He made a fist and held it out, and darkness squeezed between his pale fingers. It dribbled onto the floor, more and more of it pooling around his feet, spreading in all directions.

"Interesting technique," I said. "By which I mean, that's disgusting."

"The river is the river." He opened his palm, welcoming me to step into the slick of oil he'd made.

I sighed, trying to pretend it wasn't so different from tapping the floor, like Yama did. "If Mindy isn't in one piece, I'm sticking this knife in your eye."

"Now *there's* my little valkyrie," he said with a smile. "But knives don't work in the afterworld, even on the living. And I wouldn't touch her for the world."

And he stepped into the puddle of black goo.

I clutched the knife, held my nose with two fingers, and followed him down.

The River Vaitarna carried us a short distance, no more than a minute's journey. The passage was steady, but thick with cold and grasping things. We emerged from the river into some kind of basement, its concrete floors glimmering with damp. The walls were tangled with pipes and junction boxes, and the only illumination came from flickering lights on panels full of switches and dials.

"I don't see my friend."

"She's here." The old man gestured vaguely at the space around us, as if Mindy had been boiled down and painted onto the walls.

"What do you want from me?"

He nodded happily at this, as if I'd asked the right question. As if it were up to *me* to figure out what was supposed to happen next.

"Do me three favors, and I'll give her back to you."

My grip on the knife tightened. "You kidnapped her. That's not how favors work."

"Perform three labors, then. Or grant me three wishes. Whatever you want to call them, the first is very simple: kiss my hand."

He extended his hand to me, palm down, its pale flesh gleaming with psychopomp shine. His glittering eyes narrowed to colorless slits.

It was all I could do to suppress a shudder. "Why do you want that?"

"To make our connection stronger. A convenience, nothing more."

The way he said "convenience" brought the lurking shudder out of me. It wrinkled my body, twisting my muscles around themselves, forcing out a hiss of breath.

"I don't want to be connected to you. I don't want you to come near me ever again."

"You misunderstand. I can reach you at any time, Lizzie Scofield. But I want our connection to go both ways. I want you to be able to call *me*."

A dry laugh pushed itself from my lungs. "Not going to be an issue."

"You may need me one day, little valkyrie. I'm good at so many things your dark-skinned friend is not. He may be older than me, but I can show you tricks he's too prim and proper for. And if I'm wrong about you, and you never call . . ." He spread his hands. "You won't ever see me again."

That promise was almost tempting. But three wishes and a kiss sounded too much like a fairy tale, one of those old-school, unedited Grimm stories with a horrible ending. They were always full of arbitrary rules: Don't leave the path. Don't eat the faerie food. Don't kiss the scary psychopomp's hand.

Not to mention, the thought of touching my lips to his pale skin was revolting.

"What else will kissing you do to me?" I asked.

"Nothing at all." He raised his right hand. "I swear."

I stood there, wishing I could ask Yama. But if I called him, the old man would disappear, along with any hope of finding Mindy.

"Listen, girl. If you don't want to play, we can always do this later. Say, ten years from now?"

"Ten *years*?"

"We can both live as long as we choose. So yes, a decade is the price for annoying me. Or you can kiss my hand right now."

"How do I know you won't just keep Mindy? You collect children like her, don't you?"

He shook his head sadly. "Not like her. She doesn't have what I want."

I remembered what he'd said the first time we met. "But what about all those memories of birthday cakes, of bedtime stories? Are you saying Mindy doesn't have those?"

"I'm sure she does, but I've already had a thousand birthdays, my dear. I've graduated to collecting endings. Sweet, beautiful ones that fade like sunset."

"What the hell are you talking about?"

His voice took on a singsong cadence. "You know when you finish a book, and it feels like all of those people in it have gone away to a party without you? That ache is in my pockets."

"What the hell does that have to do with children?"

"That's what I take from them, Lizzie," he said. "The ones who died too young, the sweet way that they slip away. Those sick little children, smiling up at their parents, knowing they're loved even as they fade into darkness."

I could only stand there, staring at the old man. He looked so happy, his bleached eyes radiant as they stared into the middle distance. His words had reached into the cold place inside me, the spot that had never warmed since Dallas, no matter how many times Yama's electricity coursed across my skin.

The old man wasn't a child stealer, not quite. He was some other kind of monster. Maybe there were simply no words for what he was.

His smile had drooped. "I'm afraid your little Mindy's end was quite dreadful. So, no, I have no taste for her."

"What made you like this?" I said.

"The war," he replied simply, his hands smoothing his pockets. "There were so many orphans. Every time I was called to another burning city, I found their little ghosts wandering, having died in terror all alone. Hundreds of them."

I stared at him in silence. It still didn't make sense.

"Knowing there are children who died loved, that helps to fight the memories." His face hardened. "But that's enough of a history lesson, girl. Make your choice."

At that moment, part of me just wanted to start stabbing him and not stop until my arm was too tired to move. Then I would look for Mindy until I found her in that basement or somewhere nearby. She was a ghost. She couldn't starve. I would keep searching if it took a thousand years.

But the old man knew how to disappear in an instant. And was it even possible to kill someone—another liver—on the flipside?

So I didn't stab him. Instead, I said, "If you're fucking with me, you *will* be sorry."

I must have put what I was thinking in my voice. His eyes widened, like translucent fish puffing themselves up to scare off a predator, and when the smile came again, it looked strained. But he extended his pale, shiny hand.

It hung in the darkness between us, one last chance.

"This sucks," I muttered to myself, and took a step forward. Then another step, keeping my eyes from the growing expression of satisfaction on his face.

I took his wrist, touching only his patched coat, the knife ready in my other hand, just in case he was lying about that too.

As I bowed my head, panicked thoughts crowded my mind. Fairy tales again: Was this some kind of afterworld trick to play on the unwary? Was I dooming myself to eternal servitude by kissing his bare flesh?

Of course, if that were true, then I was already Yama's slave a thousand times over.

I forced my head to descend the last few inches, until my lips brushed the back of the old man's hand. His skin was as cold as marble, but carried the same buzz that I'd felt traveling across Yama's, or my own. The old man's electricity was darker, though, as bitter as a pencil tip.

I dropped his hand and stumbled back, another shudder forcing its way through me. I gasped for air—I'd been holding my breath.

"Done. Are you happy?"

He breathed out a sigh. "Very."

"What else do you want?"

"For my second wish, I want you to say my name." He bowed. "I'm Mr. Hamlyn, Miss Scofield. Pleased to meet you properly at last."

"That's it? Just say your name?"

He nodded. "You'll need to know it, to find me when the valkyrie inside you wakes up. Perhaps if you said it a few times, just to be sure."

This was much less repulsive than kissing him, so I did what he asked, repeating his name quickly, trying to sound offhand about it. But a fresh trickle of nerves was moving through me. Maybe he'd just been warming up.

"Okay? What's the last one?"

"I want you to tell your rather impressive friend something. What's his name again?"

"Yamaraj."

The old man smiled. "Tell him I'm hungry."

With those words, he flickered out of sight.

I stood there, staring at the spot he'd occupied, a sudden emptiness in the darkness of the basement.

What had just happened? It had all seemed too sudden in the end, too easy, as if the old man had been scared off by something. I looked around—there were no sparks in the darkness, nothing but the scent of rust.

This didn't make sense.

But then I heard a whimper, the sound of a child snuffling.

"Mindy?" I cried. "It's me!"

For a moment there was no answer, but then a form emerged from the shadows. Her eyes were wide, her pigtails tangled and wild. She stared up at me through gray, teary eyes. "Lizzie?"

I ran to her and dropped to one knee, wrapping my arms around her. She was cold and trembling, her muscles limp beneath my grasp.

"It's okay, Mindy."

Her arms hugged me in return, but timidly, as if she were afraid I would change into something else. "You promised no one would get me."

I pulled back, looking into her eyes. "I'm sorry."

Mindy stared back at me a moment, and then her eyes scanned the darkness. "The bad man was here."

"No, it wasn't him. It was just . . ." I didn't want to say his name. I didn't want to think it. "Just some pomp. He's gone now."

But I still had no idea why the old man had disappeared, or if he was coming back. So I stood and took Mindy's hand.

"Let's go home. We'll be safe there."

She nodded, her hand small and cold in mine, and let me take her down into the river.

★　★　★

When we came up into my bedroom, I peered through my open door into the kitchen. My mother wasn't there, and the pot of water hadn't boiled over yet.

I wondered how long I'd been away. Those minutes in the basement had seemed like ages.

"I have to go make dinner," I whispered. "But you can watch if you want."

"It's okay. I'm going to Anna's closet."

I nodded, letting myself slip across into the real world. With my heart beating so hard, it was instantaneous. Colors bled into my room, and the smell of rust and blood faded from my nostrils.

Mindy still stood there, looking up at me.

"I'll never let that happen again," I said softly. "I promise."

"You can't promise."

"Mindy . . . ," I began, starting to explain that she was safe from Mr. Hamlyn, who didn't want little girls like her. But she was right—there were other bad men, old and young, living and dead and some halfway between. Too many to make promises.

"But you came and saved me." Mindy stood on her tiptoes, and gave me a real hug this time, her cold arms tight around me. "That's what matters."

I heard the sound of my mother coming down the hall. But I let Mindy stay wrapped around me even as I heard the hiss and sputter of the pot boiling over in the kitchen, my mother's arrival in the kitchen, and her annoyance that I'd left the water to burn.

CHAPTER 31

THE TOUR CONTINUED FOR SIX MORE DAYS—INTENSE AND insane, unreal and unforgettable. The pendulum swung from the boundless energy of public events to the muted stasis of airports and hotel lobbies. From exhilaration to exhaustion, from the heights of human connectedness to sitting in traffic jams.

But then it was over, and Darcy and Imogen found themselves at Chicago O'Hare saying good-bye to Stanley Anderson. It was as heart-shredding as the tearful end of summer camp, and as they walked down the jet bridge, Imogen said to Darcy, "The absence of old friends one can endure with equanimity, but separation from one's new book-tour buddies is unbearable."

The plane urged itself into the air and back to New York City, where Imogen and Darcy fell into bed for several days, the echoes of a thousand zealous readers in their ears. Before long they were back to work, because there was a new ending of

Afterworlds to write, and both *Phobomancer* and *Untitled Patel* to begin at last.

"This is your worst idea ever," Darcy said.

"Research!" said Imogen, walking around to the back of the rental car. She squeezed the key fob in her hand, and with an obedient beep, the trunk popped open. "That's weird. I don't even know what to call this thing."

Darcy crossed her arms against the early November chill. "It's called the trunk. Duh."

"No, this." Imogen opened the trunk a little wider, then closed it halfway again. "This thing in my hand, the thing that moves. Is it the door to the trunk? The hatch?"

Darcy realized she had no idea. Writing often did that—made her aware of all the different parts of things, and how many words she didn't know. "Great question. Let's go home and google it."

"Very funny." Imogen zipped up her leather jacket. "I'll look it up while you're driving around. My phone should work in there, right?"

"We're not going anywhere with you in the trunk! I haven't driven since I left Philly!"

"Bad driving is good. The guy who kidnaps Clarabella is drunk, remember?"

"Bad driving is not good! I mean, do you want me to tie your hands behind your back too? We might as well go all the way."

After a moment's thought, Imogen shrugged. "Didn't bring any rope."

"Can't you find someone else? At least if *they* kill you it won't be *my* fault."

Imogen smiled. "It's your fault anyway, because you stole my closet scene."

This statement was true enough to silence Darcy. If *Phobomancer* still began with Clarabella stuck in a closet, Imogen could have researched the scene safely at home.

For two months now, she'd been complaining that her opening lacked realness, because she'd never been locked in a trunk. So tonight she'd lured Darcy out into the mid-November cold with the promise of a new twenty-four-hour ramen place. It had all been a ruse.

"What if I have a wreck?"

Imogen shrugged. "Just go slow. It's safer in a trunk at twenty miles per hour than in the passenger seat at fifty-five."

"You're just making that up."

"Yeah, but I thought it sounded pretty good."

Darcy let out a groan. Imogen would not be dissuaded by personal danger. This was a woman who'd climbed buildings at college, and who still rode on the shifting platforms between cars when the subway was too crowded. Darcy had only one card left to play. "If we get into a wreck and you die, they'll arrest me for kidnapping. Probably murder!"

"Nope. I left a video explaining the whole thing on my laptop. You won't get worse than involuntary manslaughter."

Darcy hesitated. "Does this mean I get to look in your computer if you die?"

"Only the video folder! If you so much as peek in my diary, I will haunt your dreams."

With these words Imogen climbed into the trunk, and Darcy

was forced to come around to the back of the car. It was one of those roving rentals that occupied special parking places on the street. Imogen had unlocked it with her phone and found the keys waiting in the glove compartment. The whole process had been dangerously efficient, too swift for the brakes of sanity to take hold.

Imogen was curled around the laughably small spare tire, her neck at an angle that already looked broken.

"Maybe I should have gotten a sedan."

"Imogen. Do not do this. Please."

"Wouldn't be so bad if this jack wasn't jammed into my spine."

"I am *not* helping you kill yourself!" Darcy shouted. A man walking a large black dog glanced at her from across the street. The dog looked intrigued, but the man only turned away and coaxed it back into motion.

"Just a few miles. Ten minutes in here is all I need."

"I refuse," Darcy said. "I was promised *noodles*."

Imogen shrugged, or at least tried to in the confines of the trunk. "So you want me to ask the next person who walks by? It's three a.m., the hour of weirdos. I'm sure I can find *someone* who'd be into driving a stranger around in a trunk."

Darcy stared at her. "I can't believe you."

"And *I* can't believe how long I've banged my head against this scene!" Imogen unwound herself from around the spare tire, managing to kneel. "And it has to be perfect. If this book isn't fucking amazing from page one, Paradox won't publish it!"

"What do you mean? They bought the whole trilogy."

"They can still cancel the rest of the contract." Imogen slumped a little. "I got a call from my agent today. *Pyromancer*'s tanking."

"That's crazy, Gen. I saw you sign hundreds of copies."

"Yeah, there was a spike while we were on tour. But it's not selling at the chains, or anywhere else. They have two months of data now, and everyone's freaking out. My agent was at this big meeting at Paradox on Monday, with blame flying in all directions—too much red on the cover, the weird title, the mention of cigarettes on page one." Imogen let out a sigh. "And of course the girls who like girls."

"That *one* kiss?"

"And the famous dribble of candle wax. But it doesn't matter where they put the blame. The book's in trouble, which means the series is in trouble!"

Darcy shook her head. "But the middle book, whatever you call it, comes out next. *Phobomancer* doesn't come out for *two years*. By then, everyone will have realized how awesome you are!"

"I don't have two years. My agent wants me to give Nan a first draft in a few months, a really solid one, to show her what she's fighting for." Imogen gripped the front edge of the trunk. "And I'd be doing this anyway. This is where Clarabella starts to control her phobias."

Darcy stood there, unbelieving. All those booksellers and librarians, all those Standerson fans—they'd all loved Imogen. Since then, at least fifty rave reviews of *Pyromancer* had appeared online, and another half dozen in actual printed magazines and journals. Two of them with little stars beside them!

What more had Paradox been expecting?

"Okay," Darcy said. "I'll do it."

Imogen's smile lit up the darkness beneath the trunk door, or hatch, or whatever it was called. She tossed Darcy the keys and curled up again.

"Watch out for bumps."

"I'll watch out for *everything*." A slow, deep breath. "You ready?"

Imogen gave her a thumbs-up, and Darcy softly closed the trunk. She walked to the front of the car, wondering if anyone had been watching from an apartment window above. They must have thought this the world's oddest abduction.

Darcy sat for a moment in the driver's seat. The car was much smaller than anything she'd driven before. Her parents always said that big was safe. Though, as Nisha liked to point out, what they meant was safe for the Patels and not the other people on the road. But with her girlfriend curled up in the trunk, Darcy would have been happy with that kind of safe.

The pedals seemed too far away, but the driver's seat wouldn't budge. She gave up and started the car, then guided it forward at crawling speed.

It was strange seeing the city from the front seat instead of the back of a cab. Even stranger, driving evoked memories of high school. Her mind flashed back to senior year, to drunken passengers and arguments over radio stations. To making people hold their cigarettes out the window, and her father checking the odometer when she got home. To Nisha demanding trips to the mall, because with great automotive power came great sisterly responsibility. Darcy wanted to turn to Imogen and tell her everything.

But Imogen, of course, was in the trunk.

"Can you hear me?" Darcy shouted.

There might have been a thump from the back. But had it been an answer? Or was it just the death flailings of carbon monoxide poisoning?

At the next red light, Darcy pulled her phone from a jacket pocket. But as she brought up Imogen's number, she noticed a car in the rearview mirror.

A police car.

"Oh, crap," Darcy muttered.

The police had no reason to stop her and search the trunk, of course. She'd hardly gone above fifteen miles an hour. Could they pull you over for driving too *slow*?

Of course, making calls while driving *was* illegal. Darcy placed her phone on the passenger seat and stared straight ahead—the model driver.

Then she realized that the traffic light had turned green. How many seconds ago had that happened?

Darcy eased the tiny rental forward. The police car followed.

"Okay, going a little faster now," she murmured. Her grip tightened on the steering wheel as she increased her speed to twenty-five. What was the speed limit in the city, anyway? She'd never seen any signs. Did everyone just *know*?

The police car was still behind her. Not passing, not turning off.

Imogen hadn't foreseen this little problem with driving around in the middle of the night—there were *no other cars*. Darcy was a lonely and obvious target for law enforcement.

"Crap, crap crap," she muttered.

A thump shook the car. It had come from inside. . . .

"What is it?" she yelled.

No answer. Darcy's eyes darted down to her phone. Nothing.

"Are you okay?" she screamed as loudly as she could. "For fuck's sake, call me!"

But she didn't dare stop. The police car was right behind her, lurking and watching, and the wide lanes of Delancey Street were looming ahead. Darcy turned right, because right was easier.

The police car followed.

"Fuck!" she screamed, banging on the steering wheel. Another bump from behind the backseat came in answer. *Why was Imogen signaling?*

With a massive effort of will, Darcy pulled one white-knuckled hand from the wheel and grabbed her phone. She held it low, touching Imogen's name and turning on the speaker, then dropped it into her lap.

"Dude!" Imogen's voice answered. "It's called a *lid.*"

"*What* are you talking about?"

"I just googled that thing that goes over a trunk. It's called a trunk lid. Pretty stupid, right?"

"Why are you bumping the backseat?" Darcy screamed.

"Research! I wanted to know if you could hear me over the engine."

"I thought you were dying!"

"Seriously? Relax."

"There's a cop car right behind me!" But as Darcy cried out the words, a presence loomed on her left. The police car had pulled up beside her, and the officer in the passenger seat was watching her yelling to herself.

Darcy stared back at him, wide-eyed and terrified.

Imogen's laughter filled the car. "Awesome."

SCOTT WESTERFELD

"Shut up!" Darcy hissed through her teeth.

The officer gave her a slight roll of his eyes, and the car pulled ahead. Darcy kept the steering wheel in a death grip, driving straight until the police car turned off an endless mile later, disappearing back toward Chinatown.

A sigh escaped her. "Okay, they're gone."

"Good. I think this is all the research I can stand for one night."

"Great. Except . . ." Darcy stared ahead. Rising up before her was the Williamsburg Bridge, massive and inescapable, thanks to a row of orange traffic barrels to her right. "I think we're going to Brooklyn."

"Very funny."

"No, not really."

The tiny car was already climbing the slope of the bridge, and Darcy saw a pair of headlights approaching fast from behind. She accelerated, trying to match their pace. She was up to fifty miles an hour when the other car shot past.

"Dude," came Imogen's voice. "This feels like serious speed. Would you not?"

"No choice!" Darcy cried. "Matching traffic!"

The bridge was carrying her up, lofting her as high as the towers of Brooklyn ahead. The car that had passed sped off into the distance, and the sky flickered around her through a grid of suspension cables. For a moment Darcy found herself alone at the bridge's midway point, suspended above the glistening river.

It was really quite beautiful.

"I'm sorry your book isn't selling," she said softly.

She wasn't certain if Imogen had heard, but then a sigh came through the phone. "I know, right?"

420

"Why Paradox is freaking out already? It's only been two months."

"Because if this book doesn't sell, stores won't order my next one. Which *still* doesn't have a decent title."

For the millionth time, Darcy racked her brain for a better name than *Cat-o-mancer*. She wanted so much to help. "I'm sorry I stole your scene."

"Don't worry," Imogen said with a laugh. "It's *way* more interesting back here than in a closet."

Darcy allowed herself to smile. Maybe she had managed to help a little, and at least she hadn't killed Imogen tonight.

"We're almost across. I'll pull over the first place I see."

"Thanks for doing this."

"You're thanking me?" Darcy asked. "Like you didn't *make* me do it?"

"Did I put a gun to your head?"

"You threatened to use some random stranger! That's emotional blackmail!"

"I was *kidding*."

"Yeah, right." At last an exit had appeared, and Darcy slowed and drifted into the exit lane. A moment later, she was on a quiet street with wide sidewalks and shop fronts covered with roller doors. She brought the car to a halt and turned off the engine, then took a moment to flex the sore muscles of her hands, breathing deep and slow. Her whole body was a snarl of anxious tendons.

"Feel free to let me out *anytime*," announced her phone. "It's cold back here."

"Coming!" Darcy got out and went around to the back of the car. She scanned the pictograms on the key remote, then squeezed.

The trunk popped open.

"Fuck a duck," Imogen said, kicking the lid up with a booted foot. She uncurled herself and sat there for a moment, cracking her neck.

"You okay?" Darcy asked.

"It's just a crick. You didn't kill me."

As Imogen stood, Darcy stepped into her arms, needing the realness of her, the softness and the muscle beneath the leather jacket. "No, but I missed you."

When they pulled apart, Darcy realized that the street wasn't completely empty. Two guys in fedoras sat on a stoop nearby, and a young woman was skateboarding past. All three were staring.

"Never seen anyone get out of a trunk before?" Imogen muttered.

Darcy just giggled and handed her the keys.

They drove the car back to the same parking space, and Imogen did phone magic to return it to communal use. Then she announced something wonderful. . . .

There really was a new twenty-four-hour ramen place nearby.

She led Darcy around a corner, down an alley, and up a half flight of stairs. This late, the restaurant's rough wooden tables were empty except for a Japanese-speaking foursome on a very giggly double date. In the corner was a plastic good-luck cat as tall as a parking meter, tirelessly waving its paw.

Darcy ordered pork ramen with boiled eggs and bamboo shoots, and a beer to calm her frazzled nerves.

"Thanks for tonight," Imogen said when the waiter had left.

"It was fun, I guess. Once it was over."

"For me, too. Maybe I'll finally nail this scene."

"So what was it like back there?"

Imogen thought a moment. "It smells like a car, but greasier. And it's really uncomfortable. I guess we've spent a hundred years engineering car seats, and they soak up all that momentum pretty well. Trunks, less so."

"Lucky I didn't crash, then." Darcy spun the coaster in front of her, wishing she had a beer to put on it. "But Clarabella wouldn't be worried about comfort. She's just been kidnapped."

"Yeah, but being back there makes you feel like luggage. Scared luggage. You can't see out, so you're just tossed around without any warning."

"Sorry."

"Don't be silly. I forced you to kidnap me at emotional gunpoint."

Darcy smiled. "At last a confession. Did you get carsick?"

"Too much adrenaline." Imogen rubbed her neck. "And there was a draft in there—all that cold night air hitting me in the face. I could hear the tires against the road, and feel how the asphalt changed texture on the bridge."

As the beers arrived, Darcy considered these details. They had a realness that was missing in Imogen's current draft.

"To research," she toasted.

"Research!" Imogen drank and pulled out her phone, grinning as she tapped notes to herself.

Darcy took a long first drink, wondering what research her own draft was missing. Should she lock herself in a closet? Visit the dunes of White Sands? Go to an airport at midnight and wander the empty corridors? Or a gun range where people were firing automatics?

She looked around the ramen place, noticing the jar of pickled eggs on the counter, the pale blue Christmas lights strung along the ceiling beams. The world always had more details than you could remember, more than you could even see, and a thousand times more than you could ever write down. You were always deleting and forgetting far more than you could express in words.

It was that moment that she remembered what Imogen had told her tonight, which her mind still rejected as unreal. It seemed impossible that *Pyromancer* was tanking. Surely it had sold millions of copies, and this was all some accounting mistake that would be cleared up by morning.

As Darcy watched Imogen tapping at her phone, she mulled her outrage and disbelief, and also felt a small, formless fear growing inside her. It was the merest piece of something larger, a tentacle creeping beneath the door.

What would happen when her own book came out?

Nisha had texted today: *323 days till publication! Nervous yet?*

Imogen looked up and saw Darcy's expression. "I bummed you out, didn't I?"

"No. I'm just angry at the world for being stupid. And . . ." A shuddery breath. "This might sound kind of selfish, but I'm also scared. If your book can't find an audience, what's going to happen to *Afterworlds*?"

Imogen put her phone down and reached across the table. "Who knows? It's just random sometimes, I guess. Or maybe it *is* my superobvious flame-red cover, or the girls kissing, or the dread mention of cigarettes."

"Ariel doesn't even smoke!"

"But she hangs out in the smokers' den, as I foolishly mention on page one. But you don't have any red flags to worry about." When Darcy sighed at this, Imogen added, "And not because *Afterworlds* isn't gritty and real! It's just that you stayed away from the obvious hitches."

"Except an unhappy ending?"

"You're going to nail your ending, happy or not."

Darcy put down her beer. "This is crazy. I should be comforting *you*."

"I don't need comforting," Imogen said. "I need a killer opening scene. And a decent title for book two."

"Fucking *Cat-o-mancer*," Darcy said, casting an accusing glance at the giant plastic creature in the corner. The little engine inside was still making its arm wave, beckoning good luck, or prosperity, or whatever plastic cats were supposed to bring. "What's Japanese for 'cat'?"

Imogen thought a second, then shrugged and tapped at her phone.

"*Neko*," she said a moment later.

"*Neko-mancer*?"

Imogen laughed. "Manga fans might get it, but Paradox's marketing department?"

They tried other languages—*Gatomancer, Chatomancer, Katzemancer, Maomancer*—which produced amusement, but nothing useful, title-wise.

Two bowls of noodles arrived, steaming and fragrant. Darcy warmed her hands against her bowl as Imogen snapped apart both sets of chopsticks.

"At least I got noodles tonight," Darcy said.

"And I got an opening." Imogen lifted a piece of pork from the bowl and blew on it. "Maybe you should borrow all my scenes, so I have to write better ones."

Darcy groaned. "I'll never steal your ideas again, I promise!"

"Once a klepto, always a klepto," Imogen said with a shrug. "Hey, it's not like I hate thieves. I just wrote a whole book about a cat burglar."

"Wait," Darcy said, her first bite frozen halfway to her mouth. A lighter was clicking somewhere deep in her brain, trying to ignite.

Imogen finished chewing. "What?"

"Your protagonist in *Cat-o-mancer*, you just called him a cat burglar."

"He's a thief with catlike powers. So?"

Darcy waved a hand for silence. She stared into her bowl, willing her mind to penetrate the thickness of the broth, the tangle of noodles and shredded pork.

"Catlike powers . . . which he uses to steal things."

"Did someone say your sleeper-agent code word?"

Darcy shook her head slowly, until finally her disordered thoughts clicked into place. "*Kleptomancer*," she said softly.

Imogen paused a moment, then put her chopsticks down.

"You know, that's . . ." A longer pause. "That's pretty good."

"Because 'klepto' is a real word!" Darcy cried. "Everyone knows what a phobia is, and what a pyromaniac is. But none of those other titles *meant* anything."

"And kleptos are obsessive-compulsives." Imogen stabbed her chopsticks into her bowl and swore. "How did I not think of that?"

"You got too obsessed with cat ladies." Darcy smiled at the giant plastic cat.

Imogen lifted her bowl with both hands and bowed. "Thank you for your inspiration, Neko-chan."

"Hey! No praise for inanimate objects while I'm sitting right here!"

Imogen turned her beaming smile on Darcy. "Thank you, too, my love."

"You really like it," Darcy murmured, and felt her debt for the stolen scene finally lifting. "I guess you owe me a title."

"How about a name instead?"

Darcy shook her head. "A name?"

"Audrey Flinderson," Imogen said softly.

It took a long, confused moment for Darcy to understand. "Is that your real . . . I mean, your old name?"

Imogen nodded.

Darcy waited for something to change, for her inner machinery to shift so that Imogen became Audrey. But nothing happened.

Imogen was Imogen.

"So I can look you up now? Online and stuff?"

"You can." Imogen shrugged a little. "But you might not want to."

Darcy stared into her ramen bowl, wondering if she could expend an effort of will and cast the name away, like a dream forgotten on awakening. It didn't seem likely.

"Were you really that bad?"

"I was mostly pretty good. But when I wrote mean things, they traveled farther and stuck around longer. That's kind of how the internet works."

"Are you *trying* to be cryptic?"

"No, I'm succeeding." Imogen took a thoughtful drink. "But I should have told you my name earlier. I should have trusted you. I'm sorry."

A little stab of pain went through Darcy. "I thought you *did* trust me. Like, always."

"You were younger than me. You still are. And like I said, changing my name is one of the best things I've done." She took a slow breath. "But I'm trusting you now, that it won't change the way you see me."

"I promise it won't, Gen."

"The funny thing is, I kind of thought you already knew."

Darcy frowned. "Your name? How could I?"

"We were on tour together for a week, on a plane almost every day." Imogen waited for a reaction, didn't get one, and went on. "And you have to fly using your legal name, you know?"

"Crap," Darcy said. Sneaking a look at Imogen's ticket had never occurred to her. Of course, she'd never dug through Imogen's wallet either, or hired a private detective. This was what she'd wanted. To be told.

Imogen was trying not to laugh. "I guess it's good you don't write spy thrillers."

"Very funny."

"You're going to google the hell out of me, aren't you?"

"Probably."

"Thought so," Imogen sighed. "Just remember, the things we write, they aren't always really us."

CHAPTER 32

WE SAT ON AN OUTCROP OF ROCK, BLACK AND SHARP-RIDGED.
that rose up from a white sea. The surface of the snow was frozen
into glass. Wind-borne flurries uncoiled across it, the high sun casting halos in them, like gray rainbows. The mountains tumbled jag-
gedly away in all directions, down into parched and sandy valleys.

I didn't have a jacket, just a sweater, but from the flipside I felt
only tendrils of the cold. Still, the sight of that bright expanse of
snow was enough to make me shiver.

"You've got a thing for bleak places," I said.

Yama smiled. "It might be bleak, but it's almost silent."

Almost silent. That meant a few people had managed to end
their days up here, maybe unlucky mountain climbers haunting
the peak where they'd died. I hadn't seen any ghosts wandering
around, but Yama could hear their voices in the stones. This was
his mountaintop in Persia, one of those desolate places that Yama

needed to stay sane. How long would it be before I started needing them too?

I shook off that thought.

"I'm worried about Mindy. She spent all day in her closet."

"She's been afraid for a long time."

"This is the worst I've seen her." When I'd checked on her that evening, Mindy had been crouched in the deepest corner, behind the dresses hung in dry-cleaning plastic. Her hair had been tangled, her clothes unkempt. "Her voice sounds softer. Like she's fading away."

"She can't fade, Lizzie. She has your memories of her to keep her together, and your mother's."

"But what if she decides she doesn't *want* to exist, because it's too scary?" I turned from the snow-bright view to face him. "Can ghosts *make* themselves disappear? Like, spectral suicide?"

He shook his head. "She'll go back to the way she was. Ghosts aren't really affected by what happens to them. They only change as the memories of the living change."

"Then why is she totally traumatized?"

"Because of what happened years ago. That's still part of her."

I turned away from Yama. I could see what he was saying—Mindy was still eleven years old, still afraid of the man who'd murdered her so long ago. But I hated the idea that she was trapped with her fear forever. It didn't seem fair to give the bad man that much power.

And if the afterworld kept ghosts frozen in time, what would it do to me?

"We can change, right?"

"You and me? Of course."

"But do you *feel* seventeen? Or really old?"

Yama shrugged. "I'm not sure what 'seventeen' feels like. I was fourteen when I crossed over, almost old enough to take a wife."

"Now, see, that's just creepy."

"It was the way of my people." He said this a lot.

"Your people and mine are different." I said this a lot too. "But you don't really seem much older than me. You seem seventeen. Of course, that's probably what your people called *middle-aged*."

His crooked eyebrow rose, carrying a challenge. "In my village, people went from young and healthy to old and frail in a few seasons. There wasn't enough middle age to have a word for it."

"Okay, that sucks." It wasn't fair to make fun of people who'd lived in the late Stone Age, but sometimes it was just too easy.

"It takes some getting used to," he said. "Losing time. You're already days younger than you should be."

I blinked. That was a weird thought, that on my eighteenth birthday I'd be cheating, not really as old as my driver's license claimed. But much stranger was that I could live forever if I wanted.

"Mr. Hamlyn told me he never comes out of the afterworld. Like, he's worried he could die of old age any minute."

Yama sat up straighter. "He told you his name?"

"Yeah." I took a slow breath, realizing it was time to go into detail about how I'd rescued Mindy. "That was one of his conditions for letting her go. I had to learn his name."

"He wants you to call him."

"He thinks I'll want to, for some reason." I scratched my arms. Mr. Hamlyn's weird energy was still on me, like phantom insects.

"He also made me kiss his hand, to make sure we're connected. Was that some kind of trick?" I tried to laugh. "I mean, does he get my firstborn now?"

Yama smiled a little, put an arm around me, and answered with a kiss of his own. The warmth of his lips danced on my skin, erasing for a moment the lingering taste of the old man. The touches of freezing air softened around me.

When we pulled apart, he said, "It was no trick, but it's odd. Why does he think you'll want to call him?"

I just shrugged, not even wanting to guess. "His last demand was that I deliver a message to you: 'Tell him I'm hungry.' Does that make any sense?"

"It sounds like a threat."

"But he's scared of you."

"Of me, but not my people." Yama's voice faded a little. "I protect the dead, and he preys on them."

I waited for more, but Yama was lost in thought. As the silence stretched out, I started to wonder if I should go. Sometimes in these desolate places of Yama's, I felt like an alien, a cactus transplanted to the tundra. It was midnight back in San Diego, noon here in Persia, and a jet lag fuzziness was hitting me.

"I can see why psychopomps don't bother with sleep." I leaned my weight into Yama, closing my eyes.

He held me. "You still need to sleep, Lizzie. It will keep you from changing too quickly."

"We'll go in a minute," I said, but in the end it was longer than that.

★   ★   ★

When Jamie drove me home from school the next day, we found a strange car in the driveway. It was a two-door. Sleek, dark red, and very shiny.

"Looks like your mother has company," Jamie said as we pulled in.

"She's supposed to be at work." I looked up at the house. "Till seven."

"Okay. Weird." Jamie stared at the mystery car. "Those are dealer plates. You think she bought a new car?"

"Are you kidding?" I stepped out, looking around for anyone the car might belong to. No one was waiting at the front door. Nobody was in sight at all. "Since my dad left, we haven't even bought new towels."

"That's too bad." Jamie was out now, walking around the car. "It's a pretty sweet ride."

"Yeah, but why is it *here*?" I pulled out my phone. "I'm going to call Mom."

"Hang on." Jamie reached over the hood and pulled something from the windshield. "It's a note, Lizzie. For you."

She came around the car and handed it to me—a blue envelope. My name was written on it, but nothing else.

"Open it!" she cried.

"Okay," I said, but part of me was afraid. Something weird was going on.

I tore the envelope open, and a single piece of paper slipped out. It was a printed-out email, from my father to a Chrysler dealership here in San Diego. A passage in the middle was highlighted in yellow.

Dear Lizzie, this is for you, because of everything you've gone through . . . I had to stop there and stare at the car. Seriously?

"It's from my dad."

"I *knew* it!" Jamie cried. "The second I saw the dealer plates, I knew that this was some kind of terrorism-related guilt gift!"

I shook my head. "No way. My dad wouldn't *do* this."

"Clearly he has. What else does it say?"

I stared down at the paper, which had turned everything I'd thought about my father completely sideways. But as I kept reading, everything turned sideways again.

. . . especially now with your mother's diagnosis. I wish I could do more.

They'll slip the keys under the door. Love, Dad.

"No," I said softly.

Jamie was still laughing, her fingers stroking the curving lines of metal. But my mind went rushing back to two nights before, when I'd been making ravioli with Mom. What she'd said about my father: *You'll need him one day.*

This is what she'd been talking about.

"My mom's sick."

It took a long, twisting moment for Jamie's laughter to fade. "She's what?"

I held out the piece of paper, unable to speak. Jamie pulled it from my hand and read, her expression showing everything I was too shocked to feel.

"What diagnosis? What's he talking about?"

I shook my head.

"But you'd know, Lizzie! I mean, your mom would never tell *him* anything before she told *you*."

"She said something the other night," I managed. "About me needing him."

"No way." She crumpled the paper in her hand. "He must be fucking with you."

I wanted to believe Jamie, but my mind was still flashing back to everything Mom had said two nights before. *Jamie doesn't want to talk about herself. She wants to be there for you.*

My mother hadn't meant Jamie. She'd been talking about herself.

"She thinks I can't take it," I said softly.

Jamie shook her head. "Even if she's hiding something, Anna would have told him not to tell you! Not even your dad would just *forget* something like that."

As I stood there, some cold, impassive part of my mind worked it out. It was easier to tease apart my father's motivations than to think about what the note had just told me.

"He wanted to spoil me."

Jamie looked at the car. "You mean, to be nice?"

"Not that kind of spoil. This was a *spoiler*." I was breathing hard now. "He wanted to show that he found out Mom was sick before me. To make the point that *he knew and I didn't.*"

Suddenly my legs were too weak to hold me, and I sat down right there on the driveway. It wasn't like falling, just a slow collapse into a heap. I wrapped my arms around my knees, and my eyes closed.

A second later, Jamie was right next to me.

"It's okay, Lizzie."

"It's not."

Her hand smoothed my hair. "You don't even know what kind of diagnosis. It could be, like, for a root canal or something."

I didn't even bother to argue with that. People don't use the word 'diagnosis' for root canals. Nor does anyone buy a car for you when your mother requires dentistry.

Instead I said, "What if it's me?"

"What do you mean?"

"The attack in Dallas, whatever disease my mom has."

I opened my eyes and looked at her pleadingly. She didn't answer.

"What if it's all because of *me*?" I asked. "I'm not a valkyrie at all. I'm a fucking grim reaper."

"You're talking crazy, Lizzie." Jamie's voice was calm but stern. "You didn't cause what happened in Dallas. That was those guys from Colorado. And whatever your mother has, it's because of a bacteria or something. *Not you.*"

I shook my head. Jamie didn't know what was inside me, the cold place that resonated with the darkness of the afterworld. She didn't know that I could see ghosts, could cross over to the flipside, and could see the dead histories of things dancing in front of me. She hadn't seen the little girls, the way they looked at me, wanted me.

She didn't know that I was part of death now.

"It's inside me, Jamie."

She pried one of my hands loose from my knees and held it. "What is?"

"Since Dallas. There's something different about me."

"Of course there is. But nothing that can make your mom sick.

We should call her and find out what this is all about."

"Maybe it's always been with me." I squeezed Jamie's hand. "I grew up with Mindy. She's been here since before I was born."

"Wait. Who the hell is Mindy?"

Suddenly I had to explain it all. "My mother's best friend, when she was little. She was murdered. It changed my mother's life."

Jamie was just staring at me. I could hear that I was barely making sense, but somehow I couldn't stop talking. I'd hidden so much from her, from everyone, and I had to say it aloud now.

"I think it changed me too. I grew up with the ghost of that little girl."

Jamie stared at me a long time. "Are you serious? That really happened to Anna?"

"When she was eleven years old, her best friend disappeared on a trip with her parents. But they found Mindy buried in her own backyard. That's why my mom's always afraid for me."

Jamie dropped my hand. "You mean, like on that field trip last year, when she texted you every five minutes?"

I nodded.

"Crap," Jamie said. "I made so much fun of you about that."

"Mindy's always been here, since before I was born. That's why I'm changing so fast." Even if half the stuff coming out of my mouth sounded crazy to Jamie, it was helping me to say it out loud. I was a natural psychopomp, just like Yama had said.

Jamie squeezed my hand harder. "You know there's no such thing as ghosts, Lizzie. But why didn't you ever tell me about this little girl?"

"I didn't find out until after Dallas. Mom hid it from me." I looked down at the crumpled note, now on the ground. "Just like she hid being sick."

"Lizzie. We should call your mother."

"Sure." I put my hand on the bumper of the new car, pushed myself back to standing. I knew what I had to do now. "But not while she's at work. I bet she hasn't told them either. We can't just drop this on her."

"But it got dropped on *you!*"

"That's not her fault."

Jamie didn't look like she agreed, but said, "Okay. But I'm staying with you till she gets back."

"You don't have to." I took a deep breath, forcing myself to smile at her. "I mean, I kind of need to be alone. Please."

She stared at me, and I stared back. The cold place inside me was growing, keeping me calm.

"Are you really okay?" she finally said.

I nodded and gave her a hug.

Eventually Jamie was convinced, and I watched her drive away, smiling and waving at her. Then I walked to the front door and opened it. There on the floor was another blue envelope. I knelt and picked it up. Metal clinked inside.

"Lizzie?"

It was Mindy, peeking out of the hallway that led to my mother's bedroom.

"Everything's okay," I said.

"You look funny."

I nodded. No doubt I did look funny, like someone ready to calmly tear the world to pieces. The blue envelope ripped in half like tissue paper, the car keys dropping into my hand.

"I have to go away tonight. But I'll be back tomorrow, I promise."

"Okay," Mindy said hesitantly. "Where are you going?"

"To fix things," I said.

The new car had a fancy GPS system, which blinked to life when I started the engine. But instead of simply taking me to Hillier Lane in Palo Alto, the car wanted to dither and delay, to regale me with operating instructions and helpful hints and endless safety tips, as if it wanted to *get to know me.*

It had picked the wrong day for that. Two minutes in I switched it off and asked my phone for directions.

The cold place inside me had made me logical, somehow, and I had realized something. In some way—deep in his brain, in his heart, in his spirit—my father saw me the same way that Mr. Hamlyn saw ghosts. The same way the two of them saw everyone, as pieces in a game. Our emotions were just threads to weave amusing patterns with.

I couldn't fix my father, or what he'd done to my mother over eighteen years of marriage. And I couldn't fix Mr. Hamlyn either.

But I could fix the bad man.

It was almost three in the morning when I found Hillier Lane.

It shouldn't have taken eleven hours to get there, but I'd begun my journey at the start of rush hour, on a route that led me through the treacly heart of Los Angeles. It was also possible that I made a few wrong turns.

My phone's battery had started to fade two hours into the trip, so I'd switched it off and followed I-5, and then highway signs the rest of the way to Palo Alto. In the end I'd done something even more old-fashioned, asking a gas station attendant for help. It hardly mattered how long the trip took. I was a valkyrie. I didn't need sleep.

It was strange, seeing the bad man's house in the colors of the overworld. The bungalow wasn't gray, it turned out, but painted a sunny saffron orange, like runny egg yolks. But it wasn't a cheery sight. My valkyrie eyes were like a cat's—half on the flipside—and I could still see the dead girls paired with their gnarled little trees.

As I got out of my shiny new car, they turned to face me. But they didn't make me nervous anymore. I walked straight into them, and knelt next to one of the trees.

"I'm going to fix this," I announced, and began to dig.

My hands clawed at the neat circle of wood chips around its base, tossing them aside. The little ghosts looked on, curious and silent, as I worked. My hands reached loose dirt, then packed soil full of stones and bugs. I wondered if there were any neighbors watching as well, wondering what the hell I was doing. I wasn't so sure myself. I only knew that I was driven by a burning need to find the truth buried beneath those trees.

But then my fingers were grappling with the tangled roots of the tree, thick and gnarled and unbreakable. I swore, and looked up at the ghost looking down at me. It was the one in overalls with sparkly barrettes in her hair.

"Don't worry," I said. My hands were covered with dirt, and they ached from digging. "He's not getting away with it."

I rose and steadied myself, my eyes fixed on the bad man's front door. I willed myself across to the flipside as I climbed the porch steps. A moment later I was inside.

His bedroom was as tidy as ever, and the bad man was sound asleep beneath thick blankets. It was cold up here in northern California. I hadn't even noticed.

I stared down at him, for the first time unsure of what to do next.

Maybe I'd expected my anger alone to be enough. As if I could unwind the bad man with a glance. But reality was slowly seeping into my body. My muscles were cramped from driving all those hours, from digging with bare hands. My head pounded from grinding my teeth, and part of me wanted to turn my phone back on and call my mom. She would be worried senseless by now.

Instead I stared down at the bad man, listening to him breathe.

I couldn't just leave him sleeping peacefully. He'd done so much damage, and every moment he lived did more. It was the bad man's memories that kept Mindy's last hours alive.

I slipped my bottom lip between my teeth and bit down hard. The pain threw me back into the real world, and color rushed into the room. Like the outside of the house, the bedroom was full of color now—the curtains turned yellow, the walls a light russet, the blankets were patterned in dark greens. Even in darkness, the room seemed joyful.

I remembered the shovel under the bed. Maybe I could still find my evidence.

I knelt to peer into the shadows, and my eyes found the shimmer of metal. My reaching hand grasped the handle and pulled the shovel slowly out. Its blade slid, a giant fingernail against the wooden floor.

I stood up again, the weapon in my hands.

The bad man hadn't moved, but I couldn't hear his snoring anymore.

Was he lying conscious beneath his blanket, wondering at the sounds that had awoken him? Or had he only come halfway out of sleep, stirring a little before he slipped back into dreams?

I waited to find out, watching him.

Then I noticed the eyes staring back at me through the bottom of the bedroom windows. The curtains hung a bit too short, maybe so the bad man could peek out at his trees, his trophies. Lined up across this sliver of glass were five pairs of eyes, all of them peering at me, wondering what I was going to do next.

A shudder went through me, the realization that I wasn't here just for Mindy. It was so these little girls could fade at last, unremembered. With those eyes on me, I didn't have a choice anymore. Digging up their bones wasn't enough.

The sharp sound of a breath went through the room.

It was the bad man, peeking out from beneath the covers. Not at me, but through the gap under the curtains. He was staring out at his precious trees.

And he had seen the hole.

In the moonlight, it would be easy to spot that black opening, crude and dug by hand, as if something had scrabbled its way out from the cold ground.

"I'm here for you," I hissed.

He spun around, tangling himself in his bedclothes, staring at me with wide eyes, like a little kid seeing a monster in his room.

Fair enough. I was a valkyrie, after all.

"Why?" I asked him.

He stared up at me, shook his head a little, as if he didn't understand. Or maybe he didn't believe in me.

"Why do things to other people? We aren't your toys."

He didn't answer. The cold place was in my voice now. It didn't sound like me.

"We aren't here to be played with, or kidnapped, or shot at in airports because you have some fucking death wish!"

The bad man turned away from me. A pale hand emerged from beneath the blankets, reaching for the pill bottles next to his bed.

I raised the shovel at last, and brought its blade down flat on the bedside table. Wood and plastic shattered with a beautiful *crack*, and pills shot in all directions, skittering into the shadows like insects in a sudden light.

The bad man's pale hand hung there in midair, trembling, searching for the pill bottles, as if he still couldn't believe that any of this was happening. Then from his lips came a sound, a series of short little gasps.

I climbed up onto his bed, straddling the bad man, trapping him under the blankets. With both hands on the shovel, I pressed it down hard against his chest. The gasps grew sharper, until his whole body shook, shock waves traveling beneath me.

Through the bottom of the window, the little girls' eyes gleamed.

I could feel what was happening to the bad man. I could sense it in the air, the smell of rust and blood.

After a few minutes, his shaking and shuddering passed.

"Mr. Hamlyn, I need you," I said.

CHAPTER 33

"YOU HAVE FAILED TO TEXT ME ENOUGH," NISHA SAID STERNLY. "The purpose of this call is to inquire why."

"I text you every day!" Darcy put in earbuds and tucked her phone into her pocket. She'd been hanging up laundry to dry when Nisha called, an activity that made the big room look unwriterly. But bringing home wet laundry saved quarters, and at least now she had a distraction.

"You text with budgetary concerns, Patel, but not with *all the gossip*."

Darcy laughed. "What? So you can spill the beans to Mom?"

"I do not spill the beans, Patel. I *manage* them, selecting only the choicest for the parental palette. I am the mistress of beans."

"You are the mistress of bullshit," Darcy said.

"Only when I need to be. Now spill."

Darcy sighed, hanging one of Imogen's T-shirts over a chair.

Her little sister wasn't going to stop until she got gossip. And really, Darcy should have told Nisha about Imogen ages ago. "Okay. But this information is for verbal discussion only. No texting."

"I'm aware of the security issues."

Darcy lowered her voice, though her parents were a hundred miles away. "I'm with someone."

"I knew that," Nisha said.

"You did not!"

"You hooked up, like, five months ago."

Darcy only glared at a set of her own soggy pajamas.

"Let us review the evidence," Nisha said. "One: you haven't mentioned anyone. I mean, you live all alone for the first time ever, and you encounter no cuties? No one crushworthy in *all* of New York City? That's weird, Patel, even for you."

"Um, I guess."

"Two: you never come back and visit. Which means you aren't missing my shining wit, the only thing better than which is . . . ?"

"True love?" Darcy ventured.

"Precisely. And three: when I asked Carla if you liked anyone, she said, 'No comment.'"

"You asked Carla? Isn't that kind of cheating?"

"It's not cheating if you already know the answer. So I ask myself, why the secrecy? Why are we almost whispering?"

Darcy sighed. "You must have theories."

"Two of them. This person is older than you, right? Old enough to squick the elder Patels."

"Wrong! Well, maybe a little bit. But she's only— Oh, fuck!"

Nisha's laughter poured down the line. "*She?* So *both* my

theories are correct. Is there a German word for always being right?"

"I think it's *obnoxobratten*."

"This was so easy. You complete me, Patel."

Darcy lowered her voice again. "You haven't shared these theories, have you?"

"No, but you know they won't care, right? Or has Imogen not come out?"

"She's totally out, but . . ." Darcy groaned. *"Stop doing that!"*

"Can a shark stop swimming?"

"Yes, when it is *killed*. How did you know?"

"Pfft. Figuring out who was the easy part, since you never shut up about her. So was that tour thing with her real? Not just . . ." Nisha made a suggestive noise.

"It was publisher approved!" Darcy cried, then realized that her parents would be wondering the same thing, once they found out. "Shit. I was going to tell you guys at Thanksgiving. But it never came up."

"Um, I think you have to *bring* it up, Patel. You think Mom's just going to ask if you're gay?"

"I was going to, but Lalana was in Hawaii, and she kind of wanted to be there too."

"Wait. Aunt Lalana knows? You told her first?" A stormy silence filled the line, and Darcy realized that she'd made a terrible mistake.

"It's just, when she cosigned my lease, she made me promise to tell her everything!"

"This is a serious betrayal, Patel. There will be consequences."

AFTERWORLDS

"Sorry." Darcy lowered her voice still further. "But there's something I wanted to talk to you about, something Lalana doesn't know. It has to do with Imogen's name."

"Her name?" Nisha said with a snort. "No one in the family cares that she's not Gujarati. Well, except Grandma P., and she'll probably be more worried about the not-having-a-penis thing."

"No, not *that*. The thing is, she wasn't born Imogen Gray. It's a pen name, and she never tells anyone her real one."

"That's weird. Why not?"

"Because of stuff she wrote when she was in college. She doesn't want her readers finding it online. I guess she didn't want *me* finding it either."

"So you don't know your girlfriend's actual name?"

"No, she told me. But I haven't looked online yet. Just in case it's . . . weird."

"Aren't you scared she's a murderer or something?"

"Um, I think they would have arrested her. She uses her real name to fly and stuff. Also, she didn't *have* to tell me any of this."

"So why did she?" Nisha's voice dropped to a whisper again. "Her fake name is Gray! What if that secretly means Graybeard!"

"What?"

"Like in that fairy tale, the pirate who gives his new wife all those keys to the house. But there's one she can't use, because it's for the room where all his murdered wives are! What if this is like that?"

"That's Bluebeard, stupid. Greybeard is Gandalf's last name. Are you going to tell me she's a wizard now?"

"No. But you should totally turn that key." Nisha sounded dead

447

serious. "And you should probably do it before you come out to the parents. You know, just in case."

Darcy considered this. She'd thought she was being virtuous, not snooping on whatever Imogen had put behind her. But what if she was just being a chickenshit again?

Maybe Nisha was right, and it was better to get it out of the way.

"Okay, I'm going to look at it now. I'll text you when I'm done."

In the end, there weren't that many hits for "Audrey Flinderson."

Most of the results were from Imogen's blog in college. Darcy read a handful, and the only striking thing was how boring they were. She could see glimmers of Imogen's future style, but the sentences were shapeless, the stories rambling and uncertain.

Nearer the top of the first page were Imogen's movie reviews, more recent and better composed, and funny in a way that *Pyromancer* never tried to be. They were full of profanity, but nothing Imogen hadn't said in front of bookstore audiences. Darcy would've been mystified why Imogen had hidden her old self, except for the essay sitting at the very top of the search results. It was for a shared blog, and had the title "Unpopular Opinion: My Ex-Girlfriend Is a Bitch."

Darcy saved it for last. She read it slowly and carefully, with her heart beating slantwise in her chest.

It was brilliant, in a way. Scathing and caustic, witty and droll. The essay was about an unnamed ex in college, someone jealous and selfish and jaw-droppingly vile. It was a deft and savage portrait, dripping poison from every word. The essay was full of obvious exaggerations, but somehow it made Darcy believe the unbelievable about its subject.

It was horrifying but, like a bloody accident on the side of the road, Darcy couldn't look away. She was too wrapped up in the guilty pleasure of watching a stranger shredded in public. An awful person, who deserved it, and who somehow Imogen had loved for a while.

When Darcy was finished, she leaned back from the screen, a tremor in her breathing. The scary thing was, she'd seen hints of Imogen in every sentence—her passion, her intensity. She had even imagined the motions of her hands as the rant unfolded. This was essential Imogen, distilled by anger and betrayal.

And she'd been rewarded for it. The essay had over a thousand comments, and had been shared countless times. It would probably always be the first result for a search on "Audrey Flinderson."

Darcy tried to imagine reading this five months ago, the day after she and Imogen had first kissed. It was searing enough now. Back then, it would have been boiling oil poured on naked skin.

At least the secrecy made sense now. As Darcy sat there, she murmured Imogen's warning from the other night. "The things we write, they aren't always really us."

That was true, wasn't it? Maybe this essay was partly in character. Maybe Imogen had only been playing at being this wounded, vicious person, like when Darcy imagined herself as Mr. Hamlyn. All writing had some element of fiction in it, after all.

Unless, of course, it was the other way around, and Audrey Flinderson was only playing at being Imogen Gray.

Darcy shuddered that thought away, and pulled out her phone.

It was just a scary story, she typed to Nisha. *Nothing real.*

*   *   *

Winter spilled out its white heart on New York City. Frost spider-webbed the windowpanes in the big room, and fallen snow shushed the growl of trucks and cars outside. No matter how hard the ancient radiators clanked and wheezed, apartment 4E stayed cold, keeping Darcy in sweaters and Imogen in fingerless typing gloves. But the two never complained, because a chill in the air was a small price for all those windows, that view of the rooftops of Chinatown sharpened with glittering icicles.

It was the ending of *Afterworlds* that made Darcy shudder at night.

She'd rewritten the last three chapters many times now, a dozen tries at keeping Yamaraj alive and her romantic couple together. In some of the attempts, Lizzie gave up her human life, descending into Yamaraj's underworld kingdom to live forever in splendor, cold and gray. But those endings always left Lizzie's mother and friends grieving somewhere in the background, and Darcy's realization that guys with castles were sort of Disney had never faded.

In other versions, Yamaraj would give up immortality to live with Lizzie in the sunlit real world. These endings didn't leave Lizzie's friends and family hanging (and had no castles) but they introduced the nagging problem of Yamaraj's people and his sister Yami. All those ghosts were left behind, fading in the novel's rearview mirror like thousands of unwanted puppies on the side of the road. Even worse, in removing Yama from the underworld, Darcy would be erasing the last traces of Hinduism from her invented world.

Darcy had to find a third way, an ending that kept both characters' lives intact while still resolving the story (and leaving something for *Untitled Patel* to explore). She had to make Yamaraj deeper, more than just a prize to be won.

Those perfect last chapters had to be out there in the writing ether. But no matter how many rewrites Darcy began, or how hard she stared out the big room's rimed windows, this ending wouldn't come.

She asked for another extension, and got it, to the end of January. But Nan Eliot laid down the law—this was a final deadline, a drop-deadline, a line beyond which even a lord of the dead could not pass.

"My parents asked me about Christmas," Darcy said one night when her writing wasn't going particularly well.

"Yeah?" Imogen didn't stop typing.

"Well, 'asked' is probably the wrong word. They *expect* me to come down and visit them for a week. And it's not really Christmas. We celebrate Pancha Ganapati. It's a five-day thing, in honor of Ganesha."

Imogen looked up, her fingers pausing. "I thought your family wasn't religious."

"Not really," Darcy said. "But we put twinkly lights on pine boughs and give each other presents on the last day, which happens to be December twenty-fifth. Because the whole thing was invented to make little Hindu kids shut up about Christmas."

Imogen let out a laugh. "This sounds like a flexible religion."

"It's pretty fun, actually, and it's not like I have a choice about going." Darcy paused for a moment. This conversation was proving harder than expected. "So I was thinking, do you want to come with me?"

"That depends."

Darcy waited for more, but nothing came. "Um, on what?"

Imogen gave her a look. "Do they know about me?"

"Oh." Darcy's throat tightened a little. "No. I mean, I talk about you all the time, of course, so they know who you are . . ."

"But not about you and me."

"Nisha knows." Darcy sighed. It was always frustrating when her new life bumped up against the one she'd left behind in Philly.

"Yeah, she texted me about that." Imogen closed her laptop and leaned back in her chair, which meant this conversation was serious now. "Obviously it didn't come up when you were down there for Thanksgiving."

"I was going to say something, but my Aunt Lalana was with her boyfriend in Hawaii. She wanted to be there when I told them."

Imogen nodded, but looked a little tired. "Okay."

"Look, it's *not* okay! You're the most important person in my life, so it's not okay that they don't know. I just . . ."

It was hard to explain. Darcy's parents weren't going to freak out and disown her for dating a girl. If anything, they would giggle at her for having hidden it for so long.

But here in New York, everyone figured out on their own that she was with Imogen. Most of the people they met already knew about the two of them from the publishing grapevine. If anything marked them out as a couple, it was the fact that they were both YA novelists. Darcy loved how the first thing everyone said was, *Oh, you're those two writers.*

But in front of her parents, being in love with Imogen would be reduced to a phase, just like her writing "career."

"I just . . . ," Darcy started again, but it took a moment. "It doesn't feel right, having to *tell* my parents."

"They're just supposed to guess?"

Darcy shook her head. "It's so easy up here. And when I compare this new me to the old me back in Philly, it feels like I don't deserve who I am. Like when I showed up in New York, they gave me an adult card without checking. Everything gives me impostor syndrome."

"I think what you're trying to say is, you've been lucky so far."

"How is this about luck?"

A truck rumbled past below, its tires tempered by the snow into a long, exhausted sigh.

"I figured out what I was halfway through high school," Imogen began. "I had to explain it to my father while I was still living under his roof. I had to deal with friends who didn't like me anymore, with teachers who were mostly assholes about it, and with a school bus full of gossips and jocks and other assorted fuckwads, every single morning. And the cherry on the top was a vice principal who already pretty much hated me, so imagine his excitement when I added a girlfriend with a habit of *setting things on fire*."

Darcy stared at the floor. Having snooped her way through Imogen's high school yearbook, she should have figured most of this out already. "That sounds pretty crappy."

"It was the hardest thing I've ever done. Not all of us make it, you know."

The big room was quiet for a while, except for the whispers of car tires down on Canal Street. Darcy's hands curled into fists, because on top of her usual mix of clueless and ashamed, she was

453

angry now, for what a bunch of total strangers had done years ago to Imogen White and Imogen Gray.

It was Gen who spoke again first, her hands spreading. "But we all have different experiences, all equally valid. I guess."

Darcy looked up. "Even us lucky little shits?"

Imogen smiled at this, but her jaw was still a hard line.

"Do you want to come home with me or not?" Darcy asked.

"For Christmas with the family?"

"Not Christmas, Pancha Ganapati. And Carla comes over for most of the holiday stuff, so you won't be the only non-Hindu in the house."

"But I'll be the only person who's lying about why they're there."

Darcy didn't answer. She hadn't thought about keeping this secret as a lie, but of course it was. She was careful how she mentioned Imogen to her parents, and often had to change details in her emails to them.

"Is this because you looked me up?" Imogen asked. "You don't want them to know about me?"

"Of course not." This was the first time either of them had mentioned the essay aloud since the night Imogen had revealed her name. "I haven't thought about Audrey Flinderson much. Really, Gen, I don't care what you blogged about in college."

Imogen let out a sigh. "Well, good. So this is just you being a chickenshit."

"It's not about being afraid!" Darcy cried. Suddenly all that mattered was that Imogen understand her, completely. "When I sold *Afterworlds*, I didn't just get a book deal. I got a whole new life, one that came with no assumptions about who or what I was. And

I know how lucky that is, like winning the lottery. But it's still *my* lottery ticket, and I don't want to give it up! And part of that is not having to define myself."

Imogen was shaking her head. "You define yourself all the time, Darcy. You hold my hand when we walk down the street. You think people don't notice that? You never hear it when some homophobic fuckhead says something?"

"Of course I do." Darcy reached across the desk. "But holding your hand is like breathing—it's easy. It always has been. That's the way it *should* be, right?"

"Of course," Imogen said. "But it doesn't always work out like that. Back in the hallways of Reagan High, holding Firecat's hand was like setting off a bomb."

"That sucks, but that isn't how it's been for me," Darcy said. "And I like my life the way it is. I don't want to see my parents being *understanding*. I want everything to stay exactly the way it is between you and me and our friends up here in New York. *I like it in fucking YA heaven!*"

Imogen listened to all this, and then sat staring out the window for a long time. Her fingers were twitching just a little, as if she were typing to herself.

"Sure," she finally said. "Who wouldn't want that?"

"So you understand?"

Imogen nodded. "This is your dream life, and you don't want to mess with it. But it's not my dream life to sleep alone in your parents' guest bedroom, or steal kisses from you when no one's around. I don't want to spend Christmas being your five-years-older secret girlfriend."

"Pancha Ganapati, not Christmas," Darcy said, quite clearly. "And what does this have to do with your being older than me?"

"It makes the whole thing more embarrassing." Imogen stared out the window again. The radiator beneath the desk began to tick and wheeze, building up to another burst of warmth.

Darcy managed to smile. "*Now* who's being a chickenshit?"

"*You* are! The chicken is officially *you*," Imogen said. "But if I go along with you and lie to your parents, then I'm one too. And I'm supposed to be older and wiser."

"Older and wiser than me? That's not saying much."

"Look, we all feel like impostors sometimes, but you don't have to about *this*. If you want to make your dream life real, you have to connect the new Darcy to the old one." Imogen's voice dropped. "Just like I had to connect Imogen Gray to Audrey Flinderson. I had to tell you, even if it made you hate me."

"Never," Darcy said, squeezing Imogen's hand. "That's not what this is about. It's just that finishing my book, telling my parents, and the rest of growing up—everything's taking longer than I thought."

The morning of Darcy's first full day back in Philly, she and her sister were busy stringing pale yellow lights around the Ganesha painting that their mother had brought down from the attic that morning. Lord Ganesha stood with one heel in the air, ready to dance. But he was also meditative, his palms open and facing upward. A pair of freshly cut pine boughs arched over him, giving off a bright forest smell and shedding needles on the beige carpet.

"Twinkling or not?"

Nisha stood back, surveying their work. "Twinkling, clearly."

"Okay, here we go." Darcy plugged in the lights.

After a moment, Nisha shook her head. "This is mere blinking, Patel. It's way too slow to constitute twinkling."

"Maybe they need to warm up?" Darcy's father had always been in charge of the lights. But both her parents were in the kitchen, flooding the house with the smells of roti and coconut and sugar at high heat. "Why is Dad cooking, anyway? I thought he wasn't allowed to when guests were coming over."

"I think they want us to have quality time together." Nisha lifted one foot, half imitating Ganesha's pose. "In other words, they want me to acquire gossip."

"Seriously?"

"You should hear Annika every time I get a text from you. She wants details. She wants *analysis*."

"Ugh. I thought they were getting better." Darcy lay back on the carpet. "Dad hasn't bugged me about going back to college in, like, a month. Driving me home from the train last night, he even asked me how my *career* was going!"

"Yeah, I talk about your 'career' all the time, mostly to annoy them. But now they've started saying it too." Nisha placed her hands in prayer position and bowed at the waist. "You're welcome."

"Thanks," Darcy said. "But can I point out that it really *is* a career? Like, with actual money?"

"So you say. But without my parental engineering, the elder Patels would be visiting you once a week." Nisha paused to wipe away an imaginary tear. "And in return I am given no twinkling lights."

It was true, the lights were still only blinking.

"But I brought you presents!" Darcy pointed to a pile of boxes wrapped in bright orange and waiting to be deployed around the shrine. The presents had been painstakingly selected over the last few months, because Nisha was notoriously honest about gift quality. They included a subway map phone cover, train tickets to New York for spring break, and a T-shirt emblazoned with a death-metal version of Glitter-Mane, Nisha's second-favorite Sparkle Pony.

"Those are mere objects, Patel. You made me guess all the good gossip."

Darcy rolled her eyes. This was all because Aunt Lalana had found out about Imogen first.

"So do you only like girls now?" Nisha asked.

"I don't know."

"That answer bores me, Patel. You must *look* at people now and then. Like, random hotties on the street. Are they ever boys?"

"I don't *look* at anyone else. I don't think about it that way." The lights were speeding up a little, almost twinkling now. "Maybe I'm Imogen-sexual."

Nisha snorted. "I believe the technical term is 'adorkable.'"

"Why do you care, anyway?"

"I'm just curious. Plus, the elder Patels are going to ask these questions after you leave. It's my job to have the answers!"

Darcy took a deep breath. "I don't know if I'm going to tell them yet."

"Don't be a chickenshit, Patel."

There was that word again. For a moment, Darcy wondered if Imogen and Nisha were coordinating their attacks.

"Seriously, it's the first day of Pancha Ganapati," Nisha said. "Perfect timing!"

It took a moment for Darcy to understand. Ever since they were little kids, she and Nisha had always focused on the last day of Pancha Ganapati, when presents were opened. She'd half forgotten that tonight, the end of the first day, was about clearing up misunderstandings in the family, about making things right.

"When did *you* get all religious?"

Nisha shrugged. "I'm in it for the math."

"What math?"

"Dude. We invented zero. And there's this mantra from three thousand years ago—it's just the powers of ten, from a hundred up to a trillion. How cool is that?"

Darcy raised an eyebrow. "It's possible that you and I have different interests."

"Listen. Dad gave me this book for Hindu kids, and it said that if you burned every copy of the Vedas, the same truths would be rediscovered. That only makes sense if you're talking about the *math*."

"Huh." Darcy glanced at the painting of Ganesha. The lights had finally started to shimmer. "That's what all this is to you? Just numbers?"

"*Just* numbers?" Nisha snorted, and her face took on a look of adamantine certainty. "The universe is math on fire, Patel. That's my faith."

Darcy didn't answer, thinking of Sagan and his Angelina Jolie Paradox. Maybe that was the point of truth—you could erase it all you wanted, and it was there to be discovered again.

*   *   *

For dinner that night, Annika Patel had gone into full Gujarati feast mode, arraying half a dozen small dishes before each place at the table. In addition to the usual okra and chickpeas, there were curries made of ivy gourd and bitter melon. The roti was homemade, as attested by its charred edges and the loud cursing of Darcy's father all that afternoon.

Even for Darcy, who had rejected the family's vegetarianism so long ago, the smells rising up from the table were mouthwatering. And as still more side dishes arrived, she was hit with a pang of missing Imogen. It would have been wonderful to explain the nuances to her, to help her dissect the yogurt-soaked dumplings and steamed taro leaves, and watch her sample the sinus-clearing chutneys.

To know a family is to eat its feasts, Darcy thought, deciding that next year Imogen would be here.

She glanced across the table at Aunt Lalana, who had arrived just before dinner. She was looking back at Darcy with expectation in her eyes.

Great. More pressure.

"This looks amazing, Mrs. Patel," Carla said, and Sagan nodded. The two were traditional guests for the first night of Pancha Ganapati, and both were back from a semester of college looking older and wiser. Carla's hair was cut short and sleek, and Sagan had replaced his glasses with contact lenses. Such superficial changes, but they reminded Darcy that her friends were growing up at least as fast as she was.

When her mother asked what courses they were taking, Carla

launched into a disquisition on the British eighteenth-century novel. "There was this whole genre called the supernatural explained. It's not even the 1800s yet, but all these writers are already sick of paranormal. So they start writing horror novels where everything creepy turns out to have a logical explanation. Well, sort of logical."

"You mean, like every *Scooby-Doo* ending ever?" Sagan asked.

"Exactly! They *want* the genre tropes, but they can't *handle* the genre tropes."

"Those meddling kids," Sagan said, tearing a piece of roti in half.

"I always hated that when I was little," Darcy said. "Are the books any good?"

Carla shrugged. "The sentences are crazy long. But it's like Shakespeare; you get used to it in fifteen minutes."

"I suppose Darcy will be an English major too," Annika Patel said. "Imagine, getting to read novels all day long."

There was a quick exchange of glances among the teenagers at the table. Darcy's college career was still a given, of course. But it wasn't her mother's assumption that made Darcy bristle. It was the fact that she already read several novels a week. Maybe she hadn't plowed through any eighteenth-century gothics lately, but half of what she read hadn't even been published yet. Surely that was more interesting than being forced to swallow proto-*Scooby-Doo*.

She was about to make this point when her mother spoke again.

"Speaking of novels, I have an announcement." Annika paused a moment, gathering everyone's attention, then turned to Darcy. "I finally read your book."

There was another pause, another exchange of glances.

"You were supposed to wait for it to be published!"

"That's what I was going to do. But then I realized it wasn't coming out till *next* September."

"Only two hundred and seventy-six days," Nisha said brightly.

"I mean, really," Annika said. "Does it take eighteen months just to make a book?"

Darcy's mind flooded with answers—sales conferences and copyedits, advanced readers' copies and cover designs—because she'd asked the same question herself many, many times.

But what she said was: "And you read all of it?"

"Did you think I wouldn't make it through?" Her mother laughed. "It takes more than a little violence to scare me off."

"She read that first chapter out loud to me," her father said, all smiles. "Very chilling."

"Thanks." Darcy waited for the rest. Not more praise, but her mother's recognition of Rajani's ghost.

"I loved how they could go anywhere in the world, just by wishing."

"The river isn't exactly *wishing*, Mom."

"I suppose not. But it was clever of you, using the River Vaitarna. I didn't know you were still interested in religion."

Darcy blinked. She'd been thinking about her parents' faith for the last six months of rewrites. "So you didn't mind that I used Lord Yama as a character?"

Her mother waved a hand. "He wasn't really Lord Yama. He was just some boy."

"Oh," Darcy said. "But what about Mindy?"

The others were all watching carefully, though only Nisha knew about Annika's murdered childhood friend.

"She was cute. And funny."

"Funny? And cute?"

"Because she was such a little 1970s kid. I could just *see* those braids. And corduroys!" She turned to her husband. "Remember when you used to wear them all the time?"

He laughed. "I think I've still got a pair somewhere."

"Um, but there wasn't anything else *familiar* about her?" Darcy asked.

Annika Patel frowned. "How do you mean?"

Darcy sat there, not sure what to say. Kiralee had been right, of course—it was a terrible idea to talk about Rajani aloud, at least until the series was finished. But Darcy couldn't believe that her mother had missed the parallel entirely.

It felt like a failure of her writing. Or maybe her mother simply wasn't haunted by her past. Maybe she had left all that behind in India.

"I just thought you might have noticed . . ."

Darcy couldn't go on. Bringing up Rajani at a crowded dinner table risked exorcising her from the quiet, gray place in Darcy's mind where the story had been born. It risked every page of *Untitled Patel* being somehow different, somehow broken by the revelation.

But why was her mother being so clueless?

"What is it, dear?" Annika Patel asked.

The whole table was staring at her now. She had to say something, anything to protect her little ghost.

"Um, I have a girlfriend."

The moment of silence wasn't very long, but it felt timeless and huge and echoing. Everyone's eyes shifted from Darcy to her parents, the only two at the table who hadn't known already. They looked more baffled than anything else, but to be fair, the statement had been a giant non sequitur. Aunt Lalana was smiling with approval, at least.

Nisha was the first to speak. "Smooth, Patel."

The spell broken, Darcy said, "I wanted to tell you guys. We've been together for a while now. I really like her."

In a strange way, it felt like her first performance as an author on the stage of Avalon High School. There hadn't been time to get nervous, so the words she needed had simply appeared in her mouth.

"A girlfriend? Well, I didn't expect that." Annika Patel's smile looked skittish for a moment, then settled. "You know we love you, Darcy, always."

"Of course I know," Darcy said, and she always had, but the hearing of it struck her somehow. She skipped a breath, and the lenses of two unshed tears alighted on her eyes, making everyone at the table look sharper, clearer.

"Salubrious occasion is salubrious," Sagan said softly.

Then a puzzled look crossed her mother's face. "Wait. Was I supposed to get that from reading *Afterworlds*? Did I miss something?"

"Not about that. It was just . . ." Darcy didn't know where to go from there. "Imogen's really nice and I think you'll like her. And I'm sorry for taking so long to tell you."

Her father spoke up. "You chose the perfect time, Darcy."

She smiled back at him, as if she'd told them on the first night of Pancha Ganapati on purpose, and not just because she was a lucky chickenshit. After all, the timing *had* been perfect.

She was fine with being lucky—this family, this made-up holiday, this certainty that she was loved.

This was her faith.

CHAPTER 34

MR. HAMLYN WAS ENRAPTURED WITH THE LITTLE DEAD GIRLS, until I explained that they wouldn't be to his taste. They had not been loved at the end.

"And you leave me with *that*?" he asked, pointing at the ghost cowering in the corner.

The bad man's spirit had risen up a few minutes after his body had gone still. He was skinnier than I'd expected, in flower-patterned pajamas and white socks. He'd hardly noticed me, too busy staring out at the five little girls in his front yard. Maybe he'd always suspected they were out there, and thought his nightmares were coming true. Or maybe he thought the nightmare was hap-pening now. He hadn't said anything, just crawled into the darkest corner of the room and covered his eyes.

"Yes," I answered Mr. Hamlyn. "I killed him. Now cut him to pieces, please."

The old psychopomp looked me up and down, at the dirt beneath my fingernails, the shovel in my hands. His smile grew and grew, until it seemed twisted and wrong, too big for his face.

"I knew you had it in you, girl."

I pointed the blade of the shovel at the bad man's ghost. "Teach me how to take his memories apart."

Mr. Hamlyn gave a theatrical little shudder. "They're very *nasty* memories. You should start with something sweeter."

"I'm not going to make a quilt out of him. I just want him *gone*." I looked out the window at the little girls. "And to set them free."

"He's dead. His memories won't hold anything for long." A shrug twisted his frame. "But I suppose we can hurry things a bit."

That was when Mr. Hamlyn showed me what was in the pockets of his patchwork coat.

It was a piece of memory he'd found, something awful. It was so rare, he said, that I could travel the river for a hundred years and never feel one brushing against the back of my neck. But I would certainly notice if that ever happened—the shiver that holding it gave me was very particular, like an eel wrapped around my spine, cold and squirming.

He said it was like a diamond, forged under unimaginable pressures, so that it cut lesser memories to pieces. Such threads formed only when something unimaginable happened, like the death of a whole city by fire. He had seen it happen half a dozen times.

"Be very careful with it," he said. "Anything that can cut a ghost can cut you too, even in the afterworld."

It was the perfect tool for psychopomps like him.

The little girls faded as we worked. The bad man had remembered them best of all, better than their own families, even. As his ghost parted into bright, shimmering strands, the girls dwindled and sputtered, finally departing one by one.

Free at last, or simply gone.

I saw more than I wanted to that night, the bad man's whole grisly career flashing past as his threads pulsed in my hands. But as awful as those visions were, there was something elegant in Mr. Hamlyn's work. Like a cross between a surgeon and a storyteller, he teased out and sliced away single threads from the tangle of a life.

But he had no desire to collect anything so foul, and in the end we cast all those carefully cut pieces into the Vaitarna. That's all the river was—endless millennia of human memories boiled down to black sludge. I wondered how it could smell so sweet.

"Thank you," I told Mr. Hamlyn when we were done.

"There's no thanks better than being right."

I looked at him. "Right about what?"

"That you would call me." He smiled. "Though I admit, it was sooner than expected."

I started to say that there was no way I'd ever be calling him again. But how could I be sure? My future was up in the air, both as a valkyrie and as a human being.

Everything changes when you take a life.

It would have been easy to let the river carry me home, but my real body was here in Palo Alto. I couldn't leave it behind, or my shiny new car, for that matter.

When I turned on my phone for directions back to the highway, it woke up sputtering: six messages from my mother and fourteen from Jamie.

Maybe if they'd left only one or two, I would have listened to them. But the thought of all those voice mails growing steadily more anxious made me switch the phone back off. But first I texted them both:

I'm okay. Will be home this morning.

The highway was easy to find, and there were plenty of signs pointing to Los Angeles. But my timing was terrible once again. After four hours of driving I found myself approaching LA smack-dab in the middle of morning rush hour.

It was also breakfast time, and I hadn't eaten since lunch the day before. Maybe I didn't need sleep anymore, but here in the overworld food was not optional.

I stopped at a place called the Star Diner in North Hollywood, choosing it for the parking spot right in front. A mercifully efficient waitress brought me scrambled eggs and toast, which I devoured in about three minutes. Eating simple, ordinary food edged me back toward reality.

Morning sunlight slanted in through the diner's picture windows, as if the afterworld didn't exist. The tables were trimmed in cheery, glittering chrome. Sitting there drinking coffee, I didn't feel like someone who'd cut apart a ghost last night. I wasn't sure how I felt, exactly. Not angry anymore, because the bad man was gone, but not triumphant either. I should've been exhausted from driving all night, but even that was missing. It was as though I'd excised some part of myself along with the bad man's memories. Only the cold place remained.

Then I reached into my wallet to pay, and a business card slipped out. It had a blue seal in the upper left corner, and the name Special Agent Elian Reyes in the center. I remembered what he'd said to me on the phone:

You should always report murders, of course.

And that's what I'd just done: committed murder. What else would you call breaking into an old man's house in the middle of the night, waking him up, and leaning on his chest until he has a heart attack?

It hadn't been an accident.

The business card was frayed and soft from being in my wallet. I'd memorized the information ages ago, figuring that if you have your own personal special agent, you should know his number. Learning the digits by heart had seemed funny at the time.

It didn't seem funny now.

You should always report murders, of course.

What would happen next back in Palo Alto? Someone would find the bad man's body, sooner or later. The police would be called, and couldn't fail to notice the smashed bedside table and the pills scattered across the floor. They would ask the neighbors if anyone had seen something strange, like a car pulling up at three in the morning. Maybe a wild girl digging up his lawn with her hands.

As I sat there staring at the dirt under my fingernails, the eggs in my stomach began to squirm. I'd turned on my phone in front of the bad man's house, and sent two texts, and made that collect call from near my house. In a phone company databank somewhere were numbers connecting me to his mysterious death.

The kicker, of course, was my fingerprints on the handle of

his shovel, which I'd slid back into its spot beneath the bed before leaving.

A dry little laugh forced its way out of me. I wasn't a particularly clever murderer, was I? Nor was my defense going to be the sanest thing ever heard in a California courtroom: "I did it to free five little dead girls, and so my ghost friend doesn't have to worry about the bad man ever again."

I took a slow breath, letting the fear of being caught flow through me. It was better than feeling nothing. Better than letting the cold place grow until it swallowed up the rest.

There were so many things I couldn't change: what had happened to those people in the airport, whatever was wrong with my mother. Last night, at least, I'd done something rather than nothing.

And you can't put a valkyrie in jail. We can walk through walls.

If there was a punishment for what I'd done, it wasn't going to come from the world of phone records and fingerprints, of laws and prisons. It would come in the transformations taking place inside me. As Yama had tried to warn me on that lonely island: whether ghosts were real or not didn't matter, what mattered was what we decided to make ourselves.

I slipped Agent Reyes's card back into my wallet, and left the waitress a big tip.

My mother was waiting on the front steps when I got home.

"Nice car," she said when I got out. I think she meant it.

"I know, right?"

We took a moment together, amazed that my father had spent real money on me. I sat next to Mom on the steps, still uncertain how to feel. *In trouble* seemed wrong, like something for little kids, not murderers. I couldn't tell whether she was angry, or sad, or exhausted. Or maybe just sick.

"Did Jamie tell you about Dad's note?" I asked.

"Of course."

"Then what is it? Your diagnosis?"

"Not yet, Lizzie." She held up a trembling hand. "You disappeared for twenty-one hours. You don't get to set the terms of this conversation."

Angry, then. I didn't answer, just nodded.

"Where the hell did you go?"

"Driving."

"For *twenty-one hours*?"

"Yeah, I know." I still wasn't tired. I wondered if I would ever sleep again. Probably not without Yama's lips to help me, and would he ever touch me again after what I'd done? "Driving helps me think. It's a pretty comfortable car."

Mom took a deep breath. I could *hear* her biting back harsh words.

"Jamie told me you have a boyfriend."

"She did? Seriously?"

A grim smile crossed my mother's face. "She didn't say anything until this morning, when you still weren't home."

I sighed. Fucking LA traffic. "Yes, I have a boyfriend. But this had nothing to do with him. I just needed to get away."

She gave me a long, appraising stare. But she turned away with a sigh, as if I were something unknowable.

Fair enough. I didn't even know myself.

"Are you going to die?" I asked.

"Not any time soon. But we'll get back to that, and to your boyfriend."

Not any time soon. If that counted as good news, then the world sucked.

Mom stood up and went over to the car, opened the driver's door, and leaned in. "Jesus. A thousand miles, Lizzie?"

"Like I said, it helps me think."

She shut the car door and came back to the porch. She stood over me, a parent over a child. "Where did you *go*?"

Only the truth would do. "Palo Alto."

"Is that where your boyfriend lives?"

"No. I went to your old neighborhood."

She stood there staring at me, her anger blunted for a moment. This telling-the-truth business was oddly effective.

"You know that old photo in your room?" I asked. "I needed to see the house where you grew up."

She shook her head. "Why?"

"Because you never told me about Mindy. She was haunting you and you didn't tell me. But she was *there*, Mom." I could feel the cold place retreating as I spoke, so I kept going. "Every time I played outside when I was little, she was there. And even now when I'm traveling, or when we drive anywhere, she's there in the way you worry. Every day of my life, her ghost is with us. Every day!"

Mom didn't answer, but I didn't have any more words, so we were silent for a while. I wondered if Mindy was standing on the other side of the front door, listening.

Finally my mother said, "You don't know what it's like, when your best friend disappears."

"Maybe that's because you *never told me about her.*"

"I'm not going to apologize for that. Not today. And it wasn't something I could just tell my child about. They found her in her own backyard, Lizzie. You have no idea."

I nodded, even though I knew better than she did how horrible it had all been. I'd seen every detail played back in the bad man's memories. The only thing I didn't understand was why my own mother had hidden it from me.

"Look, I get that it was awful. But—"

"If you get it, then why would you disappear for *twenty-one hours*? Why would you drive away and turn your phone off? You vanished, just like she did!" Something shuddered in my mother's chest. "At three this morning I got up and checked the backyard, Lizzie, in case you were buried there!"

Her voice broke at the end, and the sound of it was awful, like every fear she'd ever had was tangled in her lungs.

"Oh, right," was all I could manage.

She was staring at me, waiting for more, and I wanted to say how thoughtless I'd been, how I would never disappear again. I wanted to break down and cry.

But I kept seeing what *I'd* been doing at three that morning.

"I'm sorry," I said at last. "Really sorry."

She nodded at that. "Good."

"But I'm not Mindy. Okay?"

My mother thought about this, as if it were something that could be debated. But finally she nodded again. Then an odd look crossed her face.

"I never told you her name."

"Really? Maybe I looked it up online."

Mom shook her head. "But that was her nickname. In the newspapers they called her Melinda."

"Then you must have told me."

I could see her weighing this, and not quite believing it. But it was the only possible explanation.

"Mom, will you just tell me about your diagnosis now? *Please?*"

"Okay." She nodded and closed her eyes. "You know how I've been tired all the time? My doctor thought it was anemia, not a big deal. That's why I've been taking iron tablets."

"You have?" My voice was weak. Now that she was finally telling me, I wasn't sure that I wanted to hear this.

"But iron didn't help, and my blood counts kept getting worse. A lot of conditions can cause this, so there were a lot of tests— lupus, hepatitis, HIV." She opened her eyes. "It wasn't any of those. It didn't make sense to tell you until I knew something for sure."

"But you told Dad."

She nodded. "With my blood counts, it might've been something that could cause heart failure. Maybe out of the blue. So yeah, your father had to know."

"Heart failure?" I shook my head. "You said you weren't going to die any time soon."

Mom nodded. "My heart's fine. The diagnosis went in another direction. What I have is called melody . . . crap." She cleared her throat and tried again. "Myelodysplastic syndrome, it's called. Everyone just says MDS."

I took my mother's hand. "What does that mean?"

"It means my blood's all messed up, right at the source. They finally got around to testing my bone marrow. There are stem cells in there that make your blood cells. Mine are broken."

"Broken? How the hell does that happen?"

"They don't know. When I was a couple of years younger than you, I worked as a house painter. We used benzene to strip the paint back then. We should've worn masks, I guess."

"And *that's* what did this to you? Some chemical you inhaled, like, thirty years ago?"

"We don't know." She took both my hands in hers. "But the important thing is that it's not genetic. You don't have to worry about this happening to you."

"But I *do* have to worry about it." The reaper was in me, sweeping across my life, across the lives of everyone around me. It was in the marrow of my mother's bones. "So what happens next?"

"Well, nothing wonderful. Blood transfusions, maybe a stem-cell transplant. We're talking about years of dealing with this, and we don't know how it'll work out. But I'm younger than most of the people who get this disease, which is lucky."

Lucky, like surviving a terrorist attack.

"Real luck is taking another flight," I said softly.

My mother didn't hear me, or she didn't understand. "I've got decent health insurance, so we probably won't lose the house. And this is not going to make me an invalid, so you don't have to be chained to your mother. You'll be off at college for most of it." She looked at me. "Are you following all this, kiddo?"

I shook my head. "I got lost somewhere between blood transfusions and losing our house."

"Right." She took a slow breath. "I guess you didn't sleep last night."

"Not at all."

"Maybe we should go into details later. Along with that boy-friend conversation we're going to have."

"I'd like to go to bed."

My mother hesitated, just to show that she was within her rights to make me sit here apologizing for the rest of the day, but had decided to be merciful. "Okay. But you know I have to meet him, right?"

I nodded. "He's really nice and I think you'll like him."

"I hope so." She hugged me then, hard and long, and when we finally pulled apart, she was smiling. "I'm glad you got home in one piece."

I felt forgiven, at least a little, even if my mother only knew a tiny slice of what I'd done the night before. Her absolution fell on something darker than she knew.

She held out a hand. "Keys."

So I gave her the keys to my shiny new car, as if that made up for everything, and told her I was going to bed.

Mom stayed outside, giving the new car another once-over, so I slipped into her room.

"Mindy?"

No answer, and the closet was empty. I had an awful thought: What if the bad man's memories had been the only thing keeping her from fading? What if I had just erased my ghostly friend?

But then I heard a giggle behind me.

I turned and saw a shadow scampering away. Following the giggling to my own room, I found Mindy sitting on my bed.

"Finally!" She smiled, patting the blanket for me to sit beside her. "I thought Anna was going to yell at you *forever*. She's pretty mad, huh?"

"Yeah, she was upset."

"You're naughty, sneaking away like that."

I stared at Mindy. Her hair was combed straight again, tucked neatly into two little pigtails. She looked so happy, more at ease than I'd ever seen her. It was as if she already knew that the bad man was dead.

"You didn't used to be bad," she said, still smiling.

"I had something important to do. Remember how I said I'd fix things?"

"Like what?" she asked, patting the blanket again.

I sat down, speaking softly. "Last night I went back to your old neighborhood, and I got rid of the bad man. You don't have to worry about him."

"What bad man?" Mindy asked.

It took me a moment to speak again. "What do you mean?"

"What bad man did you get rid of?" She giggled a little. "And why was he so bad?"

"Because he . . ." I didn't finish. "You don't remember him?"

She made a show of thinking, squinting her eyes. "Not unless you mean your dad. He was pretty annoying."

Of course. The part of Mindy that had been terrified all these years had existed only in the bad man's head. All that remained of her now was what my mother remembered, the carefree child of eleven.

Things were fixed far better than I'd imagined.

I swallowed something hard in my throat. "Yeah, he was annoying. But he's gone now."

"It's just us three!" Mindy leaned across the bed and wrapped her arms around me. Her embrace was still cold, but there was a spark along her skin that had been missing before. When she pulled back, she was giggling again. "So what's Anna going to do to you for running away?"

"She took my car keys. In fact, I'm pretty sure she took my car. Who knows when she'll let me drive it again."

"What a drag." Mindy frowned. "Wait. When did you get a car?"

"Yesterday. Lost it pretty quick, huh?"

Suddenly we were both laughing together, not holding back at all. After the last twenty-four hours, I desperately needed to find something funny. It was probably lucky that my mother was still outside, out of earshot.

But there was something freaky about how happy Mindy was. Her three decades of fear had been erased overnight. It felt almost as if Mr. Hamlyn were right, and ghosts weren't real people after all. And if Mindy wasn't really herself anymore, it was my fault. I'd taken away the hours that had made her the ghost she was.

I decided to test something. "You know what my mother told me?"

"What?"

"That your real name is Melinda."

A thoughtful expression crossed her face, and it took a long moment until she finally nodded. "That's right. That was my name."

Was, she'd said. Mindy was her real name now, because my mother's memories were all that she had left.

"Did you know my mother was sick?"

She shrugged. "Sometimes she talks to doctors on the phone, about how she's tired all the time."

"Okay." Maybe stem-cell diseases weren't an easy concept for an eleven-year-old. "But that's it?"

"I guess. Is Anna going to be okay?"

I nodded. "They figured out what's wrong. And she's going to get it fixed."

Mindy smiled, and I knew that lying had been the right thing to do. If my mother died, Mindy would have no one left who remembered her as a living girl. What did that mean to a ghost?

In any case, it was easier for me to pretend that my mother was okay.

CHAPTER 35

"SIX MONTHS!" DARCY CRIED. "I HAD SIX MONTHS TO DO THIS, and now I've only got six days!"

Imogen didn't answer. She was busy in the kitchen, filling the house with the scent of simmering meat. It was four thirty in the afternoon, but Imogen's stew required hours of cooking. Of all their experiments in the Chinatown markets, from fried whelks to sea urchin to salted duck tongue, short rib stew had proven the most successful.

Even in her deadline panic, Darcy felt herself getting hungry.

"This is just like high school," she muttered to herself. "I always did everything the night before."

"That's the curse of being clever!" Imogen called out.

"What is?"

Imogen stepped from the kitchen, her hair in a headband, wearing an apron emblazoned with a black velvet painting of

Shimmer-Tail (Nisha's favorite Sparkle Pony). "All those years of doing schoolwork the night before, and still getting an A. Now you're stuck with the habit."

"That's not fair. I've been trying to rewrite this stupid ending for months!"

"Yeah, but in your heart of hearts, you know it doesn't really count until the night before it's due." Imogen smiled evilly. "If you were a little less clever, you'd have a much better work ethic."

Darcy back stared at her. "Are you complimenting my intelligence or insulting my character?"

"Just working out my own issues." Imogen disappeared back into the kitchen.

Darcy didn't bother to answer that. Lately, Imogen was overwhelmed with her own anxiety about the first draft of *Phobomancer*. Two deadlines in the house at once was perhaps one too many.

Open on Darcy's laptop screen were a dozen documents, the twelve best versions of the end of *Afterworlds*. Some were dark and melancholy, some light and uplifting, and some straight-up Happily Ever After. Darcy felt as though she'd written every possible ending for the book, and now it was simply a matter of picking one.

"I'm a writer, not a decider," Darcy mumbled to herself. The words danced in her head for a while, as meaningless as the burble of boiling water from the kitchen.

Maybe she was afraid to pick an ending, because once this book was finished, the die was cast. She would either be a success or a failure, all her realness determined by that single throw.

Or maybe it was because she wasn't so much a writer as a thief.

She'd stolen her little ghost from her mother's childhood, a kidnapping scene from her girlfriend, and the love interest from her own religion. Maybe she had no perfect ending because there wasn't one to steal.

Imogen popped out from the kitchen again, a paring knife in hand. "What do you think of River Treeman?"

Darcy looked up. "Who's that?"

"No one, yet. But how do you like it as a name?"

"Sounds like they had hippie parents. Or is this person an elf?"

"Crap. Never mind." Imogen disappeared again.

Darcy shook her head, staring again at her laptop screen.

If only Kiralee Taylor had just *told* her how to end her book, or shamed her into fighting for her original tragic ending. But she'd made the whole experience a test of skill, in which Darcy either had to write a happy ending that went with the unhappy themes of her novel, or an unhappy ending that kept her unhappiness-hating publisher happy.

The word "happy" had started to sound wrong in Darcy's head, like a random collection of Scrabble letters.

"What about Amanda Shearling?" Imogen called from the kitchen. "As a name."

"Sounds like a really rich person."

"Ugh."

Apparently, Imogen's mechanism for dealing with stress was to make up bad character names and cook. Of course, both were probably more useful than Darcy sitting here staring, as if her eyes could arrange the letters on the screen.

What if it was too late? What if she'd already written so many endings that she would never find the right one? Like kids who've told so many lies that they can no longer remember the truth.

"Gen?" she called. "Once the stew is stewing, I think I need you."

It wasn't long before Imogen emerged from the kitchen again, pulled out the chair opposite from Darcy, and sat down.

"The ribs are stewing, the mushrooms soaking. What's up?"

"All my endings suck."

"How many pages are we talking about exactly?"

"The last four chapters. Lizzie's killed the bad man and chopped his memories up, then returned home and found out what her mom's disease is. But after that . . ." Darcy stared her laptop. "Maybe the book's already over. Killing the bad man is the climax, and confronting her mom is the denouement. Maybe I'm just waffling for another ten thousand words. Maybe *I'm already done*."

Imogen didn't look convinced. "This isn't an action movie, Darcy. You don't kill the bad guy and then roll the credits."

"If it's not an action movie, what it is? A horror-slash-romance? A Bollywood musical? An indie film about a wilted helium balloon?"

"It's not a movie at all, Darcy; it's a *novel*. And novels are messy and tangled and complicated. If you end it right after the bad man dies, then we never find out what happens between Lizzie and Yamaraj."

Darcy shook her head. "Maybe the book's not really about him. Maybe Kiralee's right, and he's just there for purposes of YA hotness."

"That's not what she said. And what about the death cult? You want to leave that up in the air? And Mr. Hamlyn? And Anna's disease?"

"Maybe all that stuff can be in *Untitled Patel.*" Saying the non-title of her sequel filled Darcy with despair. She only had seven months left to turn in a first draft. How had she gone from someone who could write a whole novel in thirty days to someone who took half a year to rewrite *four chapters*?

"When you finish this book, then you can worry about *Untitled Patel.*" Imogen pulled off her Sparkle Pony apron, wadded it up, and cast it aside, all business now. "You can't forget about Yamaraj. He's the key to your ending. Your book is all about facing death!"

"Okay." A little shudder of relief went through Darcy. Maybe if she just listened to Imogen talk, she might understand her own novel again. "What does fear of death have to do with Mr. YA Hotness?"

"People don't just fear death. They get hot for it too. That's why teenagers love slasher films—fear and excitement and lust, all wrapped up around getting killed. That's why Lizzie wants Yamaraj."

"Because she's in love with death?"

"Not in love with, *hot for.*" Imogen was shredding the air with her hands now. "In those moments at the airport, Lizzie faces her own mortality. And Yamaraj is the guy who's already faced it. He can hear it in the stones, smell it in the air. If she holds on to him, maybe death won't be so scary! That's why Mr. Hamlyn collects the memories of dying little kids, because it makes him feel like he has control over death. But of course it never works. That's why you can't end with killing the bad man. That isn't even a victory, because you *can't win against death.*"

Darcy stared back, dazzled as always by Imogen's rantings. But behind the intensity was something subtle and true, a new facet of Yamaraj that Darcy had never glimpsed before. He was beautiful, not because he was hot, and not only because he'd faced down his own death. But because he was noble. Every day, he fought a war that he knew he would lose.

But she had to ask, "So they aren't really in love?"

"Maybe she needed to love someone, after what happened to her. But love isn't always a forever thing."

Darcy sighed at that. Even though it was probably true, it went against everything books were *for*. In novels, love was perfect and without end.

"Can you just write this for me?"

A laugh came from Imogen. "Too busy making stew. And coming up with names. What do you think of Ska West?"

"Ska, like the music?" Darcy shook her head. "What are these for, anyway? Are you adding a bunch of new characters to *Phobomancer*?"

"They aren't for characters," Imogen said. "They're pen names."

"For who?"

"For me." Imogen stood up and left the table.

Darcy sat there, stunned for a moment, but then pursued Imogen into the heat and sizzle of the kitchen. "Gen. Why do you need a pen name?"

Imogen began to chop, her knife slicing through daikon and scallions. "For when I have to start over. For when Paradox pulls the plug on my series, and no bookstore ever stocks me again."

"That's crazy."

"Writers do it all the time. It's better than dragging around a busted sales record."

Darcy took a step closer. The thought of Imogen writing under another name was horrible. As if it would change her into someone else.

"They're not going to cancel your series, Gen."

"I'll be glad when they do," Imogen said. "Like in those hard-boiled crime novels, when the criminals are relieved to be caught."

"Stop it, Imogen! You're not a criminal, or an impostor, and Paradox isn't canceling your series. And you don't need a pen name, because Imogen Gray is going to be a famous bestselling author!"

Their eyes locked, Darcy challenging Imogen to dispute her. There was silence in the kitchen, except for the burble in the pan.

"I've already got a pen name," Imogen finally said.

"No. Imogen Gray is your real name. That's who you are."

"I remember when you didn't think so."

"I was wrong."

Imogen reached out to brush Darcy's shoulder, her lips playing with a smile. But a moment later the expression soured, and she turned back to the cutting board. "This isn't about me, it's about business. Books fail. Writers fail. It's not all YA heaven."

The last two words stung, as they had ever since the argument over Imogen coming down for Pancha Ganapati.

"Where's all this coming from, Gen?"

"My agent doesn't like the new opening."

Darcy shook her head. "You sent it to him?"

"Yesterday, to get him all excited about *Phobomancer*. Not a good move, it seems." Imogen turned away to push her wooden spoon around the pan. "He says the inside of a car trunk is the wrong place to start a book, because there's nothing to see."

"But that's the point!"

"Then the point is not clear." Imogen let out a sigh. "He also says it's not scary. Which is true, and makes perfect sense. I'm not really claustrophobic. When you drove me around in the trunk, *you* were the one who was nervous. I was having a blast!"

Darcy closed her eyes. It was true—Imogen wasn't afraid of anything.

"I wish I could fix this for you."

"Yeah, I know. You wish everything was YA heaven."

There it was again, the magic words for mocking little innocent Darcy, who thought everything was easy, because she'd never had it hard.

She made herself swallow the insult. "Your career isn't over, Gen."

"Not yet. But you never know."

"True. You could get hit by a bus tomorrow," Darcy said, accepting that the real world was gritty and brutal, that life could suck. Sometimes, she wondered if Imogen's pessimism was designed to toughen her up. As if Darcy was a project—*hard work*, as Gen had said on the night she'd found out about Imogen White.

"Or a taxi," Imogen pointed out.

"Do you want to read the opening to me?" Darcy asked. "Sometimes out loud helps."

Imogen looked down at her stew. "I read, you stir?"

"Perfect. And if it still sucks, I'll think of some way to scare the crap out of you, I promise."

Imogen smiled at last, and Darcy gathered her into a hug.

"Let me take a shower first. Gotta wash away the stench of failure." Imogen pulled away to face her. "Thanks for talking me down."

"I didn't just piss you off more?"

"Only at first," Imogen said, giving Darcy another smile. She handed over the wooden spoon. "Keep it simmering and skim off any foam."

She headed for the bathroom, pulling off her T-shirt as she went.

Darcy took a slow breath, feeling more settled than she had all day. Helping Imogen through a freak-out had made her own crisis seem surmountable. Six days was long enough to make an ending. The main thing was not to panic.

Darcy focused on the simmering pot, letting her mind drift away from the various endings of *Afterworlds*. Maybe her subconscious would come up with something brilliant while she skimmed and stirred.

But her reverie didn't last long, because watching stew simmer was boring. Darcy went to get her laptop, propped it open on the kitchen counter, and checked her email. There was a query from Rhea, her editor's assistant: *Can Nan call you tonight before she leaves work? She wants to see how the new ending's going.*

It had been sent only minutes ago. Darcy sent back a yes, and a moment later the reply came: *She'll call you in five.*

The message set off a slow-building panic in Darcy, as if Imogen's fears had leaked into her mind. Did Nan have some editor's intuition that the work was going badly? What if the failure of *Pyromancer* had created a new policy at Paradox, that books were canceled before publication unless their authors could explain their rewrites in vivid detail?

"That's just silly," Darcy said aloud. Nan just wanted to make sure the new ending was on track for the deadline. But *which* ending?

Then Darcy realized: her phone wasn't in her pocket. She hadn't used it that day, except to read Nisha's text informing her that *Afterworlds* would be published in 241 days. Where had she left it?

Darcy turned the flame beneath the short ribs down a nudge and went into the big room. Her phone wasn't on the writing desk, or any of the windowsills. It wasn't on the comfy new couch that she'd blown her January budget on. (Revised budget: according to Nisha, her spending was well into August by now.)

Darcy went back into the kitchen and checked the counters again. Nothing.

She flung open the door of the bathroom. "Gen!"

"Did you get bored and burn my stew?" came the reply from a cloud of steam.

"Not yet. Do you know where my phone is?"

A pause. "Did you check your pocket?"

"Yes!" Darcy groaned, slammed the door, and headed for her bedroom. No phone there, nor in the closet-and-bookshelf room.

She imagined Nan at her desk, tired after a long day's work, dialing and getting no answer. How annoying. How like those clueless little debutante authors who knew *nothing* about rewriting books, only monkey typing.

The five minutes was surely up. Unless Rhea's email had said Nan was going to call *at* five . . .

Darcy went back to her laptop and checked. Nope. Five minutes, three of which were gone.

"Shit, shit, shit." She dove at the new couch again, flinging aside cushions. She found only dust, seventy-five cents, and an earring Imogen had lost a week before.

One minute left now!

When Nan called, the phone would make itself known, unless the ringer was off. Sitting on the desk was Imogen's phone. Darcy swept it up, turned it on to call her own number . . .

. . . and found herself staring at the yellow background of Imogen's diary.

"Never," she murmured. But her eyes, unbidden, were already reading the first line.

After all this hard work, another bitch.

Darcy read it again, but the words stayed separate and meaningless, the letters spiders on the screen. She whispered the sentence aloud, but it still didn't make sense. She turned the phone off and placed it softly back on the desk.

As Darcy sank onto the couch, she closed her eyes. Her hand still burned where she'd held the phone. How had she been so stupid? Like a character in a fairy tale who only has to follow one simple rule, and fails.

Once you turn the key, you can never forget what's in the closet.

Darcy reasoned with herself. The words could have referred to anyone, really. There hadn't been a name or any other clues.

But Darcy Patel was the only person who Imogen ever called

"hard work." And "*another* bitch"? That was Audrey Flinderson talking.

"Crap," Darcy said. This was why diaries were private.

A sound reached her ears then, a muffled shrieking close by. She sprang to her feet, turning her head to triangulate its source. It came again, and a moment later Darcy was on her knees, reaching through the dust bunnies already gathered beneath the new couch.

She pulled out the phone and answered too loudly, "Yes!"

"Nan Eliot here."

"Of course. I mean, hi. How are you?"

"Very well, Darcy. And you?"

She was panting. Her heart was pounding and thrashing, like a spin dryer with a brick inside. "I'm good."

"I just wanted to ask how the rewrites were going."

"They're great." In her own ears, Darcy's voice broke and trembled. *After all this hard work . . .*

"I see." Nan paused. She'd heard the uncertainty. "You know this deadline is very important. If you miss it, we won't have advanced copies ready for BookExpo America. You're already on the schedule there."

"Of course." Darcy realized that the shower had turned off. She couldn't face Imogen yet. She turned away from the bathroom door, staring out at the rooftops of Chinatown. "It's not going to be a problem. I've got it under control."

There was another pause. Darcy wasn't convincing Nan or herself.

"I mean," she stumbled on. "I've already got the ending done. It's just . . . there's more than one."

"Interesting. Do you need help choosing?"

Darcy heard the bathroom door open and shut her eyes. "I'll know what to do."

"It's a little scary, isn't it? Letting go of your first book."

Darcy didn't know how to answer this. Fear was part of what she was feeling, but the uncertainty was worse. The sentence in Imogen's diary had exposed a fault running through her new life, a split in the sky of YA heaven.

"I'll be okay."

"I'm sure you will, Darcy," Nan said. "But there's something I always tell my debut authors. Your first novel is like your first relationship. You won't really understand the decisions you make until years later." She laughed. "And you'll probably screw up the ending."

"Um, I . . ." Darcy's voice failed her. "My first what?"

"You remember your first sweetheart, right?" Nan asked.

"Sure."

"Oh, of course." Nan laughed again. "It probably wasn't as long ago for you as it was for me. So you must know what I mean. First love is amazing and wonderful, but a kind of panic underlies it, a sense of not knowing what you're doing. First novels are the same way."

Darcy swallowed. There was a lump in her throat the size of a thimble.

"So how do I fix that? My book, I mean."

"You do the best you can. But remember, it's not going to be the most polished novel you ever write, or the wisest, or the best-selling. That would be a shame, after all, to peak with your first. We at Paradox expect great things from you, Darcy, well beyond these two books."

"But even if it's my first, I still want this to work."

"Of course. And luckily you have one superpower right now, something you don't need experience to find."

"What?"

"Honesty. Just write the most honest ending you can."

Darcy closed her eyes again. She didn't want anything to end.

"Can you do that for me?" Nan asked.

"What if it doesn't have a happy ending?"

Nan sighed. "Just consider this, Darcy—real life doesn't have many happy endings. Why shouldn't books make up the difference?"

Darcy stood at the window for a while after Nan had hung up, holding the phone at her head, half pretending to be in conversation. Staring out at the bustle of Chinatown, she slowly gathered herself, until she felt strong enough for the long walk back to the kitchen.

"Sorry, Gen. Did anything burn?"

"It's fine." Imogen didn't look up from the stew. "Who was so important?"

"It was Nan."

"Checking in on you?" Finally their eyes met. "Jesus. Is everything okay?"

"Yeah," Darcy said, which was a lie, and honesty was all she was good for.

"What the hell did Nan say to you? You look awful."

Darcy realized she wasn't ready to have this conversation.

"She was telling me not to sweat it, I guess." Darcy swallowed the hard and bitter taste in her mouth. "She said that no matter what, I'm going to look back on my first novel with embarrassment."

"Whoa. She really said that?"

"Not quite. It's more like she was telling me not to panic."

"Doesn't look like it worked."

"No," Darcy said, and couldn't stop herself from asking, "Are we okay? You and me?"

Imogen put down the wooden spoon and wrapped her arms around Darcy. "Sorry I've been so crazy. It's not you, it's the writing. You know that, right?"

"Of course." She held Imogen tighter. "I know we're good."

More lies, but maybe lies were better than the truth.

CHAPTER 36

THE NEXT MORNING I SEARCHED THE LOCAL NEWS SITES FOR Palo Alto, and the web editions of both San Francisco newspapers. There was nothing about a murder investigation, or a man found dead in his house.

It was weird to find nothing in the news, not a word. Of course, the bad man hadn't exactly been a social butterfly. It could be weeks before anyone found him in his bed. That wasn't a pretty thought.

Before leaving for school, I cleared the search history on my laptop, in case Mom was checking up on me. That was enough to keep my mother from asking questions, but what about the police? What if there was still a clue somewhere on my hard drive? Or evidence pointing back at me from those news websites?

I sighed. If anyone was doing serious forensics, I would've already been busted in a dozen other ways. The calls from my phone, maybe the data in my car's GPS. In crime shows, it only took a tiny clue to get the murderer caught.

But on TV there was always a clear motive. Who would imagine that a high school student had driven all night to kill some random stranger? Unless that student was already famous for a horrific brush with terrorism, the sort of experience that might leave someone obsessed with death.

I'd always have an insanity defense, at least.

When I got to school I looked for Agent Reyes's car, but it wasn't around. He hadn't shown up since that first day back from winter break. Which was fine. Now that I was a criminal, not being of interest to the FBI was probably a good thing. If Special Agent Reyes had been there, I would've been tempted to ask him another string of hypotheticals about serial killers. Not such a good idea anymore.

I went to the attendance office first, to hand them a note from my mom. It explained that she was seriously ill, and that I might be missing some school for the next few months while I helped her out. Mom was scrupulously honest, so the note said nothing specific about my absence the day before. But everyone made the expected assumptions, and they were all very sympathetic.

I was a senior. My transcripts had already been sent off to colleges. People like me were supposed to blow off their last semester. That I had a really good excuse would only make it easier.

Jamie was waiting for me in the hallway outside.

"Hey." She greeted me with a tiny wave, looking guilty. I'd

almost forgotten that she'd spilled the beans about my secret boyfriend.

I gave her a hug. "Hey, yourself. Sorry I disappeared like that."

"I get why you needed space, but Anna was totally freaked out. I had to tell her *something*."

"It's okay, Jamie."

"So I don't suck for telling her about your boyfriend? It's just, I thought it would be better if she knew you had a place to go. Instead of thinking you were driving around all night doing crazy stuff."

A laugh forced its way out of me, because "doing crazy stuff" didn't begin to cover it. Jamie took the sound as forgiveness, and we hugged again.

When we pulled apart, she still look worried. "You were saying all that weird stuff, about grim reapers. What *was* that?"

"Nothing." I shrugged. "It was just the bad news about my mom, freaking me out."

"So how sick is Anna?"

"I'm not sure." It occurred to me that I could have spent the morning googling MDS instead of my own crimes. But I was about as good a daughter as I was a criminal. "Her blood's messed up."

"Like leukemia?"

I shook my head. "It's something I'd never heard of before. She says it'll take a long time to treat it. And a long time before we know if she . . ."

My voice faded. Saying all this aloud had made me unsteady on my feet. The second late-bell rang, and the hallway emptied around us.

Jamie put a hand on my shoulder. "Should you even be at school today?"

"Mom was pretty sure," I said.

"Oh. You must be totally busted."

"Yeah." We hadn't had any specific conversation about punishment, but Mom had taken my new car to work today. I was fairly certain that I wouldn't be driving it anytime soon. "But, whatever. Even if she grounds me till I'm eighteen, that's only three months."

Jamie smiled. "Your rebellion was well timed. She must want to meet your mysterious boyfriend."

"Thanks to you."

"Does that mean I get to meet him too? Finally?"

I stared at her. "So *that's* why you told her?"

"Never." She crossed her heart. "But I'm glad I did. Anna needs to know stuff like that, especially now."

"I guess so." I wondered what the chances were of Yama sitting down for dinner with us. Especially after I'd confessed my murder to him.

Jamie took my hand and led me toward my first class. "You two need to stop hiding stuff from each other. You know that, right?"

I nodded, unable to say more. There was so much now that I would never tell my mother, or Jamie, or anyone else here in the overworld. It didn't feel as though I could ever be completely honest again.

That night Mom and I cooked together, and we talked a lot too. Not about her disease, but about my father, the person he'd always been. The odd thing was, we hadn't talked about Dad in any serious way since he'd left us.

"He sees people as pieces in a game," I said at one point, thinking of Mr. Hamlyn, too. "Like we're here just to amuse him."

Mom frowned at this, almost as if she wanted to come to Dad's defense. But she only shook her head and said, "I'm sorry. I was young."

We wound up staying up late, my mother sharing a glass of her wine with me. We toasted to how great the rest of the year was going to be, because we'd clearly had our share of disasters already. Mindy watched us from her corner the whole time, happy to be part of the family, so I didn't bring up anything about my mother's childhood. Now that Mindy had finally forgotten what had happened thirty-five years ago, it seemed cruel to remind her.

By the time Mom sent me off to bed, Mindy was full of energy. She wanted to take the river to New York City and spy on my father.

"Some other night. I need to see someone."

"You mean your pomp boyfriend?" She shrugged. "He can come too if he wants."

It took me a moment to understand—this was the new Mindy, unafraid of bad men. But the things I had to explain to Yama weren't for her ears.

"Not tonight. I'll be back before dawn."

Mindy grumbled a little, but finally headed off to roam the neighborhood by herself, a fearless little ghost.

I stood in the middle of my bedroom and slipped across to the flipside, ready to face Yama and confess what I'd done. But as the magic words from the 911 call faded in my mouth, I heard a voice floating on the rust-scented air of the afterworld.

"Elizabeth Scofield . . . I need you."

It sounded like a young girl, maybe Mindy's age. My heart froze—what if one of the five girls I'd freed still existed, and still wanted me? But then the words came again, and I heard the faint accent in them, like Yama's.

It was the ghost of his sister Yami.

The river knew what to do.

I'd always wondered how Yama arrived so quickly when I called him. But the river's current was driven by connections, by desires. The Vaitarna was roiling with my need to know why Yami's voice had called me instead of her brother's. The moment I released myself to the current, it took me, furious and spinning.

It had to be a simple reason, nothing horrible. Hadn't my mother decreed that there would be no more disasters this year?

I swirled to a halt in a part of the river that I'd never seen before. The familiar formless plain stretched in all directions, but the sky was wrong. Instead of starry black it was the red of a fading sunset, rusty and muted. It was strange seeing a wash of color above the boundless gray.

Yami stood there waiting, her large eyes dissecting me.

"Long time no see," I said.

"We've both been occupied." Her hands adjusted the folds of her gray skirt. "When my brother chooses to neglect his people, someone has to take his place."

"Right." Yama had said something about his sister not approving of us. "Sorry if I've been distracting him."

"I doubt that," she said.

I frowned. "I haven't been a distraction?"

"You have. But I doubt you're sorry."

All my clever rejoinders foundered on the fact that she was right.

"Yami, why did you call me? Is your brother okay?"

"He regrets that he can't come to you. His people need him." She paused a moment, weighing her words. "They are besieged."

"Wait. You mean, there's a battle down there?" I shook my head. "The underworld has wars?"

"Something smaller than a war, but equally deadly. A predator."

It took a moment to understand the word. But when I did, monsters came to mind. "Okay. That's scary."

"Lord Yama is not afraid, but perhaps you can . . ." She held out her hand. "My brother will explain."

"You're going to take me to the underworld?"

Yami's reaction was to raise an eyebrow, as if I wasn't worth a yes.

Yama had told me about his home, how beautiful it was. But the thought of going that far down into the underworld scared me. The few stray ghosts at school still made me uneasy. I couldn't imagine a city of thousands.

I looked up at the strange bloodred sky. "We're close, aren't we?"

"This is the deepest part of the river." When I still hesitated, Yami snapped the fingers of her outstretched hand, and a single drop of black oil fell from them. "Come, girl. Or don't you want to go to hell?"

"Nice of you to put it that way." I stared down at the spreading black pool between us.

"Pardon my English," she said with a smile. "Do you prefer 'Hades'? It isn't a bad place, you know. Just a quiet one."

"With predators."

She nodded. "At the moment. But my brother seems to think you can help."

It was hard to argue with that, and I needed to see Yama and tell him everything that had happened in the last two days.

I reached out to take her hand.

We went farther down, deeper than I'd ever gone.

The light was different here. A ruddiness infused everything—the sky, the ground, Yami's skirt and blouse—the color almost vivid compared to the endless gray of the flipside. The air was different too. My lungs had to work hard to take it in, like being in a small room full of cut flowers whose scent was rust and blood.

We alighted on a balcony that overlooked a skyline of jumbled shapes. The buildings didn't match, more a collage than a city. They seemed to have been plucked from every epoch, from stone hovels to columned mansions to towering modern apartment blocks. A panopticon of windows stared back at me, reflecting the bloodred sky.

It was magnificent, like a city constructed over thousands of years with nothing ever torn down. Like every city that had ever existed on earth put together.

"Who built all this?"

"It is remembered, not built."

Ghost buildings. Of course.

I stepped to the edge of the balcony and leaned out over the city of the dead. We were only a few stories up, and I could see that the edges of the structures were blurred, the details indistinct. Faded memories given form.

And it was lifeless. The wide avenues stretched out empty in all directions. No litter stirred in the low and constant wind. There were no vehicles, no traffic lights.

"Where are all the people?"

"Where they usually are when there's a wolf at the door. Inside."

I turned to her. "A literal wolf? The ghost of an animal?"

Yami shook her head, but didn't speak, as if she wanted me to guess.

I wasn't in the mood. "Where's Yama?"

"Yama*raj* is out there, where he's needed. He'll return when he can."

"You said I could help. How?"

Yami thought about this for a moment, and then she said, "Shall we have tea?"

She went inside through the balcony doors, which were as wide and tall as a soccer goal, leading me into a room as big as my entire house. A huge patterned rug lay at its center, surrounded by dozens of cushions. Candled chandeliers hung above us. As we entered, men in knee-length robes and loose trousers stepped forward from the shadows, lighting the branches of the chandeliers with smoking tapers. These servants were as gray-skinned as Yami—ghosts, of course. They didn't talk, though one met my eyes with an expression of disquiet, then looked away.

Yami settled on one of the cushions and pointed to the one across from her.

"Sit, girl."

"My name is Lizzie."

"You should show more respect for your name, Elizabeth. Names are important here."

I didn't sit down, taking in the beauty of the room around us.

The arched ceilings were painted in russet curlicues, held up by carved and fluted columns, and the candles in the chandeliers flickered like stars above us.

Then Yami said, "The predator takes only children."

That made my knees buckle. I sat, unable to speak for a moment, staring at the rug, which was woven in a pattern of zigzags, diamonds with interlocking vertices. It made my vision pulse with my heartbeat.

Only children.

Yami clicked her fingernails, and two servants stepped forward again. Instead of burning tapers, they had silver trays in their hands, each with a steaming teapot and a small porcelain cup with no handles. Yami watched them work, thanking each by name as they served us. A smell like roses and burned sugar filled the room, making the air even thicker.

"The predator," I said. "It's one of us, a psychopomp."

She nodded, waiting for more.

"And the children . . . they all died peacefully, with their parents caring for them. Back when they were alive, I mean."

"So it's the man who troubled you before." Her words came slowly, clearly. "The one who sent my brother a message."

I nodded. *I'm hungry*—a warning.

"How did you lead him here, girl?"

"Why would I do that? I've never even *been* here before!"

"How else would he have made a connection to my brother?"

"A connection?" I tried to remember what had happened in the basement, the night Mr. Hamlyn had given Mindy back. "I kissed his hand, but I told Yama about that."

"Think harder, Elizabeth." Yami pronounced every syllable of my name.

I closed my eyes, and heard Mr. Hamlyn's voice again.

I want you to tell your rather impressive friend something. What's his name again?

And I'd answered.

"Yamaraj," I said. "I told Mr. Hamlyn his name, kind of by accident."

Yami stared at me a moment, then raised her teacup and blew across it. Steam coiled from her lips.

I could hardly breathe the heavy, blood-scented air. Mr. Hamlyn had trailed me to New York because he knew my name.

"I didn't know not to. Nobody told me!"

"My brother didn't tell you." Yami closed her eyes. "Because you're a distraction. Because he didn't want to scare you with all the rules of the afterworld. Because you turn him into a *fool*, just by existing."

I shook my head. Yama had told me many times that names were important here, just not clearly enough. Maybe after three thousand years, it seemed obvious to him. You couldn't explain everything to clueless novices, after all. There was too much they didn't know.

My mouth was suddenly dry. I reached for my teacup, but it was empty except for steam.

"Only memories," Yami said. It took me a moment to realize that she meant the tea. Memories were all they had in the underworld, like when children play at tea parties with empty cups.

"How many children?" I said.

"Three, so far."

"What can I do?"

Yami shook her head, as if I was being as thick as the air. "You said you kissed him, and you know his name."

"Of course! We're connected." I stood up on shaky legs. "I'll call him, or track him, or however it works."

Yami held up a hand. "Wait for Yamaraj. This is his justice to serve."

CHAPTER 37

THE DARKNESS SPILLS DOWN THE VALLEY AND ACROSS TO THE distant hills, a blanket of midnight. No campfires are in sight, and in dry season there are no bright slivers of freshet to reflect the sky. But Darcy Patel spots a single bright coin flicked into all that velvet—a waterhole.

Her dry tongue scrapes across sorely fissured lips, but she makes no haste, first measuring out the stars of Corvus and Crux. She has to keep a straight path to reach that patch of wet silver before the sun rises again. The last seventeen days have brought an avaricious heat, taking the expedition's oxen, the convicts, and the freemen in that order. The native guides wisely slipped away a week ago.

Her course determined, Darcy stumbles down the ragged slope, setting a thirsty pace. The night is long, her eagerness tempered by hard falls from watching the constellations overhead instead of looking to her own feet. Empty runnels crisscross the valley, and her muscles soon burn with every dusty scramble down and up again. The scent of jerky from her pack simmers in her head, but her mouth is too parched for dried meat to do her any good.

In the coldest moment of the night, just as the horizon has begun to glow, a glimmer of water appears ahead. At first, Darcy doesn't dare believe in it. But the ground grows softer under her feet, and her nose catches traces of hook-leaf and mint bush in the air.

She hears a splash in the distance, perhaps a rock wallaby down for its first drink of the day. But fresh meat is a concern for later—at this moment Darcy is made of thirst. She's already running, falling to her knees in the red mud. As her face touches water, she shivers with passion. The sores on her lips finally cool, the cracks in her throat stealing the first gulps before they can reach her stomach. It is a full minute before she's had her fill, and tries to rise up from the mud's embrace.

But the mud will not let her go.

Darcy pushes herself up on her elbows, but that's all she can manage. Her arms, her legs are trapped by some insuperable viscous force. Even stranger, inches in front of her face, the water is sliding away. Something huge is stirring beneath her, the land itself lifting up.

She hears splashing all around and cranes her neck. In the rosy light of dawn a dozen wallabies retreat in all directions, fleeing whatever the great lump of mud beneath her has become.

The sucking grip on her arms and legs softens, and Darcy manages to struggle to her feet. For a moment, she stands upright on a swelling hill of mud. But suddenly the red earth beneath her turns to treacle, and she's sinking into living, pulsing warmth. Slow and inexorable, the mud covers her knees, consumes her body, and finally fills her lungs.

As the red earth enfolds her, Darcy hears a shudder deep inside it, a rumble of ancient gasses at its core, a sound almost like a word. . . .

Bunyip.

Darcy woke with a start, gasping for breath, thrashing in the tangled sheets. It took her long moments to realize that she was safe and sound in her own bed, not suffocating in the sacred, hungry mud of an outback waterhole.

It had been ages since she'd had the bunyip nightmare. But lying here in a sheen of sweat, Darcy perfectly recalled the Kiralee-inspired night terrors of her early teens. And in that moment she realized that the black oil in *Afterworlds* was suspiciously similar to the living red mud of the Taylor mythos.

Funny that Kiralee had never mentioned that. Had she even noticed? Or was she simply used to being borrowed from?

Imogen lay curled on her side of the bed, undisturbed by the nightmare. It was only nine in the morning, hours before she usually stirred. In the five weeks since sending off *Afterworlds*, Darcy had stopped staying awake all night, sometimes going to bed as early as two a.m. But Imogen still wrote till dawn, trying to make the first draft of *Phobomancer* too astounding to ignore. Their sleep schedules were gradually falling out of sync.

After all this hard work . . .

Darcy slid out of bed, put on a bathrobe and slippers, and

padded to the kitchen to make coffee. It was Imogen's percolator waiting on the stovetop, Imogen's brand of espresso in the fridge. Their possessions were entangled, their tastes entwined. But on mornings like this, when Imogen was still asleep and Darcy was alone in the early March chill, she felt fallen.

Cast out of YA heaven, and living with Audrey Flinderson.

She measured the grind, filled the percolator, and watched the flame bloom. As she waited for the gurgle of coffee, Darcy warmed her hands over the heat.

In some other universe, she'd chanced on another part of the diary—a research note, a plot idea, or one of Imogen's ridiculous pen names. The Darcy in that world was still blissfully ignorant, no doubt excited to face a new day of writing. But this Darcy hadn't typed a single word of *Untitled Patel*.

The night before, not for the first time, Imogen had caught her staring out the window, brooding. Imogen had closed her laptop with a sigh and said, "There's nothing wrong with flailing after you finish a novel. It's just postpartum depression. But the cure is to start the next one."

This wasn't bad advice—*Untitled Patel* was due in less than six months. But Darcy was still wrung dry from her final days of rewriting. She'd thrown away all her previous efforts and gone in a new and crazed direction. She'd sent her characters to hell, sliced them up, and killed one of her favorites. And she'd left Yamaraj finally feeling like a proper death god, wounded in his heart and freighted with eternity.

The result wasn't exactly a happy ending.

The weird thing was, both Moxie and Nan Eliot loved it. Darcy should have been celebrating . . . after all that hard work.

But Imogen hadn't read it yet, not in the endless weeks since Darcy had finished. She kept delaying, saying she needed to focus on the first draft of *Phobomancer*. Once that was done, she could give Darcy's new ending her full attention.

Or maybe she was sick of hearing about it. Sick of everything Darcy Patel–related.

Maybe it was all just hard work now.

The coffee burbled and sputtered on the stove, promising solace and caffeine. Darcy poured, cupped the warmth of the mug with both hands, and joined her laptop at the writing desk in the big room.

Waiting in her in-box was an email from Rhea:

Hey, Darcy! Attached are the copyedits and style sheets for AFTERWORLDS.

We fast-tracked these edits, and Nan says that if you can get them back to us by Friday, the advanced copies at BEA can be copyedited. Yay!

A glimmer of excitement stirred in Darcy, her gloom lifting. There was something pleasingly official about being copyedited, and frightening as well.

She opened one of the style sheets. It was a list, the names and attributes of every character in *Afterworlds*.

Lizzie: 17, short for Elizabeth, white, only child, hair color unknown

Yamaraj: appears 17 (3000?), Indian (brown skin), crooked eyebrow, beautiful, brother of Yami

Darcy frowned. The details of her protagonists seemed so sparse and flat. Surely Lizzie's hair color was mentioned somewhere in the book. She opened the file and did a quick search on the word "hair," but discovered only that Lizzie's was long enough to push behind her ears when wet.

"Crap," Darcy said aloud. Then she read the next description.

Jamie: 17, has car, lives with father

"'Has car'? That's *it*?" she cried out. No hair color, no brothers or sisters? No particular race? Hardly anything at all. But as *Afterworlds* had unfolded, Jamie had grown into someone quietly amazing. Not just a friend, but a touchstone of normal life that kept Lizzie from leaving the real world behind.

And she was nothing but a cardboard silhouette.

"Fuck!" Darcy yelled.

"Hey," said a sleepy-looking Imogen from the bedroom door. "Are you yelling at yourself?"

Darcy nodded. "Copyedits. Turns out I suck at characters."

Imogen scratched her head, sniffed the air. "Is that coffee?"

They sat across from each other at the desk, perusing printouts of the style sheets.

"This timeline rocks," Imogen said.

"I know, right?" The copyeditor had sifted through *Afterworlds* for every reference to time (Was it a school day? Nighttime? How many weeks had passed?) and put them all into one place. Darcy marveled that she hadn't made so obvious and useful a document herself.

Another document, the Paradox in-house style guide, was more arcane than helpful, though. Paradox demanded serial commas, and wanted "recalled dialogue" to be set in italics. Numbers one hundred and below had to be spelled out, but for anything higher numerals were used. Unless the number appeared in dialogue or was a big round number, like a million. There were so many issues Darcy had never thought about. But these decisions, at least, had been made for her.

When Darcy turned to the manuscript itself, she found the tricky questions, the judgment calls. There seemed to be hundreds of queries, several on every page. Darcy drifted through the document, reading the copyeditor's notes at random.

"What does this mean, Gen? 'Can't hiss without sibilant.'"

"Where is that?" By now, Imogen had her own copy of *Afterworlds* open on her laptop.

"When Lizzie's in her kitchen with Mr. Hamlyn." Darcy followed the dotted line leading from comment to text. "The paragraph that says, '"Be quiet!" I hissed.' What the hell does 'without sibilant' mean?"

"It means there's no *s* in 'Be quiet.'"

"Oh. You can't hiss something if there's no *s* in it?"

"I can. *Be quiet!*" Imogen hissed, her voice sinking into a fierce whisper, her neck muscles tensing, her teeth bared like a snake's.

"Whoa," Darcy said. "You totally hissed that."

She created her own little comment box, and typed "stet." Kiralee had taught her this word, a magic spell for making edits go away.

"One down, a million to go." Darcy read further. "Okay. Here's a note that says, 'You seem ambivalent about ghosts. Are they people or not?'"

"Wait. The copyeditor queried the whole moral dilemma of your book?"

"Yeah. But she's right, Gen. Lizzie keeps worrying about Mindy being a real person. But when those five little girls disappear, it's no big deal!"

Imogen shrugged. "That's because they're minor characters, like the guys in war movies who die in the background. Novelists are evil psychopomps, basically. We treat a few characters as real, but the rest of them are cannon fodder."

"But if the copyeditor's asking about this, it must be confusing. Maybe my book has a fundamental lack of ethical coherence!"

"Or maybe copyeditors just hate ambiguity," Imogen said.

"Very true," Darcy hissed, not as snakily as Imogen. "Stet."

They read in silence for a while, Darcy still adrift among the endless queries. Tomorrow she would start at the beginning and address each in order, but at the moment sampling them was daunting enough. She didn't want to panic and ruin this moment here with Imogen.

Darcy had missed working together at the same desk, the quiet tap of keys, the shuffle of paper. Imogen was still in her pajamas, her hair bed-mussed and growing raggedly out of its last cut, beautifully unkempt. Maybe once Darcy was writing again, the words she'd found in the diary would fade from her mind.

"Good coffee, by the way," Imogen said.

"Thanks." Darcy stared into her own empty cup. "And thanks for doing this. I know you're busy with *Phobomancer*. But I'd be going bat-shit without you here."

Imogen smiled and gave her a lazy cat's-eye blink. "You should enjoy this, Darcy. Copyedits are the fun part! You get to sit here for a whole week, poking around in the *Oxford English Dictionary*, pondering whether a semicolon or an em dash is better."

"Your idea of fun and mine are somewhat different," Darcy said. "I mean, what does all this have to do with *stories*? Does a semicolon ever make the difference in a novel having the juice?"

"Dude. Semicolons *bring* the juice."

"Once in my creative writing class in tenth grade, I called them winkies out loud."

Imogen's eyes widened. "Don't ever tell Kiralee that. She will disown you and never blurb you again!"

Darcy giggled. She'd completely forgotten about winkies. But then she said, "Hang on. She'll never blurb me *again*? Is Kiralee giving me a blurb?"

"Crap. That *was* a secret. Kiralee wanted to tell you herself, because she really likes the new ending. She called it 'suitably brutal.' But I'm hoping that phrase won't be in the blurb."

Darcy felt a smile on her face, the gloom of the last weeks lifting again. "I'm so glad you told me, Gen, even if you weren't supposed to."

"So when Kiralee calls, can you, like, *pretend* to be surprised?"

"That shouldn't be hard. A big chunk of me is still amazed that Kiralee Taylor even *read* my book, much less is going to blurb it."

Imogen smiled. "I'd blurb it myself, but I don't think my name would sell too many copies."

"But you haven't read it," Darcy said.

In quick succession, flickers of surprise, embarrassment, and annoyance flitted across Imogen's face. Darcy hadn't meant to say it like that, or to have sounded so deadly serious, her voice breaking a little on the final word.

"Not the new ending, anyway," she added lamely.

"Yeah, I'm sorry." Imogen raised her hands. "I've been crazy, I know."

"It feels like you're mad at me."

"Don't be silly. I'm pissed at fucking *Phobomancer*, not you."

Darcy tried to stop herself, but the words kept coming. "You keep saying I'm such hard work!"

"I do?"

"Well, maybe you only said it once, when I was snooping in your high school yearbook. But it kind of stuck in my head, because . . ." Darcy squeezed her eyes shut. Crap. This was it, the time to be honest. "I sort of looked at your diary."

Imogen said nothing. Darcy opened her eyes.

"It was an accident. Nan was about to call me, and I couldn't find my phone."

"So you used mine." Imogen's voice revealed nothing. It wasn't angry, or disappointed, or intense. Her face was impassive, her eyes motionless. For a moment, she looked like a cardboard cutout.

Imogen: 23, white, tall, short dark hair

"I didn't mean to look at anything, Gen, I swear. I was just going to call my own phone—to find it. But I saw a page of your diary by accident. And you called me hard work, and a bitch. Just like that other girl."

Imogen shook her head slowly. "No, I didn't."

"Yes, you did." Now that her honesty had finally arrived, Darcy had no choice but to give it free rein. She needed to say everything. "Do a search. Find the words: *After all this hard work, another bitch!*"

Imogen drew the phone from her pocket, tapped at the screen with slow deliberation. Darcy sat there, aware of her own heartbeat in the corners of her vision, the room warping with every angry pulse. When she blinked, a single tear trickled from her eye.

After an endless silence, Imogen raised an eyebrow. "Huh. I never noticed that."

"Never noticed?" Darcy shook her head. "How could you not *notice*? You typed it!"

"Not really." Imogen's voice was still infuriatingly flat. "That wasn't about you, Darcy. It was about my opening. The version my agent didn't like."

"That makes no sense. Why would you say that about a scene?"

Imogen stood slowly. She was all in slow motion now, a statue come to life.

"*B* is next to *H*," she said quietly, and walked away across the big room.

Darcy knew that she should follow, should keep arguing until everything was out in the open. This wasn't about her spying on some precious diary, it was about the two of them knowing what they really thought of each other. It was about honesty, not secrets.

It was about whether Imogen/Audrey was writing another savage screed in her head, or in her diary, this time about Darcy Patel.

But somehow she couldn't make herself move. She was too angry, too astonished that Imogen was responding in nonsense phrases.

B is next to H. What the fuck did that mean? In what universe could that diary entry have referred to the opening of *Phobomancer*?

B is next to H . . .

Darcy's fingers twitched, and then, quite suddenly and completely, she understood. Not with her mind, but in the marrow of her hands, the muscles informed by the millions of words she'd typed in her life, all the emails and school papers and fan fiction, all the discarded drafts of *Afterworlds*. Her fingers twitched again, spelling out the words, telling her what Imogen had meant.

Darcy stared at the open laptop in front of her. On its keyboard the *B* was, in fact, just below the *H*. She closed her eyes, and saw the words again . . .

After all that hard work, another hitch.

Imogen's finger had slipped and hit the *B*. Or one of the other letters in that little cluster—*G, N,* or *V*—and software had brought the error home.

"Fucking autocorrect," Darcy hissed.

She stood up and made her way to the bedroom door. Imogen had changed out of her pajamas into street clothes. She was stuffing T-shirts into a plastic bag.

"Please don't, Gen. I get it now. It was just an accident."

Imogen turned. "Just a hitch, I think you mean."

Darcy tried to smile, but it felt wrong on her face. "I'm sorry."

"Me too," Imogen said, and cleared her throat. "I could deal when you snooped in my old yearbook, Darcy. It made sense. You just wanted to learn more about me. And you had every right to know my real name. You were going to find that essay sooner or later, after all."

"Imogen . . ."

"And in the end, it wasn't that big a problem that you stole my scene. You didn't mean to. Shit like that happens when writers live together, I guess. It was all okay, really, as long as I could have one thing that was my own. My fucking diary."

"I know. But it was an accident."

"How long ago? When did you read it?"

Darcy stared at the floor. "Six days before my deadline. The night Nan called. I was just looking for my phone."

"Sure. But you didn't forget it. And you didn't tell me you'd read it for six weeks! That's why you've been so depressed, right? Because you keep thinking about that essay."

"Yes," Darcy said. She had to be honest from here on out.

"Because those words from my diary became the most important thing for you, because they were supposed to be my secret. Because they were *mine*." Imogen turned away, stuffing a handful of underwear into the garbage bag. "Nothing else I've said to you in the last six weeks really mattered, did it? It was the words in that diary that you believed. The fucking *typo* that you trusted! Not me."

"I trust you, Gen."

"No you don't! Whatever I hide will always be more important to you than what I say and do. Whatever I give you will matter less than what I keep to myself. You'll always want more than what's in front of you. You'll always want my innermost thoughts, my writing ideas, my real name."

"Imogen Gray is your real name."

"Not really. I'm Audrey, who wrote that pathetic, *spiteful* essay. That's how you see me."

"I see you as Imogen."

"That's just my pen name, and it might not even be that for very long."

"Please stop saying that. And please stop *packing*." Darcy leaned back against the wall, sliding down until she was on the floor. "Talk to me."

"Okay. Do you want to know what I really think? What my diary really says about you?"

"Yes . . ." Darcy heard her own voice trail off. "I mean, except if you don't want to tell me. Keep any secrets you need to, Gen."

"I never thought you were a bitch, Darcy. Never once. You're the opposite of that—a really sweet kid. Maybe a little lucky, a little sheltered, but smart enough that you didn't really need the world to beat you up." Imogen had stopped packing, but she had gone still again, her voice flat, her face expressionless. "Smart, but maybe not as lucky as you seem. I think you got published too young."

"Oh," Darcy said softly. Her heart had just broken.

"Not because your writing isn't ready, but because *you* aren't. You don't trust me, and you won't trust your own novel when it gets out there and people start to write about it. Thousands of people, some brilliant, some stupid, or vile and hurtful. I'm so scared for you, Darcy. There are pages and pages in my diary about how scared I am for you."

"I had no idea," Darcy said.

"That's because I didn't want my fears to become yours. Because they're *mine*. And I was right about keeping them a secret too, because you've spent the last six weeks freaking out over one fucking typo! What'll you be like when a thousand people start picking apart your novel?"

"It'll be okay," Darcy said. "Because you'll be there."

"Maybe."

Darcy didn't understand the words. She couldn't. She shook her head.

"I think you also met me too young," Imogen said. "That's in my diary too. You want something more epic than this relationship, something fantastical and heavenly. You want us to read each other's minds."

"No, I don't. I just wanted you to *read my fucking ending.*"

"Yeah. I'm sorry about that." Imogen's stone facade had cracked. She looked defeated now, her hair in disarray, her face flushed, like someone who'd lost a fistfight. "But right now my opening still sucks, and I haven't gotten any work done in the last month. And I really need to get my head clear, so I have to go home. I have a book to write."

Imogen turned away, stuffing a last few things of hers into the plastic garbage bag—her phone charger, a handful of rings, a signed copy of Standerson's latest from the tour, and the box of matchbooks that she'd brought over for writing purposes, full of random jobs and settings and potential fires.

Darcy tried to stand, to stop her girlfriend from leaving. But gravity held her to the floor with an avaricious force. The air was thick, and it was impossible to speak a word.

Imogen went past without saying good-bye, leaving Darcy sitting there, trying to breathe. For her whole life, her good luck had been a trick, a bait-and-switch, a setup. The fact was, Darcy's luck was shit.

She had met the love of her life too young, and because of that she would lose it all.

CHAPTER 38

YAMA WAS BACK SOON, HIS HEAT SPILLING BEFORE HIM, SETTING the chandeliers flickering over our heads.

"Lizzie," he said, and for a moment it felt good to hear my name.

But then I had to tell him, "It was me. I led him here."

A look passed between Yama and his sister. His was of sadness, hers a cold expression of triumph.

"I'm so sorry," I said.

He shook his head, but he didn't cross the floor, didn't reach out to me, just stared at his sister. For a moment I saw how similar their faces were. Despite his added years, they really did look like twins, except that her skin was gray, and his warm and brown.

Finally he turned to me. "I should've taught you more."

"It was obvious." My words tasted of the rusty air. "You kept telling me that names are important."

"It was my fault."

"Enough!" Yami clapped her hands, and black oil scattered across the floor. "There's time for penance when our people are safe."

I nodded and held out my hand. The droplets of oil were skittering beneath our feet like black mercury, seeking one another. They joined into a single pool, as smooth and shiny as a disk of onyx.

"How do I find him?"

Yama took my hand. "Don't say his name. It'll only give him warning. Just think about when you kissed him."

A shiver went through me, but I remembered the bitter electricity of Mr. Hamlyn's hand against my lips, the cool dryness of his skin. I let myself hate him for tricking me, for fitting so perfectly into my murder of the bad man. For being exactly what I'd needed that night. I felt my hatred became a connection between us.

I pulled Yama into the dark pool and let the current take us.

We stepped out of the river into hell.

The sky was on fire here, too blinding to look at, crowded with a hundred suns. The air slid into my lungs as thick as syrup, the rust and blood a taste in my mouth now, not just a smell. A roaring filled my ears and shook my bones, and I knew that we were someplace even deeper than Yama's underworld city.

Beneath our feet was broken pavement, cratered and pitted. In all directions lay the remains of a modern-looking city, the buildings half-destroyed, the skyline as jagged as broken teeth.

I couldn't see Mr. Hamlyn anywhere. It was too bright, too loud.

Yama stared at the broken cityscape, shading his eyes from the searing sky. "These are his memories. But of *what*?"

My eyes were tearing up in the heat. "He kept talking about a war, how whole cities died at once—adults, children, everyone. This is what made him a psychopomp."

Yama was looking up in awe. "Death falling from the sky."

I understood it then—the thunderous drone that made the air shiver and melt, it was the sound of a thousand propellers, the whistle of bombs falling through the air. It came from overhead, but also from the shattered ground beneath our feet, leaking from every stone.

I realized that it had to be the Second World War, and a strange thought struck me. "He's a lot younger than you, isn't he?"

"Some are old when they cross over." Yama turned to me. "Can you find him?"

I shut my eyes against the burning sky and felt it, the pull of my hatred leading me to Mr. Hamlyn. He was inside the shell of a building right in front of us. It had been six stories tall once, but only the outer walls stood, the windows looming empty.

The hot, smoky air made it hurt to talk, so I pointed. We made our way across a hundred yards of crumbled asphalt and in through a gaping hole where a doorway had been. The interior was full of rubble, and the roar of airplanes and bombs echoed from the jagged walls.

Yama drew me to a halt. "We should be careful. The wolf is a lion in his own den."

I looked up. There was no roof, just more blazing sky. "You mean, he's *comfortable* here?"

"These are his memories of where he was made."

I shook my head. By that logic, I'd be happy in an airport, the air full of screams and the floor slick with blood. I didn't want to imagine that place ever again.

But the old man's recollections were vivid, I had to admit.

"He's up there." I pointed at a ragged set of stairs that clung to one of the remaining walls. They led to a corner of the building that was more or less intact. As we climbed, I could feel the roar of bombs and airplanes, as if the stairs were about to crumble beneath our feet.

At the top was a landing, where a section of roof was still attached, blocking out the fiery sky. We stumbled into its shade, half-blind for a moment.

Mr. Hamlyn was waiting there for us. He sat on a broken block of stone, a needle and thread in his hands. Scraps of cloth lay in a pile at his feet, the beginnings of a new patchwork coat. A shudder went through me as I realized: his clothes were patched together from the pickings of a bombed-out city.

"Ah, you're here." He didn't look up from his work. "Not just young Lizzie but the impressive Mr. Yamaraj."

Neither of us answered. The floor trembled beneath our feet.

"I suppose you're upset about your missing children."

"Are they here?" Yama asked.

Mr. Hamlyn looked up and smiled. "Only in spirit. But I'm sure you have more for me to taste."

Yama made two fists, and sparks began to drift from his skin. The air grew even hotter around us.

"I'm not going to kill you," he said. "But I can burn you."

Mr. Hamlyn's eyes were bright. "You mean, we'll be connected?"

"You'll bear my mark. And if you trouble my people again, I'll find you, anywhere you run."

The old man spread his hands, the needle still held daintily between forefinger and thumb. "But I like it here just fine, and young Lizzie is welcome anytime. You, on the other hand, are starting to annoy me."

Yama didn't answer, walking toward him, sparks cascading from his clenched hands. Mr. Hamlyn only smiled up at him.

That's when I started to worry. The old man had fled in an instant when Yama had confronted him before, and had even seemed scared of me. But here in his own private hell, Mr. Hamlyn was unmoved by threats.

He placed the needle carefully beside him, and reached for a tangled ball of thread at his feet.

At last I saw the pattern of shimmering lines crisscrossing the floor. They were threads of memory stretching from wall to wall. Each glistening strand led to the tangle at Mr. Hamlyn's feet.

"Yama!" I cried, just as the old man's hand clutched the ball of thread and pulled hard. The crisscrossed lines on the floor sprang into the air, suddenly taut, a shimmering spiderweb leaping into form around us.

One of the strands bit into my thigh, cutting deep. I staggered away, but two more went taut across my path, and I barely stopped myself in time.

I didn't dare move. The threads were all around me, vibrating with the sound of the airplanes overhead. Yama was trapped in the center of the web. His hand was bleeding, his black silk shirt sliced open in half a dozen places.

"Don't move!" I cried. These were the same cutting memories I'd used on the bad man's spirit. The souls of people who'd watched their entire city burn in one night, countless yards of them wrapped around us.

"You should listen to our young friend," Mr. Hamlyn said. Blood dripped from his hand that held the ball of thread, but he didn't seem to notice. "Funny that you haven't seen this little trick before. I suppose they didn't have incendiary bombs in your day."

Yama just stared down at the glittering lines that trapped him, astonished.

"Meet the population of my hometown." When Mr. Hamlyn spoke, the threads shimmered around us like plucked strings. "Funny what watching everyone you know die can do to a ghost, and what the threads of that ghost can do to *us*."

The old man pulled the ball of thread tighter. The glowing lines closed around Yama.

He could barely move now, but his voice was steady. "What do you want?"

The old man laughed. "Everything! I want all those ghosts you've been collecting for me. Thousands of them! Especially the ones who died young and loved."

"Stop!" I cried. "Please, don't hurt him."

Mr. Hamlyn turned his colorless eyes on me. "You I would never hurt, my little valkyrie. But you heard your friend. He's very angry with me, and very dangerous."

"I'll never bring him near you again, I promise!"

"But I need his people, Lizzie. All those memories tended through the centuries, just waiting for me." The old man shook his head slowly. "Think of what I could weave from them."

Yama growled, and a spray of sparks shot from his clenched

fist. The old man pulled the threads tighter, and new cuts opened on Yama's flesh.

"Stop it!" I cried, and they both looked at me. A glowing strand shuddered inches from my face.

"Get out of here, girl!" Mr. Hamlyn said. "I don't want to hurt you. I want to teach you things."

"To hell with you!"

"Lizzie. You should leave." Trickles of blood were pooling beneath Yama's feet. He stood in an awkward position, trying to keep the glowing lines from cutting deeper.

"Yes, go," Mr. Hamlyn said. "Before I get bored."

I hesitated. Here at the periphery of the glowing spiderweb, there just was enough space to make my way out. But if I did, the old man would slice Yama to pieces.

"Okay," I said softly. "Just a second."

I visualized my way through the web before I moved, cataloging every deadly thread. Then all at once I took three steps—each awkward and dangerous—closer to the center.

The old man sighed. "You think you know more tricks than me, girl?"

"I don't know any tricks." I reached out a hand and placed it on Yama's shoulder. "But if you want to kill him, you'll have to kill me too."

"Lizzie," Yama whispered. "Don't."

A growl came from Mr. Hamlyn. "What makes you think I won't?"

I locked my eyes with his. "Because I want to learn from you."

The words came out as if I meant them, because some part of

me did. I wanted to know how he made the sky burn, and how the razing of a city decades ago could be woven into a deadly web of light.

The old man stared back at me, and he saw that I wanted everything.

"You tempt me, girl."

"I won't bring him here again. And even if I did, I'm sure you've got more tricks."

"Flatterer." He smiled at me. "You'll keep him under control?"

I nodded. At that moment, I didn't care about the ghosts the old man had taken. I just wanted Yama to live.

"For you, then," the old man said. "And because I need him alive to keep his ghosts from fading. Be careful with him. Cuts are tricky, down here in the afterworld."

I ignored him and snapped my fingers—a drop of oil slipped from them. It fell through the shimmering lines and splashed into Yama's blood. Slowly it expanded, turning the dusty stone beneath us black.

We began to sink into the floor, and for a moment Mr. Hamlyn looked as though he was about to pull his web tight and cut us into pieces. But in the end he didn't, and a few long moments later we were in the river.

When we reached his palace again, Yama collapsed into my arms. His shirt was in pieces, and he bled from countless cuts.

I set him gently on the cushions, looking around. No servants in sight, and his sister was gone.

"Yami!" I called, then turned back to her brother. Blood pooled beneath him, soaking into the gray pattern of the rug. It was bright red, and there seemed to be too much of it. Had the old man's web sliced open an artery?

Then I felt the trickles on my own body, and looked at my arm. The blood was flowing too fast, like water from my veins. A wave of light-headedness swept over me.

"Yami!" I cried again.

"We have to go," Yama murmured. "Home."

"We're there. But something's wrong!"

"Not my home. Yours. Quickly."

A blur of gray servants flickered in the corners of my vision, and I heard Yami's voice. "What happened? Yama!"

"The old man was setting a trap." I stared at my arm, from which the blood still flowed. "He cut us. Something's wrong."

"Take my brother to the overworld," Yami cried. "Now!"

I looked up. "What? Why?"

"You can't heal here, you idiot girl!" She clapped, and black droplets fell like rain from her hands. "Your body is halted!"

I stared at her—and it slowly started to make sense. We didn't grow old, or tired, or hungry in the underworld, nor could we heal. Our blood wasn't coagulating.

Yama's skin was growing pale. We were both bleeding to death.

"But this isn't even my real body," I murmured. "I thought this was some sort of astral projection."

"My brother has been able to travel in his own body for three thousand years," Yami said. "And you're much stronger than you know. Now go!"

*   *   *

A moment later we were in the river again, its current spinning out of control and purposeless, a reflection of my panic. I couldn't think of any hospital I was connected to—all my memories of childhood accidents were too fuzzy, and my head was light from blood loss.

But I remembered what Yama had asked earlier, for me to take him home. I thought of my bedroom, willing us there. Maybe I could stop the worst of his bleeding on my own, and then drive him to a hospital.

At first the current obeyed me, taking us steadily up toward the overworld. My arms stayed wrapped around Yama, protecting him from the river's needy wisps of memory.

But then, all at once, a new force shook the current, something stronger than my will, and yanked us in another direction.

"Yama," I hissed in his ear. "What's happening?"

"The river's calling you." As he spoke, tendrils of his blood carried into the raging current. "It's sooner than I thought."

I screamed into the river. Whatever disaster was happening in the overworld, it couldn't happen *now*.

Yama's head rolled back, and his muscles went slack against me. I held him tighter, as if that would keep his blood inside.

It was long minutes later that the river finally set us down . . .

. . . into chaos.

Gunfire and blinding lights came from every direction, and smoke filled the air. We were deep in a forest, surrounded by pine trees that climbed into the sky, their branches laden with snow. It was nighttime, but searchlights lanced through the smoke and mist. Among the trees sat squat little cabins. Black-clad figures ran among them, stopping to fire rifles into the trees.

Why had the river brought us here? This didn't look like any-place I'd ever seen before, or anywhere I'd ever imagined.

But Yama was still bleeding. He had to cross over into the real world now, or I'd lose him. There was only one scrap of safety that I could see—a corner where two of the cabins had been built beside each other. I dragged him across the snow and into the shadows there.

"You have to cross over," I whispered in his ear.

He didn't answer. His face was as pale as the snow on the dark ground.

"Yama!" I cried. Still no response.

I remembered what Yami had said: *You're stronger than you know.* And, of course, I was bleeding too. Which meant my real body had been down there in Mr. Hamlyn's war zone.

Maybe I could do this. . . .

I wrapped my arms around Yama and shut my eyes, focusing on the crack of rifles around us, the panicked shouts.

"Security is responding," I muttered to myself.

A moment later I felt it happen, both of us breaking through the bubble of the flipside. The fresh air of the overworld surged into my lungs, along with the half-remembered smell of tear gas and gun smoke. It was suddenly freezing cold, my breath coiling in front of my face. The sound of gunfire turned sharp and deadly. But I had done it, traveled on the river in my real body. . . .

Straight into a battle.

I didn't have time to worry about bullets. I pulled at the places where my shirt was already sliced, tearing off strips of cloth to bind Yama's wounds. The gashes looked deep and brutal, but at last the red was thickening, flowing like blood instead of water.

By the time I had tied his cuts as best I could, I was half-naked. I pressed myself shivering against him, trying to keep us both warm. The gunfire had tapered off, but shouts and the roar of vehicle engines came from all around.

Then I saw the body in the shadows beside us.

It was a young man, probably in his twenties. He lay faceup, both his hands wrapped around his own throat. Blood trailed away from between the motionless fingers, red and thick in the snow. He'd been shot in the neck. His eyes stared straight at me, as if he'd been trying to speak, to get my attention in his last moments.

As I stared back at him in horror, his spirit stirred.

I'd seen this before, when the bad man had died. But I'd been ready for that, and this caught me by surprise. A second version of the young man, pale and stone-faced, pulled itself up from the body on the ground.

He turned and looked at me, strangely calm.

"You're dead," I said to him, because that was the only thing I knew for sure.

He nodded, as if this made all the sense in the world.

A shudder went through my frame. The cold was seeping in.

I turned from him, and saw more of them. More ghosts, spirits freshly torn from their bodies and set wandering loose on the snowy ground.

"I think I'm here to help you," I said.

Psychopomps were needed here, so the river had brought us.

"You're an angel, then?" the ghost asked.

I had to laugh at this. In my shredded shirt, I probably looked more like a madwoman than a heavenly creature. I was certainly no valkyrie.

"I'm just a girl."

"But the prophet said there would be angels to greet us. Angels of death."

A chill went over me as I realized the obvious. The river had brought me to the mountains of Colorado, to the home of a certain cult with an Armageddon mentality, an isolationist dogma, and a charismatic leader. A place that had been surrounded for the last week by two hundred federal agents—a massacre just waiting to happen.

But right now I didn't care much about souls who needed guidance to the underworld. What I cared about was keeping Yama alive. And, strangely, the dead cultist had just given me a glimmer of hope.

There were FBI agents here. They had to have doctors with them.

"I'll be back soon," I said, pulling myself gently from Yama's side.

He opened his eyes, nodding weakly, but awake again. The overworld and my crude bandages had helped a little, at least.

The ghost was kneeling now, his hands clasped together in prayer. I ignored him and stepped from the shadows into the searchlights sweeping the compound. My arms were wrapped around me in the cold, but I pried them loose and forced myself to hold my hands in the air. Freezing cold was better than bullets.

"Hello!" I called into the darkness. "I need help!"

A moment later a dozen flashlights pointed at me from the trees, like the glimmering eyes of beasts.

An amplified voice called back at me, "Down on the ground!"

I hesitated, staring at the snow and wishing I was wearing more than a shredded shirt. But the voice had sounded impatient, and I dropped to my knees, then face-first into the snow.

"My friend needs help!" I shouted. "He's bleeding!"

They didn't answer, and it seemed to take forever before boots thudded across the hard ground, surrounding me. Rough hands pulled my arms behind me, and the click of handcuffs reached my ears. By then I was too cold to feel the metal against my skin.

They pulled me up into a sitting position, and finally I could see them. Six men and one woman in bulky vests with FBI in bright yellow across them.

"My friend's bleeding, unconscious, unarmed," I said through chattering teeth, and jerked my head toward the cabins. "Please help him!"

"Check it out," someone ordered, and three of the men headed toward Yama.

I looked up at the man who'd spoken, trying to utter some kind of thanks, but the words died in my mouth. Behind him was another agent. He stood among his fellows, looking a little confused. His raid jacket was full of bloody holes, and he cast no shadows in the floodlights angling through the trees.

"I'm so sorry," I said.

He looked at me, a little surprised that I wasn't ignoring him like all the others.

I wanted to tell him it was okay, that there was more beyond the veil of death. That some of the underworld was sane, well tended, even civilized. But the cold had frozen my tongue by then, and a moment later someone shoved me back down into the snow.

CHAPTER 39

"FOR FUCK'S SAKE, PATEL. YOU'RE TEN MINUTES LATE!"

Darcy sighed. "Nice to see you too, Nisha."

"This place is terrifying."

Darcy looked around, shrugged. Penn Station was a bit cold, and crowded, and the marble floors were streaked with rain tracked in from the streets outside, but it wasn't scary at all.

"Is it the sandwich shop that frightens you, little sister? Or the Lox Factory?"

"It's everything." Nisha presented her duffel bag to Darcy, and took the handle of her rolling suitcase for herself. "The general ambiance distresses me."

Darcy smiled. She'd never thought of herself as tougher than Nisha, or tougher than anyone, really. But it was true that almost ten months of living in New York had left her with no dread of shabbiness, underground tunnels, or crowds.

Then the weight of the duffel bag hit. "What the hell, Nisha? You're only staying a week. What did you bring, bricks?"

"Books. You know, in case your fancy friends want to sign them. At my cocktail party."

"What cocktail party?"

"Carla and Sagan got a party."

Darcy let out a groan. "That was my housewarming. And I haven't been doing parties lately."

"All the more reason to have one now." Nisha headed off through the crowd.

Darcy followed, wondering why the heavy books weren't in the rolling suitcase, and why she'd been stuck carrying the duffel bag, and how Nisha had, annoyingly, chosen the exact right direction out of the warren that was Penn Station.

Half an hour later they were in apartment 4E's guest room. Nisha was unpacking her suitcase, displacing Darcy's dress jackets from their hangars in favor of a wide selection of gothic attire.

"That looks like a lot of clothes for seven days."

Nisha paused. "Are you having second thoughts about my visit, Patel?"

"Of course not," Darcy said, though her conversation with their mother the night before had been somewhat daunting. Phrases like "in loco parentis" had been thrown around. Phrases like "cocktail party" had not.

"You don't look very happy, is all."

Darcy shrugged, but didn't answer.

"I mean, you've got an apartment in New York, your first

novel coming out in five months, and me visiting for a whole week! You should be as happy as a unicorn fully jacked on Zoloft, all rainbows and bliss. But you look like someone just drowned your bag of kittens."

"Way to mix your metaphors," Darcy said.

"Those were similes. I thought you writers knew that stuff."

Darcy stared at her little sister, wondering why she was being so clueless. Nisha knew everything that had happened a month before, thanks to dozens of texts and emails and three long phone conversations. It seemed cruel of her to pretend ignorance, unless she simply needed to hear it in person.

Maybe the subject was unavoidable. These days, the breakup was measured not in the weeks since it had happened, but in the minutes after awakening it took Darcy to remember it was real.

"I miss Imogen."

Nisha nodded sagely. "You still haven't seen her?"

"Only by accident, last week on Canal Street. We talked and were polite and everything. She hugged me at the end."

"Hugs are good, right?"

"Hugs are crap! Hugs are zero."

"Yeah, hugs are the worst," Nisha dutifully agreed. "But I thought you guys were still emailing each other."

"We are. But not the screeds we should be writing. Just these stupid little notes that say nothing—hugs in email form. Imogen says she has to focus until she's done with her book. We used to work together, but I'm no longer conducive to work. I am drama. I am turmoil."

Nisha listened to this quietly, then sat down cross-legged on the floor, her position of wisdom. "But she hasn't written a savage and lengthy essay about your faults, has she?"

"No. She wouldn't do that." Darcy had always been certain of this.

"For that matter, she hasn't even officially dumped you."

"She says it's just until she finishes her book. She's trying to be nice, I think, but it's just taking longer and hurting more." Darcy flopped back on the guest futon and stared at the ceiling. "Like jumping off the Chrysler Building and hitting all the flagpoles and gargoyles on the way down."

"Why would she do that, Patel?"

"Because I'm too young for a proper dumping! Imogen thinks I'm too young for anything."

"Yeah, that is kind of a general problem with you."

Darcy raised her head to glare at Nisha. "You *are* younger than me, you know."

"Not for my age."

"Crap," Darcy groaned, her head falling back onto the futon again. "You're probably right. I fucked up everything. I snooped on her all the time, and I didn't tell her when I was upset, or listen when she needed space."

"So you told me in great detail." Nisha drummed her fingers on the floor a moment, then asked, "But snooping isn't a dumpable offense, is it?"

"I guess the really bad thing was not trusting her."

"So trust her now."

Darcy sat up. All these questions were making her restless. "How do I trust someone who barely talks to me? What's there to trust?"

"The one thing she's telling you: That this isn't the end. That she just needs space to write."

"But that's what we did together," Darcy said. "That's who we *were*. If we can't write together anymore, what's the fucking point?"

Nisha was silent for a long moment, as if she was really considering this. Her supercilious tone had shifted into something else. Something more mature.

"Did Imogen say she never wants to write with you again?"

"I guess not. She claims it's just this book making her crazy. But it was *me* making her crazy, Nisha."

"Not if you trust her, Patel. Don't give up just because she can't be with you right now."

Darcy didn't answer. She wasn't giving up. Not in a hundred years.

But she was ranting in despair at her little sister, who'd only walked through the door ten minutes ago, which was pathetic. The weird thing was how calm and collected Nisha looked, as if events were unfolding exactly as she'd planned.

"Is this how you wanted to spend your time in New York?" Darcy asked with a sigh. "Listening to my misery?"

"I'm here to learn. And what you have taught me is to avoid love as long as possible." Nisha rolled her empty suitcase into the corner. "Is there food anywhere?"

Darcy managed a smile. "This is Manhattan. There is food."

Their first stop was the ramen restaurant with the giant cat statue. It was one of the places where Darcy had lurked back in the lonely days just after the breakup, hoping to bump into Imogen. Things had never worked out that way, but Darcy still felt a little trickle of hope whenever the bell above the front door jangled.

Also the noodles were exceptional.

"I named a book here," Darcy said after they'd ordered.

Nisha looked up. "*Untitled Patel* finally has a name?"

"Alas, it remains untitled," Darcy said. It remained mostly unwritten as well, except for a few rough ideas. "But this is where I came up with *Kleptomancer*. That's the name of Imogen's second book. Pretty good, huh?"

"Dude." Nisha shook her head. "Can we talk about something else?"

"Sure. Whatever. How about my budget? That should be fun."

"Indeed." Nisha produced her phone and flicked at the screen, always happy on the familiar ground of numbers. "I have all the details right here."

What followed was unpleasant.

It wasn't just the prodigious rent of apartment 4E, nor the many one-way plane fares purchased while tagging along on Imogen's tour. There were also the clothes that Darcy had bought for the tour, and various furnishings acquired over the last nine months, and her curious inability to keep her daily expenses under seventeen dollars. (Food was so delicious. Beer so necessary.)

But the worst thing, it turned out, was the fact that she hadn't kept any of her receipts for business expenses, and her first-ever income tax return was due in a week, along with a titanic check. According to Nisha's calculations, Darcy was almost an entire year ahead of schedule when it came to running out of money.

"Why so surprised, Patel?" Nisha said when her presentation was done. "Sooner or later there had to be a reckoning."

"Yeah, but it's all reckonings these days." Darcy snapped her chopsticks apart, and splinters flew in all directions. "I think my whole life might be reckonings from here on out. I just got my lease renewal form. My rent's going up, starting in July. Ten percent."

"Whoa." Nisha made notes on her phone. "I told you to sign a two-year lease, Patel."

"I think Lalana would've noticed."

"What are you going to do?"

Darcy shrugged. "I still love my apartment. But it isn't like it was."

"So find a cheaper place. Or come home!"

"Nisha, I love you guys, but I have a sequel to write. I'm not going to get anything done sitting in my old bedroom."

"You wrote *Afterworlds* in your bedroom. In thirty days!"

"That was easy—I didn't know what I was doing."

Nisha shook her head. "Patel, you've got almost three months left on your lease, and you have no love life anymore. So why not get writing for real and see what you can do? I mean, *after* you're done entertaining me this week."

"Maybe." It seemed like a decent idea.

"You know," Nisha said. "The elder Patels still think you're going to Oberlin in September."

"That's unlikely. The application deadline was three weeks ago."

Nisha blinked. "I thought you had a place saved?"

"Yeah, I missed that deadline too. Like, almost a year ago."

"You're pathetic, Patel." Nisha laughed a little. "Not that it matters. Your financial aid is a smoking crater anyway."

"What do you mean?"

"They don't just look at this year's income, Patel. They look at this year's *tax return*. Which shows the money you made *last year*."

Darcy swallowed. "You mean, the money that's mostly gone?"

"You've got more payments coming in for publication, and for *Untitled Patel*, but those will be an issue if you apply to Oberlin next year. As your accountant, I advise you to stick with the plan of being a writer for three years."

"Um, could you have mentioned this earlier? Like, back at the start, before I tossed away my college career?"

"You said that's what you wanted! And I didn't know you were going to blow your advance on rent and noodles."

Darcy slumped down into her seat. She was doomed.

The food came then, but Darcy found no solace staring into the murky and expensive broth of her ramen. First Imogen's phone and autocorrect had conspired to destroy her life, and now her landlord, the IRS, and her future college were joining in. It was only a matter of time before the entire universe was arrayed against Darcy. Even her chopsticks were misbehaving, letting the udon noodles slip away, flicking broth into her face as they slapped the surface.

But the ramen's taste was exquisite, and soon the two sisters were talking about less depressing things: Nisha's classes at school, her plans for college, the foibles of the elder Patels. Darcy filled her in on all the gossip from Carla and Sagan, whom she'd talked to almost daily since the breakup, one of the small silver linings of the last month.

Darcy wondered if she should look for more silver linings. Nisha was right about her not having a life. Perhaps writing was something she could still do alone.

"I just wish another idea would hit me," Darcy said. "Something big and weird, like when I found out about Mom's friend getting murdered."

Nisha looked up from her empty bowl. "Oh right, about that. You know how she didn't say anything when she read your novel?"

"Yeah? Did she talk to you about it?"

"Not a word, ever. So I did some research, and it turns out that was a different Annika Sutaria."

Darcy stared at her sister. "What?"

"It turns out that India is, like, really *populated*. As a result, many people share the same name. The Annika who knew that murdered girl is a month older than Mom. You suck at research."

"Fuck," Darcy said. The little ghost had never been hers at all.

Or maybe this meant that Mindy really *was* hers, because she'd invented her from a case of mistaken identity. Or perhaps it meant she'd used a tragedy she had even less right to steal. And what if by now that other Annika was also dead, and Darcy was the last person to remember Rajani at all, the last keeper of her ghost?

Darcy knew only one thing for certain: a ghost with a mistaken identity wasn't a bad idea for *Untitled Patel*.

"Can we go to a bookstore?" Nisha asked.

Darcy's mind clicked back into the present. "You know, I've sort of been avoiding the publishing thing."

"You've got a book to write, Patel. How can you avoid the publishing thing?"

"That's the *writing* thing," Darcy sighed. "The publishing thing is book blogs, YA Twitter feeds, mock Printz Awards, reviews. I've been offline for weeks." Everything reminded her of Imogen.

"Yeah, well, bookstores are the *reading* thing. Come on."

Book of Ages was one of the last big indie bookstores in Manhattan, more than half its floor space dedicated to young people's lit. The walls were covered with vintage children's art, the shelves thick with YA and middle-grade. There was a graphic novel section the size of half a tennis court, centered around a red-and-white-checked Tintin rocket as tall as Darcy. A visit to the Ages had been a highlight of every family trip to New York when the two sisters were little.

"So are you, like, a rock star here now?" Nisha asked as they passed through the doors.

"I am a rock star nowhere," Darcy said. "I don't even have a book out yet, remember?"

"A hundred and sixty-eight days and counting! So they won't recognize you? Will there be no discount?"

Darcy glanced at the woman behind the counter. She wasn't one of the handful of Ages employees that Darcy had met. "Sorry. Full price."

"No books for you then, Patel. As your accountant, I declare you officially penniless."

"Can I charge you a dollar every time you say 'as your accountant'?"

"I doubt it would help," Nisha said, then came to a halt, staring at an end cap display of a dozen paperbacks, all with the same flame-red cover. "Hey, isn't that . . ."

Darcy nodded. It was *Pyromancer.*

"Weird," she said, picking one up. "This wasn't supposed to be out in paperback till summer."

"Is that good or bad?" Nisha asked.

"Not sure." Darcy turned the book over. On the back was the old blurb from Kiralee, and also the starred reviews, all the mountains of praise that had never seemed to sell any copies. "But Paradox is still trying, I guess."

Whatever the meaning, it felt good to see Imogen's novel here in quantity at the front of the store. Darcy turned to the author photo on the back cover: Imogen looking happy, her hands tucked safely in the pockets of her leather jacket to prevent head touching.

A stone formed in Darcy's throat as she remembered the day of the photo shoot. The Imogen in this picture had spent every day with Darcy by her side.

"Knock yourself out with that," Nisha said, and headed off toward the Sparkle Pony pop-up section.

Darcy opened to the first page.

Her favorite part of setting fires had always been the matches. She liked the way they rattled, stiff little wooden soldiers in a cardboard box, and the way they bloomed into hot flowers between cupped palms. She loved the ripping, fluttering noises they made as they fought the wind. Even their remains were beautiful— spindly, black, and bowed—after they'd burned all the way down to fire-calloused fingertips. . . .

The words shivered on the page, just as they had the first time she'd read them. She heard the author's voice in the cadence of the sentences. For a moment, she expected Imogen to walk up behind her and lay a hand on her shoulder, or a kiss on the back of her neck.

"Good timing, huh?" came a voice.

Darcy spun around. It was Johari Valentine.

"Oh, hi." They embraced, pulled apart again. "It's been ages!"

"I've been back home in Saint Kitts." Johari shook her head. "Couldn't stand another winter up here. Bad enough, writing about the cold without living in it!"

"Oh, right. When does *Heart of Ice* come out?"

"October." Johari rapped her knuckles against the wood of the nearest shelf, a little spell to ward off doubt.

"Mine's late September," Darcy said. She glanced at the end cap. "What did you mean, good timing?"

"Imogen's paperbacks, they came out just in time."

"For what?"

Johari frowned. "You know, the president's daughter? The photo?"

Darcy shook her head. "I've been kind of . . . out of it."

"Mercy, girl. I must have been out of it too!"

Johari looked astonished. Apparently nobody had told her about the breakup. It seemed strange that there could be anyone left who didn't know.

"What happened?" they both asked at once.

After a moment of standoff, Darcy sighed and went first. "I haven't seen Imogen for a while. We're taking a break, I guess."

"I'm so sorry, darling. You two were so sweet together."

"We *are* sweet. It's just for a while." Darcy took a steadying breath, trying to heed Nisha's advice to trust Imogen's word. "No big deal. But did you say something about the president's daughter?"

Johari's eyes widened. "Yeah, someone took a picture of her walking to the helicopter, and she was carrying *Pyromancer*. It was easy to tell, because of that red cover."

A startled laugh jumped out of Darcy. "That's kind of funny."

"It was, at first. But then some political blog made a big deal out of it, because of the 'questionable content.' You know. Girl starting fires, kissing other girls." Johari chuckled, shaking her head. "Then some news channels followed along, and for a while, everyone was talking about Imogen."

"Seriously? How did I miss this?"

"It was only three days ago? Four? The silly people have moved on to talking about something else by now. But I suppose people who read novels have longer attention spans, because it's still selling."

"Whoa. What a lucky little shit she is."

This set Johari, who never swore at all, laughing again.

Darcy laughed along, already composing a congratulations email to Imogen, and wondering if her good luck was still around after all. Maybe Imogen had just borrowed some of it for a while.

CHAPTER 40

THIRTY MINUTES LATER I WAS SITTING IN A MAKESHIFT CAMP half a mile from the compound. The air buzzed with radios and the rumble of a generator, which powered huge floodlights shining into the trees. The lights were hot enough to melt the snow in the pine boughs above, and a soft, glistening rain misted down into their beams.

Sitting on my crate, I was close enough to benefit from the warmth of the floodlights, and was wrapped in two mylar blankets. My cuts had been bandaged, and pronounced too minor for me to be taken to the medical tent. I had a mug of coffee nestled between my hands, which a very kind FBI agent had given me. My walking-through-walls magic had made short work of the handcuffs, but nobody seemed worried about that. Maybe it was because I was a half-frozen, half-naked young girl, or maybe because the situation was secure, with no gunfire for the last fifteen minutes. Whatever it was, everyone had stopped pointing guns at me.

Soon I would slip away, down into the river and back to my warm bedroom. But not until I was certain Yama was okay. I didn't know where the wounded were being treated. I was afraid to ask, in case someone noticed I was free and handcuffed me again, which would mean taking my hot coffee away. So I sat there just waiting, numbed by all I had seen.

The freezing cold had reached all the way inside me, joining with the place that had been there since Dallas. I wondered if I would ever be warm again.

Then I realized that someone was staring at me. I looked up from the depths of my coffee.

"Oh," I managed, my heart sinking. The grim reaper that had swept through my life had kept on going.

"Miss Scofield. How odd to see you here."

I nodded. "I guess everything must seem a bit odd to you right now."

Special Agent Elian Reyes stared at me, uncertain, confused. But after a moment, he sat down on another crate, and we stared off into the trees together. The cold place inside me, and the real-world cold that had joined it, was dampening my reactions. It all seemed very normal, somehow, sitting with him.

Of course, comforting the dead was my job now.

"I forgot you might be here," I said.

"I almost wasn't. It's only been four hours since I landed in Denver." He looked down at his hands, as if he didn't recognize them. "Last one here, first one through the door."

I nodded. "It's all about timing. You miss your flight, and everything turns out different."

"You know, I almost did, but for once there was no traffic on the way to LAX." His laugh was short and dry. "Or maybe if I'd been a little faster on my feet."

"Don't blame yourself, Agent Reyes. Everyone blames themselves."

He looked at me. "Are you okay, Lizzie?"

"Really cold, is all."

"Cold? So you're not . . . like me, are you? But you can see me."

I shook my head. "I can see ghosts, because of what happened in Dallas. It changed me. This is my new calling."

Agent Reyes was thoughtful for a moment. "You seem a bit young for that job."

I nodded in complete agreement, wishing that I was eleven again, not knowing anything about how the world worked. Not about bad men, or the secrets of death, or even that my father would be leaving us soon.

But there was no going back.

"I'm supposed to guide people, I think. I'm not quite sure how exactly, but I'll try to help you. Though maybe . . . you could help me first?"

"Of course, Lizzie. I always wanted to help you more than I could."

"I guess I knew that." It took a moment to speak again. "My friend was here, another guide, and he was hurt. They must have taken him wherever the doctors are."

"I was just at the med tent." Agent Reyes pointed into the distance, at another glow among the trees. "Your friend will be there, unless they've airlifted him out. I'll take you."

He held out his hand, and as I took it, I let myself slip across. It wasn't as cold on the flipside, and now I had a ghost to guide me.

Special Agent Reyes and I found Yama in the medical tent, his wrists handcuffed to the metal rails of a stretcher. He still looked pale, and a bag of plasma hung from the IV stand beside him. His wounds were hastily bound in white gauze, with black stitches peeking out from the sides.

But his eyes were open. "Lizzie."

I stepped forward, took his hand. My voice wasn't working. For a moment, it was tricky keeping myself here on the flipside. The tent was full of wounded agents and handcuffed cultists, and two bodies lay in the corner, sheets pulled over their heads. Agent Reyes's gaze drifted toward them.

"Thank you for saving me," Yama said.

A strangled laugh forced its way out of me. "I led you into a trap."

He shook his head. "That was my mistake. We're even now."

A medic lingered by the stretcher, probably wondering why Yama was murmuring to himself. He fell silent as she flicked a light into each of his eyes, checked the IV bag, and took his pulse.

"Do you get used to being invisible?" Agent Reyes asked me.

"Sort of." I stared at Yama. He had saved me in the airport, and now I'd saved him, but my stupidity had cost the afterlives of three of his people. It didn't feel even to me.

The medic moved on.

"Have the doctors said anything? Are you going to be okay?"

"They don't say much to me." Yama rattled his handcuff against the stretcher rail. "I appear to be in disfavor."

"On behalf of the bureau, I apologize." Agent Reyes looked genuinely sorry. "We don't have any protocol for spirit guides, I'm afraid."

"I won't be here long." His eyes turned to me. "I have a city to protect."

"Of course," I murmured. Without Yama to guard them, his people were easy prey. "Can I do anything to help?"

He nodded weakly. "Yami will call you."

I wondered for a moment what Agent Reyes was making of our conversation. But he was staring at the sheet-covered bodies in the corner of the medical tent.

I turned back to Yama. "I'm not afraid of Mr. Hamlyn."

"You don't need to be. I think he likes you."

My breath caught. Yama had heard the truth in my voice when I'd said I wanted to learn from Mr. Hamlyn. The man who had taken his people.

"I know he's bad."

"One can learn from monsters, Lizzie. After all, I wasn't the best teacher."

"Don't talk in the past tense, please. You're not going to die!"

"No, but I'll have to stay in my city now. The predator won't leave my people alone."

"You'll have to stay there . . . all the time?"

"Every minute I'm away, he'll hunt them."

I shook my head. All those hours we'd spent together, on bleak mountaintops or his windy atoll, were suddenly precious.

"And my sister was right," he said. "I've been lazy."

I swallowed something hard in my throat. "But it's okay if I visit, right?"

"Lizzie, you can do more than visit. You can come and live with us." A slow and beautiful smile overtook his face as he spoke, but I couldn't answer it.

Yama's city was magnificent, but also gray and silent, and I was already so cold inside. I could think myself into the afterworld, and smell rust and blood in the air. Death had been with me from the day I was born, and on top of all that, I was a murderer now.

What would living in the underworld do to me? Would I forget what sunlight felt like? Or start to hear the voices of the dead in every stone?

There was so much I'd meant to tell Yama tonight, but there hadn't been time. Around us, the medical tent was growing busier as more wounded were brought in.

I reached out my hand and brushed his cheek. With him in the real world and me on the flipside, the electricity of his touch was only a fleeting thing.

"My mother needs me now."

"There's no rush for you and me," he said.

Of course not. Yama planned to live forever. He could wait a hundred years, until my mother was a distant memory, my oldest friends all dead and buried.

But *I* couldn't wait for *him*. Not for a hundred years, not for a hundred days. Since when was love something you didn't rush? I leaned forward and kissed him, and the spark of his lips was still there, even through the veil of the flipside.

But when I pulled away, he let out a gasp.

"Lizzie. What happened?"

"What do you mean?"

"You did something." His voice had gone soft and harsh, and the shouting and bustle of the medical tent came rushing into the quiet.

He knew. He had tasted it on me.

"The bad man. I went back to his house."

Yama shook his head. The color was draining from his face, as if his wounds were flowing again.

"He was keeping those little girls there. And his memories were inside Mindy, making her scared all the time. But I fixed it. He's gone, cut to pieces."

"By the predator?"

"Yes, by Mr. Hamlyn." My gaze fell to the dirt floor again. It was glistening beneath my feet. The space heaters in the medical tent were melting the frozen ground. "But it was me who killed him."

Yama closed his eyes, his face twisting with pain. A hard and bitter moan seemed to leak out from his whole body.

Yama had sensed murder on me.

I'd become like the stones that smelled of blood, and whispered with the voices of the dead. Stained, like the rest of the world, except for that moon-shaped sliver of island in the great southern sea.

"You've never killed anyone, have you?" I asked.

"Of course not." His eyes opened, glistening with tears. "Don't you understand, Lizzie? Whatever comes after, life is priceless."

I stood there, silent. Almost dying had, in fact, taught me that, but it had taught me too many other things at the same time. All of it was jumbled in my brain now, a mess of strange rules and unexpected horrors. In the end, my anger had won out over the rest of what I'd learned.

Yama had kept his hands clean for thousands of years, and it had only taken me a month to kill someone.

"I'm sorry," I said.

Yama gave me one last look of horror, and turned his face away.

"You should go help Yami."

"Of course." I would have done anything for him. But when I closed my eyes and listened to the still air of the flipside, there was nothing. "It's just . . . she hasn't called me yet."

"She will soon." He closed his eyes again. We were done.

I took a step backward, away from his stretcher. A medic rushed past, running to help with a wounded agent being carried through the open tent flaps. As she passed through me, I felt the spark of her intensity, her resolve to save the man's life.

I turned from Yama and walked away.

Committing murder was so much worse than giving away his name, because it had changed *me*. All he'd ever wanted was a respite from death. For a few hours on a mountaintop, or a few moments when our lips touched. And now that was gone between us.

"Lizzie." It was the ghost Agent Reyes, following me out of the tent. "Are you okay?"

I nodded, still walking.

"Your friend, I overheard the medics. He's going to be fine, once he's got some plasma in him."

"Thank you." My voice sounded broken.

Agent Reyes stood in front of me, forcing me to stop. "I heard what you were saying to him, about a bad man. That's why you called me, isn't it?"

It took a moment to understand that he didn't mean a call on the current of the Vaitarna River, or the way this gun battle had called me here to Colorado. He only meant a phone call.

"Right. When I asked you about serial killers."

He nodded. "That wasn't hypothetical."

His gaze was too steady, his gray eyes too sharp, and I had to look away. "I guess you're not an FBI agent anymore, right?"

"No. The bureau doesn't employ ghosts."

I nodded. "Well, there was this serial killer, and I helped chop him into pieces."

"Is that part of your calling now, Lizzie? Avenging the dead?"

I shook my head. I had no calling, no purpose. I wasn't a valkyrie or a spirit guide. All I wanted was to go home. "It was just a mistake, an awful one. But it's okay. My fingerprints are on the murder weapon, and I texted someone from right in front of his house. They'll catch me."

At that moment, I wanted to be caught. To be punished, not for what I'd done to the bad man, but to Yama. To us.

Special Agent Reyes's hand took mine, just for a moment, his expression sad and steadfast.

"We don't catch everyone," he said.

I spent all night in the flipside, sleepless, numb, waiting for Yami's call.

Mindy was still full of energy, and took me on a tour of the neighborhood, regaling me with all the gossip she'd picked up over years of spying. She didn't notice how quiet I was.

It was unsettling, unreal almost, how much of her personality had disappeared when I'd killed the bad man. As if the deepest parts of her had been erased.

As if she wasn't a person anymore at all.

The hours passed and dawn drew near, and I started to worry about Yami. I knew she didn't like me very much, but I was all she had to protect her brother's city. Why hadn't she called by now?

She had died young and slowly in that field of bones thousands of years ago. Maybe Mr. Hamlyn wanted the threads of her life, and had already taken her.

I thought about going back to Colorado, to tell Yama that she hadn't called. But if his sister was in danger, he would leave his bed in a heartbeat, and that would be the end of his healing. I didn't want to imagine him guarding his people, pale and stitched and bloodless, like some zombie king in a gray palace.

But finally, just as dawn broke over the Andersons' yard, I heard a faint call on the winds of the flipside.

Elizabeth Scofield . . . come here.

It was Yami's voice. She hadn't said, "I need you," like the first time she'd called. This was a command.

I didn't hesitate, didn't even say good-bye to Mindy, just let the river take me. It was a short and furious trip, much quicker than my first journey down to the underworld. And when the black oil of the river passed from my eyes, there was no gray palace to greet me, no red sky.

Just a too-familiar street in Palo Alto.

Yami was waiting for me on the bad man's lawn. Around her, the gnarled and stumpy trees marked where the little girls had stood for so long. It was strange to see them gone.

"What is this?" I asked. "What are you *doing* here?"

"I have news for you." Yami sat down on the grass, cross-legged. "Come and join me, girl."

I took a few steps closer, but didn't sit.

"Don't be afraid, Elizabeth. It's only dirt."

"Do you know what's buried down there?"

"The dead are buried everywhere." Yami stroked the gray blades of grass. "The earth is a graveyard."

I supposed she was right, but I stayed on my feet. The place I had dug away with my own frantic fingers was smooth now.

"Yami, what did you do?"

"We buried the past."

I took a step backward, looking up at the house. The windows of the front bedroom stared balefully down at me. "You buried . . . the bad man?"

Yami let out a sigh. "Don't be absurd, Elizabeth. He's far too heavy. And if the police found him in the ground, it would cause a stir."

"Heavy? But you're a ghost. You can't carry *anything.*"

"Of course not." Yami opened her palms on her knees, as if she were meditating. "Mr. Hamlyn was most helpful."

My heart beat sideways once. "Mr. Hamlyn?"

"Sit down, girl. You don't look well."

I finally obeyed her. I didn't feel well either.

"After you left Yamaraj, my brother called me to his side," Yami began. "You managed to save him from the predator, it seems."

"Um. You're welcome."

She arched an eyebrow at this, and continued, "He told me to return home, and to call you down to help protect our city. Obviously I did not. There was work to be done there in Colorado. Souls to be gathered."

I stared at the ground, realizing that I'd done nothing to help the ghosts at the gun battle. I was a crappy psychopomp on top of all my other failings.

"There was an FBI agent there," I said. "Elian Reyes. Did you help him?"

Yami was smiling now. "We helped each other. He told me what you'd done, chopped someone to pieces. It was obvious that the predator had helped you with that. So when I returned to our city, I waited. He came soon enough, hungry, as promised."

"But why didn't he just . . ." My voice faded as Yami placed her hand firmly on mine. "Sorry. Go on."

She set to rearranging the fabric of her skirt across her knees. "Fortunately, Mr. Hamlyn is not the sort of man who rushes things. I was able to explain what Agent Reyes had told me. About your fingerprints, your phone messages, your general incompetence."

I stared at her. "It *was* my first murder, you know."

"And a very useful one, Elizabeth. I let Mr. Hamlyn understand that if your crime were ever found out, you would have to flee the overworld. Which would mean you coming to live with my brother." She shook her head slowly. "Neither of us wanted this to happen."

I shook my head. "Why does Mr. Hamlyn care?"

"Think harder, girl. If you come to live in the underworld, my brother has no reason to leave his city unprotected. So the predator loses his prey."

"So Mr. Hamlyn covered up my crime, hoping that I'll distract Yama?"

"Exactly." Yami smiled again. "Whereas I know that my brother will stay where he is needed. Because he loves his people more than he loves you."

I didn't answer that. After what I'd done, she was probably right.

In the corner of my eye, I noticed the cat, the one that lived nearby, watching us. It was crouched in a hunter's pose behind one of the gnarled little trees—chest and forepaws down in the dirt, its rear up in the air, muscles bunched and ready to spring. But in that way that cats sometimes do, it just stood there frozen, never coming after us.

I looked at the unsettled ground. "So what did Mr. Hamlyn bury here?"

"A few smashed bottles of pills, evidence of a struggle. When they find your victim, he'll be an old man who had a heart attack in his sleep, rolled out of bed, and landed hard. Nothing worth investigating, and even if they dust for fingerprints, Mr. Hamlyn polished the shovel. He and I have a wager. Will my brother choose his people, or you?" Yami sighed. "Mr. Hamlyn thinks rather highly of your chances. I'm not sure why."

I stared at her. "But why did he bother making a bet with you? Why didn't he just . . . eat you?"

"His tastes are rather specific." She held out her hand, showing me a soft scar in her gray skin. It was a half-moon shape, and I remembered the shard of bone that had cut through her. "I may have died young, but it was in terrible pain."

"Right. I'm sorry."

She nodded, receiving it like an apology that was her due. Then she reached out and brushed my scar, the tear-shaped one on my cheek. Her fingertips had a fiery spark, like a snap of static electricity, sharper and meaner than her brother's.

"It's unfortunate, this path you've taken, Elizabeth."

"I didn't really have a choice."

"You've made a few." Yami sighed gently. "Sometimes I wonder whether my brother was right to follow me. My parents lost two children that day."

"But you want him to stay with you now?"

"Lord Yama chose his path." She stood. "Choose yours, Lizzie. Life is priceless."

She snapped her fingers, and droplets fell to the grass around us, glittering like black diamonds.

Before she could depart, I said, "You're probably right. He won't abandon you, or his people. Not for me, anyway."

Yami stared at me a moment, then shrugged before she slipped away.

"If I knew the answer for certain, it wouldn't be a proper bet."

CHAPTER 41

IT STARTED SLOWLY AT FIRST, LONG DAYS OF STARING AT HER computer screen with nothing to show for them. But Darcy forced herself to stay at her desk, hour after hour, until the words at last began to come. For a week they dripped, like water from a broken tap, but gradually they came faster, until whole chapters flowed onto the page each day. She reached the terrific speeds she had back in that fateful November eighteen months before, and then surpassed them.

In the end *Untitled Patel* consumed her, drowning out her own dramas in the clamor of Lizzie's continuing story, and that of a ghost who was mistaken for someone else. Darcy lost herself in scene structure and syntax and semicolons, in plot and conflict and character, the elements of story contesting with each other for space on the page. She sprang up in the middle of the night to write, not because she was afraid she would forget her ideas, but because her head would explode if she didn't write them down. She wrote straight through her nineteenth birthday, and hardly noticed.

The month passed quickly in the end, at such a gallop that she hardly felt the absence at the center of her days, the empty chair across from her. She never grew weary of store-bought ramen, or worried about money and the other fleeting details of real life. And as the middle of May approached, she found herself completing the first draft of her second novel, the sequel to *Afterworlds*. It was messy, downright chaotic at the end, and still untitled, but there was time to fix all that.

As far as Darcy could tell, it was a real book, or close enough. There were even flickers of the juice. And a week before BookExpo America, she emailed it to Moxie Underbridge and collapsed into several days of sleep.

Books were free here. It was magic. It was huge.

Darcy had woken up early, anxious about her first public event for *Afterworlds*, a signing of advanced readers' copies at BEA. Her nerves had only sharpened when a chauffeured car arrived to take her uptown and deposit her in front of the Javits Convention Center.

Inside, the main hall was vast and buzzing. The ceiling was a hundred feet above her head, and the rumble of thirty thousand booksellers, librarians, and publishing pros shivered in the air. Darcy felt small and overwhelmed.

But books were free here.

Some were piled in modest stacks of twenty, and some laid like bricks to form book forts big enough to hide inside. Some were handed to you if you showed a flicker of interest, and some were arranged in spirals, almost too pretty to ruin by taking them. Almost.

Half an hour before her signing, the empty duffel bag that Darcy had brought was already overloaded, and she cursed herself as a neophyte. She could have brought a duffel bag full of duffel bags instead.

Of course, how would she lift all those books? How would she even read them all?

Still, they were free. Not just the YA novels she'd been able to scam out of her fellow authors over the last year, but historicals and cookbooks and category romances, thrillers and science fiction and even graphic novels. All of their publication dates were months away, and they all had that beautiful freshly printed smell.

By the time Rhea called her and told her it was time to meet at the Paradox booth for the signing, she had almost forgotten to be nervous.

At one end of the cavernous hall was the signing area, a cattle yard of stanchions guiding hundreds of people toward a long row of authors. Giant numbers hung above each aisle, lending a stamp of order to the industrial-size muddle of the crowds.

Debut author Darcy Patel, signing her novel *Afterworlds*, had been assigned aisle 17. She approached the signing area in the tow of Rhea, who had kindly stuffed the duffel bag full of free books into the nether regions of the Paradox booth. Darcy was wondering how many Paradox bags she could scam.

"There are self-pubbed romance writers on both sides of you," Rhea was saying. "They'll have long lines, but nothing crazy. You were supposed to be next to this former child actor signing his self-help book, but we managed to get you moved."

"Because his huge line would embarrass me?" Darcy asked.

Rhea shook her head. "We just don't like movie stars next to our authors. It's distracting. Their heads are too big!"

She led Darcy behind a giant black curtain, into the setup area for the signings. Boxes were piled everywhere, and a fully loaded forklift whirred past as they made their way toward the rear entrance to aisle 17. Darcy was wearing the cocktail dress her mother had given her on that first day in Manhattan. The dress had always brought her luck, but it felt out of place here among the freight and scurry of backstage.

"Good news: your books made it." Rhea pointed at a stack of boxes covered with Paradox logos and the words "*Afterworlds—Patel.*" "What kind of pen do you sign with?"

"Um." Darcy tried to remember the sage advice that Standerson had given her last year. "Uni-Ball . . . something?"

"Vision Elite? Jetstream? I prefer Bic Triumphs." Rhea was rummaging in her bag. "Take three of each, and a Sharpie for casts, show bags, and body parts."

"Thank you." Darcy meekly accepted the handful of pens.

"We've got five boxes to get through. That's a hundred copies, give or take." Rhea knelt and slid a box cutter down a seam of tape. The folds leaped open, revealing the familiar cover, which now wore both Kiralee's and Oscar Lassiter's blurbs.

Darcy knelt beside Rhea. A single advanced copy had arrived at apartment 4E a week ago, but it was staggering and wonderful to see her novel in quantity. The real books didn't come out until September 23, four whole months from now, but these advanced copies were somehow more precious. Each was marked: NOT FOR SALE.

"A hundred of them?"

"Yep. That's about thirty seconds per customer."

Darcy looked at Rhea. "Am I really going to have that many people? I mean, who's heard of me?"

"A ton of people downloaded the galley. There's buzz." Rhea smiled. "And these are free, after all."

Darcy swallowed. What if you gave away your books for nothing, and still nobody came?

The appointed time arrived, and Darcy found herself in front of the black curtain, perched on an unusually high chair behind a signing table. Rhea was at her side, stacking up copies of *Afterworlds*, and in front of Darcy stretched a line of people who actually wanted her signature.

But it wasn't a very long line—maybe twenty-five people. Not a hundred, surely.

"Ready to go?" Rhea asked, and Darcy nodded dumbly.

The strange thing was, a lot of them had already read *Afterworlds*.

"I downloaded that galley the first day," said a librarian from Wisconsin. "My teens just *love* anything with terrorism. Can you sign it, 'Congratulations Contest Winner'?"

"Great first chapter," said a bookstore owner from Maine. "But I was hoping there'd be more about the death cult. Those cults are a real problem, you know?"

"I love ghost romances," said a blogger from Brooklyn. "Lizzie should have got with that FBI agent, especially after he died. Which was kind of her fault."

There were more comments and suggestions, and much polite

praise. But already the reactions were so varied, and sometimes a little strange.

"There's a sequel, right?" asked a bookseller from Texas. "Lizzie and Mindy should start solving other people's murders. It would be so *cute*."

Darcy smiled and nodded at everything that was said to her, signing her name with the new autograph she'd been practicing all week. The *D* was huge and sweeping, sprawling across the full title page, swelling with pride.

But signing here in this convention hall somehow had the feel of business, with none of the glamour, intensity, or love of Standerson's events. Not that Darcy had earned such adulation yet, but part of her was impatient for actual teenagers to start reading her novel. These were gatekeepers. She wanted zealots.

And there weren't enough of them. Only twenty minutes into Darcy's hour, the line trickled down to nothing. She tried to keep the last man talking, but he hadn't even wanted a dedication, only a signature, and soon he was gone. For an uncomfortable moment Darcy and Rhea stared at each other, saying nothing.

"Crap. Should I just sneak away?"

"Of course not! Just don't sign so fast. More people will show up. They'll drift over from the other aisles." Rhea smiled. "In fact, here's two more."

It was two of Darcy's sister debs, Annie and Ashley. They wore matching T-shirts emblazoned: 2014!

"Hey," Darcy called as they approached. "Sister debs!"

The smile crumpled on Ashley's face. "My book got bumped till next spring. I'm not really your sister deb anymore."

Annie put a comforting arm around her. "I told you, you can still wear the shirt."

"I'm so sorry," Darcy said. "But thanks for sending me *Blood Red World*. I loved how complicated the politics were. And those make-out scenes on Mars! Would low gravity really work that way?"

"I *hope* so." Ashley was staring at Darcy's pile of books. "How was your signing? You must have been mobbed!"

"Mildly," Darcy said. "But everyone was really nice."

"Your cover's so great," Annie said, picking up a copy of *Afterworlds*. "I love the whole roiling smoke thing!"

"Teardrops are the new black," Ashley added.

"Thanks." Darcy wondered if their covers were out. She hadn't kept up with any cover releases in the last two months, nor had she ever pursued the promised interviews with Annie, or put anything else on her Tumblr. She was a bad sister deb, and felt a sudden need to make up for it. So she said, "I'm nineteen, by the way."

"That was my guess!" Ashley began a dance. "Score!"

She looked so happy that Darcy didn't point out that she had been eighteen back when the sister debs had laid their bets. Instead, she signed their copies of *Afterworlds*.

As they headed off, Kiralee Taylor and Oscar Lassiter came winding through the empty corral of stanchions.

"I've been told there's some sort of Hindu death-god book available here?" Kiralee called. "Can such a thing be true?"

Darcy laughed. She hadn't seen Kiralee in person since the blurb had been bestowed. "Very true, and it's free for famous authors!"

"Having fun?" Oscar asked.

"I was. Then business tapered off."

"More will come," said Kiralee. "For the moment, you've got some stiff competition down the way."

"You mean Big Head?" Rhea frowned. "My sister and I always hated his show."

"Not him," Kiralee said. She was wearing a mysterious smile. "And don't worry, I've tweeted your august presence. Prepare to be positively *swamped*."

Rhea slid Darcy a book, already opened to the full title page. For a moment, Darcy froze, the Uni-Ball Vision Elite a thick and clumsy thing in her hand.

"K-I-R—" Kiralee began.

"Hush!" Oscar said. "She's *thinking*."

This was only partly true. There was a glimmer of cognition in Darcy's head, which might have been translated as, *Oh shit, I'm signing a book for Kiralee Taylor*. But really it was nothing but a buzzing in her ears.

The book splayed out before her was real. Kiralee standing there waiting for a signature was real. The rumble of the crowds and the smell of freshly printed and bound paper was real. Darcy Patel was a published author now.

"Well, this is a bit awkward," Kiralee said a moment later.

"Ignore her," Oscar said gently. "Take your time."

And Darcy suddenly knew what to write.

Thanks for all the nightmares of red mud.

She signed it with a flourish, and then moved on to Oscar's.

Writing is a lonely business, except for Drinks!

The two of them were very kind about what she'd written and, still kinder, they stuck around until the line built up again, attracting strays from the other aisles and a handful of Kiralee's followers. Soon Darcy was signing again, careful never to rush, pausing to talk to everyone, at least until more people waited behind them. The line ebbed and flowed, until, quite suddenly, the hour was done and Rhea was packing things away.

"Great job," she said. "Only a box and half left!"

Darcy was stunned. It hadn't felt anything like seventy people, but her right hand was marvelously sore.

"Oops, two more. You sign, I'll pack." Rhea dropped a pair of books on the table and began to kick-slide the leftover box away behind the curtain.

Darcy looked up. It was Carla and Sagan.

"Where did you guys come from?"

"From our dorms, where we live," Sagan said. "We decided to road trip down this morning."

"Road trip!" Carla yelled. She was hugging a dozen books to her chest already.

"How did you get in?"

"Imogen weaseled us day passes from Paradox," Sagan said. "Like, in case you needed friendly faces at your signing."

"Sorry we're late," Carla said. "But the *free* is strong in this place!"

"Wait. Imogen got you in?" Darcy blinked. She hadn't checked the schedule, but of course Imogen would be here somewhere. It was strange, how on busy days Darcy could go for hours without noticing the missing pieces of her heart. But when memories did come, they hit all at once.

"Why the sad face?" Carla asked.

"She didn't come to my signing."

"No shit, Sherlock." Carla fumbled a book out of her hoard. Its cover was filled by a black cat, the eyes shining a familiar flame-red. "She's busy down on aisle 2. That's why we're late."

"Seriously?"

"We went to tell her thanks," Sagan said. "And she had this *huge* line! It took us forever to get over here."

Darcy pulled the advanced copy of *Kleptomancer* from Carla's hands. She'd read the first draft almost a year ago, but had never seen the cover. "I forgot these would be here. Did I ever tell you how I—"

"Named that book?" Carla and Sagan said in unison, then burst into giggles.

"You guys suck."

"Oh, really?" Carla snatched the copy of *Kleptomancer* back. "Is that why we haven't heard from you lately."

"I was madly writing. I got a whole draft done!"

"In a month?" Sagan said. "That's, like, old-school Darcy behavior."

"So what are your plans now?" Carla asked.

"Hang out with you guys, obviously. After the Paradox party."

"Not tonight," Carla said. "Now as in . . . the future. Are you going to Oberlin? Staying here forever?"

"Yeah," Sagan said. "You never told us what you did with that lease renewal."

"Oh," Darcy said softly. "I kind of forgot about it."

"So you get kicked out on July 1?"

"I guess so." Over the last month, Darcy hadn't focused on her apartment situation, or the future in general. The first draft of *Untitled Patel* had consumed her mind and soul, along with certain household details like laundry, cleaning, and paperwork.

"Smooth," Carla said with a laugh. "I'm glad that living on your own has made you so mature."

Darcy sighed. She'd tried hard to grow up a little in her time alone in apartment 4E. But maybe she was doomed to be forever adulthood-challenged.

She opened one of the books on the table. "How about, 'From your loving high school best friend. Thanks for all the maturity advice'?"

"Sucks!" Carla and Sagan said in concert.

"You guys have to stop doing that. Talking together is creepy-twins."

"I have an idea," Carla said. "How about you write—"

"No! I have expertise in this now. This is my *job*." Darcy stewed in silence for a moment, then lifted up her pen.

*Without you guys, all that reading wouldn't have
been half as fun.*

She wrote the same in Sagan's copy.

"Time to saddle up," Rhea said from behind her. "The next author's waiting, and the party's in half an hour."

"Sorry!" Darcy leaped up from the seat. It belonged to someone else now.

"By the way, can we stay with you tonight?" Carla asked.

"Duh. See you later," Darcy said, and handed over her keys.

* * *

The Paradox party was only a half-hour walk away, but it was a hot day, and the broad expanse of Ninth Avenue offered no shade at all. Darcy was sweating in her little black dress by the time she and Rhea arrived at the bar.

"Guinness, right?" Rhea asked as she headed away.

"Yes, please!" Darcy called after her. It was mercifully cool and dark here, but she was in serious need of a drink. The restaurant was crowded with Paradox authors and editors and people from marketing, publicity, and sales. All of them were important to her future, and most she'd only met for the first time today. Luckily, they still had their name tags on.

But she lingered at the edge of the crowd, not yet ready for more small talk after her hour at the signing table. Darcy found herself glancing at the restaurant doors, wondering if Imogen was coming. She wouldn't spurn her own publisher just to avoid an ex, would she?

"Darcy! How did your signing go?" said Moxie Underbridge, sweeping from across the room.

Darcy winced a little. Since sending off her first draft of *Untitled Patel*, she'd begun to wonder if it wasn't a bit too first-drafty, a lot too chaotic. Moxie hadn't responded to it yet, which seemed like a bad sign.

"Pretty good, I guess. Maybe sixty people?"

"Seventy-three!" Rhea corrected as she sailed by, depositing a cold Guinness in Darcy's hand, not waiting for thanks.

"Not bad for your first signing," Moxie said.

"Better than I expected. Weird too. People have actually read me now, which was kind of scary. They had *opinions*."

Moxie laughed at this. "Opinions mean they want a sequel. Which is in lovely shape, by the way. Just finished the draft last night."

"It's okay?" Darcy took a steadying drink. "I was thinking you might find it a bit . . . shaky."

"Shaky?" Moxie shook her head. "It's so much better than the first draft of *Afterworlds*. You've grown a lot."

"Are you kidding? It doesn't feel that way."

"You probably don't even remember how *Afterworlds* started. Those two chapters at the beginning, in the silly underworld palace, and that maudlin last scene on Yamaraj's deathbed? Nan was worried you'd never get the ending right."

Darcy blinked. "You never told me that."

"Well, it's not my job to frighten you, darling. Debutantes need careful handling."

"But if Nan was worried, why did Paradox give me so much money?"

Moxie shrugged. "Because they knew it might be a huge book. And Sales loved that first chapter."

"That's *all* they liked?"

"Of course not. But it showed great promise, so Paradox committed. And now it's paying off! You've got great buzz, and it'll only get bigger after today." Moxie patted Darcy's shoulder, but then sighed. "Of course, we probably wouldn't get that much money these days. It was a different era."

"Um, it was only a year ago."

"That long? Good heavens." Moxie fanned herself and took a long swig of her martini. "It feels as though you've been with us forever, Darcy."

Darcy smiled. On good writing days it did feel that way, as though she'd been born in New York City, or had somehow risen up through its sun-baked asphalt, a fully formed novelist. But most of the time, she still felt like a kid.

"Hey, you." The familiar voice went fizzing through Darcy, and she turned.

It was Imogen, of course. She was dressed up for her signing, in a crisp white shirt, her fingers strewn with sparkling rings. A black jacket was slung over one arm from the heat of the walk here, and she had a sweating beer in her other hand.

There was always a part of Darcy's brain that expected to run into Imogen—on the streets of Chinatown, in the subway, at some restaurant they'd both loved. So over the last two and a half months, she'd crafted a hundred artful versions of what to say next.

But what she said was, "Hi."

This greeting seemed to please Imogen. "Good signing?"

"It was great. Yours?"

"Pretty decent."

"Decent? Carla and Sagan said your line was *huge*." Darcy laughed, because she could tell by Imogen's embarrassed expression that it was true.

"Weird, huh? Just some random photograph, and everything changes."

"It wouldn't have changed anything if your book wasn't great," Darcy said, then cringed inside at the earnest tremor in her voice. She took a drink, pulled herself straighter. "Thanks for getting my friends in. I didn't even know we could do that."

Imogen's smile returned. "Writerly superpowers, tiny but potent."

Neither said anything for a moment, but the chatter of the crowd didn't rush in to fill the silence. An invisible barrier seemed to hover in place, shielding the two of them from interruption. Moxie had simply disappeared.

"I loved your ending," Imogen said at last.

A rushing sigh escaped Darcy, as if she had been holding her breath for a long time. "Really?"

"Yeah. You totally brought the darkness."

"I was feeling dark that week. Kind of gritty and real."

A laugh bubbled up out of Imogen. "And brave, too, with Kiralee Taylor herself telling you to write a happy ending. I'm proud of you."

Darcy's eyes opened and closed, a deliberate blink to test if this were the real world—it was. In fact, this bubble of conversation with Imogen was the only world. None of Moxie's praise for the first draft of *Untitled Patel* mattered, nor did the kind words she'd heard at her signing. Not next to this.

"I'm glad you liked it."

"It was suitably brutal."

Darcy laughed. Kiralee had actually used those words in her blurb, and she hadn't let Marketing edit them out. "Speaking of brutal, I just finished the first draft of *Untitled Patel*. Did it in a month!"

"That's great, Darcy." Their glasses met with a sharp, bright sound. "I got worried when you weren't writing. You aren't designed for not writing."

"Yeah, I kind of suck at it. I won't make that mistake again."

They held each other's gaze, and again Darcy was only half aware that there were other people in the room.

"So *Untitled Patel* still doesn't have a title?" Imogen finally said. "Don't I owe you one of those?"

"I stole your scene. I think we're even."

Imogen still smiled, but she looked away. "I'm sorry I had to leave."

"But you had to." Darcy wanted to keep going, to explain that she understood everything now, even if she hated every minute of being apart. That she could need Imogen with every scrap of her being and still give her room for her secrets, or the space to stay away. But that was too much too soon, and wanting too hard had been Darcy's problem from the start.

So she said, "How's *Phobomancer* going?"

Imogen breathed a little sigh of relief. "Really well. I'm almost done."

"Tell me it still starts in the trunk of a car."

"Of course. My agent loves that part now! He says it's finally got some actual fear in it."

Darcy felt herself shiver. "I knew you'd nail it, sooner or later."

"It was easy once I figured out what I was afraid of."

"You're not afraid of anything, Gen."

Imogen didn't answer this at first, and Darcy felt earnest again, like someone flailing their way through their very first relationship. This was not the moment to be young and foolish.

But then Imogen took a step closer, her voice almost fading into the hubbub of the party. "Turns out, I was afraid you wouldn't wait. That you'd give up on me."

"Never," Darcy said at once. "I trust you, Gen."

"I didn't mean to make it some kind of test. I just wanted to get my book right before dealing with us. But it was selfish, staying away this long."

Darcy had only heard a single word of this. "You said *was*."

"What?"

"You used the past tense, Imogen. It *was* selfish to stay away. Does that mean you're not anymore?"

Imogen nodded, took her hand.

"Oh," Darcy said, her heart unbroken in her chest.

There was so much more to fix—her apartment situation, her muddle of a first draft, her disaster of a budget, her absence of a college career. And there was, as Nisha had pointed out in a text that morning, the small matter of maintaining her sanity for the hundred and seventeen days until *Afterworlds* came out. And the possibility that people had better things to spend their money on than a debut novel by an unknown teenager.

It was also possible that she and Imogen hadn't changed *that* much in the last two and a half months. In real life, transformations were reluctant, piecemeal, and slow.

Imogen still needed her secrets. Darcy still needed everything.

"I'm running out of money," she said.

"I'm suddenly in demand," Imogen said.

"I won't have an apartment in two months," she said.

"We can write together anywhere," Imogen said.

"I might go to college. Somewhere cheap."

"That might be a good thing. I'll visit."

Darcy nodded. Maybe the trick was not to panic. In life, as in the bewildering business of writing stories and flinging them out into the world, you had to focus on the page in front of you.

"I'm sorry I dropped the ball," she said.

"The ball bounces."

"You don't think happy endings are stupid anymore?"

"Your question is irrelevant," Imogen said. "This isn't the end."

CHAPTER 42

A WEEK LATER I FOUND MYSELF IN A HOSPITAL AGAIN. NOT IN a field tent in the snow, but a bright and shiny chemotherapy ward in Los Angeles.

My mother wasn't getting chemo—not yet, anyway. She was hooked up to a blood bag, which was filling her with extra red blood cells. She had to do this once a week until her tests looked better, merely the beginning of a long process with many more treatments and tests and machines.

After the nurse had set everything up, he left us alone and we were quiet for a while. Mostly I was trying not to look at where the tube went into my mother's arm. The doctors had put a piece of plastic in her, called a port, which let them slip an IV in without making a fresh hole. I didn't mind needles, but the thought of Mom needing a permanent valve in her skin gave me the creeps.

She claimed she liked it, because it made her feel like a cyborg.

"Does it hurt?" I asked.

"Not really. The most annoying thing is, I can't eat red meat for a while."

"That's weird."

"With all this red blood getting pumped in, I have to watch out for something called 'iron overload.'" My mother laughed. "Sounds kind of heavy metal."

"Which is so *you*," I said, doing a quick search on vegetarian recipes on my phone. "Okay. How about I make a cauliflower frittata tonight?"

"Seriously? We don't have to be vegetarians. Just no red meat."

I scrolled some more. "Maybe some kale stew?"

"Are you trying to kill me? Kale has more iron than beef! Parsley is also deadly."

"Wow. 'Parsley is also deadly.' I bet no one's ever said that before." To test my theory, I typed the phrase into my phone. The top result was something called the Parsley Massacre, in which twenty thousand people had been killed. Everything was about death if you looked closely enough.

I put away my phone.

Another patient was brought into the chemo ward. He was much older than my mother, and shuffled past with a young nurse on his arm. His hair was wispy, his skin stretched tight over the bones of his face.

Walking behind him was a young girl. Her flowery dress looked old-fashioned, and no shadows played in its folds. She seemed not to notice me and my psychopomp shine. She kept her head down, smiling a little, like a child at a somber ceremony trying not to giggle.

My mother and I watched in silence as the nurse hooked the old man up. When she was done, he put in headphones and lay back with his eyes closed. His hands twitched in time to the music in his ears. The ghost girl watched, tapping her feet as if she could hear the music too.

I took a steadying breath. "I've deferred college for a year."

My mother stared at me, the muscles of her arm gone tight. For a moment, I thought the IV was going to pop out of her skin.

"You can't do that, Lizzie."

"It's done." My voice stayed firm. "The call has been made."

"Call them back! Tell them you've changed your mind."

"That would be a lie. And I can't back out now, anyway. They already gave someone else my spot."

My mother groaned. "Lizzie, you don't have to do this. I can lie here with a tube in my arm without your help."

"You don't want me here?"

"I want you in college!"

"For now," I said, readying my mental list of arguments. I'd been preparing myself for this conversation since my first college acceptance letter had arrived. "But once you start chemo, you'll need someone to drive you up here. And to help you remember which pills to take."

She rolled her eyes. "I'm not senile. Just sick."

"But some of your meds affect short-term memory. And you're not going to feel like cooking for yourself most days. And because the deferment's for medical reasons, my spot is a hundred percent locked in. And don't forget, you won't have much income for a while, so my financial aid app will *kick ass* next year. There's nothing but upside."

She stared at me for a long moment. Across the ward, the other patient was humming along with his music. The ghost was sitting motionless, hands folded.

"You've thought about this way too much," Mom said.

"By which you mean, my logic is irrefutable?"

"By which I mean, you could have included me sooner in your thinking."

"You'd've told me not to think about it at all."

My mother sighed in defeat, staring off into space. "Okay, Lizzie. But only one year. You can't give up your life for me."

I took her hand. "Mom . . . *this* is life. Right here in this room, with you, is life."

My mother surveyed the room—the blinking lights of the transfusion machine, the fluorescents in the tile ceiling, the tube in her arm—and gave me a droll look. "Great. Then life sucks."

I didn't argue. Life sucked all right. It sucked hard, because it was random and terrifying and too easily lost. Life was full of death cults and psychopaths, bad timing and bad people. Life was broken, basically, because four assholes with guns could kill an airport full of people, or some microscopic error in your mother's marrow could take her from you far too soon. Because you could make one mistake in righteous anger, and lose the person you most loved.

But everything that sucked about life also proved that it was priceless, because otherwise all of that wouldn't hurt so bad.

"I want to be here for you," I said.

My mother smiled. "That's sweet. But are you sure this isn't about staying near your boyfriend?"

My reaction must have showed on my face.

"Oh. He's not your boyfriend anymore?"

"I don't know. I haven't seen him for a while."

On our way out to the hospital parking lot, we went through the waiting area for the emergency room. My mother had to stop and pee, so I was alone for a moment in a crowded, bustling hallway. I leaned against the wall watching the floor, hoping not to see any more ghosts.

But something must have made me look up.

A paramedic was passing by, pushing an empty folding wheelchair. He was young and handsome, with a freckled shaved head and a whisper of a mustache. A radio was slung over one shoulder, and his uniform was rumpled, like he'd been working a long shift.

He looked up at me as he passed, our eyes catching for a moment, and he slowed. His skin shone, luminous even under the harsh fluorescents in the hospital hallway.

A smile cracked his tired face. He'd seen my shine as well.

"Need any help?" he asked.

It took me a second to realize what he meant.

"No, I'm fine. I'm just here with my mom." I glanced at the bathroom door.

"Gotcha. It's just, you look like you caught a gnarly one." He took a quick look both ways down the hall, and lowered his voice. "Round this place, you can run into some pretty fucked-up wraiths. Some real Do Not Resuscitate assholes."

"Yeah, I guess so." A shiver passed through me. "But it's cool. It's just been a tough few days."

"Ain't they all," the paramedic said, and placed his hands on the wheelchair's handles again. "Hope your mom's okay. Let me know if there's any wheels you need greased around here. I've got *connections.*"

"Really?" I finally managed to smile. "Thanks."

He winked. "Us shines, we gotta stick together."

With a grin, he turned and pushed the wheelchair toward the ambulance bay, and it occurred to me that most of his days were probably tougher than most of mine, whether his patients lived or died.

And I realized I finally had a better word than "psychopomp."

As we drove back to San Diego in my new car, Mom talked about all the stuff she was going to do when she stopped working. She wanted to paint the garage and remodel the kitchen, start an herb garden in the backyard. I didn't ask where she would get the money, much less the energy, to do these things. I didn't point out that she wasn't an actual cyborg now. I didn't want to kill her buzz.

We cooked together that night, with Mindy watching, a strange but happy little family. All the futures I'd imagined for myself might be closing down, but somehow that made the present more precious, more real.

It must have been exhausting for my mother, or maybe the transfusion had taken something out of her, because she went to bed early. From her bedroom door she called, "You really thought about how my illness would affect your financial aid next year? Well played, kiddo."

After I'd cleaned up the kitchen, Mindy was still bouncing, so we went for a walk. I decided to steer us past the ghost school, just as an experiment.

It had faded since I'd seen it last. The line of the terra-cotta roof was indistinct against the gray sky. Maybe someone who'd gone to school here had died in the past week, leaving one less living memory to hold its shape.

"Remember this place?" I asked.

"Of course, silly. We went in there once." Mindy took my hand and squeezed. "It was pretty scary."

"Yeah, no kidding. What did that voice say again?"

"*I can heeeear you up there,*" she sang softly, and collapsed into a fit of giggles.

It was weird. Mindy knew exactly what had happened here, but she sounded like someone retelling a scary movie, not a little girl talking about a man who'd kidnapped her. It still seemed like part of her was missing.

I shivered a little myself, recalling the sound of the old man's fingernail traveling across the floorboards of my room.

Mr. Hamlyn hadn't troubled me since our visit to his private hell. Maybe he was keeping his promise to wait for me to call him. And maybe one day I would need his knowledge again. For the moment, though, the scars his web had left on my arms and legs were reminder enough of who and what he was.

"How was Anna today?" Mindy asked as we headed home. "Was she grumpy about having a transfusion?"

I looked down at Mindy. She might not remember her own awful past, but she kept careful track of my mother's illness now.

"She was grumpy, but not about the treatment. I told her about putting off college."

"*You're in trouble*," Mindy sang, and threw her arms around me. "But I'm glad you're sticking around."

"Me too. As long as Mom doesn't call the admissions office and find out I was totally bluffing. I've got sixty days to change my mind."

"You always were a fibber," Mindy said. "Like that time you convinced Jamie that there were two moons in the sky, but one was invisible."

"Huh. That was, like . . . eight years ago."

"Yeah, but did you know Jamie only pretended to believe you? I heard her tell Anna about it the next day. They were both laughing at you!"

I came to a halt, stung a little by this bygone humiliation, but more astonished that Mindy could remember it. She'd never said anything like this the whole time she'd been afraid of the bad man.

Maybe the part of her that had been emptied by his death was slowly filling up again, but with less horrible things.

When we got home, Mindy wanted to go exploring. She was officially bored with our neighborhood, and had started spying on the people who lived on the next block over. She was hungry to make her world larger, so I let her go on alone.

I stayed awake in my room, lingering on the flipside, hoping to hear a voice on the currents of the river. Yama had to be back in the underworld by now. He had a city to protect, after all.

I stared at my hands, wondering if someday I would be able to smell the blood on them. Maybe, as my shine powers grew, the murder I'd committed would slowly become visible, like the black stain of squid ink on my palms.

Did Yama still think about me? Did he wish he could leave his gray city unprotected and take me someplace windswept and silent and alone?

His absence was a new cold place in me, a hunger on my skin, a fissure in my heart. Without his lips to calm me, I didn't sleep much anymore, and my world seemed smaller than it ever had. The walls of my bedroom had shrunk around me.

So when, just after midnight, a voice reached me on the rusted air of the flipside, at first I didn't believe that it was real. But then it came again.

"Lizzie, I need you."

It was Yamaraj.

By now I knew the moods of the river well enough to know that it wasn't taking me down to the underworld. The voyage was too quick, the current too calm and steady. So he wasn't inviting me to his gray palace. I could deal with that. Any place was fine with me.

When I alighted, it wasn't another windswept mountaintop. It was somewhere I'd been once before, definitely a place to which I was connected.

Dallas/Fort Worth Airport.

Yama waited for me beneath a wall of blank television monitors. We were just beyond the metal gate that had stopped everyone from escaping that night. It was two hours later here than in San Diego, well past midnight, so the gate was rolled down, just as I remembered it.

My heart beat sharply in my chest, and flickers of color pulsed in the corners of my vision. But I kept myself under control.

"Why here?" I asked.

"I'm sorry, Lizzie. This must be hard." His voice was ragged, like he'd been arguing with someone all night. "But you're needed."

I stared through the gate, at the place where so many had fallen. It looked almost the same as it had just before the attack. A few dozen people waited, bored and restless, for their flights to be called.

There was only one addition. Just outside the security gates was a gray block of stone enclosed in a glass cube about ten feet across. It was blocked off with scaffolding, still under construction.

A memorial for the attack, I remembered now. When the design had been published, some reporter had called Mom to see if I had a comment about it, and she'd told them that I didn't.

"Are you sure I'm needed here? It feels like all of this has gone ahead without me."

"Not all of it," Yama said.

I stared at him. He looked older, as if the short time he'd spent in the overworld to let his body heal had been much longer. A scar lay across his cheek, looking fresh and pink, and his skin was a little pale.

He was still beautiful, though. My skin was thirsty for him, my head dizzied by his presence. Tsunamis of black oil didn't faze me anymore, but Yama did.

"There's someone I need you to meet," he said. "But only if you're up to it. We can do this later."

"Now is fine." To be here, the setting of all my nightmares, with him was better than being anywhere else alone.

He held out his hand, and I reached for it. The heat of him, the fire on his skin, came surging into me. The cold places inside me grew warmer for a moment.

I had to say something to keep from sobbing. "Aren't you afraid Mr. Hamlyn will visit while you're gone?"

Yama shook his head. "He hasn't been snooping around for a while. He's playing a long game, waiting me out, thinking I'll grow lazy again. And this will only take a few minutes."

"Oh." Only a few minutes.

I focused on the feel of his hand in mine, the way his silk shirt moved across his skin.

As we passed through the gate where I'd almost died, a trickle of remembered panic went down my spine. But the metal grid was as flimsy as smoke in sunbeams. I could walk through mountains now, if I wanted.

We reached the security area, the place where it all had started. This late, the metal detectors and X-ray machines were mostly shut down. A few bored TSA agents waited around, and two National Guardsmen in body armor stood watching, backs against the wall. The bloodshed in Colorado was still recent, and Jamie had told me that security was high everywhere. Maybe a little more so here.

I didn't look at the memorial. It was for the other eighty-seven people here that night, not me.

"I still don't get it. Why do you need me?"

Yama answered with his eyes, glancing at a boy my age waiting in one of the big plastic chairs. I'd hardly noticed him there in the corner. He was muttering to himself, his cap down low over his face, almost huddled in his football jersey.

He was gray-skinned and shadowless. But he looked so crisp,

his outline clearer than any ghost I'd ever seen. And I realized that millions of people still remembered who he was, what he had done.

I'd tried to forget every detail of that night, but even I knew his name.

"Travis Brinkman," I said.

He looked up at me, a little alarmed, a little defiant, like a kid caught doing something suspicious. "Do I know you?"

I shook my head. "We never met. But I was here that night."

"You were?" He thought for a long moment, and shrugged. "Don't recall you. Guess that was a bad night for making friends."

"It was bad for everything." I looked back at Yama, wondering how I was supposed to help. He gave me a soft smile of encouragement.

"Don't know what else I could've done," Travis said. "Nobody was doing *anything*. Just letting those guys shoot."

"Yeah. It didn't seem real at first." It was strange, talking to someone who'd actually been there, something I'd thought would never happen. "No one was moving, because it didn't make any sense. And everyone being frozen just made it more unreal."

He clenched his fists. "I know, right? But when those guys were out of ammo, I thought everyone would *move*. So I moved."

I sat down next to Travis. I'd gone through what had happened that night so many times in my head, imagining myself calling for help faster, or leading the crowd in a safer direction, or simply missing my plane from New York and not being here at all.

How must it have felt for Travis, who'd actually *done* something? Who'd come so close to stopping them?

"Too bad it was just you," I said.

"Nobody else helped." He was muttering to himself again, his hands jerking a little with every word. "But if I could've got one of those guns . . ."

"At least you tried."

"Didn't make any difference. They got me. They got everybody."

I stared at him. Probably ghosts didn't read newspapers. Maybe he hadn't heard the whole story about the symbol of hope.

"Travis. They didn't get me."

He looked up, face wide open, his hands still for the first time.

"You kidding?"

I pointed at the metal gate. "I was over there when it started, on the phone with my mom. And while everyone else was getting shot, I called 911."

Can you get to a safe location? The words flickered like static through the air around me, making my breath catch. Color trembled through the world. But I had to stay here. I had to keep telling Travis my story.

"The operator told me to play dead, and right that second a bullet went past my head. So I fell down."

"You played dead?" He stared down at his hands. "Damn. Wish I'd thought of that."

"It wasn't my idea. The woman on the phone told me to." I stared at him, recalling how close I'd come to being shot. "My brain was barely making sense of everything, and she told me what to do just in time. That was time I wouldn't have had, except for you."

Travis gave me a hard, disbelieving look, then jerked his thumb at Yama. "That guy tell you to say all this?"

"No. I was here that night, for real."

Travis didn't look convinced. "He always used to come around here and argue with me. Kept telling me I was a hero."

"You are."

He rolled his eyes. "Even he got bored of saying it. Hadn't seen him for a while."

"It doesn't matter what you want to call yourself," I said. "The guy was aiming straight at me when I finally realized what I had to do. It was all down to those last few seconds. . . ."

He stared at me, and I could see how deep his disbelief ran. He'd been sitting here for months with that fixity of mind that ghosts had, thinking he'd failed somehow. That was the story that the papers had told—he was the hero who'd died bravely, but in failure—and it was how the living remembered him.

No one had ever realized that I'd needed Travis Brinkman to survive.

Not even me.

"Thank you," I said. "For everything I have now."

"You sure I helped?" he asked softly, and I saw it in his eyes then, a bright shard of hope that lingered there. The same one that had sent him running unarmed against the guns.

"I'm sure. Maybe you only delayed them a few seconds, but if you hadn't, I'd be dead."

"Hell, had to do *something*." Travis glanced at Yama. "He an all-right guy?"

I nodded.

"What about where he wants to take me?"

"It's kind of weird, but beautiful. And a lot better than this airport."

"Yeah. I hate airports."

"Me too," I said. "They suck."

"Yeah." His hands slapped down onto his knees, and he stood up and looked around. "I guess I'm about ready to get out of here."

"Okay, good. But, Travis, do you mind if I talk to my friend first?"

For a long moment Yama and I were silent. It was too hard for me to speak, and he was probably worried about his sister, his city.

But finally he said, "Thank you for doing this, Lizzie."

"I owed it to Travis. You must know that." I looked up at him. "Why didn't you bring me here before?"

"You weren't ready."

"Maybe not," I sighed, looking around the airport. "But how's that any different from everything else that happens to me?"

"I didn't want to hurt you, Lizzie."

I stared at him, unsure what to say, whether to apologize or beg forgiveness. I just didn't want him to go away yet. "How's Agent Reyes?"

Yama gave me a sad smile. "Very much in charge of our city watch. He hasn't faded at all. He must be well remembered among the living."

I swallowed. "Please thank him for me, for everything. And your sister, too, I guess."

Yama nodded rather somberly at this, and I realized that he knew what my thanks were for—covering up the murder I'd committed.

My vision started to pulse with color. "I'm sorry, my love."

"Me too." He touched the tear-shaped scar beneath my eye.

"Is this forever, the way you feel about me?"

"Only death is forever, and even it changes over time."

I stared at him, wondering what that meant. That the scent of my murder would fade? That there was something I could do to erase what had happened?

But Yama didn't make it easy for me. He didn't give me any straight answers, just kissed me once, kindling a fire on my lips.

"I will see you again," he said, and for the moment that was enough.

On my way home, I had a realization: I couldn't face my bedroom again. It was too empty, too small. For the last week I'd been huddled there waiting for Yama's call, avoiding everyone except my mother and Mindy. But it was time for a change. Not just of scenery, but of everything.

So I gave myself over to the river, letting it listen to my subconscious and take me where it wanted. For a moment it spun, slow and directionless, but then something firmed inside me, and a few swirling minutes later I had reached my destination. It was somewhere the river had never brought me before, but a place I'd been connected to for a long time.

Jamie's room was in its usual state of disarray, her physics homework piled on the floor, her clothes draped over the chairs, shiny brochures from half a dozen colleges spread out across the bed.

She sat at her computer, wearing pajamas and a bathrobe. I saw that she was cropping a photograph of herself, and quickly turned away. I had vowed never to use my powers to spy on my friends. I walked through her bedroom door to the other side, passed into the real world, and knocked.

"Yeah, Dad?"

I opened the door. "Hey."

"Oh, hi." Jamie blinked. "Did my dad let you in?"

By reflex, I almost lied to her then. But I had an idea why the river had brought me here, why my own mind wanted this, and it had to do with being honest.

"No, I let myself in."

Jamie laughed. "At this hour? Creeper. What's up?"

"Not too—" I stopped myself again, took a slow breath. "A lot, actually."

She turned her chair around, and made a clear space on her bed for me with a sweep of her arm. The smiling faces of excited college freshmen wafted to the floor like leaves.

I sat down hard, feeling a little weak in the knees. Maybe I didn't have the right to say all this out loud, to burden someone else with what I knew. But I couldn't keep doing this alone.

"I should have called you," Jamie said.

I looked up. "What?"

"You've been so bummed all week. But I didn't want to pressure you. I didn't know what to do. Sorry."

"Oh." I shook my head. "Don't worry about it. You've been great. Through everything, really. It's just that things got worse this week."

"Your mom? Or your secret agent?"

A pang went through me. "Not secret, special. Yeah, it's partly about him. But that's not all."

"So did you guys break up?"

"We were never . . ." I took another breath. "That is, I broke up with my . . . boyfriend, but the special agent was someone else."

Her eyes went wide. "Dude. There were two of them? No wonder you've been so stressed!"

"No!" I raised my hands, wishing I'd thought this story out before starting to tell it. That was the problem with letting your subconscious make decisions for you. But it was too late to back out now.

"Take your time," Jamie said. "It's going to be okay."

I tried to smile. Everything was so muddled between Jamie and me, I didn't know where to start. I only knew where I wanted to wind up.

"Can I show you something?" I asked softly. "It's kind of weird."

She nodded solemnly.

I closed my eyes, murmuring the words I never thought I would utter before a normal living person. "Security is responding."

The slightest sound came from Jamie, her breath catching in confusion.

I ignored it. "Can you get to a safe location?"

"Lizzie?" She sounded scared now.

"Wait," I breathed, then, "Well, honey, maybe you should pretend . . ."

I felt it happen, the soft and certain passage over to the flipside. The smell of rust and blood, the flattening of sound. The strange feeling that I belonged here now, just as much as I did in the real world.

And a soft utterance from Jamie: "What the actual fuck."

I took a sharp breath, letting my heart beat wildly with all my misgivings, my uncertainties about doing this. I opened my eyes, and color bled back into the world, the clutter of Jamie's room suddenly bright and welcoming again.

She was staring at me in horror.

"I'm sorry," I said. "But I didn't know how else to start."

"What the hell *was* that? What did you just . . ."

Jamie shuddered in her chair, but then she gathered herself. Her lips pressed firmly closed, and she made a guttural sound, like the determined clearing of her throat. "Okay, Lizzie. You've had your fun. Now you need to fucking spill."

As I opened my mouth to speak, something about her expression made me incredibly happy. She didn't look scared, or astonished, or even confused that I'd just turned myself invisible before her eyes.

In fact, she looked thoroughly *annoyed* at me.

How perfect.

"It's called the flipside," I said. "It's where the dead walk, and I'm going to tell you how it works, and about the underworld, and shines, and ghosts. From now on, Jamie, I'm going to tell you everything."

ACKNOWLEDGMENTS

For their wise words, anecdotes, and writerly suggestions: Holly Black (whose research ethic inspired the trunk scene), Debbie Chachra, Deborah Feiner, Javier Grillo-Marxuach, Alaya Dawn Johnson, Maureen Johnson, Justine Larbalestier, E. Lockhart, Anindita Basu Sempere, and Robin Wasserman.

For perspective given and lines stolen: *Highsmith: A Romance of the 1950s*, by Marijane Meaker (also known as M. E. Kerr); *Manhattan, When I Was Young*, by Mary Cantwell; *Goodbye to All That*, edited by Sari Botton; and the essay of the same title by Joan Didion.

And for making the world of YA so awesome: every bookstore that has ever put me onstage; every teen librarian and tireless zealot; you readers young and old, lovely and cantankerous; my steadfast agent, Jill Grinberg; my wise publisher and editor, Bethany Buck (who has never demanded a happy ending); and the amazing team at Simon Pulse, who have supported me since the early days.

AUTHOR'S NOTE

When Darcy receives her editorial letter in chapter 21, her editor complains that the second and third chapters of the book are "all exposition." So Darcy decides to rewrite those chapters, setting them in the airport, with the gun battle still raging around Lizzie, instead of in Yamaraj's underworld palace.

This is exactly what happened to me. (Except that I realized that Darcy's second and third chapters weren't working *before* I finished my first draft and sent it to my editor. One of the advantages of age is that we see our mistakes more quickly.) I decided to rewrite the book much as Darcy does, and when I got to the chapter where she gets her editorial letter, I used my own mistakes for hers.

So what follows is the original version of chapter 4 (which is chapter 2 of Darcy's book-within-a-book), in which Lizzie wakes up not in the airport but in Yamaraj's underworld palace. As you can see, this earlier version is much less interesting, and I'm sure you'll be glad that Darcy and I rewrote it completely.

CHAPTER 4

WHEN I OPENED MY EYES, THE AIRPORT CEILING WAS GONE.

The light was wrong as well—trembling firelight instead of fluorescents. The air smelled clean, no blood or smoke, and the gunfire had been silenced. Two figures hovered over me, silhouetted against flickering gray stone overhead.

I still wasn't breathing, and nothing made sense.

"What do you mean, a faker?" a man's voice said.

"Every once in a while, someone's clever enough to think their way in." That was a girl's voice again. As her face came into focus, she drew back a hand and slapped me across the cheek. The pain lit something inside me, and my lungs sucked in a startled gasp. My body started up like an old car, in jerks and shudders.

"Sit up!" the girl said. "Or do you *like* being dead?"

I managed to push myself up, still coughing and heaving. I felt as though I'd breathed in all the darkness I'd fallen through, and had to push it out of my lungs.

"Do you speak English?" the girl asked. "Your clothes look American."

I stared at her, trying to make sense of the words. She had a strong accent that I couldn't place. My vision was fuzzy, as if everything were covered in a gray gauze, but I could see that the girl was young, maybe fourteen. She wore a leather jacket over a sari.

"Yes, I speak English," I said, and coughed again. "Give me a second."

"She sounds American," the man said. He had the same accent as the girl, but not as strong. "And you really think she's alive, my lady?"

She nodded. "Look how red her blood is."

"Of course I'm alive!" Shouting hurt my throat, but it pushed aside a little of the thick, heavy cotton in my head.

The man was staring at me, and I stared back at him. Even in the firelight he looked wrong. His skin was a soft gray, as if he were a pencil drawing come to life. He wore an old-fashioned tailcoat, a bow tie, and a derby hat—all the same color as his skin.

I looked around the room. The walls were gray marble, and chandeliers hung from the arched ceiling, candles burning in their branches. There were no chairs, no furniture at all except for the dark slab of stone I'd woken up on. A few flowers lay scattered on the floor.

The blow to my head had done something to my vision. All I could see were shades of slate and charcoal—even the flowers were gray. I touched my free hand to my forehead and felt the stickiness of blood.

When I looked at my fingertips, they were smudged with red.

My color vision seemed to come and go. The girl was as gray-skinned as the man, but she wore a pale blue jewel on her forehead, and her leather jacket and sari were shiny and black.

"Who are you?" I asked.

"This is the lady Yami," the man said, bowing a little. "You may address her as 'my lady.'"

"What the hell is happening?"

The man sputtered at this, but Yami silenced him with an upraised finger.

"That depends," she said. "What is the last thing you remember?"

I closed my eyes a moment, and the noises and smells of gunfire came rushing in. I snapped them back open, my heart pounding again.

"There were men with guns, killing everyone."

"You see, my lady?" the man said. "She's surely dead."

Yami reached out for my forehead. Her palm was marked with a half-moon of white scar tissue. Her fingertip was cool.

"And yet still bleeding," she said. "The dead don't bleed."

"Wait! Just wait!" I scrambled back from both of them on hands and heels, slipped from the stone slab onto the floor, then scrambled unsteadily to my feet. My running shoes skidded on smooth marble, and I looked down. My footprints were streaked with blood.

But as I watched, the red faded to gray.

"Don't worry. That isn't yours." Yami held up her hand, showing a smudge on one fingertip. "Yours is still quite red."

We all stood there a moment, the man in the derby hat looking perplexed, Yami and I just staring at each other. I didn't see the point of saying anything. None of this was happening. I'd fallen asleep in one of those plastic airport chairs. Or maybe I was still in Manhattan in my father's guest bed.

I thought about all the reasons I could be having this nightmare. Because my mother worried too much when I traveled. Because part of me wanted to stay in New York, on the pillow of my father's wealth.

But the salt tears on my lips tasted very real. I stared at the gray streaks my shoes had left on the floor, and something hard and cold rose in my throat.

"They were killing everyone."

"Not everyone. You have your wits to thank for that." Yami turned to the man and waved a hand at him. "Wake Yamaraj."

As he scurried away, I felt my pockets. No phone, but I remembered the woman who'd saved me.

"It wasn't my idea. Someone told me to play dead."

"You played too well," Yami said.

She led me down a long veranda in the open air, a row of columns separating us from the dark night outside. A cool breeze pushed between them, and I could smell grass and sickly sweet flowers.

A city stood in the distance, a cluster of black spires rising up against the stars. The towers looked modern, made of steel and shimmery glass, but were too tall and spindly to be real.

"Where am I?"

"An afterworld."

I came to a halt, and Yami stopped and turned to me.

"You've nothing to worry about. Haven't you been listening? You're still alive."

Anger surged through me then, frustration at everything being senseless and confusing and just plain *wrong*.

"We're standing here talking. Of course I'm alive!"

"I am not," she said simply. "I have been dead for four thousand years."

"That doesn't even . . ." My words faded as my gaze drifted past her shoulder. A boy was approaching from the other end of the veranda.

He was older than her—my age. He'd clearly just woken up, with his disheveled hair and black silk pajamas. The man in the derby hat walked behind him, still looking as gray as a corpse, but the boy's skin wasn't gray. It was as brown as mine at the end of a long summer at the beach, and his face shone in the flickering candlelight. He was beautiful.

Yami glanced at them over her shoulder, then straightened as she turned back to me. "My brother, Yamaraj. And your name is?"

"Lizzie," I said softly. As he grew closer I noticed that the boy's shirt was unbuttoned, or maybe it was a short robe loosely tied. As he walked, the silk rippled in the firelight, like black liquid rolling across his skin. His thick midnight hair fell just above his shoulders, and his brown eyes were luminous.

"So many corruptions of Elizabeth." Yami muttered something in a language I didn't recognize. "You living should show more respect to your names."

I wasn't really listening to her. The boy was looking straight back at me now, our eyes locked across the firelit darkness.

"My lord, this is Elizabeth," Yami said, bowing at his approach. "She appears to be alive."

Without thinking, I bowed a little too, which felt ridiculous. His eyes traveled up to my forehead.

"And hurt, it seems. Mr. Basker, fetch some water and a cloth." As the man pattered off again, Yamaraj turned to his sister. "Really, Yami, our guest is bleeding. And you're marching her about in the cold?"

She gestured at my forehead. "I wanted you to see."

"I've seen blood before. Let's get her inside."

"It's not that cold," I said softly.

"You have to send her back, brother," Yami said.

"Soon enough." The boy took my arm, his hand warm through the sleeve of my hoodie. I shivered a little in his grasp, and he smiled. "Don't worry, Elizabeth. You're safe here."

For a moment, I heard the woman's voice on the phone. *Can you get to a safe location?*

The boy led me through a pair of arched doors as wide and tall as a soccer goal, into a room as big as my mother's entire house. A dozen cushions were arranged like chairs around a gray-patterned rug at its center, and candled chandeliers hung just above head height. As we entered, men in knee-length robes stepped forward from the shadows, lighting the branches of the chandeliers with smoking tapers. These servants were as gray-skinned as Yami. They didn't talk, but one met my eyes with an expression of disquiet, then looked away.

The boy settled me on a cushion and then sat beside me, his hand steady on my arm. He kept glancing up at my wound.

"Does it look that bad?" I asked.

"Not at all. It's just that . . . we rarely see such colors here."

"What he means is, you'll survive." Yami sat on the other side of the rug from us, her arms crossed.

"What I meant was," the boy said, "it's edifying to see someone so alive."

I stared at him a moment, wondering if that was supposed to be a compliment. It seemed to be, and certainly his soft brown eyes were more comforting than Yami's cool stare.

"This must be confusing," the boy said softly. "But if you please, can you tell me how you came here?"

I swallowed, looking down at the rug—a pattern of zigzags, like diamonds with interlocked elbows. A tremor of exhaustion passed through me, and I realized that it was after midnight. At least it was back in reality.

Because of course the attack had been real, and this was all a dream. My subconscious had a pretty weird idea of safety.

The man in the derby hat—Mr. Basker—appeared beside me, kneeling to place a bowl of water on the floor. He handed a towel to Yamaraj, who dipped it in the water.

"May I, Elizabeth?" he asked.

I nodded. "Call me Lizzie."

"Lizzie? Charming." He pressed the cool wet cloth against my forehead. Something relaxed inside me; the simple knowledge that someone was taking care of me took hold with a tiny shudder. "Can you tell me what happened?"

His expression was one of awe, as if I were somehow as beautiful as he.

"I was at an airport, and there were men with guns. They wanted to kill us all."

"A war?"

My voice grew soft. "Not really. I don't know who they were."

He squeezed my arm, and pressed the cool cloth against my head again. I could feel my heart beating in the wound.

"We tried to get out." It took me a few slow breaths to continue. "But the gate was locked. There was nothing I could do but play dead."

"Ah." He lowered the cloth and squinted at my forehead. "So you thought your way here."

"She's just like you." Yami was curled up on her cushion now. I suddenly saw how alike brother and sister were, how beautiful she was. But her skin was that strange gray, and his such a warm, healthy brown.

I looked down at my hands—my skin was always pale this early in spring, but it didn't look gray at all.

"I'm alive," I said to him. "And you are too, right?"

"Of course." His grin made me smile back at him, as if having vital functions were our own private little joke. "That's why I'm the raja here."

I nodded, though none of it made sense. My eyes were growing heavy again. I'd been so ready to sleep on the plane.

Yami leaned forward. "You have to send her back soon, brother."

"Of course," he said. "Will you be safe, Lizzie, if I send you back?"

My breath caught at the thought of returning to the real world.

How long had I been having this vision? A few minutes? Half an hour? This place was bizarre, but there was order here, and warmth, and the candlelight made everything softer. Back in reality I was lying on a cold airport floor with bullets flying over me. Whatever this was—a dream, a delusion, a near-death experience—I needed it to keep going a little longer.

"I don't think it's safe yet."

"Then we're in no hurry," he said, a smile on his face again. "But you can't fall asleep."

"You think I've got a concussion?"

He pressed the cool cloth against my forehead again. "Don't worry about that. But if you fall asleep here, it will be a long time before you leave again. Would you like tea?"

Across the room, Yami sighed.

The sound made me angry, and I pulled away from the boy and said, "What I'd like is for someone to tell me where the hell I am! Seriously!"

"Of course." Yamaraj wrung the bloody cloth over the bowl, and watched with fascination as the water turned pink in the candlelight. "Now that you're here, you want to know the secret of death."

I shook my head. What I wanted to know was why reality was broken.

"Death is mysterious," the boy continued. "But I can tell you the story of how we came to this afterworld. It may help you understand your own journey."

"My journey?" I stared at Yamaraj. He had something steady in his eyes. Looking at him made the world almost make sense.

I settled into the cushion, and the muscles in my core that had been clenched since the first gunshots relaxed a little. Somewhere in the back of my mind, terror was still churning. I had seen people murdered tonight, but I was safe with Yamaraj.

"Okay," I said. "I'm listening."